...otorcycle engines; ...n led him, perhaps inevitably, to qualify as a solicitor and emigrate to Somerset, where he specialised in death and taxes for seven years before going straight in 1995. Now a full-time writer, he lives in Chard, Somerset, with his wife, one daughter and the unmistakable scent of blood, wafting in on the breeze from the local meat-packing plant.

Find out more about Tom Holt and other Orbit authors by registering for the free monthly newsletter at www.orbitbooks.co.uk

By Tom Holt

EXPECTING SOMEONE TALLER
WHO'S AFRAID OF BEOWULF?
FLYING DUTCH
YE GODS!
OVERTIME
HERE COMES THE SUN
GRAILBLAZERS
FAUST AMONG EQUALS
ODDS AND GODS
DJINN RUMMY
MY HERO
PAINT YOUR DRAGON
OPEN SESAME
WISH YOU WERE HERE
ONLY HUMAN
SNOW WHITE AND THE SEVEN SAMURAI
VALHALLA
NOTHING BUT BLUE SKIES
FALLING SIDEWAYS
LITTLE PEOPLE
THE PORTABLE DOOR
IN YOUR DREAMS
EARTH, AIR, FIRE AND CUSTARD

DEAD FUNNY: OMNIBUS 1
MIGHTIER THAN THE SWORD: OMNIBUS 2
DIVINE COMEDIES: OMNIBUS 3
FOR TWO NIGHTS ONLY: OMNIBUS 4
TALL STORIES: OMNIBUS 5
SAINTS AND SINNERS: OMNIBUS 6
FISHY WISHES: OMNIBUS 7

THE WALLED ORCHARD
ALEXANDER AT THE WORLD'S END
OLYMPIAD
A SONG FOR NERO
MEADOWLAND

I, MARGARET

LUCIA TRIUMPHANT
LUCIA IN WARTIME

NOTHING BUT BLUE SKIES

Tom Holt

www.orbitbooks.co.uk

First published in Great Britain by Orbit 2001
First published in paperback by Orbit 2002
This edition published by Orbit 2005
Reprinted 2005

ISBN 1 84149 058 X

Typeset in Plantin by M Rules
Printed and bound in Great Britain by
Clays Ltd, St Ives plc

Orbit
An imprint of
Time Warner Book Group UK
Brettenham House
Lancaster Place
London WC2E 7EN

For two disparate Jans,
Fergus and Yarnot:
Friends indeed

CHAPTER ONE

For men in dark grey suits and black sunglasses climbed
out of a black, fat-wheeled Transit and slammed the
doors. The noise woke up the proprietor, who staggered out
of the little shed that served him as an office. He blinked at
them.

'Mr Denby?' said one of the strangers.

The proprietor shook his head. 'No,' he added, in case of
doubt.

'But this is Denby's boatyard, right?'

'Yes.'

The four men exchanged glances and nodded. 'You build
boats?'

'Yes.'

'That's good. We want a boat built.'

If the proprietor was surprised by that, he didn't show it.
(But then again, he never showed surprise at anything.
Simple demarcation. If you want emotions registered, go to
an actor.) Instead, he carried on looking weather-beaten and
authentic.

'Yeah,' said another of the strangers. 'Can you do that for us?'

The proprietor's shoulders moved about a thirty-second of an inch, which in the boatbuilders' dialect of body language means something like: *Of course I can build you a boat, you fool, assuming that I can be bothered and you don't mind waiting a year or so, and what would a load of dickheads like you be wanting with a boat, anyway?*

'Cool. Of course, we need it in a hurry.'

This time, the proprietor allowed his lower lip to twitch, somewhere between fifteen and twenty thousandths of an inch.

'Like, we need it in three weeks, finished and ready to roll. Can you manage that?'

'Depends.' The proprietor half-closed his eyes, as if performing miracles of mental quantity-surveying. 'What kind of boat do you boys want?'

'Ah.' For some reason, the strangers seemed uncomfortable with that question. 'We thought we'd leave that to you, really. Like, you're the expert here, you don't keep a dog and bark yourself, all that shit. A boat.'

'A boat.'

'You got it.'

'What kind of boat?' the proprietor asked again.

To look at the strangers, you'd think they had something to hide. 'A big boat,' one of them said. 'Not that we're trying to dictate to you in any way, shape or form; I mean, if it's gotta be a certain size, that's the size it's gotta be. Hell, last thing we want to do is come in here telling you how to do your job.'

'A big boat,' the proprietor said.

'Yeah.' The tallest and grey-suitedest of the strangers nodded assertively. 'A big boat's just fine by us. Something in the order of – and this is just me thinking aloud, you understand, there's nothing carved in tablets of stone or anything –

something round about, say, 300 cubits by fifty cubits by thirty. There or thereabouts,' he added quickly.

'Cubits?'

'Sure. Why not cubits?'

This time, the proprietor actually frowned; easily his most demonstrative gesture since 1958. 'What's that in metric?' he asked.

'Metric?'

One of the other strangers nudged him in the small of the back. 'He means, like, French.'

'Ah, right. OK. Trois cent cubites par cinquante par . . .'

The proprietor's eyes snapped wide open, like a searchlight switching on. 'Are you boys French, then?' he asked dangerously.

'Us? Shit, no. No way. We're—' From the way the man's head moved a fraction to the left, you might have been forgiven for imagining he was reading notes scribbled on his shirt-cuff. 'We're English, same as you. You know: Buckingham Palace, afternoon tea, Bobby Charlton—'

By now the proprietor was staring at them as if trying to melt holes in their faces. 'Where did you boys say you were from?' he asked.

'England,' the stranger repeated.

'Ah. What were you saying about cubits?'

The stranger took a deep breath, as if making himself relax. 'I was just thinking, three hundred's a good round number, for length. By, you know, fifty. By thirty. Give or take a cubit.'

'Mphm.'

'And,' the stranger went on, 'something else that's just occurred to me, like a real spur-of-the-moment thing, dunno where in hell I got this from, but don't you think it might be pretty damn' cute if you built it out of gopher wood?'

'Gopher wood.'

'Yeah. Gopher wood rocks, is what I say.'

The proprietor breathed in deeply through his nose. 'Gopher wood,' he repeated. 'And rocks.'

'Nope, just gopher wood. And while you're at it,' another stranger put in, with an air of almost reckless cheerfulness, 'wouldn't it be just swell if you pitched it, inside and out. Like, with pitch?'

'Hey!' His colleague's face instantly became a study in wonder. 'That's brilliant, man. Definitely, we want to go with that. Will that be OK?' he asked the proprietor. 'Pitch?'

'Pitch.'

'And,' the other stranger ground on, 'what say we have like a window, say one cubit square? And a door in the side? And – get a load of this, guys – lower, second and third storeys—'

The proprietor let go the deep breath. 'You mean like Noah's ark,' he said.

The strangers looked at each other.

'Who?' they said, all at once.

'Noah. Like in the Bible.'

'Sorry,' said the tall stranger, 'we don't know anything about any Noah. We're just, you know, sparking ideas off each other here, brainstorming . . .'

The proprietor's head moved from side to side, a whole four degrees each way. 'You want Noah's ark,' he said, 'and you want it in three weeks.'

'At the most. We're kinda on a schedule here.'

Lunatics, the proprietor thought. *Mad as a barrelful of ferrets*. Then he looked them up and down: the suits, the Ray-Bans, the thousand-dollar shoes, the brand-new custom Transit. *Still*, he thought, *it takes all sorts*.

'All right,' he said.

If the strangers were trying to conceal their relief, they weren't very good at it. 'Hey,' one of them said, 'that's great.'

'Awesome,' said another.

'But it's going to cost you,' the proprietor said.

The tall stranger nodded. 'Sure,' he said. 'We guessed it

would.' He nodded to one of his colleagues, who was holding a big aluminium case, the sort you transport expensive cameras in.

'Do you reckon five million dollars'd cover it?' he asked earnestly. 'In cash,' he added, 'half now and half on delivery?'

'In three weeks,' another of them pointed out.

It's very hard to stay looking weather-beaten, authentic and taciturn when, inside, every fibre of your being is shouting YES! YES! YES! YES! YES! But the proprietor managed to make a pretty decent job of it.

'All right,' he said.

The dragon glowed in the silk like daybreak, wild in symmetry, exuberant in formality, a flash of two-dimensional lightning, storm and thunder frozen in amber. As they stared at it, even the schoolchildren were quiet for a while, as if they were grateful for the sheet of stout plate glass that separated them from it. Only the guide seemed not to notice that the dragon was looking straight at her, amused and affronted—

'In Chinese mythology,' the silly woman was saying, 'the dragon symbolises the element of water, and it was believed that dragons were responsible for bringing rain. In its aspect as the source of all fertility and increase, the dragon was adopted by the Chinese emperors as a royal emblem; in particular the dragon with five toes or claws on each foot, as in this example, painted on silk during the Ming dynasty, depicting the Dragon King of the Yellow River teaching the first Emperor the Chinese written language. Notice the distinctive colour tones, typical of the period . . .'

At the back of the group, Karen yawned, trying without much success to be discreet about it. She knew that yawning was likely to distract the rest of the group and spoil their pleasure, and she felt bad about that. But she couldn't help it. The reaction was entirely automatic, being the result of too many deathly boring teatimes spent gawping at interminable collections of family albums – here's one of us outside the temple, now here's your uncle standing in front of the main gate, and here we both are looking up at the gate, and this is just inside the gate, though really it's a bit too dark to see anything. Ordeals like that leave an indelible mark on a child's mind, triggering involuntary reactions; so, even now, the very sight of a picture of a dragon made her yawn.

And besides, she told herself, *if that's supposed to be Uncle Biff, they've drawn his eyes far too close together. Makes him look like an Airedale terrier.*

She smiled. Uncle Biff wouldn't like that; not one bit. In fact, it was probably just as well for everyone living within convenient flooding distance of the Yellow River that this particular gem of Chinese cultural heritage had been looted by flint-hearted Western imperialists and carried off to a far land where Uncle Biff wasn't likely to see it; because when he got upset, did it ever rain . . .

'According to traditional Chinese beliefs,' the silly woman continued, 'each quarter of the compass is ruled by a Dragon King, who in turn is owed fealty by a complicated hierarchy of lesser dragons – thereby mirroring contemporary Chinese society – down to the smallest lake, stream and well, each of which is governed by its own resident dragon. It was believed that dragons were able to manifest themselves as fish, and also to take human form when circumstances required, so that recurring themes in folklore include the fisherman who takes pity on a fish and throws it back, only to discover that he's spared the life of an important dragon who is thereby permanently obligated to him—'

Karen couldn't help clicking her tongue. Recurring theme in folklore – once it had happened, just once. But what else can you expect when the media get hold of a story and start playing with it? As for 'obligated': do a mortal a favour and they think they own you. She played back that last thought and frowned at it; sometimes, when she wasn't careful, she sounded just like her father. Yetch.

'Another such theme,' said the silly woman, 'concerns the son or daughter of a dragon king who falls in love with a mortal—' She stopped and looked round to see what had made that peculiar noise. 'Falls in love with a mortal,' she continued, 'and takes human form in an attempt to pursue the ill-fated relationship. Invariably, of course, these episodes always end tragically, since such a pairing would represent an imbalance of the Elements, thereby violating the fundamental foundations of Chinese philosophy—'

Bullshit! screamed Karen's voice inside her head. *And 'fundamental foundations' is tautology.* Scowling furiously, she turned on her heel and marched out of the gallery before she said something out loud that might land her in court – though by rights it was the damned silly woman who should be in the dock, charged with and convicted of Contempt of Dragons—

Except that all dragons everywhere would agree with her (except one) and really, Karen had come here to get away from that particular thought. By now, true enough, she was used to the idea that her own kind didn't have the imagination to see past their silly old traditions and rubbish, which was why she was here, dressed in the monkey suit, instead of back home, where they claimed she belonged. Hearing the same old nonsense trotted out by a human, however, disturbed her considerably. Surely they ought to know better; after all, she told herself, sweeping out of the museum gates into the street, they weren't all a load of blinkered, scalebound old stick-in-the-muds who reckoned something was true just because they all believed it was true—

She shuddered and squirmed as the first big, fat raindrops slapped her face. Wet! Nasty!

Fumbling in her haste, she yanked the small folding umbrella out of her pocket and tried to get it to work. It refused, of course; she had an idea that the wretched thing had somehow recognised her, and was grimly carrying on the age-old umbrella/dragon war by means of sabotage and mechanical terrorism. By the time she managed to get its idiotic squashed-cranefly legs into place, she was pink with rage and frustration, and the rain was bucketing down—

Well, of course. Cause and effect.

Looked at one way, it was just plain silly . . . Because she'd only been a human for a few weeks, she hadn't even begun to come to terms with rain (its feel, its sudden onslaught, how squishy and cold and uncomfortable it felt as it trickled down between collar and neck), so that every time the stuff hit her she couldn't help an involuntary spasm of panic, laced with more than a dash of irrational anger. Since she was a dragon – the hell with false modesty; since she was the daughter of the adjutant-general to the Dragon King of the North-West, no less, with the hereditary title of Dragon Marshal of Bank Holidays and a maximum capacity of 2,000,000,000,000 litres/second/ km^2 when she got angry or upset, it rained.

She happened to glance down, and saw that already the paving stones beneath her feet were awash with eddying, dancing rainwater, while overhead the sky began to resonate with basso-profundo flatulence. Any moment now, there'd be lightning, and probably gale-force winds and armour-piercing hailstones to follow, and all because she couldn't make sense of this stupid goddamned umbrella . . .

She stopped trying, and slowly lowered the thing until it was resting upside-down on the pavement, its flabby fabric drinking up the rainwater. *Calm down*, she told herself. *It's all right. A little rain never hurt anybody.*

(*Please*, she prayed silently, *please don't let any of my friends from Home see me like this; especially not that cow S'ssssn, because if she were to find out I'll never hear the end of it if I live to be a million – which I already have, of course, and that doesn't make it any easier . . .*)

People, humans, were staring at her – girl with lowered

umbrella standing perfectly still in the rain, of course they were staring, and as the embarrassment began to bite, so the rain thickened. (They'd scrambled the B-92s now, the big, fast saturation-grade raindrops with the enormous payload and the smart guidance system, the latest in launch-and-forget technology; humans assumed they were imagining things when they got the impression that modern rain was somehow colder and wetter than it had been when they were young, but that was mortals for you.) The frustration of knowing that she was making things even worse made her angrier still, at which point the first lightning bolt split the sky, like God arc-welding . . .

Karen closed her eyes and concentrated. It should have been easy, because all she had to do was think *STOP*—

(But that was when she was in her own body, not this cramped, largely unfamiliar right-hand-drive contraption; somehow it worked so that her instincts interfaced with the controls just fine, whereas her conscious thoughts had to stop and grind their way through the *Owner's Handbook* and the Help files in order to get the simplest thing done—)

—Which raised the questions, 'How do you think?' and 'What's the proper Think command for Stop?' and 'Which of these is the Send button, anyway?'; and struggling with all that nonsense made her feel so uptight and irritable—

At which point, someone grabbed her by the arm and dragged her, quickly and with humiliating efficiency, back into the shelter of the museum doorway. 'You're soaked,' said a familiar voice.

Sheet lightning filled the sky, thunder rattled the window-panes, drains and soakaways within a five-mile radius gave up and went into denial – indications that Karen wasn't entirely pleased to see the person who'd just pulled her in out of the rain. 'Yes,' Karen muttered, 'I am, rather.'

'You were just standing there, getting wet.'

'Yes.'

'Oh. Any particular reason?'

'I like getting wet.'

Her rescuer – imagine the Botticelli Venus dressed in a sensible waterproof jacket, of the kind they sell in camping shops – curved her lips slightly in a small, bewildered-contemptuous smile. 'Fair enough,' she said. 'Next time you might want to try swimming, though. Same net effect but your clothes stay dry.'

Karen tightened her scowl up by a click or so. 'Actually,' she said truthfully, 'I can't swim.' (Now why on earth had she gone and told her that? No idea; it had just slipped out, like a coin falling out of her pocket when she pulled out her handkerchief.)

'Really?'

'Really,' Karen replied. *Not in this body, anyway,* she didn't explain.

'Well, well. I'll have to teach you one of these days. I learned to swim when I was two.'

Too what? Karen didn't say. Another odd thing; it had nearly stopped raining, even though Karen was so livid she could cheerfully have sunk all twenty claws into the bloody woman's face.

Hard to understand, that. She could only assume it was something to do with the crushing weight of inferiority she always felt whenever she was in Ms Ackroyd's company. 'I bet,' she muttered. 'Came naturally to you, I suppose.'

'Yes, as it happens. Of course, it's always easier to learn something if you start young.' Not a drop, not a single molecule of water appeared to have lodged anywhere on Susan Ackroyd's super-polymer-monofilament-this-that-and-the-other-upholstered person. Dry as a yak bone in the Gobi Desert, she was. Typical. 'How come you never learned to swim, then?'

'Never got round to it.'

'Ah. Look, it's stopped raining. A bit late as far as you're concerned,' Ms Ackroyd added. 'See you tomorrow, then.'

Karen watched her walk away without saying a word, mostly because the things she really wanted to say couldn't readily be expressed in the effete languages humans used. If, as she asserted, she'd never really understood what love meant until she'd turned her back on the cloud-capped battlements of Home and come down to live among the humans, the same also went for hate, redoubled in spades. Oh sure, she'd felt the odd negative emotion or two in her time – she'd disapproved of evil and disliked the dragon senators who'd criticised her father's handling of various issues and taken against some of her more obnoxiodus relatives and been annoyed by several of her contemporaries at school – but hate, the real hundred per cent proof matured-in-oak-vats stuff, had taken her completely by surprise. She *hated* Susan Ackroyd with a pure, distilled ferocity she hadn't believed possible a few months ago. She hated her for her straight blonde hair, her unflappable calm, her brilliantly incisive mind, her knack of being abominably insulting while not actually saying anything rude, her ability to wear a potato sack and still look like a refugee from a Paris catwalk, the shape of her ears, her unshakeable common sense, her dry, understated sense of humour, her weakness for fresh vanilla slices, her skill at mental arithmetic, her hand/eye coordination, her rare and beautiful smile, the way she could open difficult bottles and jars with a bare flick of the wrist, her taste in shoes, the easy way she could admit it when she came up against something she couldn't do, the evenness of her teeth, her excellent memory for telephone numbers, the fact that she could swim.

Because she was the Competition.

For the sake of the unharvested crops and the water table and the already over-abused sewage systems of three counties, Karen made a mental effort not to think about that. It was, after all, her day off, when she should be happy and relaxed and at ease; nothing but blue skies. It was her day off, when she shouldn't be here at all, or anywhere, on her own . . . or where the hell was the point in having run away from Home and come here in the first place?

Humans, she decided, were much, much better at unhappiness than dragons could ever be; it came naturally to them, like swimming did to Susan Ackroyd. But, since they still retained the vestiges of a survival instinct, they'd found ways of coping with it; none of them so unfailingly effective, so elegantly simple, as the cream doughnut. Dragons had nothing like that. Thinking about it, she almost felt sorry for her tediously contented species.

The woman in the cream-cake shop recognised Karen at once, which was hardly surprising, but at least she had the tact not to make an issue out of it; she simply looked blank, as if drowned rats who asked for three cream doughnuts were something that happened every day. Once Karen was out of the shop and comfortably relaxed on the warm steps of the square – just the sight of the exuberant cream bubbling up out of the fissured doughnut had been enough to haul the sun out from behind the clouds – she felt like a completely different person. Like, to take an example entirely at random, a red-lacquer-and-gold dragon bursting through the clouds into the pure blue above, the exact opposite and equivalent of a diver plunging into deep blue water.

Homesick? After all the trouble she'd been to, getting away from there in the first place? Not likely.

Perhaps it was the doughnut; possibly it was pure logic, quietly working away at the problem like penetrating oil gradually seeping into a rusted joint. Possibly it was a flash of insight, the mental equivalent of a double six and a quick trip up a ladder; most likely that, because the conclusion arrived complete and ready to wear, batteries included. If Susan Ackroyd was here just a moment ago, it followed that she was not with Paul. If she wasn't with Paul on the morning of the Spring Bank Holiday, didn't that suggest that the two of them weren't the stone-cold definite Item she'd been assuming they were? Maybe they were nothing more than Just Good Friends. In which case (she mused excitedly, biting vigorously into the second doughnut) the game wasn't over and she was still in with a sporting chance, straight blonde hair or no straight blonde hair. The more she thought about it, the more obvious it became. If she was a man-eating vampire blonde (and amphibious into the bargain) with her hooks into some poor unsuspecting male right up to the knuckles, would she let him out of her sight on a sunny Bank Holiday morning? Would she hell as like. She'd have had their day together mapped out and precisely scheduled well in advance, with back-ups and fail-safe options in the event of unexpected obstacles and complications, all drawn tightly together into a unified game plan designed to advance the relationship to the next level of the overall strategy – she'd have drawn it all up on graph paper, neatly plotted on the X and Y axes, with each variable charted in a different colour of felt-tip pen. Wouldn't anybody, if they were truly serious about a relationship? Surely it stood to reason.

As she licked cream and sugar residues off her fingertips, the sun flipped open the lid of its paintbox and started filling in the numbered spaces with rich, glowing shades of yellow and gold. It was all fearfully symbolic, as the warmth of insight evaporated the damp residues of anger; and it had never been like this, at Home, where there simply weren't any such extremes. Maybe it was a terrestrial thing, something to do with being limited to three dimensions, one shape, one set of senses and one perspective. If they could fly like birds or swim like fish, would mortal humans still retain the ability to feel things so intensely, to concentrate so ferociously on a single issue, to love or hate a single person so passionately? Highly improbable, to say the least. Oh, but if only Daddy and all the rest of them could just have a taste of what they were missing, love and hate and cream doughnuts too, wouldn't they all be down here, on the other end of the rain, instead of up there in the monotonous, unending blue?

She'd closed her eyes at some stage. Now she opened them again, and immediately saw two very familiar faces, no more than twenty yards away. It was as if someone with a nasty sense of humour had done it on purpose.

The female – well, she was just as blonde as she had been when Karen last saw her, all of twenty minutes ago, if not blonder. And he – oddly enough, he seemed a bit shorter and somehow more meagre than he was in her mind's eye, but even so she felt the same lurching shock as always, a feeling that you get only when you see your beloved or unexpectedly bite hard on tinfoil. There they were, together – didn't they make a lovely couple, as natural a pairing as knife and fork or cod and chips, perfectly matched as if they'd been cut from the same blank. Suddenly, Karen regretted the idiotic limitations of a human body, with no proper teeth to bare or claws to spread. They were walking together towards the museum, side by side and in step like a very small column of soldiers, both of them eyes front, chins up, hands level at their sides (as if butter wouldn't melt; who were they trying to fool?) He was holding a Tesco's bag; she'd taken off her sensible coat and was carrying it folded under one arm. She said something. He laughed.

All right, Karen thought, *so I'm not really human; I am what I am, and if that's not good enough for some people, that's their hard luck*. Then it occurred to her that being what she was did have a few useful fringe benefits, and that it was the end of May, and she was by right of birth and appointment the Dragon Marshal of Bank Holidays.

What was it the humans said? When things go wrong in your private life, sometimes it helps to throw yourself body and soul into your work.

She began with a bolt of lightning that set dogs barking and nervous people skipping on the spot, followed by a stupendous rumbling belch of thunder that seemed to come from way down inside herself, followed in turn by the very latest Rapier-class air-to-surface anti-personnel rain, the kind that slices through cloth as if it wasn't there and impacts against your skin so hard you can practically hear it. This wasn't a time for gradually winding out the handles and slowly increasing the feed; if ever there was a situation that called for cracking the throttles wide open and delivering the full payload in the first volley, this was it. Maximum wetness, total viscosity, optimum drench and squelch factors, saturation bombardment; instantaneous metamorphosis from bone dry to sopping wet in the twinkling of a small, round red eye.

Daddy would have been proud of her. Faster than the eye could follow, Susan's hair went from golden waterfall to matted thatch, without any mucking about in the intermediate stages of moist, damp, sodden. Smart raindrops turned the exposed lining of her unfair-to-dragons sensible coat into a portable reservoir, so that putting it on would be the only possible way she could make herself wetter than she already was. Mortals – she'd noticed it before and for some reason it bothered her – mortals couldn't help looking ridiculous when they got wet with all their clothes on. They wore the rain like a custard pie jammed in their faces; the joke was unmistakably on them, they were the straight men and the dragons were the comics. Even Paul looked silly – endearingly, adorably silly, but still silly – with his hair plastered down over his forehead and a scale model mountain rill cascading down the slopes of his nose.

And if that didn't spoil the mood, Karen added to herself with grim satisfiaction, nothing would. If half what she'd heard about the sovereign effects of a cold shower was true—

They were laughing. Both of them. He was saying something like 'God, you're wet!' and she was saying 'So are you,' or words to that effect, and they were giggling like a couple of schoolchildren. Instead of scurrying for cover like startled rabbits – no point, since they were drenched already – they were just standing there, sniggering their silly heads off, laughing off the worst, the *best* she could do as if it didn't matter, as if a drop of rain never hurt anybody. It was sacrilege. It was an affront to everything that dragons stood for. It was so *unfair*.

Then Karen, who was also sitting out in the pouring rain without hat, coat or umbrella, realised that she was every bit as wet as they were, so wet that she could feel the rain dribbling down inside her underwear, and she wasn't laughing at all.

As soon as she woke up the next morning, Karen knew something was desperately wrong.

First, she couldn't breathe. It was as if someone had crept in during the night and stuffed cotton wool up her nose. (Her stupid, inefficient human nose; compared to the plumbing fitted to the ultra-evolved dragon body, with its multiple backups and bypasses, human pipes, ducts and conduits were downright primitive. It was a miracle the species had survived so long.)

As if the breathing problem wasn't bad enough, she was leaking. There was moisture of some kind streaming from her eyes and nose. What the stuff was – lubricant or hydraulic fluid or coolant, maybe – or where it had come from she had no idea, but it stood to reason that if it had been inside her head to start with, it was there for a purpose and she couldn't afford to lose much more of it. If the state of her pillow was anything to go by, she'd already been drained of close on a quarter of a pint; what if it was brake fluid or two-stroke oil, and when she next tried to stop suddenly her muscles were to seize and send her toppling headlong to the ground? To make matters even worse, there was something wrong with both her ears and an absolutely foul taste in her mouth, which tended to lend weight to the midnight-assassin theory.

The main thing, of course, was not to panic. First, she took a moment to check and rally those few remaining systems that hadn't been knocked out or severely curtailed by the attack. She found that she could just about breathe through her mouth (though this brought to her attention another malfunction, this time in the back of the throat, which led to convulsive coughing attacks if she wasn't very careful about precisely regulating the air flow), and that most of the motor functions in her arms and legs were just about operational, though with something like a twenty-five per cent reduction in efficiency. She dragged herself out of bed and managed to stagger as far as the bookshelf before subsiding onto the floor in a disorderly heap of limbs.

Even before Karen had made her escape from Home she'd had the foresight to realise that once she was down there among the mortals, she was going to have to cope with any injuries or illness by herself. The version of human shape assumed by dragons was believed to be a pretty faithful copy of the original in most respects, but the simple fact was that where a lot of the trivial detail was concerned, it was a case of best-guessing and figuring out from first principles. It was like trying to build a twentieth-century computer with nothing to go on except the design specifications for a twenty-fifth-century model and a photograph from a Sunday-supplement advert: no problem with getting the exterior looking just right, but the internal workings probably wouldn't fool an expert for very long – intestines the wrong colour or wound with a right-hand instead of a left-hand thread, metric instead of imperial bone-socket sizes, or something equally revealing to the trained eye. Visits to the doctor, in other words, were out of the question; which was why one of the first things she'd acquired on her arrival had been a big, fat medical dictionary.

She listed the symptoms and considered all the possible diagnoses, and came to the conclusion that what she was suffering from was something called a common cold. Terrifyingly, the book assured her that there was no known cure, and the thought of spending the rest of her life as a wheezing, gasping, seeping wreck nearly brought on a terminal panic attack; but she made herself read on, and was mightily relieved to learn that this awful condition somehow cured itself, usually in a matter of days. In the 'Causes' column, the book listed standing about in the freezing cold, or getting soaking wet, which pretty well confirmed the diagnosis while making Karen feel painfully guilty about all the rain she'd emptied on the heads of innocent bystanders the day before. Had they all caught this loathsome disease, she wondered, and were they all undergoing the same degree of suffering and discomfort as she was? The implications, not just for herself but for all dragonkind, were little short of staggering.

Well, at least she was fairly sure she wasn't going to die, so that was all right. Now all she had to do was make it through the day somehow, and then she could crawl back into bed and suffer in peace—

Which reminded her. She looked up at the clock on the mantelpiece and was horrified to see that while she'd been looking the other way, the time had sneakily scuttled on to half-past eight, and she wasn't even dressed yet.

Horrible tight human clothes, with all the ludicrous straps and fastenings and the peculiar cloth tubes you had to stuff your arms and legs into. Stupid human shoes, to make up for the hopelessly inadequate clawless human foot. Irritating human junk that had to be loaded into pockets before she dared slam the door shut behind her (keys, purse, wallet, cards, pens, handkerchiefs, combs, lipsticks, nail files—). Pathetic human lack of wings, leaving her no alternative but to run, which no upright species was ever intended to do, in order to clamber onto a crazy human bus and stand in a tightly packed human wedge while the bus crawled painfully in another typically human wedge through the blocked arteries of the city. Why, she asked herself, why this morbid fascination with the X-axis? Surely any fool could see that the surface was so hopelessly overcrowded that the system no longer functioned; in practice, it was already impossible to get from one place to another simply by trundling along the ground, whether on foot or by vehicle, whereas just above the heads and roofs of the toiling, suffering mass of travellers there was almost unlimited free transit space. It couldn't possibly be mere ignorance or lack of enterprise. There had to be some deep-rooted psychological defect that kept them rooted to the ground, in defiance of the glaringly obvious. Strange, perverse creatures. Aliens.

(Yes, but Paul wasn't an alien . . . Was he? If so, how on earth could she feel anything at all for him other than a vaguely amused contempt? However hard she tried, she couldn't find an answer to that one.)

Karen looked out at the two square inches or so of outside world that were visible past the human heads and shoulders, and saw that it was raining. Not again . . . She was going to have to find a way of controlling this, unless she wanted a whole nation of cold-stricken humans on her conscience. There had to be a way of cancelling the impulse. She'd never had this problem when she'd been a dragon. Back home there had been plenty of minor vexations and irritants, some of them as bad or worse than the things that set off downpours here on the surface, but she'd always been in perfect control, never shedding a single unintended drop. She thought about that. The only explanation was that the human brain simply couldn't handle the dragon nature; the sheer volume of thought and feeling was overloading the synaptic network, and the human controls couldn't access the dragon systems. Since humans didn't have the powers that dragons took for granted, there weren't any off switches or mute buttons to allow her to deal with them.

That, she realised, could be a problem.

It was nearly twenty past nine when she finally slithered and flopped through the door of Kendrick and Drake, Estate Agents. She arrived at her desk snuffling, guilty and wet, expecting to be shouted at, but the torrent of recrimination she'd been expecting didn't materialise; Mrs White was out viewing a property, leaving Paul and Susan (both completely cold-free) to mind the fort. Nobody here, in fact, but us humans.

'You look awful,' Susan announced, as soon as Karen had dumped the portable paddling-pool that her own angst had turned her coat into. 'Every time I set eyes on you these days, you're soaked to the skin.'

It was possible that Karen might have parried and countered this first strike with some dazzling gem of repartee, if she hadn't disintegrated in a fit of sneezing instead. By now, of course, she knew all about colds and was able to reassure herself that she hadn't inadvertently eaten a Semtex sandwich with nitroglycerine salad, but was merely clearing out her blocked nasal passages the old-fashioned quick and dirty way. Even so, the thought of the spectacle she must be making of herself was enough to send passers-by in the street outside scurrying for the cover of handy doorways. Her two colleagues, however, didn't seem unduly concerned. Paul, in fact, gave her his handkerchief, which she eagerly accepted in spite of the fact that she had two of her own in her pocket. True, she'd have preferred it if his first gift to her hadn't been a piece of rag designed for mopping up snot, but there are times when a girl's got to take what she's given.

'Thanks,' she mumbled, noticing as she spoke that her words sounded as if they were being filtered through two full-up vacuum-cleaner bags and an archery target. 'Sorry I'm late, the traffic—'

'With a cold like that I'm amazed you made it in at all,' Susan replied. 'If it'd been me, I'd have stayed in bed with a bottle of whisky and the TV remote.'

The nexus of emotions that these words inspired in Karen – basically, she was shocked that Paul wasn't as shocked as she was by this glib endorsement of dereliction of duty – took her a moment or so to get straight in her mind. Of course, no dragon would ever dream of saying anything like that. Dragons didn't call in sick (possibly because dragons seldom if ever got sick; there were only five known dragon diseases, and four of them were invariably fatal within fifteen minutes of the first symptom appearing) and if they did, they wouldn't be so damned cocky about it. Susan, on the other hand, made skiving off sound admirable, dashing, possibly even mildly glamorous; while Paul was just standing still and smiling.

Well, this was neither the time nor the place for trying to fathom the human mindset. Duty called. Lovelorn, wet and terminally bunged up Karen might be, but these were office hours and she was here to work. Even though it was by now fairly obvious that humans and dragons had rather different work ethics, she couldn't quite bring herself to work to human standards, mostly because she couldn't understand the rules. Back Home, it was easy – once a superior officer had assigned you a specific task, you didn't stop or rest until you'd done it, successfully and with a modicum of grace and flair. A word of thanks or a nod of appreciation was a pleasant bonus but not something you ever expected, since the satisfaction of a job well done was more than enough reward in itself. Concepts such as pay, or working hours, or doing just enough to get by simply didn't exist where she came from, and even if the dragon mind could encompass them, it was hard to see how you'd manage to fit them in to the sort of work dragons did – rounding up water vapour, marshalling it into clouds, escorting it to the drop zone and regulating the time, place and duration of the rainfall. The nearest equivalent she'd come across down here wasn't even done by humans, which made sense; she doubted whether they'd be capable of the mental discipline and commitment to excellence displayed by the average sheepdog.

Unfortunately, even Karen couldn't do work if there wasn't any work for her to do; she was still having difficulty with the human concept of the 'quiet day', when the junior officers are expected to sit patiently at their desks waiting for a customer to walk in through the door and give them something to do. She found it hard to imagine how a system so random and inefficient could be tolerated. What if, on Wednesday, nobody wanted to buy or sell a house all day, while on Thursday they were inundated with more business than they could handle? She'd raised the point with Mrs White at her interview, and she'd looked at Karen oddly and replied that most of the time it sort of averaged out. (A truly bizarre attitude, she'd thought at the time, all the more bewildering since it had been Mrs White staring at her as if she was a bit strange in the head, rather than the other way round.) In retrospect, she realised, Mrs White had given her a whole lot of odd looks, both during the interview and subsequently, though of course the branch manager hadn't hesitated for a moment before giving her the job, thanks to the stunning portfolio of qualifications and references Karen had presented her with—

(—A small rearrangement of history, too trivial to merit the description 'magic': for a dragon who'd come third in her year at the Academy and earned a distinction in both Applied Metaphysics and Transdimensional Badminton, fiddling about with some computer records and assimilating a few dozen textbooks had been a slice of Victoria sponge with a cherry on top. The only thing Karen had found remarkable about the training required of an apprentice estate agent was how utterly inappropriate it was – masses of irrelevant junk about how houses were built, and nothing at all about how best to pass off half-truths and downright lies to cynical and suspicious punters. It was a bit like training someone to be a lion-tamer by teaching them how to play the mandolin.)

So, when she'd answered the one letter that needed answering and filed the three that didn't, tidied up a few loose scraps of paper and washed out the coffee mugs, Karen was at a loss for anything to do. That was a nuisance. For one thing, staying busy helped her to keep her mind off the fact that she was in the same room with the man she'd forsworn her dragonhood for, and all he'd said to her all morning was, 'Do you need a hanky?' and, 'Thanks; black, no sugar.' For meteorological as well as personal reasons, that was something she didn't really want to dwell on if she could help it; nor did she particularly relish the thought of listening to the Competition telling him the apparently riveting story of how her aunt had taken back a defective pair of tights to Marks & Spencers. How anybody could hang on every word of such a pointless, boring recital if he wasn't hopelessly in love with the narrator, she couldn't imagine. Just as she was on the point of 'accidentally' yanking out the top drawer of the filing cabinet and spilling its contents all over the floor (so that she could kill an hour or so putting them all back) the door opened and someone walked in.

Under any other circumstances, the sight of a short, fat, bald, middle-aged man with a missing front tooth and bottle-end glasses most likely wouldn't have had such an electrifying effect on her. As it was, Karen was so determined to intercept him before the other two got to him that she almost knocked him over.

'Hello!' she warbled. 'Please come in. Sit down. Coffee? The kettle's just boiled. No? Never mind. How can we help you?'

The man looked up at her nervously, as if he was afraid he was about to be spread thin on toast and eaten. 'Have you got any bungalows?' he asked.

'Yes!' Perhaps a shade too much enthusiasm, passion even, in the reply. Too late to worry about it now, though. 'Yes,' she repeated, but with sixty per cent less passion. 'As it happens, we've got a wide choice of really great bungalows at the moment, in lots of wonderful locations, in every conceivable price range – I mean, some of them are so cheap we're almost giving them away free with soap powder.' That didn't sound right, either. It was at times like this that she was painfully aware of Human not being her first language. 'Not that we're having to give them away,' she added quickly. 'I mean, the demand's been so great we're practically turning people away at the door—'

The man looked round at the otherwise empty office. 'Really,' he said.

'Most days,' Karen replied. 'Today's been a bit quiet, that's all. Usually it's like a battlefield in here, with people climbing all over the desks trying to grab copies of the particulars . . . Well, not as busy as that, perhaps. But busier than this. Usually.'

As he stared at her, the man seemed to be weighing up his chances of getting past her and out of the door before she could bite him. Apparently he was a realist, because he stayed put and made a visible effort to keep still. 'Fine,' he said. 'Well . . .'

'I expect,' Karen went on, wondering if there was any way she could retrieve the situation or whether it would be better to go into the back and wait till everybody had gone home, 'you'd like to see some particulars. Yes?'

'All right,' the man said.

'Great. Wait there.'

The man froze. 'Right here,' he said.

'Yes, that's fine. I'll be back in just a second or two.'

'Will you? Oh.'

'You'll be all right if I just leave you there?'

'Oh yes, I'll be fine.'

Reluctantly she turned her back on him, just for a moment; but it was plenty long enough for him to jump out of the chair, tear the door open and slam it ferociously behind him.

By the time Karen got to the window, he was halfway down the street and running well for a man with such an obvious fitness problem.

'Hey!' Susan's voice behind her made her reluctant to turn round. 'That must've been pretty close to a record. How long do you think that was? Thirty seconds?'

'More like forty-five.' Paul's voice. It made her eyes hurt suddenly.

'Even so,' Susan was saying, 'that's pretty neat work. It usually takes me at least a minute and a half to get rid of a punter, and I used to think I was good.'

'Watch and learn,' Paul replied. 'Maybe she'll give you a few tips.'

Still Karen didn't turn round. The cold had apparently taken a turn for the worse, because she was finding it very difficult indeed to breathe.

'Sorry,' she heard Susan say. 'We're only teasing. But really, you've got to learn not to come on so strong with people. All this fire-breathing stuff—'

'We don't do that,' Karen blurted out angrily. 'It's just a myth.'

For one and a half seconds, they both stared at her without saying anything. Then Paul, having eliminated the impossible in the manner advocated by Sherlock Holmes, came to the conclusion that what she'd just said must have been meant as a joke, and laughed. Somehow, that only made it worse.

CHAPTER TWO

'My fault,' Gordon announced, making a grand if slightly vague gesture towards the pub window. 'All my fault. I admit it. I'm guilty.'

Several people turned round to stare for a moment or so. This indicated that they weren't regular customers. Most of the familiar faces didn't seem to notice Gordon's outburst, apart from one or two who took the opportunity to set their watches. Gordon, of course, couldn't see any of them. He was too deep in his own private purgatory to notice anything that didn't have whisky in it.

The barman, who'd been there seven years, grabbed some change from the till and programmed the jukebox, which started to play 'Here Comes The Rain Again'. It was an ancient and hallowed ritual, like the changing of the guard or the silly games they play in Parliament. Partly he did it because of a deep-rooted sense of tradition; mostly, because Gordon would howl the place down if he didn't.

'My song!' Gordon exclaimed. 'They're playing my song!'

It wasn't just that his money was as good as anybody else's;

Gordon Smelt's daily performance was tolerated – encouraged, even – because he was, after all, a celebrity, a TV personality, a member of the new royalty. In fifty years or so, they'd be putting up a blue plaque over the door, something like 'Gordon Smelt Got Rat-Arsed Here, 1989–2007'. There'd be a tailor's dummy in a glass case in the corner dressed up in a suit of his clothes, and you'd be able to buy Gordon Smelt sweatshirts, pens, CD covers, tastefully etched whisky tumblers, interactive Gordon Smelt multimedia drinking games; and when offcomers and ignorant Japanese tourists dared to ask, 'Yes, but who *was* Gordon Smelt?', the landlord would explain that Gordon Smelt had been a weather man – arguably the last survivor of the golden age of TV weather forecasting, or else the first precursor of the new wave (or whatever) – and press home the advantage by selling the hapless enquirer a copy of the official video, 'Gordon Smelt's Greatest Forecasts', digitally remastered into 3D with an accompanying booklet and bumper sticker. With a golden future of merchandising like that to pass on to his heirs, the landlord reckoned, it was worth putting up with the drunken shouting and the inevitable messes on the lavatory floor.

'You hear that?' Gordon was saying. 'That distant pitter-patter, like tap-dancing angels? That's rain, that is. My rain. My fault. You know why it's my fault?'

'Yes, Gordon.'

'I'll tell you why it's my fault. It's my fault because I *make the weather*, that's what I do.' He paused to empty his glass and push it across the counter, then continued: 'Which was news to me, of course. I thought I just said what I thought the weather was going to be. But oh no.'

'Same again?' the barman asked, pointlessly.

Gordon nodded without interrupting the flow. 'Oh no,' he repeated. 'I make the weather, I do. And do you know how I know that? Do you?'

'Yes, Gordon.'

'I know that,' Gordon went on, 'because every week, *twenty thousand people write in and say so*. Which means it must be true.' He grinned and picked up the glass; no need to look and see if there was anything in it. Wonderful things, rituals; a solid place among the shifting sands of real life. 'Democracy in action, that is,' he said. '*Vox populi, vox Dei*,' he bellowed, 'which, in case you're so ignorant you can't even understand bloody Latin, means "The voice of the people is the voice of God." You know what they say, in all those letters? Do you?'

'Yes, Gordon. It means the quick brown vox jumps over the lazy—'

'They say,' Gordon went on, word-perfect as ever, 'they say that Gordon bloody Smelt is a bloody rotten weather man, because all he ever makes is filthy rotten bloody weather. Get rid of him, they say. Give the bugger the push, so we can have some decent weather for a change. You know how many death threats I get on an average day? Do you? Fifty-six-point-four-seven.'

The barman nodded. 'Point four seven of a death threat must be a terrible thing, Gordon,' he said. 'Ready for another?'

'Don't mind if I do. The Prime Minister only gets six death threats a day. The bloody President of the United bloody States only gets twenty-nine. I get fifty-six-point-four-seven. And you know why?'

'Yes, Gordon.'

'Because,' Gordon said, wiping away a tear before it had a chance to dilute his Scotch, 'I don't give them the weather they want, that's why. And you know, I try. God knows, I try. Sunshine, I say, it's going to be blue skies, what do I see? Nothin' but blue skies, shinin' on me. And you know what happens when I say that?'

'Yes, Gordon.'

'I'll tell you what happens. What always happens. It rains.'

'Of course it does, Gordon. That'll be twenty-six pounds, forty pence.'

'Keep the change.' Gordon felt for the bar top with his elbow, but missed. 'The crazy thing is,' he went on, 'the stark staring barking mad crazy thing is – we don't just guess, you know. We don't just look up at the sky and say eeny-meeny-miny-mo. We're *scientists*,' he thundered, bringing his clenched fist down with tremendous force on the rim of a bowl of dry-roasted peanuts. 'We have *equipment*. In my department, we have a machine with three hundred and twenty times more computer power than NASA used to put a man on the moon, and that's just for typing up the scripts on. We've got enough hardware bobbing about in orbit to outgun the entire Klingon empire. So,' he went on, carefully picking a peanut out of his eye, 'when we say it's going to be blue skies, it's not just a guess, it's a scientific sodding *fact*. And you know what happens when we say that?'

'Yes, Gordon.'

'I'll tell you what happens.' Gordon sighed. 'It rains.' With that, the fury seemed to drain out of him, like oil from a classic British motorcycle. 'And it's all my fault,' he added softly. 'God says so. Can't fight God, you know. No point trying. I think I'll have another drink now.'

'Coming up.'

As the barman poured, he nodded discreetly to the customers at the other end of the bar, as if to say *Show's over*, while the jukebox, punctual to the second, launched into 'Raindrops Keep Fallin' On My Head'. Gordon Smelt would be quiet now, for exactly fifty-two minutes, after which time he'd make one final noise by falling off his bar stool. Throughout the pub, the atmosphere thinned, muscles unclenched, the buzz of conversation grew louder. It was, as the barman liked to describe it, the quiet after the storm.

For his part, Gordon was just about to climb into his six-teenth drink, the one that would carry him sweetly away to oblivion, when he became aware of somebody sitting next to him. This was unusual, as in unheard of. There are cocky peasants in Sicily who build houses on the lips of active volcanoes; but nobody ever sat next to Gordon Smelt in the pub.

'You Smelt?' the man asked.

Still humming along to the music, Gordon nodded.

'Thought so.' The man sat still for a second or two, then suddenly reached across, grabbed Gordon by the shoulder and turned him through ninety degrees, nearly spilling him onto the floor. 'All right,' he said, so softly that Gordon could scarcely hear him. 'Would you like to know why?'

'I'm never gonna stop the rain by— Why what?'

'Why,' the man repeated.

Gordon looked at him for a moment. 'You're drunk,' he said. 'Go away.'

The man refused to let go. There was something very disconcerting about his eyes – apart, that was, from the fact that he appeared to have six of them. Gordon squinted, adjusting the parallax, until there were only two. 'I said—'

'Shut up,' the man said, 'and listen. If you want to know why it rains, even when all the data says it's going to be ninety in the shade, I can tell you. Assuming you're interested, that is.'

Slowly and accusingly, Gordon stared into his glass. Then he put it down on the bartop, untasted. 'What are you drivelling on about?' he said. 'I know why.'

The man smiled. 'Really?'

'Course. It's because I make it rain. Because God tells me to. I thought I just explained all that; or weren't you listening just now?'

'Bullshit,' the man replied pleasantly. 'There's a perfectly simple, rational explanation. And if you want me to tell it to you, all you've got to do is ask.'

Gordon's face coagulated into a frown. 'Let me guess,' he said. 'Three guesses. Then I'll ask. Okay?'

The man shrugged. 'If you insist,' he said.

'All right, here goes.' Gordon thought for a moment. 'Global warming,' he said.

'No.'

'The greenhouse effect.'

The man pursed his lips. 'Isn't that the same thing?'

'Don't ask me, I'm just a bloody weatherman.'

'Let's assume it's the same thing. Two guesses left.'

'All-righty. El Niño.'

'Nope.'

'Not El Niño? Oh well. I know,' Gordon said, smiling unexpectedly. 'Obvious one. Secret nuclear testing.'

The man shook his head. 'Is that the best you can do?' he said. 'Secret nuclear testing. Well, well. I suppose I'd better tell you the truth, hadn't I?'

Gordon nodded. 'Fire away,' he said.

'Dragons.'

Gordon exhaled a lungful of air through his nose before replying. 'Dragons,' he repeated.

'Dragons. To be specific, the dragon king of the north-west. Or rather, his adjutant general.'

Gordon crowded his eyebrows together. 'Do you mind?' he said. 'If you hadn't noticed, *I'm* the pub loony around here. This is my turf, and if there's any gibbering to be done, I'm the one who does it. You want to gibber, find another bar.'

The man looked hurt. 'Sceptical bastard, aren't you?' he said.

'Yes. Just because I'm a paranoid drunk with a persecution complex doesn't necessarily mean I'm stupid. Which is it; practical joker or undercover tabloid journalist?' Gordon smiled hazily. 'Think carefully before you answer. Practical jokers get kicked across the bar and jumped on. I don't *like* tabloid journalists.'

The man stood up. 'Please yourself,' he said. 'I've told you what you need to know, what you do with the information is up to you. Meanwhile—' He picked up a beer mat and scribbled on it. 'Here's where you can find us, if you want to. If not – well, enjoy the rest of your life.'

'Are you crazy? I'm a *weatherman*.'

'Aren't we all,' the man replied, walking away, 'in a sense.'

The beer mat lay on the bar top, just an inch or so from Gordon's hand, right next to the full whisky glass. No more effort needed to pick up one rather than the other.

Dragons.

Well, quite.

Nevertheless, it wouldn't do any harm to look. Gordon flipped the beer mat over and saw, scrawled in green (for some reason) ink, the words:

www.stormtroopers.co.uk

– which even he recognised as being an Internet website address. He drummed his fingers in a pool of spilt beer, thinking.

Well why not? First, however, there'd be no harm in drinking this glass of fine single malt whisky.

He tilted the glass, absorbed its contents, closed his eyes and, just as he'd done every night for as long as anybody could remember after his sixteenth drink, slid gradually and with the poise of a trained judo expert to the floor. Twenty minutes later, the barman and one of the regulars scooped him up, dusted him off and laid him gently to rest in his usual eyrie in the broom cupboard.

'Seven minutes late tonight,' the regular observed.

The barman thought for a moment. 'Must be British Summer Time again,' he replied. 'Just as well you noticed, or I'd have forgotten to do the clocks.'

Snuggled upright among the mops and brushes, Gordon slept the sleep of the totally zonked. Atypically, however, he dreamed; and in his dream a great green dragon with fiery red eyes, perfumed breath, wings like a DC10 and a belly plated with twenty thousand letters addressed to *Points of View* in place of the conventional scales hovered over him, fanning him with its slow, measured wingbeats and widdling in his ear. When he tried to shoo it away by flapping an umbrella in its face, it did a double back somersault, opened its jaws to full gape and turned seamlessly into the Director General of the BBC, thereby causing the graveyard shift in Gordon's subconscious mind to file a memo recommending that in future he should avoid eating pickled eggs when going on a binge.

At midnight they woke him up and threw him out, and he wandered home in a thoughtful mood that severely impeded his ability to avoid lamp-posts. It was as he was picking himself up off the deck after a particularly close encounter that he remembered the beer mat, which he'd folded and tucked in his top pocket before sinking the last whisky.

Dragons, he thought. *Yeah, right*, he thought.

But as Gordon continued on his way (typically he walked twenty-five per cent further on the way home than on the way out; the difference between a boring old straight line and a sequence of aesthetically pleasing jags and swerves) he found himself considering, with the brand of logic that only kicks in when the brain is sufficiently lubricated, whether he shouldn't at least give the theory a fair trial. Now would be the time to do it, of course, while he was revoltingly drunk; sober, he wouldn't even contemplate doing something so utterly stupid, and so might just miss out on the discovery of a lifetime. After all, some great truths can only be fully appreciated when one's consciousness has been suitably enhanced, and if this happened to be one of them, he was ideally placed to handle it right now, being, by anybody's definition, as consciousness-enhanced as a newt.

After a mildly frustrating fifteen minutes spent trying all the keys on his keyring to see which of them opened his front door, he made it safely through to the hallway and stood still for a moment, trying to remember if he was still married. The issue was entirely relevant to the matter in hand. Jennifer would have his scalp if he started turning on lights and playing with computers at one in the morning, but he was morally certain that Jennifer had left him after the sea lion-in-the-bath incident. What he couldn't recall offhand was whether Jennifer had come before or after Trudy, and whether one or the other of them still lived here. There was only one certain way to find out and that was to turn on the light, an experiment that quickly gave him the answer he'd been looking for. Various subtle clues about the way the room looked – the trousers draped over the back of the sofa, the half-empty vindaloo cartons on the floor, the craggy yellow growth in the necks of several milk bottles – strongly suggested to the trained eye that he was once again a single man and perfectly within his rights to start up the computer any time he felt like it.

A little archaeology duly revealed the computer plug and matching wall socket, and soon the system was humming merrily – surely the whirring of a Pentium fan ranks with the soft gurgle of a brook and the distant click of bat on ball across a village green among the most soothing sounds available to a distempered mind – and the screen was urging him to buy more Microsoft products now, while stocks lasted. Somehow managing to resist the allure of these offers, he carefully unfolded the beer mat, typed in the address, hit 'Send' and went to sleep.

The common or garden office chair, as sold for computer workstation use, is a masterpiece of design, arrived at after hours of painstaking research and input from the CBI, Department of Industry and a number of consultants recruited from former members of the Haitian secret police. One of its most valuable features is the way it wakes you up, with extreme prejudice as regards the back of the neck, if you're slothful enough to fall asleep in it. The deterrent effect of this design has so far saved British industry enough man-hours to staff the next industrial revolution; but it was easy to overlook these positive aspects if you woke up in one after a night on the razzle.

'Agh,' said Gordon, and opened his eyes. He was in that uncomfortable transitional stage of being both drunk and hung-over at the same time, and the glare and movement of the screen saver was already doing peculiar things to his eyes. Experience had taught him some time ago that slapping the side of the box with the flat of his hand made the screen saver go away, so he did that, and found himself staring at the words –

WEATHER FORECASTERS OF THE WORLD, UNITE!

– in lurid green letters several inches high against a disturbingly purple background. His first reaction was that it was marginally better than pink elephants and crawling bugs; then he remembered, and narrowed his eyes to read the small print.

If you want get even, it advised him, *get MAD.*

He lifted his head and blinked once or twice. Maybe crawling bugs would have been preferable after all. He read on.

MAD – Meteorologists Against Dragons – is a direct-action organisation whose aim is to end once and for all the misery, suffering and humiliation caused to thousands of weathermen right across the globe by the recklessly malicious activities of so-called dragons. From our purpose-built headquarters securely hidden in a cavern somewhere beneath the Andean deserts of South America – the only place on Earth where rain has never fallen – we monitor dragon activity worldwide, coordinate anti-dragon initiatives, research potential dragon-prevention technology and support a far-reaching campaign of public education and opinion-reprofiling. If you want to know more about MAD and how it can help you get even, click HERE.

'Fuck off,' Gordon sighed, and went to hit 'Exit'; but the mouse slipped from his hand and landed on its own left-hand button. The screen changed.

WHAT ARE DRAGONS?

Completely potty, Gordon muttered to himself; still, he could always use a good laugh. He continued reading;

Modern scientists, assessing the ancient Chinese myth of the rain-bringing dragon, have argued an entirely plausible case for regarding the dragon as the prehistoric forerunner of the UFO. All the traditional dragon attributes – fiery objects hurtling across the sky, disturbed weather patterns and the like – almost exactly mirror the sights and sounds reported by present-day UFO spotters. From this they conclude that both phenomena represent the layman's misinterpretation of natural, easily explained occurrences such as meteorite showers and swamp gas. There are, they assure us, no such things as dragons.

Bullshit.

We, of course, know different. We know that the world is divided up into four spheres of dragon influence, roughly matching the cardinal points of the compass, each presided over by a dragon king supported by a complex and well-organised hierarchy of adjutants, marshals, signifers, lightning conductors and masters-at-arms. We have a pretty good idea of how dragons go about summoning clouds, precipitating rain at will out of a clear blue sky, and targeting rainfall to cause maximum disruption and embarrassment to the members of our profession. Make no mistake: those scaly bastards are out to get YOU, because you represent a significant threat to the veil of secrecy, superstition and ignorance behind which they've successfully cloaked their activities for countless centuries. By sabotaging our work and discrediting our members, dragons are seeking to undermine public confidence in weather forecasting in general, leading to the cutting of research and operational funding, marginalisation of weather broadcasting slots and the irreversible decline and demise of our trade. With us out of the way, dragons will once again be able to rule the skies without fear of detection and opposition.

We at MAD feel it's time we stopped these uppity critters from raining on our parade. We believe that it's not just a matter of our jobs and vocation being put on the line by a posse of overgrown iguanas. There are more public health and safety issues at stake here than you can shake a stick at; but so long as the Surgeon General, the military and the Federal Aviation Authority continue to stand by, sit back and do nothing, we get the feeling it's up to us to make sure something gets done, before homo sapiens is forced back into the dark ages of fiddling with seaweed and watching cows lying down.

To see what MAD action is planned for your region in the short and middle term, click HERE.

The icon referred to, a colourful thumbnail sketch of a dragon hanging by the neck from a lamp-post, seemed to be urging him personally to continue with the briefing. Shaking his head for as long as he could bear to do so, Gordon clicked, and was presented with a pie chart of the world, neatly divided into four quadrants. Clicking on 'North-West' brought up something that looked like a family tree, only it wasn't. Instead, it was a schematic diagram of the dragon chain of command for the north-western sector. Regarded purely as a work of art, it was quite something, with its rainbow colour-coding and elegant traceries of connecting lines and dots; if only he'd had a colour printer, he'd have run off a sheaf of copies and wallpapered the toilet with them.

Under the diagram was another block of text, headed *What YOU can do. Well,* Gordon said to himself, *indeed;* then he yawned and glanced up at the clock. If he wanted to spend more time asleep than it'd take him to brush his teeth and put his pyjamas on, he needed to go to bed now. Before hitting the kill button, however, he took the time to bookmark the page under the file name KOOKS –

– Because, he decided, he could do worse than come back to this site the next time he was filled with rage and fury against the elements. It demonstrated that he wasn't alone, that there were other weathermen out there, perched on the far shores of cyberspace, who'd been pushed even further than he had, to the point where they'd obviously dropped clean off the edge. Comparing them with himself was the most comforting activity he'd indulged in for years; indeed, just looking at the unmitigated drivel they'd come out with scattered the clouds of his anger (Freudian metaphor; so what?) and replaced the furious glare with a broad grin. As the old saying went: too many kooks spoil the wrath.

After an untroubled night's sleep soothed by dreams of blue skies, Gordon woke up with only a token hangover, which a pot of strong coffee and a pint of orange juice soon dissipated entirely, allowing him to go to work for the first time in as long as he could remember without a goblin chain-gang quarrying the insides of his skull. And, although his postbag was as full as ever and the warm, fine day he'd fore-casted was riven at frequent intervals by inexplicable electric storms, somehow none of it seemed to matter quite as much as it usually did; indeed, when he picked up an evening news-paper on his way out of the office and saw the headline ENGLAND SAVED BY RAIN on the sports page, he felt a tiny glow of pride.

Accordingly, he didn't stop off for a drink on his way home, and the regulars at the Cat's Whiskers were forced to set their watches by the TV news instead. It felt distinctly odd going to bed sober, but not entirely unpleasant. All in all, it had been a better than average day, and although he certainly wouldn't have described himself as happy – if only because he was way-wise enough to know that in the *Really Accurate Oxford English Dictionary*, 'happy' is defined as a divine dialect term meaning asking for trouble, and that admitting happiness even in pri-vate is effectively the same as twiddling a catnip mouse directly under Fate's nose – he had to concede in all fairness that he was rather less unhappy than he'd been for some time.

Gordon woke up at two a.m. with a blinding headache and various other symptoms consistent with acute alcohol defi-ciency. Fortuitously, he had a bottle or two of homoeopathic medicine about the place, and was able to prescribe himself a suitable dose; but he was realistic enough to accept that he wasn't going to be able to squeeze any more sleep out of that night. That meant he needed something to do for the next few hours.

The silly website, he suddenly thought, the one with the dragons; nothing like a little goofball comedy to help pass the time. He turned on the computer, waded through the preliminary garbage, and clicked on a promising-looking link headed *The Phantom Menace*.

The page took a long time to load, as if it wasn't happy about being woken up in the early hours of the morning. When it finally came through, however, Gordon was disappointed. The only thing on the screen was a big picture of a dragon, one of those Chinese New Year efforts, framed by the cross-hairs of an optical sight, and underneath, the words PUBLIC ENEMY NUMBER ONE, in eerily flickering blue and gold lettering. This struck Gordon as marginally too obsessive to be funny – up till then he'd still had a vague, lingering suspicion that it was all a very delicate and subtle spoof – and he was about to get rid of it when the picture disintegrated and re-formed as something rather more humanoid: a black-and-white mugshot of someone who looked like a fusion of God (as depicted by Michelangelo on the ceiling of the Sistine Chapel), Big Brother and Colonel Sanders.

Gordon was staring at this striking image and wondering why the words underneath hadn't changed when it too dissolved into a bee-swarm of pixels and came back together again as a large goldfish.

Gordon blinked three times. In an earlier, less jaded phase of his life (Marilyn, who to the best of his recollection had been after Louisa but before Trudy) he'd owned a fish tank that from time to time had contained fish. True, they'd tended to have the life expectancy of a second lieutenant in the trenches in 1914, but in between ice-cream-tub funerals he'd learned to tell the difference between, say, a bog-standard fairground-issue goldfish and a pedigree Japanese Koi – the latter had particularly stuck in his mind because of their rigid adherence to the samurai code, which led them to expire melodramatically whenever their honour was impugned by, say, a dirty water filter or economy-grade ants' eggs – and the thing on the screen, while undoubtedly a goldfish, wasn't like any other make, brand or marque of goldfish he'd ever come across.

And still the caption at the bottom of the screen stayed the same:

PUBLIC ENEMY NUMBER ONE

– which was in itself a contradiction in terms; the most any one of the three images could be was Public Enemy Number 1 (a), (b) or (c). Likewise he found it hard to imagine how a goldfish, even a bizarre mutant Ninja Koi, could be a public enemy of any description. It could die petulantly at you or it could swim backwards away from you while opening and shutting its mouth; that aside, it was as powerless and ineffectual as an MEP.

While he was trying to puzzle it out, the picture changed back into the New Year dragon, followed by a repeat of the humanoid version, with the fish bringing up the rear. Rather than sit through the show another time, Gordon clicked the kill button and turned the computer off. For some reason, though, the images stayed behind in his mind, like the forgotten guests who suddenly appear from behind the sofa on the morning after a really serious party. The human in particular; something familiar about that face – he was sure he'd seen it, or something very like it, not so long ago.

It wasn't long before the face was chasing him down a long, dark tunnel whose walls and floor were lined with viewscreens on which a goldfish in SS uniform threatened the world with storms, floods, hurricanes and tornadoes, followed by a warm front coming in from the south-west and the possibility of black ice in Hell. Fortunately, all this turned out to be a dream, from which Gordon woke with a stiff neck and a jackhammer headache five minutes after he should have left the house if he didn't want to be horrendously late for work.

All that witters isn't guilt; but a nagging conscience could be an uncomfortable companion, especially when you hadn't got much else to occupy your mind. After a day spent in making tiny, meaningless jobs for herself to do while keeping out of Paul's and Susan's way as best she could in a small, open-plan office, Karen was getting to the point where she couldn't hear herself think over the incessant muttering of the small, sharp voice inside her head –

. . . don't know how you could've been so thoughtless, going off like that without a word to anybody, they'll be worried sick, your poor father, he must be frantic, not knowing where you are, if someone did that to you you wouldn't like it, not one bit, the least you could have done was leave a note or something but oh no, you just took it into your head to go swanning off without a care in the world, typical of you, no consideration for other people, for all we knew you could have been lying bleeding to death in a ditch somewhere, most of the time you just don't think . . .

– which in turn had set off the other little guilt goblins, the ones who went –

. . . look at the state of this place, that carpet hasn't seen a Hoover in six months, dirty laundry just left lying about, it wouldn't kill you to wash up the cups and plates after you've used them, now would it, is this really what you want to do with your life, it's just as well your poor mother isn't around to see how you're frittering your time away like this. it'd break her heart. and will you just look at the dust on these shelves . . .

– in a continuous unholy counterpoint, until she'd have gone out and had her head amputated if the NHS waiting lists hadn't meant that death from extreme old age was a rather more probable outcome.

Since surgery wasn't an option, there was only one thing she could do to get rid of the nuisance. She'd have to call home and talk to her father. This would be both traumatic and extremely risky, since her father was nobody's fool and wouldn't have much difficulty in having the call traced; and before she knew what day of the week it was, she'd be scooped up by a couple of extremely polite, utterly ruthless dragons in grey suits and dark glasses, and find herself on the wrong side of the desk in her father's study being asked to explain herself; something which, for various reasons, she didn't want to do.

The trick, then, was to find a way of phoning home without being too obvious about it. Karen wished now that she'd paid more attention in class when they were doing ninja field operations at school; but she'd found all that stuff unbearably tedious, and had tended to sit at the back of the room, staring out of the window and creating entirely gratuitous rainbows to confuse and delight the world below . . . There were, she knew, many ways of bouncing signals off clouds and threading them through the eyes of storms and plaiting them into sunbeams until nobody stood a chance of figuring out where they'd come from, but she simply couldn't remember enough of them to do any good. The only technique she was sure she'd be able to get right (embedding a message in a satellite TV broadcast, with a built-in fragmentation code to separate it from the carrier wave once it hit the orbiting satellite) was so elementary that young dragons in Sixth Grade were set examples to decode for homework; there was also an inherent danger of uncontrollable secondary defragmentation, which would result in her message ending up on twenty million TV screens while her father got the second half of that day's Melrose Place.

But she couldn't think of any other way of going about it; so she resolved to keep the message short and sweet, stick to the point and hope for the best. She jotted down a rough draft on the back of some sales particulars –

Hi, Dad. Sorry I haven't been in touch before. I'm perfectly all right, so please don't worry. This is something I've got to do; I know you don't understand, but please just bear with me. I'm taking good care of myself; promise . . .

She stopped and read back what she'd written; it seemed hopelessly banal, almost meaningless, as if she'd copied out a set form of letter from a book of precedents. It was, however, the best she could do for now, and if she thought about it any longer she'd get cold claws and not do anything at all . . .

Karen closed her eyes – her two human eyes, that was. Her third eye scanned the air above the roof of the building, look-ing for the shapes and colours of a suitable broadcast signal. Most of the time, she kept her third eye firmly shut for fear of being hopelessly distracted – her human brain interpreted the messages from her dragon retina as the most dazzlingly strange and beautiful firework display imaginable, bewildering symphonies of tones and shades of colour swirling and flow-ing in ever-changing ripples and eddies –

Stop it, she told herself. *Behave. No time for any of that.* It was Indulgence of the worst possible sort to sit staring at pretty patterns in the sky; just because she happened to be wearing a human skin at the moment, that was no justification for falling into sloppy, small-minded human habits. Fancy dress or no fancy dress, she was still *herself*. Mustn't lose sight of that, ever.

She concentrated, and fairly soon caught sight of a suitable-looking signal with a hole in it about the right size. It had been a while since she'd done anything like this, even as a dragon – obviously it was harder to do with only a human body to work with, rather like trying to power an electric fence off a torch battery. But she managed in the end (she even remembered to double-fold the hem of the carrier wave and tie off the sonic wake with a Turk's head reef knot; her fourth-grade teacher would've been proud of her) and watched the tiny data packet spiralling upwards in a shower of amber, rose and emerald sparks and flares, until the distinctiveness of each shape and colour soaked away into the background and was lost. She closed her third eye, waited for a moment until the colours behind her other, more mundane eyelids had subsided to tolerable levels, opened her human eyes and blinked twice. The whole process had taken about three seconds, so it was highly unlikely that either of her colleagues would have noticed , 'Are you all right?' Susan asked.

'Fine,' Karen replied, pulling out a piece of Kleenex and dabbing at her face. 'Just got something in my eye, that's all.'

'You looked like you were miles away'

'I was.'

Susan frowned and shrugged with a fluency born of long practice – ever so many things seemed to strike Susan as reprehensibly odd, and she was ever so good at conveying her bemused tolerance for all of them – and went back to telling Paul about the man her cousin's brother-in-law's niece in Redditch had just moved in with. To judge by the fixed, snake-watching-a-mongoose expression on his face he found all that stuff utterly entrancing – a human thing, obviously, since Karen tended to find her attention wandering like Little Bo-Peep's lambs after a few minutes of similar narrations.

She stopped to think about that for a moment. Clearly, nothing fascinated humans more than the activities of other humans, and on balance that was probably an admirable trait of their species. Dragons weren't like that at all. When they talked to each other for extended periods of time (which was rarely), the subject was usually the bewitchingly perverse and unpredictable behaviour of subatomic particles, the unfathomable relationship of speed and time, the flavour of light and the many different sounds of darkness. It was almost as if dragons only discussed things with each other as a way of marshalling and evaluating their own thoughts and observations, only talked so as to think aloud. Dragons didn't bother with dragons very much, partly because most of them were pretty much alike, partly because there were so many more intriguing things to see and learn about than a bunch of flying lizards. Not so with these people. If a story didn't have human interest, it didn't interest humans, and – Karen found this bizarre to the point of perversity, but who was she to judg? – in spite of having discovered and invented a fairly creditable range of wonders and amusements (for a groundling bipedal species), what they seemed to enjoy doing most was sitting around a table talking to each other about each other. They could do it for hours. It was what they chose to do on their days off. Crazy.

(Except that she'd left Home to be with them, and all because what she wanted most of all was to be with one particular special human, for ever, always . . . Of course, it had never occurred to her to wonder what, in the event of this dream coming true, she and the wonderful human would ever find to talk about during those endless shared hours and days and months and years. Presumably, when the time came, the topics of conversation would suggest themselves naturally. Or they could just lie on their backs on the roof and count the stars.)

The telephone on her desk rang, and she pounced on it like a hungry cat.

'Hello?' The voice at the other end of the line said a name; but the entire budget for both *Star Wars* trilogies would be small change compared to the cost of typesetting it. 'Is that you?'

It took Karen a moment to recover from the shock. 'Yes,' she said, 'it' s me. How did you . . .?'

'Give me some credit, please.' The voice laughed, but there were only a few residual traces of amusement in the sound. 'What the *hell* are you doing down there? We've been going frantic. More to the point, *he*'s been going frantic. I've had my work cut out just keeping him from flooding the whole damned planet just to – if you'll pardon the expression – flush you out.'

Karen couldn't help smiling. 'That sounds like Dad,' she said, looking round to make sure the others weren't watching or listening. 'So he was upset?'

'It's a pity there's no real commercial use for understate-ment, because if there was, we could found a whole industry on you. Yes, he was upset.'

'Oh.' Karen hesitated. 'I'm sorry about that. But I'm not coming back.'

The voice on the other end of the line, which belonged to her father's chief adviser and officially designated Bearer of Vicarious Guilt, clicked its forked tongue sharply. 'Right now,' he said, 'that's the least of my problems. You do know he's vanished, don't you?'

'What?'

'Obviously not.' The voice dropped by a decibel or so. 'He went off to look for you over a week ago. We haven't heard a peep out of him since. I've bent my brain into right angles thinking up plausible lies to keep the King happy; he wants to know where his weekly returns are, and if he finds out your father is MIA—'

Karen shuddered. 'Don't,' she said.

'It's all very well you coming over all squeamish, but that's what he is. And if I was a nasty, cruel person I'd point out just whose fault that is; but I'm not, so I won't.' A pause. 'So you obviously haven't seen him,' the voice continued.

'No.'

'Silly question, really. You can tell I'm starting to lose my grip, which is hardly surprising in the circumstances. Oh, and while I think of it, what's the big idea behind all this completely unauthorised rain you've been spraying about the place? His Majesty's been asking about that, too.'

Karen winced. 'Sorry,' she said.

'You're sorry. Oh, hooray. That makes all the difference.'

'What did you tell him?'

'Oh, the usual. Fire drills. Systems checks. Dumping outdated stock before the end of the financial year. The insulting thing is, he's believed me, so far at least. What that says about his idea of how we run things up here I'll leave you to figure out for yourself.'

Karen sighed. 'So what do you want me to do? Shall I come home?'

'Only if you want to be told your fortune by the entire Legate Assembly. No, if I were you I'd stay right where you are for now and try and do something useful to make up for all the trouble you've caused. Like finding your father, for a start.'

'Oh.'

'"Oh," she says. Well, you were a bloody nuisance when you were little, so at least you're consistent. Come on, you've been down there for weeks, you must have the whole place pretty well sussed by now. I mean, it can't be complicated.'

'Well—'

'And besides,' the voice went on, 'exactly how many dragons do you think there are down there? I'll tell you. Two. Not counting you, one. In this context, I find the expression *pathetically simple* describes the task that awaits you pretty well.'

It's not like that, Karen thought, *not like that at all*. 'I expect you're right,' she said. 'I'll do what I can.'

'Oh joy,' the voice said unpleasantly, 'oh bliss. Oh yes; when all this is over, remind me to skin you alive and use your hide for a doormat, would you?'

'Of course,' Karen replied.

'That's all right, then,' the voice said. 'Goodbye.'

Karen put the phone down and leaned back a little in her chair. *Damn*, she thought. If there's one thing that gets in the way of overcoming an obsessive guilt complex, it's finding out that everything really is your fault after all.

Something else for her to do; more duty. It'd mean having to take time off from this job (leaving *him* alone with *her*), probably packing it in altogether; and by the time she got back (assuming she got back and wasn't immediately whisked off Home by the DIA) *they* would probably be living together, possibly even married, and everything she'd hoped for would have come to nothing, leaving her to face the dreadful consequences—

Indeed. And the hell with that – what on earth could have happened to her father? Dragons don't just vanish. More to the point, dragons can't just vanish – not unless they want to; but her father wouldn't want to, there was no conceivable reason why he should want to disappear, especially if he'd come Down on purpose to look for her. The only possible explanation was that something really, really terrible had happened to him, something so dreadful and unspeakable that it had made him impossible to locate Such as—

She could only think of one such-as likely to have that effect.

Karen thought about that. She thought about it for quite some time; and, because (in spite of everything she'd done and everything she'd been responsible for) she was still a dragon, when her tears began, they trickled hard and hot down every window-pane in the city.

CHAPTER THREE

The rain played drums on the roof, rattled the gutters, pressed its nose hard against the window-panes like a starving man watching the diners in a fancy restaurant; it tapped on the glass like a young lover urging his beloved to elope with him, it hammered against the french windows like a bailiff, it pawed and butted like a cat demanding to be let in.

The goldfish couldn't see or hear it, but he knew it was there; he could feel the presence of rain in the same way that you can wiggle your toes with your eyes shut. He could feel anger and frustration in its tempo, he could feel it searching for him and not being able to find him, as if he were King Richard and the rain was Blondel, singing under the castle walls. He tried to call to it, to summon it, command it (*Heel! Sit! Good rain!*), the way he'd done ever since he or anyone else could remember; but the water and the glass surrounding him insulated him from it completely, bouncing all his shouting and yelling back at him – and, since he was a goldfish, condemned by nature to hear with his whole body, he *felt* each sound crashing into him, like a misdirected trolley in a crowded supermarket.

It was ludicrous enough to be utterly humiliating; that he, adjutant-general to the dragon king of the north-west, should be trapped in a bowl of *water*. It was cruelty so delicately refined that he was amazed a dumb, blundering, tiny-brained mortal human had been able to think of it; a little pottering wingless biped, one of the tens of millions who scurry for cover at the first drop of rain, as if they were made of pure salt. Anger welled up inside him, radiated outwards and was dissipated entirely in the water, raising its temperature by five or so degrees. Having no other outlet for his wrath – no pondweed to shred with scything fin-strokes, no bits of rock to pound into dust with his tail – he hung motionless in the water and hyperventilated, the constant meaningless opening and closing of his mouth visible through the convex glass of the bowl making him look like a cabinet minister on TV with the sound muted.

Then the world went dark all around him, and his curved and bloated vision was filled with the huge, monstrous face of a human – *the* human, his jailer. An enormous eye, as big as he was, twinkled at him though the glass, making him flinch involuntarily and launch himself across the bowl with a ferocious tail-flick. Of course, he ended up exactly where he'd started.

The human was saying something, to him or at him, but the water mangled the sound and he couldn't make out a word of it or even interpret the tone of voice. There was, of course, nowhere to hide in a circular glass bowl containing only water and himself. All he could do was— Nothing.

The human made a few noises, then moved. A moment or so later the goldfish felt small disturbances in the water around him, suggesting that something was showering down on the meniscus way above his head. Rain? Indoor rain? Improbable; it was unlikely that the secret of indoor rain, which had eluded generations of frustrated dragon alchemists, should have chosen to reveal itself to a scraggy little mortal during the time he'd spent trapped in the bowl. He looked up, and noticed that the water was full of slowly downwards-drifting brown things about the size of one of his eyes – ants' eggs, falling like rain . . .

The human went away again, and the goldfish resumed his perpetual curved swimming. The worst part about his captivity, he told himself as he absent-mindedly gulped down an ant's egg, was the goldfish brain he was having to use to process every thought that crossed his mind. Quite a lot of them, mainly the ones full of anger, were too big, and had to be cut and shaped, so that by the time they'd been digested and rebroadcast, his draconian wrath had been pruned down to pique, which in turn was somehow water-soluble, like aspirin.

No; belay that. The worst thing was remembering how he'd ended up here, because that really had been *dumb* . . .

On the very first day of his search for his errant daughter (and if ever he laid eyes on her again, he'd have something to say to her; no question about that whatsoever) he'd been walking through the streets of the city which, as far as he knew, she'd run off to, when he began to get the impression that someone was following him. A human – so, no big deal; even now that he was in human shape, humans didn't frighten him in the least. He knew that stronger humans preyed on the weaker sort, beating them up and stealing their money and trinkets. If he hadn't been busy with other things, he could easily have amused himself for a day or so by strolling about looking weak and helpless so as to provoke just such an attack and thereby rid the place of a few of its two-legged predators.

This specimen, though, didn't look like the sort (he could, of course, see him quite plainly with his third eye); any humans weak enough to be preyed on by something this small and scrawny wouldn't be out and about on their own, they'd be in an oxygen tent in a hospital. The dragon found the thought mildly disturbing. If he was being stalked by something small and weedy, it wasn't just a case of picking up fleas in the flea market. This individual was far more likely to be following him, specifically, for a reason, and the only reason he could think of was because he knew . . .

But the creature was human, whatever its motives might be, and all a dragon needed to do in order to clear the streets and send the humans scampering off in all directions was to rain a little. Not too much, of course; unscheduled raining was unfortunate if unavoidable, and criminally irresponsible in all other circumstances. He started off, therefore, with a light sprinkle of fine, soft drizzle, the sort that sits on top of a human's hair like a spider in its web, rather than plastering it to the scalp. That sent a fair number of humans stampeding for shop doorways and awnings, but it didn't seem to bother his shadow at all; the little man merely drew the collar of his raincoat tight around his neck and opened an umbrella. Irritated, the dragon opened the throttle a crack or two more, enough to make the car-drivers turn up their wiper speed to maximum; the little man shuddered at the feel of water on his skin, but kept up the pace. The dragon considered that to be downright offensive – after all, this was the good stuff, from his personal reserve, some of the eighty-per-cent proof wet he'd been saving for a rainy day. He jammed the faucets wide open, so that the gutters in the street filled, overloaded and flooded the roadway, creating instant lakes for the cars to aquaplane through. Sure enough, the little man received a direct hit from the tyres of a passing sixteen-wheeler and was instantly transformed into a self-propelled pond. He stopped and shook himself, just like a dog – and then, dammit, he kept on coming, quickening his pace to make up lost ground.

It was at this point that the dragon realised that he was getting wet, too . . .

The fact that it bothered him, bothered him. If someone

had told him a week ago that a time would come when he'd feel uncomfortable standing in rain, he'd have laughed hard enough to dislocate his wing sockets. But humans were different. They didn't have immaculately contoured coats of scales, designed by nature to shed water as efficiently as possible; instead they covered their unthatched hides with absorbent materials like cotton, wool and leather, as if they were deliberately trying to catch the rainwater and snuggle it close to them for the rest of the day. The dragon wondered about that, in passing; was it a genetic throwback to the days before they had bottles and jars to carry water about in? It seemed an extravagantly perverse way of going about it. The same could, however, be said for nearly everything they did, from reproduction to gardening.

Since it would take at least ten minutes for rain of this intensity to wind down to a full stop, he decided that it would be a good idea to find shelter; not only would he not get any wetter, he'd also put pressure on his shadow, who'd also have to stop. He would make it clear to the strange little man that he knew exactly what he was doing – humans often find embarrassment as intolerable as pain or fear, so he ought to be able to make the man feel so uncomfortable that he'd give up and go away. Failing that, of course, he'd have to scare him off by a more direct and traditional method.

He turned down a side street that looked ideal for what he had in mind; on both sides rose the sheer, mountainous backs of large office buildings, and there was only one small archway that offered any kind of shelter. He darted under that, as swift and neat as a goldfish, and waited. Sure enough, his shadow was caught in the trap. His only options were to come in under the same arch and be shoulder to shoulder with his quarry, to stand out in the middle of the street, where pretty soon he'd be both painfully conspicuous and extremely wet, or to go away. To his credit, he stuck at the second option far longer than the dragon had thought he'd be able to, but in the end he turned his back and splashed through the puddles back the way he'd just come. The dragon smiled, carried on to the other end of the alley, and headed left.

Unfortunately the manoeuvre had taken him a little out of his way, and he wasn't quite sure where he was in relation to the main thoroughfare he'd been following. Trying to maintain a sense of direction in two dimensions when all your life you've been used to navigating in three can be awkward at the best of times, and the plain fact was that having to walk round the buildings instead of floating majestically over them at a height of several tens of thousands of feet made him feel dizzy and a little claustrophobic, as if he was lost in a maze. He was sorely tempted to morph back into his true shape, spread his wings and simply lift out of there, back to where there was room to breathe and perspective enough to see by. But he didn't want to do that unless he absolutely had to – not in broad daylight, in the middle of a crowded city.

The rain stopped and the sun came out; and the smell of drying cloth all around his body made him feel slightly sick. After wandering somewhat aimlessly for quite some time, he decided the simplest thing to do would be to head due south; because the river that bisected the city lay in that direction, so eventually he'd end up somewhere identifiable, even if he failed to connect with the main street he was looking for. The trouble was that it all took so long, with nothing faster than two feet to carry him, and it was also unexpectedly tiring. He'd only been walking for – what, seven hours? Eight at the very most – and already he was starting to feel distinctly weary.

South was easy enough to find; he could close his eyes and find south, thanks to the rich, dank smell of the river. Taking a direct line was out of the question because of all the masonry in the way, but ultimately it didn't matter; no more than an hour later, he found himself back where he'd started, almost exactly to the inch—

—And there was the little man, leaning against a lamp-post and grinning at him. Now that was *annoying*. The dragon scowled horribly and marched over to him.

'You took your time,' the man said.

'Why are you following me?'

'Is that a serious question, or are you just trying to scare me off?'

That wasn't the attitude he'd been expecting, not by a long way, and for a moment or two the dragon felt as if he'd just walked into an unscheduled plate-glass window. 'Why are you following me?' he repeated.

'Because I want to find out what you're up to.'

Perfectly reasonable reply for a biped; he hadn't realised they were capable of such a straightforward approach. 'Why?' he said.

'You really want me to tell you?'

'Humour me.'

The man shook his head. 'You don't scare me,' he said. 'We both know perfectly well that you won't lay a finger on me. Or a claw, come to that; and a fin I could probably deal with.'

'I don't know what you're . . .'

'If you stay human and thump me,' the man went on, with a cocky grin on his face, 'you'll get arrested; and they'll find out that you aren't in any of their records and don't actually exist, and that'll be really embarrassing for you. And you wouldn't dare turn back into what you really are, because that'd give the game away for sure. Either way, you'd be helping me achieve my objective. So, feel free.'

The dragon breathed out heavily through his nose, which seemed to worry the human a lot. 'And what would this objective of yours be?' he said.

'Oh, please.' The man smiled sardonically. 'Use your imagination, can't you? Or don't you people have them? I want to expose you, and all the rest of you goddamn' flying sprinklers. I want the world to know whose fault it really is when it rains, so that they'll start taking us seriously and do something about you. Preferably,' he added harshly, 'with cruise missiles. Or would they just bounce off those high-tensile bums of yours? I'm game to find out if you are.'

Suddenly, the penny crash-landed. 'I know who you are,' the dragon said. 'It was that nonsense you said about who's really to blame for the weather. You're one of those television people, aren't you?'

The man grinned. 'Fancy you knowing about television,' he said. 'I'm surprised. I wouldn't have thought you took that much of an interest.'

'I don't. But it's hard to ignore. I have to live in the air you people send it through.' He tightened his expression up a click or two. 'If anybody's got a right to be angry about something, it's us. How would you like it if your living quarters were constantly being saturated with other people's mindless burbling?' He took a deep breath. 'But I'm not going to have an argument with you about it,' he said. 'I haven't got the time or the energy. If you insist on trailing round after me, fine. But, if I remember correctly, you humans have got laws against that sort of thing. How'd it be if I had you arrested?'

'Be my guest.'

'You mean you'd use it as an opportunity to – what was that quaint expression you used just now? Expose me? They'd lock you up in a lunatic asylum for the rest of your life.'

'Not me.' The man's smile was starting to get on the dragon's nerves. 'I'm one of those television people, remember? A TV weatherman. Anything I do is news, particularly if I get arrested. That's how we humans are, you see; we love reading about the people we love getting humiliated and destroyed. Short of setting fire to New York, I can't think of a surer way of drawing attention to yourself than that.'

It was time, the dragon decided, to go away. The temptation simply to spread his wings and rise above the whole thing, like a cloisonnéd Harrier, was almost too strong to resist – but how could he be sure this odious creature didn't have one of his camera crews lurking round a corner or poised up on a roof somewhere? Other, stronger instincts urged him to find out by methodical experiment just how flat a human can become when jumped on repeatedly by a huge lizard; fortunately, he was able to resist them, too.

'I'm getting to you, aren't I?' the human taunted. 'You're about to lose your temper, I can feel it.'

'Certainly not.' The dragon crushed his fingernails into the palms of his soft, flabby human paws. 'In fact, I'm just starting to like you. Why don't we go and have something to eat?'

'I'd be delighted. Let's go somewhere crowded, where there's lots and lots of people. I'd really like that.'

A passer-by stopped for a moment and peered at the little weedy man, as if trying to read him upside down. 'Here,' he said, 'you're on telly.'

The weedy man smiled graciously. 'That's right,' he said. 'Thanks for watching.'

'You do the weather, don't you? After *News at Eight*.'

'That's me.'

The passer-by nodded. 'We used to watch you all the time,' he said. 'But not any more. We watch the weather on ITV now. There's less rain on ITV.'

'Ah.' The weedy man nodded gravely. 'You noticed. It's all to do with the cuts, you see. They've got the money, they can afford more sunshine than we can.'

The passer-by shook his head. 'It isn't right,' he said. 'I pay enough for the licence fee, God knows. Weren't you on that *Celebrity Squares* that time?'

'Which time?'

'I don't know, do I? I wasn't the one who was on.'

'Yes.' The weedy man dipped his head graciously. 'It was me.'

'There you are, then. Thought it was you.'

As the passer-by passed by, the dragon shook his head and sighed. 'Are they all like that?'

'All who like what?'

'Your public. The people you forecast the weather for.'

The weedy man shook his head. 'Not at all,' he said. 'Most of them aren't nearly as perceptive. Judging by the quality of insight displayed by his questions, I'd guess he was either the managing director of a major bank or the Regius Professor of Logic at Oxford. But that's not the point,' he went on, taking a step closer to the dragon, as if about to fit him with a saddle and bridle. 'They are the People, and they have a Right to Know. And I'm the one who's going to tell them.'

For the first time in his long and complicated life, the dragon felt panic starting to take hold. Mostly it was the incongruity – this pathetic specimen of a puny breed, advancing on him with a contemptuous grin on his ridiculous face, as if he was the one who could call down millimetre-perfect lightning strikes without even lifting a finger; in the face of such assurance, he couldn't help wondering if there wasn't more to all this than met any of his three eyes. He resolved on a controlled strategic withdrawal, with strategic running like buggery held in reserve as a contingency plan. The question was how—

And then he happened to look down and see, right there under his foot, a grating in the gutter. Some iron slats, a short drop, and below that a smart current of water running-off the recent heavy rain; too small for a human, let alone a dragon, but easily one small tail-flick for a goldfish.

He smiled. 'Goodbye,' he said; then he turned himself into a fish, slid through the bars and went *plop!* into the water—

—Right into the keepnet installed there by the little weedy man an hour before. Before the dragon realised what was happening to him he'd been scooped up out of the water and dumped, wriggling and thrashing, into a jam jar full of water. At once he tried to revert to his proper shape, but he couldn't; in order to make the change he needed clear, empty space around him to grow into during that all-important first three milliseconds of the process. Trapped like this in water, with the walls of the jar hemming him in, he couldn't do anything to free himself.

'Sucker,' the man said; then he screwed the lid on the jar, and everything was silent.

'Gordon?'

Gordon hesitated, his tray gripped precariously in one hand while the other tried to fish coins out of his pocket past the big bunch of keys, and looked round. 'Oh,' he said. 'It's you.'

It was a risk he ran every time he had lunch in the canteen: a disconcerting ambush by a more or less irritating colleague. There was neither time nor an obvious vector for escape, so he accepted his fate as gracefully as he could. 'How've you been, Neville?' he asked, synthesising interest like Rumpelstiltskin spinning gold out of straw. 'Haven't seen much of you since you started on the six o'clock slot.'

'Marvellous,' Neville replied, grinning. 'Come over here and sit down, I want to talk to you.'

My fault for not dying young while I had the chance, Gordon muttered to himself. He did as he was told, and started to disembark the contents of his tray onto the formica table. There weren't many places left where you could still find the genuine, original, unspeakably naff 1970s formica in its natural habitat.

'You got my message, then,' Neville said.

Gordon frowned. 'Did I?'

'Sorry for all the melodrama,' Neville replied, opening up his grin to Insufferable Level 2. 'But if I'd told you normally – you know, chatting like this – you wouldn't have done anything about it. Which is understandable enough; after all, you've always thought of me as an annoying little shit—'

'No, no.' Gordon frowned. 'Well, yes. If it's any consolation, I think of lots of people that way.'

'Me too. Doesn't matter. The point is,' Neville continued, spreading his skinny forearms across the table, 'you did as you were told and looked at the website. That's good.'

'Website? Oh, you mean *that*. How did you know I looked at the website?'

The soft gurgling noise Neville made was one of his trademarks. For what it was worth, he was a genuinely brilliant meteorologist, and he could also whistle more or less in tune. It was important to bear in mind that there was always some good in everybody. 'I don't think you really want to know,' he replied. 'So,' he went on, 'what did you think?'

'About the website?' Gordon pointed a forkful of shepherd's pie at his face, caught sight of it and put it back on his plate. 'With a certain amount of editing, it could be mere harmless drivel. I'm not saying you haven't still got a long way to go, but it's possible so long as you stick at it.'

'Drivel.'

'*Harmless* drivel,' Gordon reminded him. 'Or at least, there are several places where it aspires to be harmless drivel. Ah, but Man's reach must exceed his grasp, or what's a Heaven for?'

Neville wasn't grinning any more. 'Is this your facetious way of telling me you don't believe what we're telling you?'

'Yes. Do you want my bread roll, by the way? If you had two of them, you'd be able to bang them together and light a fire.'

'What is it you don't believe?'

Gordon sighed. 'Come off it,' he said. 'A joke's a joke, but it isn't a fence post; hammering it into the ground is not recommended. I'll admit you had me fooled for a minute or two, but . . .

Neville picked up the ketchup bottle, took the lid off, sniffed and put it back where he'd found it. 'You're saying you think the whole thing's a spoof. A leg-pull.'

'To more or less the same extent that Ronald Reagan was an actor; but yes, I think that's what you intended it to be.'

'I see.' Neville was beginning to look genuinely angry. 'Obviously I've been overestimating your intelligence all these years.'

'You mean underestimating, surely.'

Neville shook his head. 'My own silly fault. I honestly thought you had the breadth of mind, the perception, the depth of vision . . .'

'Sometimes I do,' Gordon said. 'Quite often, in fact; usually around half ten, eleven at night. Right now, though, I'm sober.'

Neville didn't seem to find that particularly funny. 'That's a pity. But we can deal with it. After all, seeing is believing.'

'Sometimes,' Gordon replied cautiously. 'Other times, it's nature's way of telling you to lay off the vodka chasers. All depends on what it is you start seeing.'

Neville pushed his chair back and stood up. 'So,' he said. 'What are you planning on doing now?'

'Eating my lunch?' Gordon caught another glimpse of the shepherd's pie. 'No, maybe not. In that case, I may as well go back to the office and do some work.'

Neville moved to block him from getting up. It was like being threatened by a Ray Harryhausen pipe cleaner. 'You mean,' he said, 'you're going straight to the fifteenth floor and you're going to tell them to fire me because I've gone crazy. That's right, isn't it?'

Gordon frowned. 'Do you want me to do that?' he asked.

'No, of course not.'

'That's all right, then, because I'd prefer not to. And besides, you only imagine the world is ruled by enormous flying lizards. By BBC standards, that makes you dangerously sane.'

People were, of course, beginning to stare. But Gordon was used to that; it was Neville who seemed disconcerted – odd, really, considering that he made his living being stared at by up to ten million people at a time.

'You'll see,' he said. 'I'll show you, and then you'll see. Meanwhile, if you so much as breathe a word about this—'

'You'll feed me to the dragon?'

Neville scowled at him. 'Don't be ridiculous,' he said. 'Dragons don't eat people. That's just a myth.'

'It is?' In spite of himself, Gordon smiled. 'You're sure?'

Neville made an uncouth noise with his mouth and walked away, leaving Gordon with his plate of congealed shepherd's pie and a few things to think about. Most of them were variations on the theme of There-but-for-the-grace-of-God; it was just as well that he'd taken to the bottle as a way of dealing with the nightmares of his profession rather than retreating inside his own head, as Neville had done.

Staring at the shepherd's pie wasn't going to make it edible. Gordon got up, spread a paper napkin over his plate as a mark of respect to the dead, and went back to his office. Even in spite of everything he'd had to suffer for its sake, he still had a spark of lingering affection for his work. Ever since he could remember, he'd had the romantic, idiotic notion of the weather being the planet's way of showing her feelings – the sun her smile, the rain her tears, mist and fog her stark, bleak moods, snow her mischievous winter grin – and according to the satellite, tomorrow ought to be a genuinely sad day, with legitimate heavy rain instead of the usual crocodile tears that he found so hard to explain or forgive. He could therefore forecast wet weather with a clear conscience; just this once, it had his permission to rain.

Once again, he passed the door of the Cat's Whiskers and kept on going. He had no illusions about being cured or having found a better way. One of the lesser reasons why he drank so much was the fact that he quite enjoyed it. He liked the taste of the stuff, the ambience of a properly dark, respectably scruffy lounge bar, the gentle relaxation of feeling his thoughts gradually getting slower and fuzzier. It certainly beat sitting at home alone in front of the telly. (Although the same could, of course, also be said of malaria or, indeed, death.) But the pub would still be there tomorrow; quite possibly the day after tomorrow, too. He'd appreciate it all the more after a couple of days away. In the same way, it made a refreshing change to wake up in the morning without a hangover.

Gordon was thinking about that last factor and reflecting on how much easier the world was to cope with when you didn't have a four-alarmer headache as he opened his front door and reached for the light switch; ironic, really, since before he was able to touch fingernail to plastic, someone stepped out of the darkness behind him and bashed him over the head with eight inches of lead-filled hosepipe.

The first thing Gordon saw when he woke up was a goldfish bowl.

Considering some of the things he'd seen a second or so after waking up (scary monsters with big eyes and horns; scuttling, crawly beetles; his first wife) it was odd that the sight of a small orange fish swimming round and round in a small glass container should have shaken him as much as it did. But this was no ordinary goldfish. This was identical to the one he'd seen on Neville's website, the one that belonged to no known species.

'Neville?' he said, as loudly as his reverberating head would allow.

'You've woken up, then,' said Neville's voice behind him.

He tried to twist round and face him, but found he couldn't. This turned out to have something to do with the blue nylon rope that surrounded him in coils like a mummy's thermal underwear and held him firmly in the armchair he was sitting on. Quite a lot to do with it, in fact.

'All right, Neville,' he said, looking round the best he could. 'I know about the ropes and stuff, thanks to the second Mrs Smelt. What's the goldfish for?'

'There is no goldfish.'

Gordon dipped his head towards the glass bowl. 'So what's that, then? One of those lava lamps they advertise in the colour supplements?'

'That's a dragon.'

'No kidding.'

The dragon was looking at them, opening and closing its mouth as it finned water. Definitely not a species he'd ever seen in a book or a pet shop. If it was a hybrid of some kind, he couldn't figure out what it was a hybrid of. It held still for a moment, flexed its gills wide and went back to opening and closing its mouth.

'Turn the sound back on,' Gordon said wearily. 'I can't make out a word it's saying.'

'You want to hear what it's saying?'

'What? Oh yes. Sure.'

'All right.' Neville took a step forward and slid back a concealed panel in the arm of a chair, revealing some kind of keyboard. 'Won't be a moment.'

'You take your time,' Gordon said. 'After all, if an impossible thing's worth failing to do, it's worth failing to do properly.'

Neville gave him a poisonous look and opened a drawer in his desk, from which he took a little net of the kind they sell in pet shops for evicting goldfish from their homes. The fish saw him coming and tried to avoid the net. It managed to make a pretty good job of it; at least three seconds passed before Neville was able to flick it out of the water and into an empty teacup. Gordon could see the poor thing squirming and wriggling—

'For pity's sake, Neville,' he said disgustedly. 'You'll kill it if you do that.'

Neville shrugged. 'He's got it coming, if you ask me. But it'll be OK, so long as he does as he's told. Right then, you. Talk to me.'

And then, to his complete astonishment, Gordon could hear the goldfish gasping and panting. It sounded almost human. 'Neville!' he shouted, and he struggled against the ropes, just as the fish was struggling against the air. Both of them were on a hiding to nothing, of course.

'Now then, your worship,' Neville was saying to the fish. 'Tell the nice gentleman who you are.'

'No,' the goldfish said.

'Please yourself. You aren't going back in the water till you do. And since you haven't got room in that cup to change shape—'

'Want to bet?'

'Yes,' Neville said pleasantly. 'Go on, then.'

Gordon heard a terrible rasping noise, one of the ugliest sounds he'd ever heard in his life. It was the fish, trying to breathe. 'Fish,' he shouted, 'do as he says, please.'

'No . . .' The voice was deep, with a strong accent Gordon couldn't place at all. The pain in it was all too easy to identify, however. For a split second, Gordon reckoned he knew what it must feel like to drown in air.

'Stubborn little thing, isn't he?' Neville sighed. 'Getting a civil answer out of him's like trying to get plain English from a lawyer; I'm not sure it can be done. We've been through this performance every day for a week, you know.'

The rasping noise was unbearable now. 'Neville,' Gordon said, forcing himself to sound calm, 'if I promise I believe you, will you put the fish back?'

Neville smiled. 'It's all very well you saying that,' he replied, 'but what makes you think I can trust you? After all,' he added, 'you're a weatherman.'

'Neville—'

Neville held up his hands. 'All right,' he said, 'I can see this is upsetting you. Come along, little fellow,' he said, picking up the teacup and dumping the fish back into the water. 'Better now?'

For a few seconds the goldfish lay in the water at a disturbing angle, motionless. Gordon was about to yell out, 'You bastard, you killed him!' when the fish dabbed feebly with its tail and pulled itself upright.

'There, you see?' Neville said. 'Right as rain, if you'll excuse the pun. Tough critters, these dragons. Strong-willed, too.'

Even now, Gordon wanted to try and reason with the lunatic; to try and explain that, even if what they'd both heard actually was a goldfish talking, all that proved was that here was a goldfish that could talk. All the stuff about dragons and rain was still— But it occurred to him that his colleague probably wasn't the most rational person in the world right now, and besides, he didn't want to provoke him into repeating the experiment he'd just had to witness. 'I can see that,' he said. 'Thank you for showing me. I don't suppose I'd ever have believed you if I hadn't seen it with my own eyes.'

Neville sat down cross-legged on the floor and looked up at him, reminding Gordon of a starved greyhound. 'Oh come on,' he said. 'I'm not stupid, you know. You aren't really convinced. You probably think it was all done with hidden microphones and rubbish. It's going to take much more than that to make you *really* believe.' He shrugged his chickenbone shoulders. 'But that's all right,' he said. 'We'll convince you sooner or later, I'm positive of that. Pretty soon—' His expression changed; remarkable, Gordon couldn't help thinking, how being barking mad could make even a complete twit like Neville look distinctly sinister. 'Pretty soon you'll have all the evidence you could possibly want; you and everybody else. And then – well, let's say it'll be interesting to see what happens.'

Gordon took a deep breath. He had no idea how one was

supposed to go about handling situations like this – doubtless there were officially endorsed techniques, taught to professional loon-handlers to A level and beyond – but he had no objection to improvising. The best approach he could think of was to try and reawaken Neville's latent inferiority complex. Neville was bound to have an inferiority complex; you couldn't be an odious little squirt like Neville for forty-odd years without acquiring one.

'Neville,' he said, trying to sound bored, 'have you any idea how stupid you sound when you're trying to do Dr No impressions? If you want to kill the fucking goldfish, go ahead; they can't put you in prison for that. But if you don't get these bloody ropes off me in ten seconds flat, I'm going to stick them, and the goldfish bowl, and anything else I can fit in there, right up your . . .'

'I don't think so.'

'Really?' Gordon laughed. 'So what're you going to do? You're going to keep me tied up here for ever? Kill me and dissolve the body in battery acid? You wouldn't even know how to get it out of the battery without spilling it down your trousers. Listen; pack it in now, while I'm still inclined to treat you as a sick but pretty funny joke, and we'll say no more about it. Otherwise it's going to turn nasty – you know, as in police and tabloids and prison? It's never worth it, Neville; even an idiot like you should be able to see that.'

The expression on Neville's face as he shook his head was little short of chilling. 'I expect you're right,' he said sadly – but the sadness was remote, as if he was expressing formal sympathy for some unfortunate victim of famine or flood in one of those funny little countries you have to look up in the atlas. 'But I stopped worrying about myself a long time ago. You can't afford to worry about what happens to you when you've got something as important as this to take care of.'

'Neville,' Gordon said; but he didn't get any further, because that was when someone kicked the door in. What with the thunderflashes and the tear gas that followed the initial forced entry, Gordon didn't get much of a look at the men who came bursting into the room – some through the door, some in through the window on ropes, as in the Milk Tray adverts – but to judge by their black balaclavas and exotic automatic weapons, they probably weren't collecting for the church roof fund.

CHAPTER FOUR

'Get real, will you?' said the pet-shop owner. 'Where am I going to get my hands on an okapi?'

The men in grey suits looked at each other. 'Two okapis,' their spokesman said.

'What?'

'We need two okapis,' the spokesman explained. 'One male and one female.'

'Do you really?' The pet-shop owner breathed out through his nose. 'Look, lads,' he said, 'why can't you just settle for a nice hamster instead? I've got plenty of hamsters.'

The spokesman frowned. 'So have we,' he said. 'In fact, we've got more hamsters than we need, really. We started off with two a short while ago, but now we seem to have lots of them. Tell you what,' he added, 'we could do a deal. All our spare hamsters for a pair of okapis.'

'That's a lot of hamsters,' pointed out his chief aide.

The pet-shop man sighed and went back behind his counter, in a manner designed to suggest that he'd lost interest in these negotiations. 'Listen,' he said. 'I'd love to be able to help you out here, but I can't. No okapis. No lemurs or ocelots or bird-eating spiders.' He picked up a thick wad of paper from the counter and held it out to the spokesman. 'None of the stuff on this list. They're lines we just don't carry. Sorry.'

'Can't you order them in?'

'No.'

'Oh.' The spokesman frowned, as if having trouble coming to terms with the concept. 'That's a shame,' he said. 'Are you sure? We'd pay cash, if that'd help.'

The pet-shop man took a deep breath. 'How about a nice kitten?' he said. 'Or two kittens? I can do you two kittens.'

'Thanks, but we've got that covered.' The spokesman thought for a moment. 'In that case, can you suggest anywhere else we could try?'

The pet-shop man grinned. 'A zoo, maybe,' he said.

'All right. Where's the nearest zoo to here?'

'I was joking.'

'Were you? I see. How about a serious suggestion?'

The pet-shop man could think of several things to suggest, some of which could easily prove very serious indeed. 'What do you boys want all these animals for, anyway?' he asked.

The spokesman took a step backwards. 'Actually,' he said, 'that's none of your business. This is a shop. We want to buy. That's all there is to it.'

'Like hell.' The pet-shop man's attitude had changed; even the spokesman could see that, and this was his first extended mission among humans. 'You know what? I wouldn't sell an animal to you people even if I had what you wanted. I don't trust you.'

'Really? That's sad. Why not?'

'Did we mention we're willing to pay cash?' added the senior aide.

'In fact,' the pet shop man said, 'I think I'd like it if you nutcases got out of my shop, before I call the RSPCA. Understood?'

The spokesman looked away and his lips moved, as if he was trying to figure out what the acronym stood for. 'If that's how you feel, we'll be on our way,' he said. 'Sorry to have bothered you.' He took three paces towards the door and then stopped. 'Oh, one last thing,' he added. 'Has anybody been in here recently trying to sell you a goldfish?'

'What?'

'Goldfish. Little orange bugger with fins and a face like William Hague. You see, a friend of ours had one stolen recently, and we just thought we'd ask—'

The question seemed to offend the pet-shop man, because he went a funny reddish colour. 'Yeah, right,' he said. 'Of course I'm in the habit of buying stolen goldfish from people who walk in off the street. That's precisely the way I run my business.'

'Is it? Ah. In that case, the next time someone comes in with one, could you possibly ring this number—?'

'Get out.' The pet-shop man was snarling now. 'Go on, bugger off, before I set the rabbits on you.'

'Actually,' said the senior aide, 'we're pretty well off for rabbits right now. In fact—'

'*Out!*'

I will be good, Karen promised. *I will control my emotions. Big girls don't rain.*

Hard enough to say that immediately after the phone call, when guilt and shock were fresh enough in her mind. Harder still, now that she was looking out of a train window, rattling away from all the reasons she'd come down here in the first place. Wingless bipeds, of course, didn't rain when they were sad. The closest they could get was a slight seepage from the eyes, a token shedding of water, as vestigial and useless as the human appendix. But she hadn't quite worked out how to do that yet, so all she could do was sit still and try not to think about it. Concentrate on the job in hand, the work that was still to do, and you forgot about the things that were outside your control, no matter how all-encompassingly awful they might seem; that was what a dragon would say, her father would say, if he was here, which he wasn't.

And if that didn't work, get on a train and go to Wolverhampton.

Simple draconian logic; Wolverhampton was near as made no odds, the centre of England, and if you were planning on conducting a thorough search, it made sense to start at the centre and work outwards. As to how one went about looking for a missing dragon, she hadn't the faintest idea. Obviously he wasn't in dragon shape, or a search wouldn't be necessary, which meant he was either a human or a goldfish. There were quite a lot of both of those in England, rather too many for a straightforward process of elimination to be practical. As far as alternative strategies went, she didn't even know if there were any. To put it another way, she hadn't a clue what she was supposed to be looking for, where it was likely to be, or how she'd recognise it if she did happen to stumble across it. Hardly scientific; but very human. After all, it was precisely the technique humans used when looking for a prospective mate, the one special person in the whole world who was meant for them, and if the bulk of human literature (up to and including the chocolate and perfume commercials) was to be believed, the technique worked for most people.

When on Earth, do as the humans do.

And it had worked for her, as far as finding that one special person was concerned. All she'd had to do was glance sideways out of the corner of her eye, as she was seeding a low cloud directly above the office where he worked. All she'd seen was a tall, rather angular human shape scurrying from the office doorway to the bus shelter, a newspaper held over his head to ward off the rain; that was all she'd needed to see. The odds against it – all the computers in Silicon Valley couldn't handle such a complex calculation, or even work out the formula needed to do the maths. But it had happened, just as it happened for millions upon millions of others.

(Nor was it particularly relevant that she was now leaving him behind, with That Bloody Woman poised like a dog begging at table to snap him up as soon as she was safely out of the way. Finding and winning were two separate operations. The fact that she'd failed in one of them didn't invalidate her success in the other. Stranger still, the finding stage was apparently the easy bit, which meant that the winning ought by rights to be so impossibly difficult that only the really clever, diligent humans ought to be able to manage it. Looking around the train compartment, however, and reflecting that each of her fellow passengers was the result of both a successful search and a successful outcome, she was amazed that there were so many brilliantly intelligent people on Earth; and if that was really the case, how come that in every other aspect of their lives they gave the impression of being so unbelievably dumb? The only explanation was that they used up so much of their reserves of cleverness on finding and winning their partners in life that they didn't have any left over for trivia such as fixing the economy or keeping out of wars. It followed that a non-human, who hadn't been trained from birth in these exceptionally difficult arts, didn't stand a chance. *Sometimes*, Karen mused unhappily, *it's hard to be a dragon, giving all your love to just one man.*)

Beyond the train window it was bright and hot, and that started her thinking. It was, after all, June. This was England, not California. Bright, hot, cloudless sky; something was definitely wrong. The obvious conclusion was that, wherever her father was, he wasn't doing his job; and she knew her father well enough to be sure that if he wasn't doing his job, it was because something was preventing him – death, injury, capture. Karen had learned long ago that Providence was easy to tempt as an ex-smoker on the fifth day after giving up, so she made a conscious decision not to speculate about the first possibility. Injury? What could possibly injure a dragon? In order to be damaged in any way, he'd have to be in one of his other two shapes. What about the third option? If he was being held prisoner somewhere, what possible motive could the captor have?

(Well, that question was easily answered. Brewers; the English Tourist Board; the Wimbledon Lawn Tennis Club; the National Farmers' Union; every sad-eyed optimist who felt a vocation towards a dry activity and then tried to make a living doing it in England – any or all of them would have an all too obvious motive.)

Nevertheless, she felt that she was getting somewhere, even if her rate of progress wasn't much better than that of the train she was sitting in. Just suppose for a moment that someone with enough at stake to take the risk had found out the truth about dragons. Capturing a dragon in his mortal guise wouldn't be terribly difficult, provided you managed to take him by surprise. Keeping him caught was another matter; probably impossible, if the dragon was determined to get free, since even in human shape any dragon would be ten times as strong as a human, seven times faster and infinitely more resourceful. As a goldfish, however, completely surrounded by hostile, energy-depleting water, he'd be virtually helpless.

Well, it was a place to start from; as, by the same token, was Wolverhampton. Now all she needed was a way of locating all the goldfish in (initially) the West Midlands, and checking them to see if they were metamorphosed dragons. At first, the scope of the problem daunted her a little, until she reflected that it was the proverbial slice of Victoria sponge compared with the statistically far harder task she'd accomplished so easily back at the start of this whole sorry adventure.

Goldfish, she thought.

Accordingly, the first thing she did after getting off the train at Wolverhampton was to find a post office and look up pet shops in the Yellow Pages. Having written out a list and bought a street map, she rehearsed in her mind what she was going to say. The words wouldn't be a problem. Pretending to be a ruthlessly single-minded public servant might be a little harder, but not hopelessly so. (After all, she *was* a ruthlessly single-minded public servant, at least when she was back home and had her regular skin on.) By the time she reached the first shop on her list, she had it all pat in her head.

'Hello,' said the man in the pet shop cheerfully. 'How can I help you?'

Karen flashed her library card under his nose. 'I'm an inspector from the Ministry of Agriculture,' she said. 'As you probably know, we're compiling a complete goldfish data-base, so what I need from you—'

'Excuse me.' There was something in the pet-shop man's eyes that suggested he'd already had a long and tiring morn-ing, which she was about to make longer and significantly worse. That made her feel bad, but it couldn't be helped. 'What do you mean exactly, a goldfish database?'

Karen stuck a suffering-fools expression on her face. 'As the basis for the National Goldfish Register,' she said. 'You know, as part of the government's new initiative to get illegal goldfish off the streets—'

The man sagged, like a suit that had fallen off its coat-hanger. 'Illegal goldfish?'

'You don't know about the goldfish initiative? For heaven's sake, you run a pet shop. You must have got the booklet.'

'No,' the man said wearily. 'No booklet.'

'Oh. Well, that's still no excuse. As part of the drive to eliminate fin-rot by the year 2006, as from the first of April next year all privately owned goldfish must be registered and inspected three times a year by Ministry ichthyologists. So,' she went on quickly, before the pet-shop man could say any-thing, 'it stands to reason we need to know who's got goldfish, how many, where they live, the height, width and breadth of the tank, details of any relevant pondweed usually kept with the fish, the serial number of the water filter, which direction the tank points in during feeding, the colour of any walls visible from inside the tank – you know, all the obvious stuff. I'll start by taking a look at your register.'

'Register?'

Karen frowned ominously. 'Please,' she said, 'don't tell me you haven't got a register.'

'I don't know anything about any—'

'A register,' Karen went on, 'of all sales of goldfish within the last seven years, consisting of one master copy for permanent reference, a duplicate copy for official use and a third copy to verify the other two copies by. Which you should have been keeping all this time, but obviously haven't. Oh dear.'

'Nobody told me anything about a—' The pet-shop man didn't bother to complete the sentence. The crushed look in his eyes suggested that he'd been there before, many times. He looked away. 'Sorry,' he mumbled. 'My mistake. I suppose you're going to report me.'

Karen clicked her tongue. 'I should,' she said. 'Really I should. But . . .'

The man looked up sharply. 'But?' he said, and the expression on his face was that of a fly caught in a web, unexpectedly told by the spider to get the hell out of there before it changed its mind. 'If there's anything I can do to help—'

'Let's see,' Karen replied. 'If you can put together a list of everybody who's bought goldfish, pondweed, fish food, anything like that over the past few weeks, I might just be able to turn a blind eye, this one time.'

The man might have considered pointing out that he didn't have that sort of information; if so, he thought better of it. Gift-horse dentistry is an unrewarding hobby; and he had bank and credit card counterfoils in his records, with names and addresses on them. 'It may take a while,' he said cautiously.

'I quite understand,' Karen replied. 'These things can take time. Tell you what; I'll give you four hours, while I make some more calls in this area. How does that sound?'

'Wonderful,' the man muttered. 'That's really very kind of you.'

'Oh, that's all right,' Karen said, gauging to perfection the amount of patronising contempt needed to make the statement sound truly authentic. 'I'm a human being, you know, not some kind of fire-breathing monster.'

After a long time in the white-walled windowless detention cell, they were led down a mile or so of ceramic-tiled tunnels and up and down another mile or so of stairs to a steel door with a four-figure number stencilled on it. The guard knocked four times, and the door opened automatically, making a very soft wheezing noise.

'You two,' said the man behind the desk 'All right, you'd better come in.'

It didn't look as if they had much say in the matter, so they did as they were told. The room's furnishings were as sparse as the audience at a poetry reading; one desk, one chair behind it, two in front of it, a light-bulb dangling from a bare flex, nothing else. Although he made it a rule always to be as optimistic as possible, Gordon couldn't help feeling that they probably hadn't been brought here to star in *This Is Your Life*, after all.

'Don't stand there like a couple of prunes,' the man snapped at them. 'Sit down.'

He was somewhere between thirty and fifty, slab-faced, blue-eyed, bald and not much wider across the shoulders than your average Mack truck. There was no reason to believe he wasn't capable of smiling, if given a direct order by a superior officer.

'You're the telly people, aren't you?' he said. 'Which one of you is Smelt?'

Gordon hesitated for a moment, then raised his hand a little. 'Me,' he squeaked.

'Fine. So you must be Wilson. Do you know why you're here?'

Neville, who hadn't said a word since they'd been captured, stuck his tongue out. The man didn't seem to notice. 'No,' Gordon said. 'Is it something to do with—?' He couldn't bring himself to say the word, the one that began with D. 'Weather,' he concluded.

'Dragons,' the man said. 'It's all right, we all know the score here, there's nothing to be gained by coming over all bloody coy. Of course you know why you're here. Now I'm going to explain it to you. Would you like that?'

'Very much,' Gordon said.

'That's all right, then. Shut up and pay attention.' He leaned back a little, and put his hands behind his head. 'Now then, let's start at the beginning. Which of you can tell me what made Britain great?'

Gordon blinked. 'Excuse me?'

'What made Britain great?' the man repeated. 'What was it that made it possible for a small cluster of islands at the unfashionable end of Europe to build an empire on which the sun never set? Well?'

Gordon bit his lip. 'Sea power?' he hazarded. 'The industrial revolution? Parliamentary democracy? Kindness to animals? The longbow?'

The man breathed out through his nose, like a Mad Cow Disease bull. 'Let me put it another way,' he said. 'What do you think prompted generations of Englishmen to leave their homes and families and set off for the furthest reaches of the globe, exploring, trading, conquering? What drove the best and brightest of the British race to quit these shores and colonise the New World, annex India, colonise Africa, settle Australia, conquer the Caribbean, plant the flag right across Asia from Egypt to Burma?' No reply. He sighed. 'All right, let's make it easier for you. Think about all those places I've just mentioned. What've they got in common?'

Gordon tried to think of an answer. 'Indigenous populations who didn't get out of the way fast enough?' he hazarded.

'Good answer,' the man replied, 'but wrong. Think harder. America. India. Africa. Australia. The West Indies. The Far East. Come on, it's not exactly difficult.'

A tumbler clicked into place in Gordon's brain. 'They're hot,' he said.

'Took you long enough, didn't it?' The man nodded. 'Correct, they're hot. Hot and dry. As opposed to the old country, which is—?'

'Cold and wet.'

'Exactly.' A thin wisp of smile residue appeared briefly on the man's face. 'The British conquered the world in order to get away from their rotten bloody climate. It wasn't just that, of course,' he added, with a slight wave of his left hand. 'The rotten bloody food had something to do with it, as well. But mostly it was the weather. The snow. The fog. The damp. The rain. All the filthy wet stuff that drops on our heads out of the sky. That's what shaped the British people, what defines us as a nation. More so than any other country in the world, in Britain the people and the climate are as one.'

'Wet and miserable?'

'In part,' the man said, nodding. 'But also hardy, strong, unrelenting, constant, driving. No nation on Earth is more aware of its weather. It's all we talk about. It dominates our lives. We even,' he added with mild distaste, 'make national heroes of our weather forecasters. You don't catch them doing that in Italy.'

'I see,' Gordon said.

'Take the Russians,' the man went on. 'So they've got snow and ice. Fair enough; they build an empire to get away from it. But it only lasts five minutes, and next thing you know they're rioting in the streets and wearing designer jeans. You want to know why? Because the Soviet Union was too big. Climate too diverse. For every province of their empire where it rained and snowed all the time, you had another where it was all sunny and warm.' (The man's face distorted with contempt as he said the words.) 'Result? They couldn't stick at it. No moral fibre, you see. No rain in the blood. Take the Americans. Ninety in the shade all the year round in California, it's no wonder they haven't even conquered Mexico yet. Now then,' the man went on, leaning forward a little and planting his elbows on the desk like electricity pylons. 'Do you know why we lost the empire?'

'No, but if you told me I'd be ever so grateful.'

'Central heating,' the man replied. 'Double glazing. Loft insulation. Cavity walls. Not to mention umbrellas and wax-cotton jackets and covered stands at football grounds. We turned our backs on our climatic heritage, and the weather turned its back on us. We made ourselves snug and comfy, and forfeited our birthright. Or are you going to sit there and tell me it's a coincidence that the last time England won the World Cup, Britain had just had two of the harshest winters in living memory?'

'That's very interesting,' Gordon said. 'I certainly hadn't thought of it that way before.'

'Don't suppose you had,' the man said. 'That's the tragedy of it, I suppose; we take our weather for granted, instead of getting down on our knees every morning and evening and thanking God for the highest mean annual rainfall in the Western hemisphere.'

'Typical,' Gordon said. 'But that's the public for you. Don't know they're born, most of them.'

The man frowned. 'But of course,' he said. 'That's the point. They mustn't know. If they knew, it'd ruin everything.'

Not for the first time, Gordon felt as if the room had just turned upside down, so that the floor was now the ceiling and vice versa. 'It would?'

'Use your head, man, of course it would. You can't expect people to do things if they know why they're doing them. The government of the country would grind to a halt. You'd have anarchy inside a week. Think about it.' The man steepled his fingers. 'It's like lab rats,' he said. 'They prod the right buffer with their noses, they get the cheese. Wrong buffer, electric shock. Perfectly valid way of doing an experiment. But if the rats knew—'

'I beg your pardon?'

'It's all right, you can't help being stupid. Look: the rats work out which buffer means cheese and which one gets them the volts. They make the system work for them, they think. If they get it right, they get fed; that's the way the world works, the way they see it. In other words, lab rats think the maze exists for the benefit of the rats. They're able to carry on believing it because they don't know about the scientists. Exactly the same with human beings. The moment people stop believing that society and the way things work are there for their benefit, they'll stop bashing their noses against the walls, and everything will grind to a halt. And that's why,' he went on, breathing deeply, 'the man in the street can't be allowed to understand about the weather. It's that simple.'

'Ah,' Gordon said.

'Which is why we need the dragon.'

'Of course. Now that you've explained it all, it makes perfect sense.'

The man shrugged. 'Anybody with the IQ of a small rock ought to be able to work it out for himself. Fortunately,' he went on, opening a drawer, 'ninety-nine point nine nine nine per cent of the British people don't quite measure up to those criteria, so the secret's still relatively safe.' He pushed a piece of paper across the desk. 'Sign here.'

'Of course,' Gordon said, accepting the pen. 'What is it, by the way? Just out of interest.'

'The Official Secrets Act, what do you think? All right,' he said, 'now your friend. Yes, you. Wake up and sign the form.'

But Neville kept his arms resolutely folded, drawing a look of extreme annoyance from the man behind the desk. 'Excuse me,' Gordon said quickly, 'but would it help if I just explained things to him? Won't be a moment,'

'Carry on,' the man said. 'Save me having to beat the shit out of him, I suppose. Not that I'd mind, only my tendinitis has been playing me up lately.'

Gordon hauled Neville to his feet and pushed him into the corner of the room.

'Listen,' he whispered. 'Obviously this guy is barking mad, but he's the one with the keys and the armed guards, so if you know what's good for you—'

'What do you mean, barking mad?' Nevilie replied. 'It all made perfect sense to me.'

Gordon closed his eyes for a moment. 'It did, did it?'

'Like he said, you've have to be pretty thick not to figure it out for yourself. Doesn't mean I'm going to stand by and let the bastards steal my dragon.'

'Of course not,' Gordon hissed softly. 'The very idea. But you're going to find it much harder with two broken arms and a dislocated shoulder to get the dragon back. So sign the bloody form.'

Neville thought for a moment. 'I suppose you're right,' he said. 'Play along, lull them into a false sense of security. Okay, I'll sign.'

Gordon looked at the steel door and thought about the M16s that seemed to be standard issue for the large number of steel-helmeted, Kevlar-clad guards they'd met in the corridors. *False sense of security*, he thought. *Yeah, right*.

'Give me that form,' Neville was saying. 'Can I read it first?'

'What do you think this is, a library?' The man stabbed at the form with a sausage-like finger. 'Sign there, on the line. That's it. Now give me back my pen.'

For some reason, Neville hesitated, so Gordon grabbed the pen from him and handed it back. As he did so, he noticed that it had the words 'A Souvenir Of Chichester Cathedral' embossed up one side in little gold letters.

'Thank you,' the man said, putting it away in his shirt pocket. 'Right, I think that's covered everything.'

'Wonderful,' Gordon said. 'Can we go home now, please?'

The man narrowed his eyes. 'Are you trying to be funny?' he said.

'Excuse me?'

'You can't go home,' the man said. 'For God's sake, haven't you heard a word I've said? This is a matter of *national security*.' He thumped the desk with his fist, creating a breeze that blew the two Official Secrets forms off the desktop and onto the floor.

For some reason, Gordon wasn't impressed. 'What do you mean?' he said. 'Are you trying to tell me we can't go home?'

'I'd have thought that was obvious.'

'For how long?'

The man shrugged. 'For ever. Well,' he added, 'in theory the restriction period comes under the hundred-and-fifty-year rule, after which I suppose you could apply to have your cases reviewed by the internal-security sub-committee. I wouldn't hold your breath, though, if I were you.'

Gordon nonetheless took a deep breath, which helped him not to fall over. 'And in the meantime?' he said. 'What happens to us?'

'Not my department,' the man replied. 'Officially you're now both under the jurisdiction of the resettlement and reha-bilitation sub-committee, whose function is to provide you with new identities, jobs, a place to live, everything you need to start a new and rewarding life without endangering national security.'

'I see,' Gordon replied guardedly.

'In practice,' the man went on, 'you aren't allowed to leave this building until the sub-committee's ruled on your case, and the sub-committee isn't due to meet again for another sixteen years. It's not as bad as it sounds, actually. There's four whole floors of disused offices up near the top of the building where we usually put people like you; last time I heard, they'd got quite a thriving little community up there. Apparently they do stuff like weaving wicker baskets and making sourdough wall-plaques. A couple of the guards' wives take them on and sell them at craft fairs. Next year, I'm told, they're planning on doing a production of *The Mikado*.'

'Sixteen years.'

'According to the schedule, yes; though, from what I gather, they may be running a bit behind. Oh, don't look at me with those God-awful puppydog eyes. There's starving refugees in Somalia who'd give their right arms for a nice office to sleep in and doughnuts on Fridays.'

'Absolutely,' Gordon said. 'Well, we'd better be on our way, then.'

The man nodded approvingly. 'Good attitude,' he said. 'Oh, and by the way – thanks for the dragon.'

'You're welcome,' Gordon said, stamping hard on Neville's foot before he could interrupt. 'We both feel sure it couldn't be in better hands.' He paused for a moment. 'I guess you aren't really supposed to tell us this,' he went on, 'but could you maybe just give us a small hint about what you're planning to do with it now you've got it?'

'Well . . .' The man pursed his lips, probably for the first time in his life. 'You're right, I'm not supposed to tell you, but since you know about the dragon already, and you've both signed the Act, plus the fact that neither of you's going to be in a position to misuse this information any time soon—' He frowned, then leaned forward across the desk and beckoned. 'We're going to make it rain.'

'I see. And?'

The man shook his head. 'No, you don't understand. We're going to make it rain *a lot*.'

'And you think people will notice?'

'Not at first,' the man replied. 'But of course, that's part of the plan. If they realise something unusual's happening, it'd spoil everything, for the reasons I mentioned just now. No; gently does it, that's the way to go. Constant drizzling rain for nine months or so; then, when everybody's fed up to the teeth and all they're interested in is where they're going for their holidays—'

'Yes?'

'We close the airports,' the man said triumphantly. 'Haven't quite decided yet how we're going to do it – terrorist scare, maybe, or we could say we're concerned about latent design faults in current-service airliners, or maybe we'll just provoke an air traffic controllers' strike. Details aren't important; what matters is that we stop everybody going on holiday and make them stay here all summer. In the rain.'

'Brilliant,' Gordon said, trying not to make it obvious that he was slowly backing away. 'And what'll that achieve, exactly?'

The man didn't smile, but he chuckled. 'Well,' he said, 'for a start it'll piss the general public off good and proper. It'll breed tension and dissatisfaction which, as you know, are the mother and father of overseas expansion. We won't do anything overt in the first two years, of course, we'll just let a good head of steam build up. Come the third year, if everything goes to plan, the British people will be so sick and tired of constant 365-days-a-year rain, they'll jump at the chance of going anywhere. And that's when we invade Australia.'

Gordon nodded slowly, four times. 'Masterful,' he said.

The man shook his head. 'That's not it,' he replied, sounding disappointed at Gordon's lack of perception. 'That's just the first step. We really only want Tasmania.'

'Tasmania.'

'That' s right. It's about the right size, you see. And of course the position's perfect; 140 degrees north, 40 degrees east. Couldn't have a better launch site if we were building one from scratch.'

'Launch site.'

'Well, yes. For when we colonise the Moon. Think about it: it's wide open, unexploited, mineral-rich, and *it never rains*. It'll be the Pilgrim Fathers all over again, except,' he added grimly, 'this time we'll do it *properly*.'

Gordon took a deep breath. 'Genius,' he said.

'I thought so,' the man replied. 'Of course, those fools in Parliament wouldn't listen; said it'd cost too much money, and the Americans might object. The hell with that; once we've built the laser-cannon installations at New Godalming, nobody's going to give a damn about what the Yanks think about anything.'

'So you're going to go ahead anyway?'

'Of course. It's one of the advantages of coming under the Home Office; we have a certain degree of discretion as to how we interpret the strict letter of the law. Like the police.'

For a moment or so, Gordon couldn't think of anything to say. 'Well,' he finally mumbled, 'very best of luck with the project, hope it all comes together for you. We'll be getting along now. Don't want to miss out on the doughnuts.'

The man shook his head. 'Doughnuts are on Fridays,' he said. 'I just told you that.'

Gordon nodded. 'Even so,' he said, 'it never hurts to get in the queue early.'

'Good point. All right, sergeant,' the man said, nodding to the guard who'd appeared noiselessly in the doorway, 'take them up to the thirty-sixth floor, they're expected. So long, then,' he added, giving Gordon a little wave. 'Remember, 'tis a far, far better thing, and all that jazz.'

'Oh, absolutely. And let me say it's been a privilege.'

'Yes.'

'It's so nice,' Gordon went on, 'to meet a man with vision. Several visions, in fact.'

'And the voices, too,' the man replied. 'They're a great comfort to me, the voices. Thank you for your cooperation.'

A doormat-sized hand closed on Gordon's shoulder. 'My pleasure,' he muttered.

'We may even name a city after you,' the man added. 'On the Moon.'

'That'd be nice.'

'Smelt City.'

'Or Smelt's Landing,' Gordon suggested. 'Got a ring to it, that has'

The man made a note on his desk jotter. 'Nice one,' he said.

'Or maybe even Smeltsylvania?'

'Don't push your luck,' the man said. 'On your way.'

Gordon waited until the guard had marched them along two corridors and into the lift. As the doors closed behind them, he decided to make his move.

'Excuse me,' he said.

The guard pretended not to have heard him, but he was expecting that and didn't let it bother him. 'Excuse me,' he repeated, 'but did you happen to overhear what your boss was saying to us? About invading Australia and colonising the Moon?'

The guard's nostrils twitched ever so slightly.

'Has it possibly occurred to you,' Gordon continued, 'that your boss is a raving lunatic? More to the point, a dangerous raving lunatic who reckons it'd be all right to bugger up the weather, start a war, maybe send thousands of people off to die on a waterless rock out in space? Would that sort of thing bother you, do you think?'

This time the guard's eyelids flickered. *Progress*, Gordon told himself. *Definite progress*.

'Of course,' he went on, 'he probably won't get away with

it; not all of it, anyway. I don't suppose he'll really be able to do much damage to the climate, because all this dragon stuff is a load of bullshit. And as for invading Australia, I don't reckon we'll actually get as far as sending in the ground troops; I expect we'll just drop a few thousand tons of bombs on Sydney and Melbourne and then call it a day, the way we usually do. Even so,' Gordon went on, after a short pause for breath, 'it seems a shame that all these dreadful things are going to happen just because of one guy behind a desk who happens to be as nutty as a Topic bar—'

This time the guard actually said something. 'Shuttup!' he said.

'But—'

'I said shut up,' the guard roared, grabbing Gordon by the collar and slamming him against the wall of the lift. 'Colonel Wintergreen is a man of destiny, and you can't say stuff like that. Understood?' He turned and scowled at Neville. 'And that goes for you too, sunshine. Got that?'

'Never said a word,' Neville replied smugly.

'Good. Keep it that way.' The guard let go of Gordon's shirt and let him slide to the floor. 'And to think,' he added, 'the Colonel's gonna name a city after you. You make me sick, you do.'

It was probably just as well that the lift doors opened before the guard had a chance to take this theme any further, since he seemed to be quite upset with Gordon about something. The rest of their journey through the maze of corridors passed, however, without further bloodshed. Eventually they came to a locked fire door, with a bell push mounted on the wall beside it. The man who answered the door was wearing a slightly different uniform.

'Sign here,' the guard said. 'And here, and here, and here, and here, and here, and here. Right, they're all yours.'

The new guard watched his colleague march back down the corridor, while massaging his right wrist. 'You're the weathermen, aren't you?' he said. 'Yes,' Gordon replied. 'That's us.'

'Follow me. Oh, and if you were thinking of trying to make a run for it – well, I wouldn't. OK?'

'It's all right,' Gordon said, dejectedly, 'we won't give you any trouble.'

The new guard shook his head. 'No, you're missing the point,' he said. 'If you try and escape, all that'll happen is, you'll get lost in these bloody awful corridors and I'll have to spend the weekend finding you. If you're sensible and come with me, we'll have you out of here in about half an hour.'

Gordon couldn't quite believe what he'd heard. For one thing, the guard sounded— Normal. Almost normal. Considerably more normal than anybody he'd spoken to since he'd left the office. That, of course, wasn't saying a great deal, but it was still enough to make his heart sing like a nightingale at a talent contest.

'Did you say out of here?' he whispered.

'Of course.' The guard chuckled. 'You didn't think we were going to leave you here with all these nutters running around loose, did you?'

'Oh, thank God.' Gordon really hadn't expected that there'd be tears, but when they came he didn't try and keep them back. 'For a moment there, when that other guard said Colonel Wintergreen was a man of destiny, I honestly thought I'd had it. Really I did.'

'Colonel Wintergreen,' the new guard said gravely, 'is potty. Crazy as a barrelful of ferrets. Come on, let's get you two out of the corridor, just in case those bastards change their minds.' The new guard shut the fire door behind them and locked it. There were four huge mortise locks on the inside of the door, along with various bolts and chains. After spending time with Colonel Wintergreen, he could understand why.

'This way,' the new guard said. 'Not very far now.'

'Wonderful,' Gordon said. 'Where are we going, by the way?'

'I'm taking you to the high altar,' the guard replied over his shoulder. 'The Grand Archimandrite wants a quick word with you before the sacrifice.'

CHAPTER FIVE

'So there you are,' the scientist said.

The dragon looked up at her. The refractive effect of the water in his bowl made the human's face look grotesque, monstrous; that and the sheer size of the enormous creature staring down at him. That huge wide mouth could swallow him whole. He felt like a human looking up at a dragon.

'Can you hear me?' the scientist went on. 'If you can, I'd like you to flick your tail or wiggle your fins or something. Will you do that for me?'

The scientist was obviously trying to speak softly and comfortably; to the dragon, of course, it came through as a rolling, thunderous wave of sound, ponderously slow and terribly distorted. Every instinct, piscine and draconian, told him to get the hell out of there, swim away as fast as he could. But there was nowhere to swim to, and besides, the scientist might interpret it as cooperation. He forced himself to lie motionless in the water.

'Are you sure you can't hear me? Or are you just playing hard to get? It's all right, I'm not going to hurt you. Really. I'm on your side.'

The dragon fought back the urge to set tail and flee. As if anything as big as that could ever be on his side . . . It took an effort to make himself remember that most of the time he wasn't just that big, he was a hell of a lot bigger. But that was different. It was different because he was one of the good guys.

'I'm going to assume you can hear me,' the scientist went on. 'My guess is that you're frightened and confused, you don't know who I am and you have no reason to trust me. I guess it's up to me to prove myself to you. Okay?'

In spite of the Spielbergesque special effects and the instinctive horror and revulsion, there was something terribly insidious about the scientist's words. Monsters aren't the only enormous things that appear in the sky and talk to you in voices like thunder. Gods do the same thing, and they're even easier to believe in than (to take an example at random) dragons. He wanted to reach out and put his fins over his ears; but his fins were too short and he wasn't actually sure where his ears were, or if he had any at all.

'First things first,' the scientist continued. 'I don't know when you last had anything to eat, but I'm prepared to bet you could use something right now. Am I right?'

The dragon stayed put.

'I'll take that as a Yes,' the scientist said. 'Now then, what would you like to eat? We've got – let's see, there's ants' eggs, some sort of crusty, flaky stuff that reminds me of what you get when you stick your finger up your nose and press hard, but maybe you guys really like it. Of course, if neither of those tickles your fancy, all you've got to do is tell me what you'd like. And yes, I know you can't talk to me through all that water, but I'm sure we could work something out. You could flick your tail in Morse code, or I could hold up little cardboard letters and when I'm holding up the right one you could do a somersault or something. If you're interested, I could see about rigging up a miniaturised underwater mike.'

The dragon hadn't eaten for a very long time and was extremely hungry, but not so hungry that he could face the thought of more ants' eggs. They tasted, he'd discovered, exactly the way a dragon would expect them to taste. He'd rather starve. The only problem was fighting down the irresistible goldfish urge to swallow the disgusting things as they drifted past his nose; it was like not blinking when someone sticks a finger in your eye, only harder.

'Ants' eggs it is, then. Oh, and by the way: if you're playing dumb in an attempt to make me think you're just a common-or-garden goldfish, hoping that I'll get bored and throw you out of the window or flush you down the bog, forget it. I know that the moment you escape from confinement, you'll change back into your regular shape and whoosh, that'll be the last we see of you. Okay? Now, are you sure you wouldn't rather have something else besides ants' eggs? I think they look utterly revolting, but what would I know?'

If only he could close his eyes at will . . . But goldfish eyes didn't work like that. All he could do was try and brace himself for the nausea that would follow on a split second after he'd swallowed the first egg. He tried to tell himself that it wouldn't be so bad this time, but without much success. He'd never been much good at lying to himself, even under the best of circumstances.

'Bombs away,' the scientist said. 'My God, you *are* hungry, aren't you? Well, at least that's one problem solved, we know what to feed you on. That's a relief. Last thing we want is for you to die on us. We'd hate that.'

The dragon couldn't close his eyes, but he could more or less close his mind; not as well as he'd have liked, because it was something only dragons could do, and he'd been stuck in this dreadful parody of his real shape so long that he was starting to forget how to do it. But he was at least able to blur out the world around him – like half-closing one eye and focusing the other on something a long way away. Instead, he opened his mind to thoughts of open air, clouds, gentle breezes filling the soft skin of his wings, thermal currents tugging at his ears as he flew. He imagined flipping over onto his back in mid air and letting a warm, firm wind carry him, of the warmth of the sun on his belly and the fresh chill of the air in his eyes and nostrils. It was comforting, up to a point; but all the time he was worryingly aware that he was a fish imagining what it would be like to be a dragon, maybe inaccurately. Had he ever actually done any of the things he was thinking about? He wasn't sure.

Rain. He tried to think about rain. He found that he couldn't. Now that was disturbing.

'Like I was saying,' the scientist went on, 'it's essential that we trust each other, or we'll never get anywhere. I won't get what I want. You'll have to stay in that horrid little bowl. I'll bet you it's really nasty being stuck in there. I mean, you're used to wide open spaces, unlimited movement; my heart bleeds for you, it really does. All right, you're saying, so why don't you let me out of here? And yes, I'd love to. Really I would. Except – well, first, I need to be able to trust *you*. I mean, what assurance have I got that as soon as you're out of there and back in your own shape, you won't flatten me and this whole building with one slash of your tail? I'm not asking for hostages or an affidavit or anything. I'd happily take your word. Any word'll do. Say anything. Say "Xylophone" or "Sideways", I don't care. For God's sake, how can we talk this over like rational creatures if you just lie there opening and shutting your mouth?'

The dragon hadn't realised he'd been doing that. He wasn't quite sure how to stop doing it, either. He'd have blushed with embarrassment if he wasn't bright orange already.

'Well,' the scientist said, 'at least I can be up front with you, and then maybe you might just feel you're able to return the favour. And if not well, I'm in no hurry. I'm not the one stuck in the wrong shape in a poxy little bowl.'

A single ants' egg floated lazily by. The dragon hated himself for swallowing it.

'You know, if I could be sure you're actually listening, this'd be a whole lot easier. Otherwise – well, here I am, a grown woman with two PhDs, talking to a goldfish. If I was me, I'd have me locked up. Anyway, here goes. Oh, this is *silly*.' The scientist walked rapidly away, becoming nothing more than a white blur on the edge of the dragon's curved vision. It was a while before she came back.

'Sorry,' she said. 'Temper tantrum, not very scientific. But you see, I've waited my whole life for this moment. I've been studying weather since I was a kid in school. All these years, I knew you existed – I didn't dare breathe a word of it, of course, or they'd have slung me out of Princeton so hard I wouldn't have stopped bouncing till I reached Utah, but I never stopped believing. And now you're here and I'm here, this is such an incredible moment for me, and you're just hanging there like an empty Coke bottle – it's so frustrating I'm ready to burst into tears. Please don't do this to me, it's so unfair. All I need is just one flick of the tail, anything to prove to myself that I'm not crazy . . . Is that really so much to ask? Really?'

The dragon concentrated. The scientist's words were tugging at his compassion almost as forcefully as the ants' eggs pulled his head round. Only by concentrating, putting all his weight behind the door of his mind and heaving, could he keep control. It was almost more than fin and scale could bear, far worse than any threats or actual pain could ever be. After all, what harm could it do, just one tail-flick . . .?

Harm beyond all measure, more damage than he could ever hope to imagine. He knew that; or at least, the dragon knew that. The goldfish believed that he'd known it once.

'Please . . .?'

He cleared his mind of the visions of air and cloud and flight; they were starting to get cloudy and vague, as the blue skies merged with blue water, the fluffy clouds became indistinguishable from hazy clouds of pondweed fronds, the currents – Instead, he thought about his daughter, and was immediately strong again. Picturing her in his mind, he knew who he was.

'All right, fish.' The scientist's voice had changed. 'This is your last chance. You're a small fish in a small pond, fish. Now, we can do this the hard way – God, I never thought I'd see the day when I'd say something like that. It's all your fault, dammit, you're turning me into the sort of person who can say 'We can do this the hard way' and not get a terminal fit of the giggles. That's *sad*, fish. I don't like it. So—'

The dragon relaxed. He could feel every part of his body now. *It's amazing*, he reflected, *how therapeutic a few vague threats can be.* One moment he was a prisoner inside a body inside a bowl; the next he was in control, able to resist, able to think clearly again. As the last few ants' eggs drifted past, he ignored them easily. As for the threats; he couldn't wait. What he really wanted, most of all, was for this silly woman to try something – anything – in the way of violent action; because in order to do anything to him, she'd have to take him out of the water first, and the moment she did that, he'd be ready.

'This is your last chance, fish.'

By concentrating really hard, calling on muscles and nerves that had never been designed for such a manoeuvre, mostly by sheer will-power, the dragon managed to curl back the edges of his lips in a teeny, tiny smile. His last chance, maybe; but he was ready.

Planning on going fishing, huh? You should have seen the one that got away.

'Just the one night?' the desk clerk asked suspiciously.

Karen nodded. 'That's right.'

'Then where's your luggage?'

'What?' Karen was too tired to be able to handle difficult concepts like luggage on the spur of the moment. 'Oh yes, right, luggage. I haven't got any.'

'None at all?'

'Everything I need is in my handbag. I'm only stopping the one night.'

Which, if the reception area was anything to go by, would probably prove to be one night too many. Admittedly, she was a trifle more fastidious than the average human (the same, of course, is true of all cats, most dogs and the leading brands of pig) but she didn't think it was totally unreasonable to object to carpet that crunched underfoot and cobwebs strong and thick enough to stand the weight of the knuckle-sized chunks of plaster that had flaked off the walls since the place was last dusted. On the other hand, it was all she could afford.

'One night, huh?' The clerk scowled. 'I know your game.'

'You do?'

'Too right I do. You're going to kill yourself.'

Not for the first time during her dealings with humans, Karen had the distinct impression that she was getting the pictures from one programme and the words from another. 'I beg your pardon?' she said.

'We get loads of your sort in here,' the clerk went on. 'You can spot 'em a mile off. No bloody consideration, that's your problem.'

'What on earth,' Karen said, 'makes you think I'm about to kill myself?'

'Oh please,' the clerk said. 'Give me some credit. I mean, look at you. No luggage. Miserable look on your face. Slumped up against the desk like that because you've lost the will to live. You might as well have a sign round your neck saying *farewell, cruel world*, it's that obvious. Well, not here you don't, because I'm sick and tired—'

'Really,' Karen said 'I'm not going to kill myself. Promise.' She smiled. 'Cross my heart and hope to die.'

'Huh! Told you—'

Karen took a deep breath. 'I give you my sacred word of honour as a—' She managed to stop herself before she said 'dragon'; then she was going to say what she really did for a living, but even as a part-time Johnny-come-lately human, she could see that 'on my sacred word of honour as an estate agent' didn't quite have the right ring to it. '—Pet-shop inspector that I'm not going to commit suicide. If it makes you feel any better, I won't even trim my toenails while I'm here, just in case I accidentally nick an artery with the nail scissors and bleed to death. Satisfied?'

The man sneered. He was very good at it, just like Elvis Presley. 'Huh,' he said. 'They all say that.'

'Really? You get a lot of pet-shop inspectors passing through here, do you?'

'They all say they aren't going to snuff themselves,' the man explained irritably. 'Then, soon as your back's turned, they're standing on chairs tying bits of rope to the light fittings. You got any idea how much it costs to get the wiring right again after some bugger's hung himself from the light flex?'

Karen thought for a moment. 'You could change over to those fluorescent tubes,' she said. 'Nothing on those things that you could get a good anchor on.'

'Yeah, and pull half the ceiling down on top of you an' all,' the clerk growled. 'No fear.'

'Hey, it was just a suggestion.' Karen breathed slowly, in, out and in. 'Look, are you going to give me a room, or do I go somewhere else? I know,' she added, 'tell you what: how'd it be if I gave you a deposit? And then, if I'm still alive at half past eight in the morning, you give me my money back. If I've gone and done myself in, you keep it. How does that sound to you?'

The man's eyes narrowed. 'How much?' he asked.

'Oh, I don't know – thirty pounds?'

'Seventy.'

'Forty.'

'Fifty,' the clerk said. 'And that's just covering paint and disinfectant.'

'All right, fifty it is,' Karen sighed. 'After all, you can't take it with you.'

'*Hey—*'

'Joke,' Karen snapped. 'Gee, if that's typical of your idea of a sense of humour in these parts, no wonder you're all in such a hurry to depart this life.'

A few minutes later, she turned the key in the lock of her room and pushed the door. It moved unwillingly, as if being asked to do unpaid overtime. The rest of the room wasn't much better, and Karen found herself wondering whether the high mortality rate among the hotel's guests wasn't just a straightforward reaction to their environment.

She sat down on the bed (slowly and carefully; it made an alarming creaking noise if you put any weight on it at all, and Karen was painfully aware that she had fifty pounds deposit at stake here) and reviewed her progress to date in the quest she'd assigned herself. That didn't take long.

Oh, she'd kept busy, no doubt at all about that. She'd walked miles and miles and miles on these quaintly impractical human feet. She'd told a lot of lies, frightened a lot of shopkeepers and fish-owners, seen one hell of a lot of goldfish. That was the problem; she'd been working flat out all day long, and she'd only just scratched the surface of goldfish ownership in one medium-sized city. At this rate, it could take decades, centuries to conduct a methodical search and that was assuming that her whole approach to the problem wasn't based on an entirely false premise. The more she thought about it, the more remote the logic seemed to be. Karen believed (on rather tenuous grounds) that her father must be trapped in the form of a goldfish, so she was looking for goldfish-owners to see if one of them had him. But (logic whispered maliciously in her ear) it wasn't goldfish-fanciers she needed to look for, it was dragon-fanciers. The nearest she could get to a firm connection was the hypothesis that whoever was holding her father in goldfish form would need to buy things like fish-food, and pondweed and air-filter car-tridges and all the million-and-one other things that underprivileged fish in seas and rivers somehow struggle on without. It was, she reckoned, a bit like trying to find a needle in a haystack by searching for the cotton it was threaded with.

She yawned like a cross-channel car ferry and lay back on the bed, kicking off her shoes with atypically human slovenli-ness. She was learning more about the critters all the time – how short their lives were, how long it took them to do any-thing, how hard they contrived to make things for themselves . . . She remembered something she'd seen in the park once, on one of the rare occasions when she'd been alone with Paul, strolling away the stub end of a lunch hour; a deter-mined-looking woman in a designer tracksuit puffing along at a brisk trot with what looked disconcertingly like small sand-bags Velcroed to her ankles and wrists. Karen found this so bizarre that without stopping to think that this was the sort of thing she was supposed to know already, she asked Paul what those funny things were that the woman had on. He replied that they were small sandbags, Velcroed to her ankles and wrists; and he'd gone on to explain that their purpose was to make the act of jogging even harder work than it was already.

In retrospect, that moment of insight was the closest she'd yet come to understanding the suckers; and there was a part of her mind that could just about follow the logic. The pur-pose of the self-inflicted burden was to make you feel confident and happy and strong when you took it off again; thus, the purpose of forming relationships or living under government was to make you fully appreciate your freedom once you'd got it back. Neat trick. But even so, it struck Karen as a rather roundabout way of achieving a fairly simple objective. Surely you didn't have to get yourself soaking wet before you could appreciate being dry.

Or maybe not. Maybe you had to, if you were human.

Maybe – this one made her wince and curl her toes – you

had to spend time as a human (or, in extreme cases, a gold-fish) in order to realise how lucky you were to have been born a dragon.

She sat up, ignoring the agonised sounds of wood and metal under intolerable stress that proceeded from the bed, and stared at the wall for a while.

'All right,' she said aloud, 'I get the message. Now, will somebody please get these things off me?'

It was meant to be a decisive moment, a point in her life where she achieved clarity, faced up to the mistake she'd made, took the implications to heart and in return was discharged and allowed to go home. Somehow, though, it didn't work quite the way it should have. She closed her eyes and waited for a minute or so; but when she opened them again, she was still there, staring at the delaminating vinyl wallpaper with the revolting stain halfway up it, whose genesis she really didn't want to think about. She was still in human shape. And, when she closed her eyes a second time, she caught herself gawping at a two-dimensional memory of Paul's face, shielded by a thick sheet of non-reflective glass.

She wondered what she'd done wrong. 'Please?' she added. That didn't work, either.

So; it wasn't as simple as that. Why was she not surprised?

Her feet were aching, and she felt depressingly sleepy. Not only that, but she was sure there was something else she'd forgotten to do; something human, routine and trivial and unavoidable. Ah yes, food. She hadn't eaten anything since breakfast.

(It was like keeping some small, helpless animal as a pet; when you weren't feeding it or mucking out its cage, you were combing its fur or clipping its claws or trying to persuade it to run round and round in its cute little wheel. All this routine maintenance humans had to do, occupying so much of their lives – so how come they still had time to be infinitely more complicated than the eternal, almost omnipotent dragons?

They were small, no doubt about that; but they were small and intricate, like a Swiss watch).

Another yawn rippled through her, starting in her midriff and working its way methodically up to her mouth. Not her problem, she decided. As far as she was concerned, she was happy to let hunger and fatigue fight it out between themselves to decide which of them had first call on her instincts. While they were doing that, she was just going to lie down on the bed and close her eyes for five minutes . . .

When she woke up, it was broad daylight and her watch had stopped. That was annoying; she'd mapped out the day's schedule in careful detail and, if she'd lost an hour or so to hoggish slumber, it'd mess everything up. She rolled off the bed, rubbed her bleary human eyes, and reached out for the controls of the ancient (late Victorian or early Edwardian) TV set that perched on top of the dresser.

She didn't have to wait long for a time check (8.45, dammit) to set her watch by. Before she could switch off, however, the irritating continuity person said something like 'And now back to that drought story we mentioned earlier', and she hesitated.

Drought?

She frowned and paid attention to the screen, on which a long, stringy blond youth in a C & A suit was interviewing a fat man, with a reservoir in the background.

'. . . One of the longest rain-free periods in a British summer since records began,' the fat man was saying.

'Seventy-two hours,' said the interviewer.

'Seventy-*four*,' the fat man replied, holding up his watch. 'And twelve minutes. Obviously, if this state of affairs continues, the government will have to take steps to conserve water reserves and prevent a drought crisis.'

The interviewer pulled his microphone back level with his chin. 'What kind of steps?' he asked, then jabbed the mike at the fat man's nose. 'Hosepipe bans?'

'Definitely hosepipe bans,' the fat man replied. 'Also bans on car-washing, window-cleaning, paddling pools and ornamental fountains. That's the first step, which we're going to introduce within the next—' (another watch check) '—thirty seconds. Phase two, which will come into effect if the drought continues past twelve noon GMT—'

(A caption flashed up under the fat man's picture, giving his name and credentials: Norman Ryder, Spokesman, Ministry of Drought, Famine, Pestilence & Death.)

'—Will consist,' Mr Ryder went on, 'of slightly more stringent measures; the contents of all swimming pools to be handed in to the police within six hours; baths to be restricted to no more than three centimetres in depth; the percentage of water in orange squash, barley water and similar concentrated beverages not to exceed ten per cent by volume. Basic common-sense provisions like that. In the longer term, we're looking into desalination plants, a substantial increase in artesian-well research and, of course, massively increased subsidies to EC cactus farmers.'

For a few seconds, the interviewer seemed lost for words. 'How would you respond,' he managed to say, 'to criticisms that the government may be overreacting slightly?'

Mr Ryder looked grave. 'I have to say that that's a rather irresponsible attitude,' he replied. 'At the present time, we have no idea how long this crisis is going to last. It's the government's responsibility to take positive action now to safeguard the public in case the position deteriorates any further. After all, for all we know, it may not rain again for *days*. It's a matter of weighing the inconvenience to the public against the potential risk, especially to handicapped people, the elderly and children. Let me ask you, which are you going to put first: washing your hair when you feel like it, or a child's life?'

Karen frowned and turned the television off. She'd been human long enough to know that they were entirely capable of getting into a hysterical panic about pretty well anything, so none of what she'd seen was impossible, or even unlikely. Something told her, however, that there was more to it than that. Generally speaking, governments only started panics that were likely to win them points in the polls. Making people take baths in an inch and a half of water, on the other hand, didn't really fit the usual definition of bread and circuses. They were up to something.

She stopped and listened to that last thought, and realised unhappily that she'd never sounded so human. *They were up to something:* you'd never catch a dragon saying that. There was a reason for that, of course. In the unlikely event that a superior officer gave an order you didn't like or couldn't understand, you asked him about it and got a straight answer. That wasn't the human way. It wouldn't work for humans, for the simple reason that there were too many of them. When you simply didn't have time to explain, you were forced to develop ways of making people do as they were told for reasons other than informed consent: fear, greed, bigotry, misdirection in all its many-hued splendour. That was why humans automatically assumed that those who controlled them were up to something; because they invariably were. The art of ruling people lay in making them believe you were up to something *else*.

She sat down on the bed and tried to concentrate. Apparently, the people who were running the country had reason to believe they were in for a long, hard drought. Coincidentally, the dragon in charge of bringing rain to the British Isles was missing; now that she thought about it, all the rain that had fallen here since he had disappeared had been her doing, the result of her inability to control her emotions.

At the very least, it implied that they knew the dragon wasn't doing his job. Draconian intuition told her it went further than that; they knew perfectly well that it wouldn't be going to rain for a long, long time because they knew where the dragon was, or what had happened to it. And the likeliest way they'd know would be if—

The peal of thunder that split the air terrified her, until she realised where it had come from. Her first instinct was to stop it – *someone'll see you, don't make an exhibition of yourself*; oh, so *human* – and she'd got to the point now where she might just be able to do that, if she really tried hard. But she didn't want to. The hell with that. If there was any chance at all that these people, these little, overcomplicated creepy-crawly little humans, had somehow managed to kidnap her father, thunder was going to be the least of their problems. The very thought of it made it hard for her to keep a grip on her human shape. She could feel her wings and tail, the way an amputation victim can still feel the missing limb. Her scales were pressing hard against the inside of her skin, trying to force their way out as if they were green shoots in the spring. There was lightning behind her eyes, desperately eager to earth itself, and the strain of keeping it back was almost more than she could bear. The hell with it; just one little abdication of control, and she'd give them more rain than they'd know what to do with . . .

Sudden clarity cooled her anger, the way cold water quenches white-hot iron. Just suppose they were holding her father, in the sure and certain knowledge that it couldn't rain without him. In which case, what would they be likely to make of *this*?

The force of the downpour rattled the windows, filling the nasty little room with the sound of rain. For Karen, it was like hearing her own language in a foreign country. She ran to the window and heaved at it till it opened, for the first time in years. Rain splashed onto her face, neck, hands and arms; it was like coming home and being greeted by an overjoyed, wet-tongued puppydog, bounding up to lick her face. The rain was a friend she'd missed far more than she'd realised;

but now that friend was here again, there was a chance that everything would be all right. An enormous grin split her face, just as the sky was split by an enormous bolt of blue forked lightning, and the roll of thunder that immediately followed it was just the echo of her own laughter. She felt an utterly basic, sensual delight in the feel of her wet hair plastered to her face and neck, of the rain soaking through her clothes to her skin. She laughed again, filling the air with static electricity—

—Which somehow contrived to jerk the ancient television into life, because it switched itself on and presented her with a vision of a weather forecaster, standing in front of a big map of the British Isles and solemnly assuring everybody that today would be another dry day in all parts of the country, with temperatures rising in some places as high as thirty-two degrees centigrade ('That's ninety degrees Fahrenheit'), with no prospect of any rain for the foreseeable future—

Karen collapsed in a fit of the giggles, which blew the TV screen out into the room in a shower of glass and wires, and fused all the electrics in the building. She was still giggling helplessly when someone came hammering at the door. It was, of course, the desk clerk.

'I knew it,' he yelled at her, pushing into the room. 'Told you I knew. You're trying to bloody electrocute yourself, and now look what you've gone and done!'

'I'm sorry,' Karen burbled through a haze of giggles. 'It was an accident—'

'Out,' the clerk was shouting. 'Go on, get out of here. You want to fry yourself, go and do it somewhere else. God knows what this is going to do to my insurance premiums.' He'd grabbed her jacket and thrown it at her; and the angrier he got, the more she couldn't help laughing, and the harder it rained.

Singing in the rain, she thought, as she sauntered down the street with her jacket over her arm, its saturated lining pointing upwards. Well, maybe she wouldn't go that far. Fairly soon she'd have to call a halt to this indulgence – dropping a hint was one thing, taking a stand directly under a huge, neon-lit sign saying HERE I AM was something else – but for now, she reckoned she owed herself a little pure pleasure, as a reward for remembering exactly who she was. Everywhere she looked, she could see the humans hating the rain; they were scurrying into doorways, crouching under umbrellas and newspapers, or trudging sullenly with their sopping-wet collars hugged tight around their necks. She felt sorry for them, but only because they didn't know what they were missing. It was like watching a small boy squirming as a girl kisses him on the cheek. *Silly humans*, she thought, *the day will come when they'll want it to rain, and maybe then it won't—*

—If she couldn't get her father back. Abruptly, she cut the rain and muted out the thunder, while her human skin crawled under the wet cloth.

A bus trundled past, crammed with humans, their strange round faces staring at her through the rain-streaked glass. Like a mobile goldfish bowl, Karen thought.

'This is all your fault,' Neville snarled.

Gordon lay on his back, staring at the ceiling, wondering what the weather was like outside. Wherever they were (he guessed they were some way underground, but that was just intuition) they didn't have a window to look out of, just four walls painted hospital-waiting-room blue and a sand-coloured lino floor. No weather in here of any kind, good or bad; and that was hugely disorientating for a man who'd spent most of his life locked in a tempestuous, destructive, Heathcliffe-and-Cathy relationship with the British climate. He was used to it spitting in his face and kicking him in the nuts; not being there at all, though, that was something he simply couldn't handle.

'They'll have that clown Julian doing my six o'clock spot,' he said aloud. 'He'll just stand there and read it off the prompt, like it's his lines in a play. Like it's *fiction*. What way is that to do the weather?'

Neville shrugged. 'Does it matter?'

'Of course it matters. Julian doesn't *believe*. It's like having an atheist vicar taking evensong.'

'You don't say.' Neville turned his back on him. 'You know, you make less sense sober than drunk sometimes.'

'I only get drunk when it rains,' Gordon replied. 'When it rains and it's my fault.'

'Definitely less sense when you're sober. They'll have to invent a whole new category of crimes to charge you with. Sober driving. Sober and disorderly. Sober in charge.'

Gordon sighed. 'Any idea how long we've been down here?'

'Up here,' Neville replied.

'What?'

'Up. We're somewhere up high, like on the top floor of a tall building. Barometric pressure,' he explained. 'I can feel it through the wax in my ears.'

'Oh.' Gordon nodded respectfully. 'Useful trait for someone in our line of business.'

'Bullshit.' Neville rolled over and faced the wall. 'High and low pressure, cold fronts moving in from the continent, isobars, cumulo-nimbus, the Gulf Stream, El Niño – it's all bullshit, as well you know. In the end it all comes down to dragons. It's nothing but big scaly lizards flying about above the clouds, pissing on our heads. Which is why it's all your fault.'

'Ah,' Gordon said wearily. 'Thank you for explaining it to me.'

'All your fault,' Neville went on, 'because you couldn't bring yourself to believe me. All I wanted to do was share the truth with you, because I knew how much they were *hurting* you. You were drinking yourself to death, and it was all their fault—'

'I thought you said it was all my fault.'

'It is. If you'd only believed in me when I first told you, we could have been out of there long before these lunatics tracked us down. We'd be free, and we'd have the dragon. Just think, will you, all the things we could've done . . .'

'Fed him ants' eggs? Watched him swimming round and round? Besides,' Gordon said firmly, 'nothing is going to make me believe that your goldfish was a dragon. Sorry.'

Neville spun round and stared at him. 'But for God's sake, you heard him—'

'All right.' Gordon held up his hand. 'Yes, I heard, or I thought I heard, your goldfish talking. Obviously you had a hidden tape recorder and some kind of proximity-operated speaker system. But even if I were naive and gullible enough to believe in a talking goldfish, how the hell is that supposed to make me believe in dragons? There is no logical connection—'

'Oh, shut up,' Neville replied. 'I suppose it's all my fault, for thinking you could possibly understand.'

'Make your mind up, please.'

Neville didn't reply; he curled up on his bunk, making himself as small as he could, while Gordon went back to staring at the ceiling. There was no light switch anywhere in the room and the light bulb was too high up to reach, even standing on a bunk. One of the first things Gordon had done when they'd been brought here was look for a thermostat or some other way of turning the heating down, because it was uncomfortably warm; at least seventy-five, quite possibly over eighty. Gordon hated it.

He must have dozed off, because he wasn't aware of the door opening or closing. The tray was suddenly there, lying on the ground near the doorway.

'Food,' Gordon said. 'Well, at least that's something. Can't remember the last time—'

He got up and examined the tray: two paper plates, a pile

of egg-and-watercress sandwiches and a jug of freshly squeezed iced lemonade. He scowled at it.

'What's the matter?' Neville asked.

'I don't like being made fun of,' Gordon replied.

Neville gave him a quizzical look. 'You're making even less sense now than you were a few hours ago. How does feeding us sandwiches constitute a piss-take?'

'Look around,' Gordon replied. 'Go on, look. Tell me what you see.'

'No, thanks. I think I'll just—'

Gordon reached out and grabbed Neville around his chicken neck. 'Tell me,' he repeated, 'what you see.'

'All right, all right – it's a room. A cell. It's not very nice. But at least there's food. Okay?'

'You're missing the point.' Gordon sat down on the bunk and rested his chin on his hands. 'They're mocking us. Everything in here is *deliberate*. Don't you see? It's a cloudless sky—' He pointed at the ceiling. 'Over a sky-blue sea.' He pointed to the walls. 'And we're lounging at our ease on golden sands, under a dazzlingly bright sun in glorious heat, about to eat our sandwiches and drink our lemonade. Couldn't ask for a better way to spend a lazy summer afternoon, could you?'

Neville's scowl melted into a wry grin. 'Not my cup of tea, beach holidays,' he replied. 'But I see what you're getting at. If you're right and it's more than just a coincidence, I'd say we're in the presence of a truly sick mind.'

Gordon grunted. 'Makes two of you.'

'Three of us. Hey,' he added, as Gordon glared at him, 'be fair. I'm not the one with the serious drink problem, remember. I don't know. Maybe we died and this is weather-forecasters' Hell.'

'I think,' Gordon said, getting slowly to his feet and craning his neck to study the ceiling, 'that it's about time we did something about this.' A smile was crawling spiderlike over his face. 'After all,' he went on, 'it's what we're here for, isn't it?'

'I don't follow.'

'Don't you? How odd. The weather is all our fault, remember. We're the guys who make it rain on Bank Holiday Monday. Well,' he went on, 'how about it?'

'Definitely three sick minds. Which,' Neville said, with a shrug, 'are proverbially better than one. What's the deal?'

'I don't like it in here. I think it'd be nice to get out. What do you think?'

'You'll get no arguments from me on that score. I take it you've got an idea.'

'I'm a weatherman,' Gordon replied simply. 'Shame there's no bedclothes on the bunks. We'll have to improvise. Give me your socks.'

'Get stuffed.'

'Do you want to get out of here or don't you? Give me the goddamn socks.'

Neville backed away nervously. 'What's wrong with *your* socks?' he said.

'They've got my feet in them. Besides,' Gordon added, 'they're nylon. Unless I'm very much mistaken, yours are cotton.'

'Cotton-rich,' Neville said. 'Which could mean virtually anything. Look, what are you up to?'

The smile on Gordon's face was reaching epidemic proportions. 'I'm going to make it rain,' he said.

'With my socks?'

'With your socks. And my handkerchief. For starters. Anyway, they'll do to get it going.'

Neville's eyes opened wide. 'You're going to start a fire,' he said.

'Precisely.' Gordon took a step closer, backing Neville into the corner of the room. 'And you know what happens when you start a fire in a government building? It rains. Or, to put it more prosaically, the sprinklers come on. And the fire alarm goes off—'

'—And they evacuate the building.' Neville relaxed, and grinned. 'Good idea. How were you proposing to light the fire? Matches? They didn't search you, then?'

Gordon shook his head. 'Lighter. Present from my secretary the Christmas before last.' He pulled off his belt and freed the buckle. 'She probably saw it in an Innovations catalogue and thought it was the most incredibly cool thing she'd ever come across in her life. I wear it so as not to hurt her feelings, and because it's the only belt I've got. Anyway,' he continued, 'the guys who searched me obviously couldn't conceive of anything as unutterably naff as a belt-buckle cigarette lighter, and here we are.' He pressed a knob on the front of the buckle, and a thin blue bud of fire duly appeared. 'Socks,' he commanded.

'Hold on.' Neville was hopping on one foot. 'You sure this is going to work?' he added. 'I mean, how do you know they've got sprinklers and alarms and all that stuff? This isn't your run-of-the-mill government office.'

'Trust me,' Gordon replied. 'They're all the same. Regulations. I remember some really boring bloke at the Met Office telling me all about it at a drinks do once. It'll be fine, you see.'

'You reckon?'

'Yes.'

'You're sure about this?'

'Of course I'm sure. What could possibly go wrong?'

'You're confidently predicting that it's going to rain in this room, and you're a weather forecaster.' Neville grinned disturbingly. 'That's all right, then,' he said. 'I was worried there, for a minute.'

CHAPTER SIX

Absence, according to the old saying, makes the heart grow fonder.

Just because an idea is old doesn't necessarily mean it's true. Other selections from the golden treasury of ancestral wisdom include the flat-earth theory and the leech as a sovereign cure for all known ailments. As far as the proximity/affection inverse ratio is concerned, however, our forefathers were definitely on to something, as Paul Willis would have confirmed as he sat behind Karen's desk, looking up an address in her immaculately ordered card index.

Odd, that a filing system should bring a lump to his throat. A flower pressed between the pages of a book, maybe; a dog-eared photograph discovered among the Visa receipts at the back of his wallet, perhaps; but a black plastic box full of neatly-inscribed cards wasn't typically one of Those Foolish Things. Then again, Karen wasn't like most people. To put it mildly.

For one thing, he reflected, as he pulled out the card he'd been looking for, she terrified the life out of him. He wasn't at all sure why. Compared with, say, Sharon Goodlet or Terri-with-an-I Ciszek or Leeona-from-Arizona or Bridget the Poison Waif – he shuddered as the memories trooped through his mind, each one leering mockingly at him as she passed. God preserve us from the memory of our lost loves, the ones who continue to haunt our dreams, especially after a late-night Indian meal. They'd all been scary, each in her own distinctive and unforgettable way, and in each instance he'd managed to jump clear at the last minute, hit the ground rolling and make good his escape with only superficial cuts and bruises. He was, in fact, something of an expert at miraculous escapes: Indiana Willis, the man who always walks away.

That was only to be expected. A man who looked like a third-generation photocopy of Hugh Grant and whose father owned twelve newspapers, sundry TV stations and a railway went through life with at least one set of cross-hairs centred on his heart at all times, and the more he tried to run away from his assigned place in the food chain, the harder his destiny pursued him. But a whole lifetime of evicting simpering blondes from his immediate environment hadn't prepared him for Karen, who didn't frighten him by her determination or rapacity. She just frightened him.

And Paul didn't know why. Most of the time, she ignored him. She avoided him as if he were a tactless topic of conversation; and yet he was certain that if someone were to ask her at any given moment where he was in relation to her, she'd have been able to reply with the exact distance in centimetres, bearings relative to magnetic north and precisely calculated grid references. It was the feel of the eyes in the back of her head boring into him that bothered him most. Maybe.

He closed the box and put it back in the drawer. Rationalised, his observations could be taken to show that she was attracted to him but didn't want to be; which was fair enough and perfectly understandable. After all, he knew better than anybody else that he was as commonplace and unexceptional an individual as it's possible to find outside of a cloning vat; so colourless as to be practically invisible when submerged in water, deep as an oil slick, complex as a hammer . . . Presumably, the reason why Karen scared him was that she actually seemed to like him (not his face or his potential value net of inheritance and capital gains tax, but *him*) and he couldn't understand why anybody would want to do that. Bizarre, almost to the point of perversity.

Now that she wasn't here any more, of course, it was much easier to like her, since she was, above all things, the sort of person who's far more attractive in theory than in practice. One of the things that intrigued him the most was that qualities he'd have found distinctly offputting in someone else (someone *normal* . . .) suited her like designer clothes. She was serious: serious about everything, as if everything she did or was involved in mattered somehow. He couldn't help finding that fascinating. Sure enough, there are a million people who keep their desks scrupulously organised and tidy, who make a note of the date and time of each phone call, who keep lists of Things To Be Done and work methodically through them till they reach the end; and 999,999 of those million people are the ones you'd gladly feed to the sharks, because you know perfectly well that they do it out of spite, to show the rest of humanity what it could have been like if only it hadn't gone so badly wrong back in the Late Bronze Age. But there's one person in that million who does it out of faith, believing that if a thing's worth doing, it's worth doing properly. That's the one person who should have been Florence Nightingale or Thomas Jefferson or Gandhi, but who ended up behind a desk in an office somewhere and still managed to keep the faith. Utterly fascinating, in a terrifying sort of a way; because you couldn't help thinking, if she cares so much about garbage like this, how much would she care about something that really mattered? Such as me . . .?

Anyway, Paul told himself, *she's gone now*; filed her last photocopy, sharpened her last pencil, backed up her last file, and left behind her a tiny, fragile model of her own perfection for him to bugger up. He frowned; he couldn't believe that anybody, even he, could be attracted to someone for her *tidiness* . . . Not that it mattered now. Gone, and just as well. Mentally he transferred Karen to the folder marked Perils Escaped From, and got on with some work instead.

'Bloody woman,' muttered Susan, at the other end of the room.

Paul looked up. 'Sorry?' he said.

'I said, bloody woman,' Susan replied. 'You don't need me to be more specific, I'm sure.'

Paul's eyebrows pulled together. 'What's the problem?' he asked.

'No problem,' Susan said. 'I wanted the OS map sheet for this site plan, and I couldn't remember what I'd done with it; and then I remembered that before she left, she sorted all the maps out, filed them in order and put them all neatly in folders where they'd be nice and handy for when we needed them. So I said "bloody woman". Naturally.'

'Oh. Why?'

'Because she's only been gone five minutes and I know for a fact that I'll forget to put this sheet away, so when I want it next time I won't be able to find it. Bitch,' she added. 'Some people have no consideration.'

Paul frowned. He knew that Karen hadn't liked Susan much – he had no idea why – and that Susan had always seemed to resent Karen, as if she blamed her for getting her into something she didn't want to be involved in. He hadn't a clue what that was all about, either. There were times when he wondered if he wouldn't have been better off getting a job as a lighthouse keeper, with no colleagues of any description to perplex him.

'You could always try putting the map back when you're done with it,' he suggested.

'Certainly not. That'd mean she'd have won, and I'm not having that.' Susan got up, dragged open a filing-cabinet drawer and pulled out a folder. 'Other people who leave on the spur of the moment leave chaos and disorder behind them,' she went on, 'which is how it should be. I feel like I'm living in a bloody museum.'

I know what you mean, Paul deliberately didn't say. 'I don't know what you're making such a fuss about,' he replied. 'There's nothing wrong with being conscientious.'

Susan pulled a face. 'There's a special place in Hell reserved for people who quit unexpectedly, leaving an immaculate system behind them,' she said. 'Probably in the Ninth Circle, along with the party leaders and the TV producers, and the people who sell lists of names to the junk-mail outfits.'

Paul was silent for a moment. 'Don't suppose you've heard anything from her, have you?' he asked.

She turned her head and looked at him. 'Certainly not,' she said. 'And I don't think she left a forwarding address, either. Why the hell would you be interested?'

'I'm not,' Paul replied, maybe a degree or so too vehemently.

'My God.' Susan stared at him, then shook her head. 'Well,' she said, 'too late now. Should've done something about it while you had the chance, though if I were in your shoes I'd be looking into the possibility of buying my guardian angel a large drink. Takes all sorts, I suppose.'

Paul wasn't inclined to respond to that. In any event, Susan was absolutely right about the one thing that really mattered: too late now. He yawned ostentatiously and went back to the mailing list he'd spent the morning putting together; more junk mail, cascading indiscriminately through letterboxes like flood water. What a way to make a living.

He'd nearly finished when the door opened and two policemen walked in.

Paul shared the instinctive fear of policemen common to all

white middle-class Englishmen, who are convinced that the police force is recruited exclusively from naturally gifted telepaths. As soon as they looked at him, he was sure they knew exactly what it was he'd done, even if he didn't; a defective brake light, a packet of crisps unwittingly pocketed in the checkout queue, where were you at 7.38 precisely on the night of 16 April? Other sections of society were more sceptical, less uptight. They could bring themselves to lie convincingly to policemen, stick their tongues out at them, maybe even throw the occasional bottle. Lucky them. Paul and his kind simply didn't have the knack.

He lurched to his feet, stammering something about how could he help them? The talking policeman (there's always one who talks and another who stands perfectly still and stares at the side of your head, watching the lies and hidden guilty secrets squirming behind the bone) said he was looking for a young woman by the name of Karen Orme, who (he had reason to believe) worked here.

'Karen *Orme* . . .' Paul's mind had gone blank, as if someone had wiped it down with a damp cloth. 'Oh, you mean *Karen* . . . Yes, she works here. Used to work here, I mean. She's left now.'

The policeman looked at him; Paul could feel his mind being downloaded, formatted, scanned and quite probably spellchecked. Shame washed over him like the spring tides, because he knew what a mess his mind was in, with random notions lying about on the floor, disorderly thoughts slung over the backs of chairs, unwashed fantasies crowding every flat surface. He felt a powerful urge to apologise, but he knew it wouldn't do him any good.

'I see, sir,' the policeman said; his eyes made it obvious that he knew Paul was lying – which was news to Paul, but if a policeman asserted it, it must be true, surely? 'Would you happen to know where I could find her?'

'I— Paul shook his head. 'Sorry,' he added, with feeling.

'No forwarding address? Did she mention a new job she was going to, something like that?'

'Sorry,' Paul repeated. 'It was all quite sudden, actually. One moment she was here; the next – gone.'

Oh my God, he realised, *now he thinks I murdered her. I didn't. Did I?*

'That sounds rather odd,' the policeman said.

'It was,' Paul replied quickly. 'Very.'

The policeman nodded. 'Had there been any trouble of any sort?' he asked. 'Any arguments or bad feeling?'

Paul's eyes opened wide. He knew what that meant: Karen had been caught stealing! That was impossible to believe – but needless to say he believed it, the way human beings always do. Besides, if she hadn't been stealing, why would the police be here looking for her?

'I hadn't realised,' Paul said. 'I mean, I hadn't noticed anything like that. I'd always thought she was like, you know, the model employee.'

The policeman nodded, didn't say anything. The conscious part of Paul's mind knew that this was one of the things they were trained to do, create an uncomfortable silence so that the hapless civilian would fill it with unguarded babble. Not that that mattered; there was probably a small part of each fish's brain that tried to point out that fat, juicy maggots didn't just hang there motionless in the water, but of course it was wasting its time. The silence was as unbearable as a full bladder, and he had to do something about it.

'Mind you,' he said, 'now I come to think of it, there always was *something* a bit odd about her. The way she did her job, mostly. Sort of – obsessive.'

The policeman raised an eyebrow.

'And definitely a loner,' Paul ground on. 'Never really got on with the rest of us – well, with Susan and me.' He turned his head towards his colleague, imploring her to join in and relieve him, but she wasn't having anything to do with it.

'Not that she was, like, strange or anything. But definitely odd.'

The policeman moved his head up and down through five degrees. 'And you're sure you don't know where she's gone? She didn't mention any family or friends who might be able to help us find her?'

'Sorry,' Paul said. 'Come to think of it, she never mentioned any family at all. And that's odd, isn't it?' The policeman hadn't blinked for over a minute; quite possibly they removed their eyelids surgically before they graduated from Hendon. 'I mean, everybody talks about their family sooner or later, don't they?'

The policeman didn't say anything for five, possibly six seconds; then he breathed in through his nose and said 'Thank you, you've been most helpful. Mr . . .?'

'Willis. Paul Willis. 78A Philby Court, Casement Road.' He told them his home phone number, too. The policeman wrote it all down in a little book, then turned and looked at Susan. 'Miss?' he said.

'Hm?'

'Could I have your name and address, please?'

Susan frowned. 'Why?'

'We need it for our records.'

'Why?'

Paul couldn't do anything except close his eyes. This was terrible. How could Susan be so *stupid*?

'In case we need to get in touch with you about anything.'

'Why would you need to get in touch with me?' Susan said. 'He's told you everything we know.'

Paul opened his eyes. The policeman was trying to read Susan's mind, but it wasn't working; he was sure he saw a little flicker of surprise on the man's face as his scanning beam was bounced back. But, oh God, why did she have to go and make an *exhibition* of herself like this?

'All right,' the policeman replied. 'That'll be all for now. Thank you for your help.'

He put enough spin on that last word to invest it with its own gravitational field, but if Susan noticed, she didn't show any sign of it. 'That's all right,' Paul burbled quickly. 'Any time.' But the policeman wasn't recognising his existence any more. He was concentrating exclusively on Susan. And not getting anywhere. After one last high-voltage stare, he turned round and marched out through the door, followed a moment later by his sidekick.

Almost immediately, reaction set in. Paul sat down where he hoped his chair was – luckily he was more or less on target – and tried not to be too obvious about shaking like a leaf. School was out in his mind, and the reactions came spilling noisily out into the playground – *bloody Susan, what the hell did she think she was playing at? My God, Karen's a thief. Or a terrorist, even. Just goes to show, you never can tell. So that's what it's like being grilled by the fuzz. Please, sir, can I be sick now?*

'What on earth,' Susan was saying, 'do you think all that was about?'

Paul lifted his head and looked at her. 'Come on,' he said. 'It's obvious.'

'Not to me.'

'What possessed you to answer him back like that?' he demanded. 'You're just lucky he didn't arrest you right there.'

'What for?'

Paul opened his mouth to reply, because the answer was obvious. Then he closed it again, thought for a moment and said, 'Obstructing the police. That's a crime.'

'Really?' Susan shrugged. 'Well, nobody could accuse you of that. You were all over him. I was *embarrassed*.'

'*You* were embarrassed?'

'Makes me wish I'd had a tape recorder handy,' she said. 'Sort of obsessive. Definitely a loner. I was waiting for you to say her eyes were too close together.'

Paul scowled. 'Well, it's true,' he said. 'Not about the eyes, but the obsessive bit. And the keeping herself to herself—'

'Dear God,' Susan sighed. 'And just half an hour ago you were dying of a broken heart. Men,' she added.

'What's that supposed to mean?'

Susan gave him a contemptuous smile. 'It's the old power thing,' she said. 'Men worship authority, it makes you go all weak at the knees. Another five minutes and you'd have been trying to lick his ears.'

Paul could feel pinkness spreading rapidly across his face. 'Don't be ridiculous,' he said, ridiculously. 'You're the one who ought to be ashamed of herself, coming over all bolshy like that. I suppose you thought you were being clever.'

Susan shook her head, indicating that the subject was closed. 'I should have made him tell me why they were looking for her, though,' she said.

'He wouldn't have told you. It's probably classified.'

Susan giggled. 'Classified?'

'Or *sub judice*, or whatever the word is. They aren't allowed to go telling people things. Stands to reason.'

'Does it really? I'll have to take your word for that.' She perched on the edge of her desk. 'So what do you think they're after her for?' she said.

Paul shrugged. 'How should I know?'

'You think she's in trouble, don't you? The Brinks Mat job. The Littlehampton pillar box bombings.'

'What? I haven't heard about any—'

'I just made them up,' Susan explained. 'God, you're so suggestible. My guess is,' she went on, 'something's happened to a close relative – father or mother or something – and they're looking for her to tell her. But she'd already heard, which is why she went off so suddenly. Doesn't that make rather more sense than Karen being the Barrow-in-Furness Ripper?'

Paul wilted a little, because of course it did. 'You could be right,' he said, 'how the hell would I know? None of our business, anyway.'

Susan took a deep breath, got up and returned to her chair. Paul didn't notice the slight frown on her face as she turned her computer monitor back on.

'Exactly,' she said.

'This is going to hurt,' the scientist said. 'A lot.'

She wasn't gloating, exactly; there was no fiendish laughter or twirling of moustaches. On the other hand, she didn't seem particularly bothered about it, either. Rule 6(b) in the heroes' basic training manual puts it very succinctly. Mad scientists aren't usually any bother; it's the sane ones you want to look out for.

'You may be thinking,' she went on, drawing back the plunger and filling the chamber of the syringe with whatever was in that small, unlabelled bottle, 'that I'm going to have real problems getting you to hold still long enough to stick this in you. But that's OK. You see this?' In her left hand she held up another small bottle. This one was blue. 'Two drops of this shit in there with you and you won't be able to wiggle so much as a fin. I guess,' she went on, smiling a little, 'this is what's known as the hard way. But as far as I'm concerned it's going to be very, very easy.' The dragon backed away until his fin hit the wall of the tank, recognising for the first time in his long, adventurous life that there was absolutely nothing he could do about the wholly superior forces ranged against him. He watched as the first blue drop hit the water, followed by the second, and the third . . .

'Hello again,' said a voice beside him. He opened his eyes—

—*His* eyes, for the first time in ages. All three of them.

'Don't try to move,' the voice advised him. 'I had these clamps specially made. Chrome molybdenum steel for tough-ness, case-hardened to eighty points Rockwell in case you were thinking of trying to chew through them. I had your teeth tested while you were under and they're only sixty-five which isn't bad, harder than a file-blade, but not good enough in this instance. If you try gnawing on these babies, you'll regret it.'

Clamps? the dragon wondered, craning his neck. *Oh*, those *clamps*; the ones that were pinning him to the hydraulic ramp he was lying on. 'Thanks for the tip,' he growled.

'You're welcome. I really don't want you hurting yourself, you know. I mean, if you get damaged, where am I going to get another specimen from?'

The dragon didn't reply; he was preoccupied with the feel of his own shape, the glorious relief of being his own size again, of having legs and wings and a proper tail instead of the drowned-moth-wing arrangement he'd been starting to get used to. 'How did you manage it?' he asked.

'Getting you back, you mean?' The scientist smiled. 'It was pretty straightforward. Not easy, but straightforward. Really, it was just a matter of pumping you full of muscle relaxant and letting your physical memory do the rest. Like letting the air out of a balloon, only the other way round. There was a twenty-three per cent chance the dosage I had to use would kill you, but since you were being so damned uncooperative I didn't really have a choice. Headache?'

The dragon shook his head. 'Dragons don't feel pain,' he said. 'Completely impervious to it, in fact.'

'Really?'

'Oh yes,' the dragon replied with more than a hint of pride. 'We deliberately bred it out of our species twelve thousand years ago as a response to – *yow*!'

'Fibber,' the scientist said indulgently, switching the electric current off again. 'It was a good idea, though – make me believe I couldn't hurt you, so I'd despair of ever getting any answers out of you. It wouldn't have worked, though. We humans have ways of inflicting pain that you people simply couldn't imagine. And yes, I know it sounds corny. The truth often is.'

The dragon growled softly. 'You'd better carry on, then,' he said. 'If it comes to a contest between your ability to hand the stuff out and our ability to take it, that might prove interesting. More so than sitting watching the tennis, anyway.'

'Actually,' the scientist replied, 'I quite like tennis.'

'Really? How extraordinary. All right, you can start now. If there's one thing I can't stand, it's being kept waiting.'

The scientist smiled. 'I haven't told you what I want yet. How can you refuse to talk when you don't even know what it is you aren't going to tell me?'

'Simple,' the dragon replied. 'I'm not going to tell you *anything*.'

'Maybe I wasn't going to ask you anything,' the scientist said. 'For all you know, I've had you brought here and forcibly restrained just so I can tell you the story of my life.'

The dragon sighed. 'Oh, I hope not,' he said.

'How sweet of you to say so.' The scientist thought for a moment. 'Actually, you've already told me something very useful indeed. Something, as it happens, that I'd never have thought of asking. Don't go away.'

The dragon scowled. It had been much easier to put up with being bored when he'd been a goldfish, because goldfish are designed to withstand tedium loadings that would kill most other life forms. Now he was himself again, he desperately wanted – needed – to be doing something. Dragons aren't your deck-chair-sunblock-and-the-new-Jeffrey-Archer types; it's all to do with being creatures of air and water, light, swift and soaring. It also explains why so few dragons become chartered accountants.

'Here we go,' the scientist said, returning after what the dragon held was a very long time, her arms full of photograph albums. 'Now, where shall we start from? The beginning, I guess.' She opened the first album. 'You know, a lot of these are really embarrassing, at least I think so. Probably everybody gets a bit uncomfortable looking at pictures of themselves as babies.'

'We don't,' the dragon said.

'Really?' The scientist didn't sound particularly interested. 'Now then, here's me at two days old. And another one of me at two days. This is me at two days old with my mother. This is me with my mother and my aunt Christine. This is me, my mother, Auntie Christine and Uncle Joe. This is me, my mother, Auntie Christine, Uncle Joe and old Mrs Tomiska who used to live next door to Auntie Christine and Uncle Joe before they moved to Baltimore. Here's me at three days old, with my mother, cousin Douane—'

The dragon rumbled ominously, like distant thunder.

'Oh,' the scientist said, 'that reminds me. In case you were thinking of trying to burn the place down with lightning or flood us out with rain, I don't think that's going to work. I won't bore you with technical stuff – at least, I'll save that for later, in case I really need to get tough with you – but there's this electromagnetic reverse-polarity dampening field surrounding the building: nothing gets out, nothing gets in. You might possibly be able to make it rain in this room, but probably only just enough to fill a kettle. So feel free. I could do with a cup of coffee any time soon.'

'We'll see about that,' the dragon said, and tried to rain. But he couldn't; it was as if there were clamps on his mind as well. After a tremendous effort that cost him a good deal of pain, he managed a single drop of condensation which fell, mockingly, on the tip of his snout.

'Told you,' the scientist said. 'Now then, where were we? Here's me at three weeks no, hang on, we've missed some. Oh well, I guess we'd better go back to the beginning and start again. This is me at two days old—'

The muscles in the dragon's neck stiffened as he drove with all his strength against the clamps. The locking mechanisms that held them in place creaked a little, but held. 'This isn't going to work,' the dragon said.

'What isn't?'

'This. We're just wasting time. Get on with the proper torture and get it over with.'

'No rush,' the scientist replied. 'Besides, I'm not sure I'm going to bother with all that now. I mean, we both know that you're incredibly tough and strong-willed, so zapping you with electric shocks and drilling holes in your scales with lasers and burning you with drops of nitric acid – all that'll happen is that you'll just get more and more ornery and I'll have a chewed-up-looking dragon instead of a pristine one. Nah.' She grinned. 'The hell with it. I'll just tell 'em I tried all that and it didn't work, and now I'm researching another approach to the problem. If I say that, they'll most likely leave me in peace for weeks. Months, even.' She patted the pile of photograph albums. 'Plenty more where these came from,' she said. 'And after we've done looking at snapshots, there's all manner of fun things we can do. Building regulations. Daytime TV. Star Trek novelisations. Computer manuals. I might even be able to persuade my sister-in-law's mother-in-law to come in and tell you about the time she went to the Royal Garden Party.'

The dragon squirmed convulsively. 'It won't work,' he grunted. 'You'll crack up before I do. After all, you're only human.'

The scientist burst out laughing. 'I'm sorry,' she said, 'but that's the funniest thing I've heard in a long while. I'm a scientist, dammit. Trying to bore me to death is like trying to drown a fish in water. Oh, talking of which, I've got a whole sheaf of notes for the paper I'm doing on photoreactive polymers that I could read to you. Shouldn't take more than sixteen hours, that is unless I give you the footnotes as well . . .'

'I can take it,' the dragon whimpered.

'Sure you can,' the scientist replied. 'Right, here we go again. Here's me at two days old. Here's me and my mother—'

*

How are you feeling?' the angel asked.

'Bloody terrible,' Gordon replied.

'It's your own silly fault,' the angel said. 'What on earth possessed you to go setting fire to a pair of socks in a room with no windows?'

Sadly, Gordon realised that the face leaning over him didn't belong to an angel after all; just a nurse, in the regulation blue uniform. 'Not my socks,' he croaked, discovering in the process that his throat was unbelievably raw and painful. 'His.'

'You were lucky you didn't suffocate,' the nurse went on. 'If Mr Harrison hadn't come along when he did, you'd have been dead ducks, both of you.'

In spite of the pain and the disappointment resulting from the nurse not being an angel, Gordon frowned. 'Sprinklers,' he said. 'Why didn't . . .?'

'What sprinklers?'

He let his head sink back on the pillow. 'Forget it,' he said. 'Not important. Where am I?'

'That's enough talking for now,' the nurse replied. 'Now, you're going to be all right, but it'll be a day or so before you're fit to be up and about again. Just lie still and quiet; I'm going to give you something to help you sleep.'

'Don't want to sl—' He felt the needle slide in and realised that for the first time in his life he was being given an injection without at least three nurses holding him down. That was worrying; if he was so weak that he couldn't even panic at the touch of a needle, he really must be sick.

The next time Gordon came round, he opened his eyes to see a plain grey plasterboard ceiling, brick walls and no nurses, let alone angels, whatsoever. He still felt awful, but he was able to get off the bed and stand up without bursting into tears or falling over. He looked round and saw Neville, still asleep on another bed a yard or so away.

'Wake up,' he snapped, slapping Neville hard across his bare instep. 'Rise and shine. What's going on here?'

Neville groaned and twisted round to face him. 'Oh,' he said. 'You're still alive, are you?'

'Apparently. Where the hell are we?'

Neville shrugged. 'Here,' he replied. 'About that brilliant idea of yours, starting a fire in a room with no windows . . .'

'Got us out of there, didn't it?'

'Yes. Into here. I expect your idea of curing a bad cold is to let it turn into pneumonia.'

'Don't be so negative. We don't even know where we are yet. Could be somewhere we want to be.'

'You reckon.'

'Could be,' Gordon went on, distancing himself from his fellow prisoner and making a show of studying the walls and ceiling, 'that this one'll turn out to be much easier to break out of. You know, a change is as good as a rest—'

'As the werewolf said to the fur-fabric salesman. You know, your buoyant optimism is starting to get right up my nose.'

'Maybe. But at least I'm not the one who believes in dragons.'

Before the discussion could develop further, a door opened in the wall – Gordon had been staring at it only a second or so previously and hadn't seen any sign of a doorway – and a man stepped into the room. He was so nondescript in every respect that, like the door, you'd have had trouble seeing him if he hadn't moved.

'And how are you two getting on?' he said.

The two weathermen stared at him. 'Who are you?' Neville asked.

'My name's Steven Harrison,' the man replied, pleasantly enough. 'I run this facility. Are they looking after you properly, or is there anything I can get for you?'

There is nothing on Earth quite so disconcerting as the perfectly normal, out of context. It was as if they'd been teleported aboard an alien spaceship and held for hours in a transdimensional stasis beam that transcended every preconception they'd ever had about the nature of existence, only to be confronted by some guy in a white suit carrying a big red book, informing them that This Was Their Lives.

'Actually,' Neville said, 'I'd love a nice strong cup of tea.'

Mr Harrison smiled. 'That could probably be arranged,' he said. 'Milk and sugar?'

'Yes, please.'

'How many sugars?'

'Two.'

Mr Harrison nodded, then turned to Gordon. 'And you,' he went on, 'would probably like to know where you are and what's going on. Am I right?'

Gordon nodded cautiously. 'I'm eccentric that way,' he said. 'Humour me.'

'I'd have said it was perfectly natural,' Mr Harrison replied. 'Just bear with me a moment, would you? Three teas,' he muttered into some kind of device strapped to his wrist. 'One with milk and two sugars. Mr Smelt?' he added, looking up again.

'No sugar,' Gordon heard himself say.

Mr Harrison nodded. 'Like I was saying,' he went on, 'it's entirely understandable that you two would want to know where you are, who I am, and what's going to happen to you. Now I'm afraid I can't tell you as much as I'd like to, because as you'll appreciate there are a number of security issues here, which means the best I'll be able to do is mark the dots and leave it to you to join them up for yourselves. But let's start with what I can tell you. I'm a perfectly ordinary civil servant, and you're both guests of Her Majesty's government.'

'Ah,' Gordon said. 'That was something I'd more or less worked out for myself.'

'Of course,' Mr Harrison replied, with a slight nod of the head. 'No great leaps of intuition required, I don't suppose. Where was I? Oh yes. My official job description is High Archimandrite and Keeper of the High Altar. To a large extent, though,' he added, as Gordon's jaw dropped like the second-hand value of a four-year-old computer, 'it's really just an honorary title.'

'Right,' Gordon said.

'Oh yes.' Mr Harrison smiled. 'It's not as if I change the flowers and polish the brassware; we've got outside contractors who do that sort of thing. I prefer to think of myself as nothing more than a run-of-the-mill High Priest.'

'I see,' Gordon said, after a very long time. 'Excuse me for asking, but high priest of what?'

'Of the State religion,' Mr Harrison replied, with just the suggestion of a frown. 'As I told you, I'm merely a humble servant of Her Majesty.'

'Ah.'

'In her fourfold aspect as maiden, warrior, mother and crone,' Mr Harrison went on, as a hatch opened in the wall and a kind of dumb-waiter arrangement slid a tray with three teacups on it onto the floor. 'I imagine yours is the one with the spoon in the saucer,' he added, giving Neville a pleasant smile.

'Hold on,' Gordon said, raising a hand. 'What was that last bit again?'

'About the tea?'

'No. Before that. The fourfold-aspect bit.'

Mr Harrison nodded patiently. 'Sorry,' he said, 'it's probably my fault for not explaining properly. Let's start at the beginning, shall we? I represent the established State religion of the United Kingdom of England, Scotland, Wales and Northern Ireland – not the Channel Islands and the Isle of Man, obviously, they come under a different jurisdiction. We worship Her Majesty Elizabeth the Second.' He paused, and frowned. 'You know,' he added. 'The Queen.'

'I have heard of her, yes.'

'Splendid.'

Gordon waited for a moment, but Mr Harrison didn't

seem inclined to add anything. 'You worship the Queen,' he repeated.

'Yes.'

'As if she was well, you know, a goddess?'

'*The* Goddess,' Mr Harrison corrected him. 'She has four aspects, but they are indivisibly One, just like the component parts of the United Kingdom. You seem puzzled,' he added. 'What else would you expect from a State religion?'

Gordon took a deep breath. 'Ah,' he said. 'I see.' He nodded, and surreptitiously nudged Neville on the shin, making him spill his tea. 'We understand now, don't we, Neville?'

'Makes sense to me,' Neville replied. 'Defender of the Faith, and all that.'

'Precisely,' said Mr Harrison, 'And of course, that explains what you're doing here.'

'It does indeed,' Gordon said. 'Well, thank you ever so much for your,time—'

'I'm delighted to know that you're both prepared to be so reasonable about it,' Mr Harrison said. 'And let me take this opportunity to mention that the procedure is entirely pain-less.'

It was unfortunate that Neville was drinking tea at that point. Quite a lot of it turned into fine spray.

'Painless,' Gordon repeated.

'Absolutely,' Mr Harrison said. 'Oh, we've come a long way since the days of obsidian knives, have no fears on that score. Basically, it's a highly refined type of lethal injection. I'm told that the actual sensation is quite pleasant, like drift-ing into a gentle sleep.'

Gordon looked at him for two or three seconds. 'That's reassuring,' he said.

'Attention to that kind of detail is one of the hallmarks of a compassionate society,' Mr Harrison replied gravely. 'After all, when you consider the very real contribution you people make to the well-being of the nation – making sure the rain falls and the crops grow, all that sort of thing the very least we can do is make sure you don't suffer unduly.'

The dropping of the penny, from a great height, made Gordon stagger slightly. 'It's because we're *weathermen*,' he said. 'Because we make it rain.'

'Of course,' Mr Harrison said, frowning again. 'You don't think we just scoop people up off the street, do you? Of course not. But weathermen; guardians of the sacred dragon – Well, I'm glad we got that cleared up. There's nothing worse than talking at cross purposes.'

'I see,' Gordon said, feebly.

'And let me say,' Mr Harrison went on, 'this won't come a moment too soon. We've already had to bring in hosepipe bans in parts of East Anglia.'

'You don't say.'

Mr Harrison dipped his head in solemn confirmation. 'And we've already announced a programme of even more stringent measures, just in case. Now, though, with any luck we won't have to go to such extreme lengths. Thanks,' he added, 'to you.'

'Well.' Gordon swallowed hard. 'I don't know what to say, really.'

'Of course. It must be a rather special moment for both of you.'

Gordon and Neville looked briefly at each other. 'You could say that,' Neville mumbled.

Mr Harrison had ever such a nice smile. 'You know,' he said, 'it's thoroughly refreshing to meet a couple of citizens like yourselves who obviously appreciate the importance of what we're doing here, and are prepared to do their bit for their country. So many of the people who pass through here can't see beyond their own selfish concerns. It's really – oh, please excuse me, I don't usually get all emotional, it's just that I'm proud of you both. Really.'

'Don't worry about it,' Gordon said; as his mind ran final checks on a battery of calculations – approach vectors, angles of incidence, degree of force required to render a middle-aged, middle-sized man unconscious with a single blow. 'It's the least we can do, I reckon.'

Mr Harrison nodded eagerly. 'It's just like the Prime Minister said in his speech to the party conference,' he said. 'About how it's up to all of us to make sacrifices if we want a better world for our children's children.'

'Sacrifices,' Neville repeated. 'Well, quite.' He took half a step back, trying to semaphore *Well, what the fuck are you waiting for?* to Gordon with his eyebrows.

Gordon got the gist of it, but something held him back; probably the fact that he hadn't deliberately thumped anybody with intent to cause pain and injury since he was eleven years old, and he hadn't been terribly good at it then. What deterred him most was the thought of how embarrassing it'd be if he sprang at his opponent with a loud cry and landed a diagonal knife-hand blow to the side of the head that either missed completely or merely caused the man to rub his ear and ask him what the bloody hell he thought he was playing at. It was enough to make him wish he'd gone along too when his second (or was it third?) wife started going to those ninja assassination techniques evening classes down at the leisure centre.

Looking back after the event at what happened next, Gordon came to the conclusion that Neville had got bored with waiting for him to make a move, and had taken the initiative himself. If so, he could say without hesitation that Neville wasn't nearly as uptight and inhibited about initiating violent action was he was. It was just a shame that he didn't have a little more science to go with his enthusiasm. If he'd bothered to consult Gordon before leaping in blindly, he'd have realised that Bruce Lee, Master Yoda, Sammo Hung and all those guys spent hours every day practising, in a purpose-built gymnasium, with a sand-filled leather bag to beat up on and a copy of the instruction manual handy, a bus ticket stuck between the pages to mark the place. Expecting to be able to do flying kicks by light of nature was, at best, naive.

But none of that seemed to have occurred to Neville, which might explain why, having uttered a blood-curdling cry of what sounded more like extreme pain than deathless rage, he hurled himself into the air, sailed past Mr Harrison by a comfortably wide margin, and hit the wall like a bug splatting itself on the windscreen of a speeding Volvo.

'Good Lord,' said Mr Harrison, hurrying across and bending over him. 'Are you all right?'

There was an important psychological difference between hitting a man facing you and planting a boot squarely in the middle of a suitably positioned trouser seat. Gordon drew back his right foot, let fly and hoped for the best; he wasn't disappointed. After a brief but spirited impression of a football, Mr Harrison crashed into the wall and dripped down it like condensation, fast asleep.

'Finally,' Neville grunted. 'What took you so long?'

'I was waiting for the right moment,' Gordon replied. 'Which you did your best to bugger up, I might add. Come on, let's get out of here before he wakes up.'

Neville hesitated. 'Aren't you going to search him first?' he asked.

'Certainly not. One, it's rude. Two, he might wake up while I'm doing it.'

'But he might have stuff we could use,' Neville argued. 'Door keys, security passes, a gun, a remote control for lowering the security net. Ten quid for the bus fare. A packet of Rolos. Maybe even,' he added poignantly, 'a pair of socks.'

Gordon shook his head. 'It'd be stealing,' he said.

'Oh, for pity's sake,' Neville growled. 'Look, you just go through his pockets, leave explaining it to St Peter on the Day of Judgement to me.'

'You're missing the point,' Gordon said, trying to damp down his agitation. 'So far, we haven't actually done anything wrong; nothing they could arrest us for once we're out of here. Let's keep it that way, shall we?'

'Oh yes?' Neville nodded toward the body sprawled on the ground 'What about assault? GBH?'

'He slipped,' Gordon replied. 'Wasn't looking where he was going. Or maybe he blasphemed against Princess Margaret and got zapped by a thunderbolt. Easier to explain away than getting caught with his wallet in your pocket. Are you really going to stand there all day waffling, or are you just trying to annoy me?'

Neville dipped his head in a slight, sardonic bow. 'After you,' he said. 'I'll be right behind you.'

'Fine.' Gordon swung round, then noticed that something was missing. The door.

'I know,' Neville said. 'I can't seem to see it either. I'm prepared to bet *he* knows where it is, but since you took it upon yourself to knock him out, we can't really ask him.' He smiled. 'I'm really looking forward to your next bright idea,' he said. 'I love slapstick humour.'

After ten minutes or so pawing at the wall in the hope of finding a minute crack or a faint tell-tale draught, Gordon gave up, slumped against the brickwork and dumped his chin in his hands. 'I shouldn't have to be doing this,' he complained. 'I'm a weatherman, not an action hero.'

'It's probably just as well we haven't managed to break out of here,' Neville replied, sitting down sociably beside him. 'My guess is that if they'd caught us wandering about in the corridors, they'd be really annoyed with us.'

'More annoyed than just injecting us with deadly poison, you mean? I guess we had a lucky escape.'

Neville laughed. 'You don't believe all of that, do you? Good Lord. A sensible fellow like you; sceptical, in fact, to a fault.'

'He seemed fairly serious about it.'

'Him?' Neville's smile broadened into a wide, untidy grin. 'He's a nutter. A loony. Just like the world-domination bloke we saw earlier. Nobody's going to sacrifice us to the Queen, just as nobody's really planning to invade Australia. This is just some old building where they lock up the basket cases. Which,' he added, his grin destabilising a little, 'is why *we*'re here.'

'That makes sense,' Gordon replied. 'After all, you're as bad as they are.'

'I wish you'd stop saying things like that,' Neville replied. 'It's a bit hurtful, even though I know you don't really mean it.'

'Yes, I do.'

'No, you don't. You're just scared and disorientated and lashing out at me because I happen to be the nearest available safe target. Basic psychology, that is.'

'Basic psychology,' Gordon repeated. 'Well, if I were you I'd write to wherever it is you got your course notes from and ask for your twelve pounds fifty back, because you don't know anything—'

Neville held up his hand for silence. 'Just a moment,' he said.

'What?'

'There, look.'

Gordon squinted. 'I can't see anything,' he said.

'That's because you don't know what you're looking for,' Neville explained, insufferably. 'That's because you never bothered to take the time to develop your third eye.'

Gordon made a sad, wailing noise and let his jaw flump back between his hands. 'Go away,' he said. 'I'm not in the mood.'

'There you go again.' Neville was on his feet now, poking at a spot on the wall. 'Being negative. A right old Doubting Thomas, you are. Well, try this one on for size. If you're right and I haven't developed my latent third eye, how come I was able to identify the dragon when I saw him walking down Leatherhead High Street?'

'You really want me to tell you?'

'You'll be sniggering on the other side of your face in a moment,' Neville said, his attention focused on the wall. 'Ah, here we are. Right, if you stop being incredibly witty for about thirty seconds, go and rummage about in Thingy's pockets till you find a small, flat black box, a bit like a pocket calculator.'

'Certainly not.'

'Don't you want to get out of here?'

Gordon sighed. 'You know,' he said, 'I really ought to stay, just to make sure you don't get loose. In a way it's comforting, knowing you're safely under lock and key where you can't do any more damage.'

'Stop babbling and find me that box.'

'Might as well,' Gordon sighed. 'After all, if I'm banged up in here with the loonies, I might just as well go mad myself.' He stood up and rolled Mr Harrison's inert body over with his toe. Sure enough, there was a small, flat black box in his top pocket.

'Is this what you're after?' he said.

'Probably. Open it and see.'

Gordon did as he was told. 'It's a pocket calculator,' he said.

'Bring it here.' Neville grabbed it with his left hand, without moving his right from a certain spot on the wall. 'Yup, this is it,' he said. 'Now, take it back and when I give you the word, I want you to key in exactly what I tell you to. Do you think you can manage that?'

'I'm sure I can. Afterwards, I can roll on my back and make noises like a hyena, if you want me to.'

'Don't be silly,' Neville said sternly. 'OK, here we go. 6-7-4-1-2—'

Gordon shrugged, and pressed the keys. A long string of

numbers later, Neville told him to press ENTER, so he did. The door opened.

'How the hell did you do that?' Gordon asked.

'Simple. Here's the lock grid, and here's the access code, written in what I suppose you'd want to call invisible ink, though really it's as plain as day to anybody with a functional third eye. That's the key pad you've got there; type in the code, press 'Go' and what do you get? One open door.'

'But that's—'

Neville chuckled. 'I told you I'd make you believe, sooner or later.'

'But I don't,' Gordon protested. 'All right, maybe I believe in you having really good eyesight and knowing a thing or two about spook technology. Maybe I might just be able to bring myself to believe in talking goldfish. But—'

'Are you just going to stand there nattering all day? Come on.'

'Still doesn't mean I believe in—'

'Come *on*. Or I'll leave you here.'

Gordon thought about it for a moment. On the one hand, he really didn't like the thought of getting out of there because Neville had been able to decipher a secret access code using his third eye. On the other hand . . . as the old adage goes, if you're starving in the desert and a headless skeleton riding a winged fiery camel swoops down out of thin air and hands you a cheeseburger, eat the cheeseburger.

'Coming,' he said.

CHAPTER SEVEN

Waiting for your enemies to come and find you was all very well, assuming your enemies had the necessary level of competence. If your enemies couldn't find a haystack in a packet of needles, a somewhat more proactive strategy might be called for.

It would also probably help, Karen thought as the train pulled out of Wolverhampton, if she were to stay put for a while; but if she was going to do that, she might just as well go back (for want of a better word) home. There at least a few people knew her by sight, so that as and when the enemy started going from door to door waving photographs and asking 'Have you seen this woman?' there was at least a moderate chance someone would say 'Yes.' Maybe she was worrying over nothing; after all, with surveillance cameras in practically every shopping precinct and at nearly every traffic junction she went past, computers able to pinpoint her every time she used a telephone or a cashpoint card and an army of blue-sweatered thugs cruising the streets in souped-up Discoveries, surely it was impossible for somebody to stay hidden long enough to blow her nose. In practice, she guessed, every spy network was only as good as the dead-heads sitting in front of the monitors – in which case, from what she'd seen of this particular strain of humanity, it was up to her to make herself as conspicuous as possible.

Which went against the carefully acquired grain, of course. How long had she been human? Not all that long, but she was starting to have trouble remembering ever having been any-thing else; institutionalised, they called it, when humans stopped fighting their environment and started thinking of themselves as part of it. Maybe when they got to thinking of one particular corner of it as home, just as she was doing now.

Home, according to one prevalent human definition, is where the heart is; was that why she was scurrying back, because the strain of being away from the human she loved was beginning to get to her? The thought made her frown. Karen simply didn't know enough about the way the human subconscious worked and, without a wiring chart or a work-shop manual, she had no way of finding out except by having one for long enough to be able to observe its habits. Maybe that was all it took to trigger a powerful homing instinct; if so, she wasn't bothered. She had to be somewhere, and home (whatever that meant) was as good a place as any.

Fortunately, sleep overwhelmed her not long after that, which saved her from having to look at Bedfordshire as it slunk past the train window. If she dreamed at all while she was asleep, she couldn't remember any of it when she woke up. But she did have a good idea about what she was going to do next.

It would only take her a moment or so; just long enough to fill in the time before the train crept into Euston. Karen closed two of her eyes, opened the third, and concentrated—

'You'll break eventually,' the scientist said. 'I know you will.

The only thing that's keeping you going at the moment is twenty million years' accrued cussedness. But it won't do you a bit of good in the long run. Do yourself a favour and give in now.'

'No.'

The scientist took a deep breath. 'Please?' she begged.

Hard to tell which of them was suffering most, the human or the dragon; but only because the dragon's pride was keeping him afloat. Break down in front of a human? Never! Even so, he knew it could only be a matter of time. Never in all the centuries of his existence had he suffered like this.

'Don't make me do this,' the human was pleading. 'Goddamit, it'll probably kill you, and what the hell am I supposed to do with a dead dragon – start a handbag factory? Assuming I survive it myself,' she added. 'And a dead scientist's no use to anybody.'

'You're pathetic,' the dragon sneered. 'Which is why you're bound to lose.'

The scientist dragged herself onto her feet, swaying as she did so. She'd worked hard, no question about that. After the family photo albums, the excerpts from her paper – that had been a mistake: not only had the dragon followed every word, he'd gleefully pointed out several mistakes in both the reasoning and the maths – three hours reading out the 'S' section from the phone book, three even longer hours reading pages at random from the latest Lynda LaPlante, a two-hour game of I-Spy that she'd had to abandon once it became clear that the only possible outcome was mutually assured destruction . . . After that it had all turned into a messy red blur in her mind, as the effects of acute tedium poisoning soaked into her system, leaving her dazed and light-headed. It wasn't a matter of torturer and victim any more; they were both victims of the dragon's mindless intransigence.

'You asked for it,' the scientist said, her voice little more than a hoarse whisper. 'God knows, it'll probably kill us both, but it's your fault. I just wanted to make sure you knew that.'

'Pathetic,' the dragon repeated, trying desperately not to slur the word, and failing.

The scientist shook her head. She was all out of words, in any case. Instead of saying anything, therefore, she fumbled a TV remote out of her pocket and pointed it at the television set mounted on a bracket on the wall, perfectly adjusted to be directly on the dragon's line of sight.

'Satellite Sport channel,' she mumbled. 'Semi-finals of the World Snooker Championship.' She giggled shrilly before adding, 'In black and white.'

'What's snoo—?' The dragon didn't have enough strength to finish the sentence.

'You'll find out,' the scientist replied, pointing the remote and hitting the button.

The screen flashed into life; the tail end of the news, with a disembodied continuity voice saying that the snooker was up next, after the weather. The scientist frowned and glanced at her watch, then shrugged. 'In just a few minutes,' she murmured. 'You'll see.'

'You know what?' The dragon managed to lift his head a degree or two. 'I feel sorry for you. All of you,' he added. 'These terrible things you've been doing to me,' he explained, 'you're right, they make a truly cruel form of torture. So much mindlessness.' He yawned, unable to control the spasm. 'So much waste of life, when you poor little things have so little of it to spare. But you can't hurt me with it, because all it makes me do is feel sorry for you.' He laughed. 'Because for every bit of it you're doing to me, you're doing a million times more to yourselves. And that's sad.'

'Oh, be quiet,' the scientist said.

The picture changed; there was a large map of the country, decorated with abstruse symbols. 'What's that supposed to be?' the dragon asked, curiosity cutting the paralysis like lemon juice in milk.

'The weather forecast.'

'Really? How . . .' The dragon stopped abruptly. There was a human on the screen now; a young human female with short, dark hair and a round face. She was saying hello.

'That's . . .'

The scientist looked up. 'What?'

'Never mind,' the dragon growled. 'Shut up, I want to listen to this.'

'You do?' Tomorrow, the human female was saying, it was going to rain. She paused, and smiled. That, she went on, was putting it mildly. It was going to rain a *lot*. Not just Bank Holiday Monday, Wimbledon Week, Second Test at Headingley rain. Not just blocked-gutters and lorries-aqua-planing-roof-high, monsoon-season-in-Delhi, thank-God-for-the-Thames-Barrier rain. (She stopped, and smiled evilly.) Tomorrow, it was going to rain like you never knew it could; so be warned, move all the stuff you value up to the attic now, steal a boat and moor it to the TV aerial, and get ready to find out just what the sky can do when it feels like it, because it's going to rain.

That was as far as it went; a moment later, the screen went blank and a worried TV voice muttered something about not knowing what had gone wrong there, normal service would be resumed as quickly as possible—

'Your daughter,' the scientist said quietly.

'Quite right,' the dragon replied. 'How did you guess?'

'Intuition,' the scientist said thoughtfully. 'That and a certain family resemblance. Can she really do that? Tap into someone else's broadcast and hijack it?'

The dragon chuckled. He was feeling much better now. 'You'll have to wait and see, won't you?' he said. 'And no, I'm not just being perverse. Really, I don't know. But if you want me to hazard a guess, I'd say yes, probably she can. If she gets angry enough.'

'Oh.' The scientist sat down on the arm of her chair.

'Excuse me,' she said, 'I've got a few calls to make. While I'm gone,' she added, 'you can watch the snooker.'

The dragon laughed; and this time there was real depth and texture to his laughter it was strong and vigorous, like a wilted plant revived by rain. 'I'm looking forward to it,' he said.

By the time they realised what she was doing and pulled the plug, Karen was exhausted. She let her head fall back hard on the seat cushion, and closed her eyes.

Big words, she thought, *for a little wingless biped.* Exactly how much substance there was to those confident-sounding threats remained to be seen. The main thing was, though, that they were bound to have noticed her. Must've done. Couldn't help but.

The train slid neatly into place beside the platform – that was something humans were good at, lining things up and fitting them together – and she climbed out, her knees feeling weak after the effort she'd been through. What she needed now was somewhere to rest and pull herself together, have a bath, probably drink plenty of fluids. She only hoped that she hadn't done the job of alerting her enemies to her presence too well, since she wasn't really in fit state to fight them right now.

She got a taxi and told the driver where to go; it was a long way, and he wanted money in advance, so she gave it to him. That made Karen smile – human lack of trust, how careful they always had to be, since they couldn't trust each other even in the little things.

Could she really make it rain like she'd threatened? More to the point, could she bring herself to do it? Personal quarrels, vendettas, wars: how much more human could she risk becoming, before she went so far that she could never get back? If she really went ahead with the threat and sent a flood, she'd be likely to do terrible damage to these fragile, feckless creatures; she'd wreck their homes, ruin their livelihoods, quite possibly kill a few of them here and there . . . *Like a human nation*, she realised guiltily, *making war on another nation over some matter of principle.* She tried to imagine what her father's reaction would be to that. *Go away, you don't belong here. You aren't my daughter any more. You aren't even one of us . . .*

Yes, she imagined herself saying, *but they started it. Dragons declaring war on humans is unthinkable, yes, but so is humans kidnapping dragons. We have the right to defend ourselves even – in the most extreme cases – even against those who are smaller and weaker than ourselves. It's all very well saying* pick on someone your own size *in that superior tone of voice, but what if the tiny, fragile psychopaths won't leave us alone? What if they're bullying us relentlessly and refuse to give it up and go away? Must the strong always be trampled underfoot by the weak?*

Yes.

Karen scowled with her third eye. *Is that all you've got to say*, she demanded, *yes? What kind of natural selection is that, the domination of the weak, the survival of the weediest?*

It's what makes humans the dominant species on this planet. They've played us at the game of evolution and won. You've got to give the little buggers credit for imagination; it's an extremely clever idea.

Karen felt her hands clench. *But it's not fair*, she yelled to herself.

Fair? Of course it's not fair. These are humans we're dealing with, and they don't know the meaning of the word. The hell with fair; the strong shall perish. The grown-up may not hit the child, the man may not hit the woman, the big country may not beat up on the little country, the rich must support the poor, and if dragons fight humans, they must do so with all four hands tied behind their backs. Nothing fair about that. How else do you think a skinny, naked little monkey came to rule an entire planet?

Well, Karen muttered sulkily, *I'm not having anything to do with it. And besides,* she added, *the rules don't apply to me. I'm human too.*

No, you aren't.

Karen opened her other eyes and stared at the back of the taxi driver's head. She felt cold, from her feet to the top of her head.

'Yes, I am,' she said aloud. 'I am now.'

When she finally got home, there wasn't much space on her doorstep. There were twelve bottles of something that had once been milk; a pile of junk mail, left outside because the letter box was jammed full with the stuff; and a human.

'Hello,' the human said, and smiled.

Karen didn't recognise him and, since he was large, rather alarming in appearance and dressed in an old, shabby Burberry, she instinctively took a step back. Human instinct, naturally.

'Who are you?' she asked.

'What? Oh, for pity's sake, Grnztxyw.'

Her mouth fell open like the tailgate of the lorry that was carrying the cheap CD player you bought in a car boot sale last weekend. The last thing she'd been expecting at that precise moment was to be addressed by her childhood nickname—

—One that only three people knew. By a process of elimination—

'Hpqzsxyzty?' she asked cautiously. 'Is that you in there?'

The human laughed. 'Of course it is, dumbo,' he replied. 'Who did you think it was?'

She could easily have burst into tears, except for a little lingering wisp of suspicion. Hpq; her oldest, dearest friend, whom she'd beaten up and chased all round the ozone layer and set fire to more times than she could remember when they were both little more than cubs together. Now she came to think of it, the person she'd be most likely to turn to in a mess like this, if only he wasn't still a dragon and a million miles away—

'Prove it,' she said.

The human looked at her as if she'd just spat in his face. 'Are you kidding?' he said. 'Grnz, it's *me*. What the hell's come over you?'

She drew the tips of her fingers down her body, from cheeks to thighs. 'This,' she said. 'And it's ingrowing, like a bad claw. Prove you're really Hpq, or I'll tear you to pieces.'

'All right.' He was staring, maintaining eye contact the way you'd want to do if you were facing a savage wild animal. 'How about this? It was when we were kids together; come to think of it, I know exactly when it was, my two-thousand-seven-hundred-and-fifty-seventh birthday. Dad threw a party for our kindergarten class. You sneaked up behind me when I was raining on the candles on my birthday cake and tied a lump of burning sulphur to my tail. Hurt like hell, until my mum put it out.'

'I remember that,' Karen admitted grudgingly. 'But there were lots of us at that party. Try again.'

'What about the time when you and I and your cousin Gndva-S'sssn skived off school to go cyclone-racing, and you dunked my head inside the magma layer of an active volcano when I wasn't looking? There was nobody else there to see us.'

'Apart from my cousin.'

'Yes, but she was helping you.'

'Okay,' Karen admitted, 'but you probably told your parents. All right, what about this one: what did I make you promise before I let you go?'

'I had to promise to be your slave for ever and ever and give you my helping every time we had truffled snow for pudding at school dinner. You know,' he added, looking thoughtful, 'when I think about it, I must be mad coming all this way to help you. You've done nothing but make my life a misery all the years I've known you.'

The lump in Karen's throat was getting so big, they'd have to draw it in the next time they revised the Ordnance Survey maps. 'It *is* you, isn't it?' she whispered.

'No, it's Norman Tebbitt. For crying out loud, Grnz, of course it's me. Who else'd be dumb enough to come all this way just to help you out of a spot of bother?'

It was almost more than she could bear; her friend, the one she'd known since before their eyes had opened. With a strangled yelp of joy she hurled herself at his chest, nearly knocking him flat on his back, and hugged him as if she was trying to squeeze his stomach out through his ears. As a final token of joy and love, she grabbed both his earlobes and twisted them savagely through a hundred and eighty degrees.

'Aagh! For pity's sake, Grnz!'

'Oops,' she said, letting go quickly. 'Human ears. Forgot. Sorry.'

'That's quite all right,' Hpq muttered, massaging the afflicted areas with the heels of his hands. 'Just don't do it again, all right? I'm a good deal less flexible than I used to be, remember.'

'Me too,' Karen sighed. 'But Hpq, it's so good to see you! What are you doing here? Shouldn't you be in North Dakota with your uncle Pvvcbdfgt?'

Hpq grinned. 'Yes, is the short answer to that. I'm playing hookey. And, yes, I'm sure to get into the most desperate trouble when I show my face again back Home. But what the hell; somehow, I've always found that trouble, suffering, inconvenience and you go together like thunder and lightning. It'll be like old times,' he added. 'Painful, and I'll wish I'd kept well clear.'

Karen could feel her eyes getting swollen and itchy, a symptom of a common human emotional disorder. It was one that had perplexed her more than most, since humans exhibited it both when extremely sad and extremely happy, as if they didn't really make a distinction between the two. 'I'm really glad you're here,' she said awkwardly, hugging him again. 'How did you know?'

'About your dad, you mean? Oh come on, give me some credit. Remember, your father is my dad's quarter-brother. By the way,' he went on, 'what on earth is that mustard-yellow stuff in all those glass bottles in front of your door, and why does it smell so revolting?'

'Ah.' Karen let go of him and stepped back gingerly, taking care not to knock over any of the bottles. 'That's milk. Or at least it was. It's stuff we put in drinks.'

There was palpable concern in Hpq's eyes as he replied. 'No,' he said. '*We* don't put it in anything. *They* do.' His brows tightened. 'How long did you say you've been down here, Grnz?'

Karen shook her head. 'Let's go inside, shall we?'

'Why?'

'I beg your pardon?'

'Why is it preferable to have a conversation in a confined space than out in the open? If you can call a landing inside a tall building the open, that is. Sorry, I'm not trying to be difficult—'

'It's all right,' Karen replied. 'I know what you're doing. You're making me notice things I've been doing without thinking for rather too long. Human things.'

Hpq nodded. 'Protective mimicry's all very well for insects,' he said gravely. 'We're bigger than that. Why are you doing this to yourself, Grnz?'

'Come inside.'

She unlocked the door, gave it a hearty shove to dislodge the maildrift behind it, and forced her way in. 'Leave the milk,' she called out. 'I'll do something about it later.'

The expression on Hpq's face as he looked round the flat was hilarious; likewise the way he instinctively ducked under a nine-foot ceiling as if he was afraid he was going to bang his head on it. Karen had done that, to begin with. 'You live in this thing?' he asked.

Karen nodded. 'When in Rome—'

'When in Rome,' Hpq replied sternly, 'leave immediately. Old dragon proverb, which you've obviously forgotten. And this isn't Rome, even. Grnz, what *are* you doing here?'

Karen sat down on the chair that didn't have dirty laundry piled up on it, and grinned sheepishly. 'I fell in love,' she said.

'You fell in what?'

'Love. Oh come on, Hpq, you know what love is.'

'I know what tuberculosis is, but I don't go out of my way to experience it. How do you mean, you fell in love? Who with? And why does falling in love mean you've got to dress up in *that*?'

'With a human.'

To his credit, Hpq managed not to say anything for at least ten seconds, after which he said 'Oh' in a completely expressionless voice. Of course, his sense of self-preservation might have had something to do with it.

'Oh,' Karen repeated. 'Thank you very much. I'd have thought you'd have understood, of all people.'

Hpq shook his head. 'Understand? Don't be ridiculous. I couldn't understand something like that in a hundred thousand years, not if I went to evening classes. As you well know. What you mean is, you'd have thought that I of all people would stick by you and do what I can to help, even though it's painfully obvious to anybody that you've gone one-wing-flapping mad. And of course you'd be right,' he added, with a wry grin, 'because I will. But understand—'

'Hpq—' Karen tried to think of something to say, but couldn't; so she threw a cushion at him instead. 'Thanks,' she added. 'I'm really glad you're here, even if you are a mindless bigot with the imagination of a roof joist.'

'You say the sweetest things,' Hpq replied. 'What's a roof joist?'

Karen made a dismissive gesture. 'Forget it,' she said. 'Now you're here, let's think what you can do to make yourself useful. Any ideas?'

'It's your adopted habitat, you tell me,' he said. 'It's as much as I can do to keep from treading on the wriggly little buggers. Even,' he added with a grimace, 'the ones who are taller than me. How the devil do you cope with that, by the way? The scale thing, I mean.'

'It just sorts itself out, after a while. Like the claustrophobia.'

'The what?'

'Fear of confined spaces. Not liking being inside buildings, stuff like that.'

'You make it sound like it's an illness.'

'It—' Karen sighed. 'For them,' she explained, 'it is.'

'At least you said *them* that time, not *us*. So,' Hpq went on, 'tell me about him. Mr Wonderful. What's the deal?'

Karen stood up and walked across the room to the window, the one with the panoramic view of a courtyard and some dustbins. 'I don't know,' she said. 'It's love, you can't rationalise it.'

'Since when? Of course you can. What is it about this joker? Smooth, shiny scales across his back and shoulders? Nice big hooked, rounded claws? Snout hairs like some ponce in a scale cream advert?'

'Nothing like that, silly. He isn't a dragon, remember.'

'I'm having no trouble at all remembering that,' Hpq said. 'You're the one with the fishnet memory. So; obviously it's not a physical thing. Or are you about to tell me this – this *anthropomorph* has a beautiful smile?'

'Actually, he does,' Karen replied stiffly. 'And it doesn't look like a guided tour of a sawmill every time he opens his mouth, either.'

'So? The sucker hasn't got any teeth to speak of. That's supposed to be a good thing?'

Karen shook her head violently. 'I don't know,' she said.

'Really, I don't. I just know I love him, that's all. Enough to leave home. Enough to want to be human—'

'Oh, for crying out loud.'

'All right, all right.' Karen looked away. 'So I know I'm going to have to make a few compromises—'

'As the pig said to the sausage machine. But,' Hpq added, holding up a hand, 'the bottom line is, that's your business and not mine. It's not even why I'm here, so let's just leave it be, before we fall out over it. Agreed?'

Karen's face melted into a grin. 'Agreed,' she said. 'Anyway, now you know what brought me here. And it's obvious that me being here's what made Daddy come looking for me. If you want to say *it's all your fault*, please do it now and get it over with.'

'Nah.' Hpq shrugged. 'What good would that do? What matters is, we're going to find him. And then I'm going to enjoy myself watching as he kicks your bum from here to Mercury.'

'As well he might,' Karen admitted. 'Do you really think we can find him, Hpq?'

Her friend, her oldest and dearest and most aggravating friend of all, grinned enormously, a reaction so typical that for a split second she almost thought she could see his face through the pink human flesh. 'We're *dragons*, Grnz. We can do anything. Well,' he added, 'we're capable of anything, which amounts to the same thing, I guess. Don't worry about it, everything's going to be just fine. I promise you.'

Karen giggled. 'That's supposed to make me believe, is it? You promise?'

'Of course.' Hpq looked at her sternly. 'When have I ever failed to keep a promise?'

'Well.' Karen started counting on her fingers. 'What about the time you promised *faithfully* that you were going to take me to the Stormtrotters' Ball; and who did you end up going with?'

'My sister,' Hpq replied stiffly. 'Duty called. But as soon as we got there I danced with you.'

'And Gndva-S'sssn,' Karen reminded him, 'In fact, "danced" isn't quite the word I'd have chosen. When I gave up and went home, you were trying to climb up her back like ivy on a tree.'

'She'd pulled a muscle in her wing-case,' Hpq muttered. I was giving her a back-rub. What's a gentleman supposed to do?'

'Not be so damned blatant about it. You know I can't stand her.'

Hpq looked genuinely surprised. 'What, your cousin Gndva-S'sssn? You're kidding. I always thought you two were inseparable.'

'Inseparable,' Karen agreed, 'in the sense that I could never get her to go away. She hung round me like garlic breath.'

'Like what?'

'Sorry, it's a human thing. No, really, I just couldn't make her leave me alone. It's because I'm the adjutant-general's daughter and both her fathers are just cloud-pushers in Ops. She never liked me, she just wanted the entrée.'

'That's not a very nice thing to say.'

Karen wilted a little. 'Maybe not. But bloody S'sssn always did bring out the worst in me.'

The telephone rang, causing Hpq to jump several feet in the air.

'It's all right,' Karen said, laughing. 'It's supposed to do that. It means someone wants to talk to me.'

'But there's nobody else here.'

'Through that.' She pointed. 'Mind out, I've got to answer it.'

'Oh? It's against the law not to, something like that?'

'Out of the *way*.' She pushed past him and grabbed the receiver. 'Hello?'

The voice at the other end of the line was warm, deep and cheerful. 'Karen Orme?'

'Yes, that's me.'

'Splendid. Look, you don't know me,' the voice went on, 'but my name's Paddy Willis. I think you may know my son Paul.'

Karen reacted as if the telephone had just licked her ear. Paul's father? Wasn't he supposed to be some multi-million-aire businessman or something? And what was he doing calling her?

'Yes, that's right,' she said. 'We used to work together.'

Hpq was pulling funny faces and making painfully-not-laughing gestures, and she realised with a certain degree of annoyance that he could hear (more properly, see, with his third eye) what Mr Willis was saying. It broke her concentration, so that she missed what Mr Willis said next and had to ask him to repeat it.

'I said,' Mr Willis told her, 'Paul's disappeared. He's been kidnapped.'

Karen didn't mean to make a sort of glugging noise in the bottom of her throat; it just came out that way. 'No!' she squealed, ignoring Hpq's query about what the matter was and frantically gesturing to him to go away, which he entirely failed to do.

'Afraid so, yes,' Mr Willis said. 'Apparently two men in ski masks dragged him out of that ridiculous office of yours, bundled him into a car and drove off before anybody could do a thing.'

'That's *terrible*,' Karen said. 'Has anybody got any idea who's responsible?'

'I do,' Mr Willis said. 'Me.'

What Karen wanted to say was 'What?' or 'Huh?', something along those lines. It didn't quite come out that way; more a sort of nasal grunt, like a pig trying to sing 'My Way'.

'It's all right,' Mr Willis was saying, 'I'm not going to hurt him, provided he doesn't try anything stupid – and I know Paul, he's much too chicken to try and escape or anything dumb like that. He'll just sit there like a battery hen, the way he used to do when he had an exam the next day. You have no idea how embarrassing it is having something like that for a son. Anyway,' he went on, 'I didn't ring you up just to bore you with my hard-luck stories. Here's where you come in. You still there? Hello?'

'Yes,' Karen managed to say. 'I'm still here.'

'Oh good. You hadn't made any of those cute stuck-pig noises for a while, I thought maybe you'd fallen asleep or something. It wouldn't have surprised me. A lot of people tend to fall asleep when the conversation gets round to my son.'

'What do you want?' Karen said.

'That's what I like,' Mr Willis replied. 'Straight to the point. Like a rat up a drain, as we used to say back in Queensland. I saw your turn on the telly last night. Well, that's not strictly true, because I don't watch that garbage. Make it a rule never to watch a station I own, it only depresses me. But one of the little people taped it for me. I was impressed. Maybe when this is all over we can line you up a show of your own. You could be the next Jerry Springer, if you set your mind to it.'

'I don't know what you're—'

'Course you do, Karen – you don't mind if I call you Karen, do you, only I can't pronounce your other name. No vowels in it, it's as bad as bloody Czechoslovakian. Odd people, the Czechs. Fall off boats a lot, if you get my meaning. Not that falling off a boat would worry you, of course. You'd just turn into a fish.'

'Hey,' Hpq muttered in her other ear, 'I like this one. He's got a bit more oomph than the rest of them.'

'All right,' Karen said, 'So you know my guilty secret. How the hell did you—?'

Mr Willis laughed. 'Don't ask me,' he said. 'Some overpaid clown from R&D came up with the actual technology; tried to explain it to me, I told him to shut up and go away. Some nonsense about a fourth eye—'

'Third eye.'

'Whatever. What matters is, we've known about your lot for quite some time – really interesting, if you're into wildlife stuff, which I'm not, though you'd be amazed how many people are. What interests me is the commercial angle, need-less to say – and of course the commercial possibilities of a resource like you lot are absolutely mind-bending. But of course, it was all pi-r-squared-in-the-sky until we finally man-aged to get our hands on a sample of the merchandise.'

Karen managed to catch the thunderstorm just in time. 'Are you trying to tell me you abducted my father?' she said.

'Us? No. It was some little nerd of a weatherman who did that. Credit where it's due, though, the way he went about it was pretty smart. We just took your old man off him, that's all.'

'You—'

'When I say we,' Mr Willis went on, 'what I should say is, Her Majesty's government. Wonderful people, the lot of 'em, and a bargain at half the price. But don't let me get started on that subject, please; I can remember when all you had to do was shove an envelope full of dollar bills under a lavatory door. Now it's all got to be contributions to party funds, that sort of thing. It's a scandal, really; I do editorials about it in my papers all the time. Anyway, that's beside the point. My boys have got your dad. He's perfectly safe and well, we're not going to hurt him – bloody stupid move that'd be, after what I've spent getting hold of him. But if you want him to stay that way – no more guest spots on the weather show. Got that?'

Karen breathed hard through her nose, swallowing back lightning.

'Because,' Mr Willis went on, 'if you make trouble for me, then it won't just be your old fella who'll live to regret it. That's how come my idiot son's being useful for the first time in his worthless life. You know I won't do anything drastic to your dad, because that'd defeat the whole object of the exercise. As far as Paul's concerned, though, any excuse. Have you got that?'

Karen closed her eyes. 'I don't believe you,' she said. 'You wouldn't hurt your own son.'

Mr Willis's laughter was warm and mellow, like good Blue Mountain coffee. 'Think about it,' he said. 'Come on, you're the superior life form, use that enormous brain of yours. It's a simple matter of obtainability. I can get myself another son any time I like – takes about ten minutes, and it's quite fun to do. You, on the other hand, can't get another father, or another Paul. But if you're a good girl and do as you're told, when this is all over I'll give you my son as a present. Yours, no questions asked, shipping and handling included. That *is* what you want, isn't it? The reason you came here in the first place?'

Karen forced herself to relax enough to be able to speak. 'I'll see you in Hell first,' she said.

'Uh-huh. Sorry to break this to you,' Mr Willis went on, 'but there isn't one. I had my research people check it out, and for what it's worth there's no such place. I've got definitive proof of it in a drawer somewhere, if you're interested. That was a whole bunch of money wasted, I can tell you. Look, I don't care whether you take my son to be your reptilian love-slave or whether he goes back to wasting his life in that poxy little office. What matters is, you care. Which is why you aren't going to do anything. Nothing at all. *Capisce?*'

'I've got an idea,' Karen said quietly. 'Take me instead. Let my father go. I'm just as much of a dragon as he is.'

Mr Willis was silent for a second or two. 'Interesting idea,' he said. 'I'll have to think about that. Meanwhile, stay put and don't do anything annoying. If you like, I can send you something to remember Paul by, such as an arm. It'd make a nice keepsake, scented with lavender. You could wear it round your neck or something. Hey, that's a thought. You could have his arms about you any time you wanted, without having to put up with the rest of him.'

The line went dead. Karen suddenly thought to look for it with her third eye, but the trace had vanished.

'It's all right,' Hpq said beside her. 'I know you weren't watching, but I was.'

'What?' Karen asked distractedly.

'Where that funny voice was coming from. I can take you there right now, if you like. It's somewhere called . . .' He closed his eyes for a moment. 'Canberra,' he said. 'Down Uncle Wzzxdydpwq's neck of the clouds. Never been there before.'

'No,' Karen replied gently. 'It's not worth the risk. He's human, remember; I don't understand his kind well enough to know what he's capable of doing.'

If Hpq noticed the significance of the expression 'his kind', he was tactful enough not to mention it. 'Up to you,' he said. 'Well,' he went on, 'at least we're getting somewhere. We know more or less where he is.'

'I suppose so,' Karen said, getting up and walking a few steps away from him. 'You know,' she went on, 'it really wasn't meant to be like this. All I've done since I've got here is hurt everybody I care about. And now you've turned up, and I've got this awful feeling—'

'Don't be stupid,' Hpq interrupted. 'Nothing's going to happen to any of us. Not even,' he added with a grin, 'this human you're apparently so fond of. Sooner or later you really are going to have to explain that to me, by the way, because I just don't get it. But,' he added quickly, before Karen could say anything, 'there's a time and a place for that. What do you want to do now?'

'I don't know,' Karen replied. 'Really I don't.'

Hpq looked at her thoughtfully. 'Now that's worrying,' he said. 'You can't have an indecisive dragon. It's impossible, like a dry waterfall. Impulsive, yes. Splat with all four feet where angels fear to tread, most certainly. That's our way. Or could it be you've forgotten that already?'

Karen shook her head. 'But we're dealing with humans,' she replied. 'They're devious. So we've got to be devious too.'

'Not necessarily,' Hpq said. 'You might as well say that in order to make fudge, you need a chocolate saucepan. If it was me, I'd be over at this Canberra place kicking their devious backsides out through their ears.'

'Well, quite,' Karen replied. 'Which is why I haven't asked you for your opinion.'

Hpq's face relaxed into a smile. 'Situation normal,' he said.

'Oh come on,' Karen replied. 'I'm not that bad, am I?'

'Yes,' Hpq said. 'Well, no. Just out of interest; did you really hate Gndva-S'sssn that much?'

'Yes. Well, no. Sometimes. Most of the time she was my best friend. But you know what it's like at that age. Just because she was my best friend didn't mean I ever liked her much.'

Hpq nodded. 'Fair enough,' he said. 'So we're not going to Canberra?'

'No.'

'And we're not going to do anything here either?'

'No. In fact,' Karen said, 'the way I see it, the best thing we can do right now is nothing at all.'

'You're joking,' said Mrs White.

Susan shook her head. 'Sorry,' she said, 'but I'm quite serious. I'll work a week's notice if you insist—'

'*One* week? Now just a minute—'

'But,' Susan went on, 'it's only fair to warn you that if you make me stay here a whole week, I'll be fretting so much about being cooped up behind my desk when I should be out there looking after my poor old grandad—'

'I thought it was your aunt.'

'Whichever. The point is, I'll be so preoccupied that I'll probably make a whole bunch of silly mistakes. You know: filing things in the wrong places, sending people to view the wrong properties, messing up the mailing list, leaving the answering machine on whenever you're out of the office, carelessly spilling drinking chocolate all over my keyboard—'

'You wouldn't.'

'It's dreadful,' Susan went on, 'how easy it is to make stupid mistakes when your mind isn't on the job. And there's so many things that can go wrong in a place like this—'

'All right.' Mrs White glowered at her, as if trying to turn her into yoghurt by sheer effort of will. 'Clear your desk and go away, if you insist. But I hope you realise that with Karen leaving and that dreadful business with Paul, and now you going off as well—'

'You're in grave danger of having to do some work. And at your age, too.' Susan beamed at her. 'There now,' she said. 'Is that rude enough to be unforgivable, or do you need me to come up with something nastier? Actually, I quite like you, but I won't let that stand in my way, I promise you.'

The only effect of that was to make Mrs White look thoughtful. 'There's more to this than you wanting to go and look after some ailing relative,' she said. 'You could try telling me what's really going on.'

Susan shrugged. 'Yes,' she said, 'but it wouldn't be any advantage to me, and I'm rather pressed for time. And now, if you don't mind, I really must be going. I won't bother with my things, if it's all the same to you – it'll be hell facing the future without my Darth Vader coffee mug and my cute furry VDU-top animal, but I guess I'll just have to be very brave. I suggest you give them to the Institute of Contemporary Arts, if the dustmen won't take them.'

'Go,' Mrs White said, making a vague shooing gesture. 'Good luck with whatever it is.'

'Thank you,' Susan replied solemnly, and left.

After she'd gone, Mrs White sat still for a while, thinking and chewing the end of her pencil. Over the years she'd been managing the branch, she'd seen ever so many bright young men and women come and, invariably, go (that was how she knew they'd been bright), but at least the reasons had always been fairly self-evident. Usually it was because they'd got a better job somewhere else, one that paid enough for a Brahmin ascetic to live on. Often girls left to spawn, boys left to tour Australia in unreliable camper vans or write novels. Sometimes they left because they couldn't stand the sight of Mrs White any longer, or because they'd had enough of estate agency and decided to go straight. At least she'd always known; this was the first time in twenty years that she simply hadn't got a clue. Her instinctive reaction was that it had something to do with young Paul being kidnapped in that deplorably melodramatic fashion; after all, what better way to provide for a secure financial future than to hold the son of one of the world's richest men for ransom? The police would be bound to see it that way when she told them. But her instincts were often wrong. It had something to do with Paul Willis, but only tangentially; more likely, it had something to do with Karen Orme (who was a much more credible suspect for the kidnapping thing— never trust someone who voluntarily washes out other people's coffee cups and then hangs the wet dishcloth over the taps to dry) and whatever it was the police had been chasing her for, several days before Paul was abducted . . .

Mrs White shook her head like a wet dog, as if trying to be rid of the whole subject. Whatever the deadly secret really was, she was fairly certain it didn't have anything to do with the business of peddling overpriced dwellings, which was the only field of activity that really concerned her. She made up her mind; first a cup of tea, then check Susan's in-tray for anything that needed doing, then a phone call to the cloning vats for a couple more junior staff. Once she'd done that, she'd be free to get on with some work, for a change.

Terrorism? Drugs? Fanatical religious cults? The CIA? Nah. They weren't the type, any of them; too clean-cut, pink and English for anything like that. Even Karen – in her memory, she'd already tagged her mental image of Karen with the *weirdo* icon; stereotyping does wonders for information-retrieval response times – even Karen the Weirdo had been weird in a typically English, boring way. The thought of either of those dreary young women being involved in anything more dangerous or exciting than putting on dark glasses to go slumming at a Chippendales gig was more than her imagination could encompass, whereas Paul – if anybody ever wandered through life with a fluorescent sign on his back reading VICTIM: PLEASE DISPOSE OF REMAINS TIDILY, it was him. Anything they could possibly have been up to would have to have been something you wouldn't mind your mother knowing about. The hell with them.

Once the kettle had boiled, and her teabag was quietly stewing on the end of its leash, she remembered to phone the police. They were very interested indeed to learn that Susan had left unexpectedly without leaving a forwarding address (she didn't bother to point out that she had given them this information a couple of days earlier, and they had it on file; it'd give them something to do, finding that out the hard way) and they did their best to insinuate that whatever it was that Karen had done, she must have been in on it too. She ignored that, as being the equivalent of a puppydog whining at her feet with its lead in its mouth, said goodbye politely and hung up; she was hot, her desk fan wasn't working and the way the sun was leering at her through the office's plate-glass window seemed to imply some kind of personal grudge. Enough of these fevered imaginings; it was a fact that English people tended to go a little crazy if they'd had to go without rain for more than ten days.

It was just after half-past five, when the office was officially closed but she hadn't got around to locking up, when the strange men in grey suits walked in. There were three of them, which puzzled her a little. Policemen arrive in pairs, or by helicopter in the small hours and wielding sledgehammers. The extra body implied that what she had here was one of the more recherché breeds of pest. This intrigued her; at the very least, they must be foreign policemen (as in the old Soviet joke; one can read, one can write, and the third one keeps an eye on the two intellectuals). Accordingly she gave them a broad smile and asked how she could help them. Were they, she enquired out of wickedness, interested in buying a nice house?

The spokesman shook his head. He seemed uncomfortable, rather uncertain when he spoke (as if Human wasn't his first language).

'Not really,' he replied. 'Actually, we were looking for someone.'

Mrs White clicked her tongue. 'I'm terribly sorry,' she said, 'but we don't sell people, just houses. I suggest you try the employment bureau, six doors down on your left; or I've heard there's quite a nice brothel in Kennedy Street, round the back of Marks and Spencers—'

'A specific person,' the spokesman said, reaching inside his buttoned jacket and producing a rather unflattering picture of Susan. 'Do you recognise this woman?'

Mrs White took the photo and studied it for a while, holding it up to the light at various angles and even turning it upside down. 'I think so,' she said.

'She works here,' the man pointed out.

'Ah,' Mrs White said. 'That'll explain why the face seems familiar.'

To his credit, the man didn't seem to mind. It was as if he wasn't really aware that she was trying to be funny, like a foreigner failing to get the point of a pun. 'Yes,' he said. 'Is she here, or has she gone home?'

Mrs White shook her head. 'She left,' she replied. 'Left as in went away for ever. Are you boys policemen?'

The man thought for a moment before answering. 'No,' he said. 'We're friends.'

Mrs White smiled. 'All three of you? How nice.'

'Friends of Susan's,' the man said, speaking a little louder, the way Mrs White would have done to someone who didn't understand English. 'She said that if we were ever in the area, we should drop by and say hello.'

'So you brought along a photograph of her so she'd know who she was. How thoughtful. Well,' Mrs White went on, 'I'm terribly sorry, but I honestly don't know where she is. As I told you, she quit her job here this morning, and she didn't tell me where she was going.'

The three men looked at each other. 'Oh,' the spokesman said. 'Isn't that—' I mean, that's unusual.' One of his colleagues nudged him and whispered something in his ear. 'Perhaps she left to have a baby,' he said.

'It's possible,' Mrs White replied. 'But if that was the case, I'd have expected her back by now. I mean, it's been over seven hours.'

'Ah,' the man said. 'Of course, yes. Well, if you do see her, please let her know we called.'

'Of course.' Mrs White nodded. 'Would you like me to tell her your names, or will she know who you are?'

'Just say her friends called,' the man replied. 'She'll understand.'

After they'd gone, Mrs White sat quite still for some time. One of the life skills that a career in estate agency teaches you is the knack of recognising the truth even when it's apparently impossible; and for what she'd definitely heard the strange men say, there was only one logical explanation. They weren't human.

She recalled the faces into her conscious mind: Karen, Paul and Susan. Boy, had she underestimated one of them!

In fact, it challenged a whole bunch of comfortable assumptions about the nature of aliens. Could it really be true that what they actually said on establishing first contact was, 'Take me to your classic underachievers'? Were they really as dumb and gullible as they'd seemed? Could any sentient life form be that gormless and still remember to breathe? It was possible; everything's possible in a curved and infinite universe. Somehow she'd allowed herself to lose sight of that fact over the last fifty years.

It was all very interesting, but what it lacked at the moment was a quantifiable financial value. That, however, was something she could change. Pulling open the top drawer of her desk she took out a small notebook, in which she'd written down the special telephone number, the one with all the 0s at each end, that Paul's father had given her when he came to work here (the idea being that when, as would inevitably happen, he got himself into some horrendously complex and expensive form of trouble, she was to ring him and let him know in good time so he could get damage limitation under way as soon as possible). She hadn't called the number before and wasn't really expecting it to work; but it did, because fairly soon after she'd dialled it, she found herself listening to a mellow, avuncular voice saying, 'Paddy Willis here.'

She hesitated for a split second. She had a feeling that what she was about to do was somehow wrong. On the other hand, she was morally certain that it would be extremely profitable. She smiled.

'Mr Willis,' she said, 'you won't remember me, but . . .'

CHAPTER EIGHT

'My third wife – no, hold on, I've skipped a marriage somewhere, my *fourth* wife, she was a redhead. Green eyes. Freckles. You know,' Gordon went on, ignoring the fact that Neville hadn't been listening for at least a quarter of an hour, 'this is a funny old country. You need to have all kinds of licences and stuff before they let you own dynamite, and yet there's women walking around with long red hair, green eyes and freckles, and nobody seems to give a damn. But when you think of all the damage one green-eyed freckled redhead can do in just one afternoon—'

'Are you sure this is the right direction?' Neville interrupted. 'Only I'm fairly sure we came this way an hour ago.'

'Don't think so,' Gordon said firmly. 'I mean,' he went on, 'with dynamite, all you can really do is blow stuff up. By contrast, the variety of different ways in which a green-eyed redhead with freckles can bugger up someone's life is pretty well infinite, especially,' he added with feeling, 'if she's wearing light blue. If the disarmament process is ever going to get anywhere, they're going to have to round up all the red-haired, green-eyed, freckled women in long blue dresses and bury them in concrete somewhere in the New Mexico desert. Otherwise, it's just asking for trouble.'

'Definitely been this way before,' Neville said. 'Look, there's that crab-shaped mark on the wall.'

Gordon stopped to take a closer look. 'That's not a crab,' he said. 'More like a horseshoe. The crab-shaped mark was just past the taped-off three-phase point.'

'You're thinking of the *other* taped-off three-phase point,' Neville replied. 'Only it wasn't, it was a vent outlet. It just looked like a three-phase point.'

They looked at each other for a moment.

'Sorry,' Gordon said, 'I haven't got a clue where we are, either.'

'Wonderful. Then why were you leading the way like you owned the place?'

'I was following you.'

'Oh, for—' Neville leaned his back against the corridor wall and slid down it to the floor. 'This is getting us nowhere,' he said.

'You know,' Gordon replied, squatting down beside him, 'just then you sounded remarkably like my first wife.'

'The blonde?'

'The other blonde. She used to take every slight navigational error as proof of gross moral turpitude. Then she'd insist I find somebody to ask.'

Neville sighed. 'They do that,' he agreed.

'And then, when you do ask someone, they give you directions that don't make sense or lead you round in a circle. And then you get spoken to for not following the directions properly.' Gordon paused, and frowned. 'I didn't realise you were married,' he said.

'I'm not. But I do have a sister.'

Gordon nodded. 'I believe sisters can sometimes be worse,' he said.

'You haven't got any sisters?'

'Oddly enough, no. I've always assumed the extra wives were to make up.' He stared at the wall opposite, as if trying to cut through it with his X-ray vision. 'I had a brother once,' he continued. 'Had him for years. But then he became a chartered actuary and moved to Canada.'

Neville clicked his tongue sympathetically. 'Don't you just hate it when that happens?' he said.

'Oh, I never liked him much. He had enormously bony knees, even as a small boy. Not his fault, of course; then again, having green eyes and freckles isn't really ever anyone's *fault*. It's what you do with them once you've got them that matters.' Gordon sighed, and breathed out slowly through his nose. 'Any particular reason why you never got married?'

Neville considered for a moment. 'I think mostly,' he said, 'it was the way all the women I asked either changed the subject or burst out laughing. The first two dozen times you just shrug it off, but after that it starts getting to you. Mind you, I'm probably over-sensitive.'

'No, no.' Gordon shook his head. 'Sensitive is good. Apparently. Though I think there must be a knack to it. Every time I tried being sensitive, I was just told to shut up.'

'Maybe there's different kinds,' Neville speculated. 'Like – oh, I don't know, direct and alternating current. Maybe you were just using the wrong one at the time.'

Gordon shrugged his shoulders. 'Who knows?' he said. 'Anyway, it makes no odds, because I'm through with all that stuff now. Particularly,' he added, tightening his face into a frown, 'if we can't find a way out of this bloody building. Do you realise we've been walking for nearly two hours and we haven't even come across a staircase yet?'

Neville looked puzzled. 'Meaning?'

'Meaning this building must be *huge*. The size of a small town. Practically visible from orbit. How many buildings that size do you think you can hide away in a small country like Britain before somebody notices?'

'Hadn't thought about it like that,' Neville admitted. 'Of course, it could be dug into something or disguised as something. Like in that James Bond film, where they built the underground hideout inside a volcano.'

'You think we're inside a volcano?'

'No, of course not. Why did you think I meant that?'

'I don't know, you're the one who's supposed to have a third bloody eye. For all I know, you can see waves of infrared radiating out of the magma core.'

'I don't think so,' Neville replied. 'I'm pretty sure I'd have noticed something like that over the last six months or so.'

'Really? In Shepherds Bush?'

'Well, obviously not in Shepherds Bush, no. But anywhere. I went to Hawaii once, you know.'

'It was just a thought,' Gordon said. 'Not that I believe in all this garbage you keep spouting, you understand.' He hesitated. 'It's just that if by some disgustingly improbable chance there is a grain of truth buried under all the bullshit, now would be a very good time indeed to dig it out.'

Neville smirked. 'I knew you'd believe me, sooner or later.'

'Now just a—'

'Unfortunately,' Neville went on, 'all I can see with my third eye right now is lots and lots more of these blasted corridors.'

'That's all.'

'Well, not quite all. I can also see several thousand lines of computer code, about a million phone messages, the repeat of this lunchtime's *Home and Away* and the shipping forecast in seventeen languages.'

'Ah.'

Neville nodded sadly. 'In case you were fretting, by the way, Marilyn is thinking seriously about moving back in with Donald, and there's force three winds expected off Rockall.

Funny,' he added, 'I haven't thought about the weather in ages. It used to be the only thing I ever did think about.'

'Really.' Gordon clicked his tongue. 'Somehow,' he said, 'that doesn't surprise me. Look, concentrate on that forecast. Can you tell where it's coming from? Which direction?'

'Not really. Why?'

'Because we know where it's broadcast from, idiot. We can use it to navigate by, like using the stars. At least we'll know whether we're going round in circles or not.'

Neville looked impressed. 'That's not a bad idea,' he said. 'All right, shut up for a moment and I'll see what I can do.'

Neville concentrating was a fairly awesome sight, especially if you happened to like a little broad comedy with your awe. Hours spent in meetings with producers had left Gordon with an almost superhuman ability not to burst out laughing at inconvenient moments, but he had to call on all his hard-won skills to keep a straight face on this occasion. Neville's face, by contrast, was about as straight as a country lane. At times his mental agony made him look like a constipated sword-swallower; at other times he beamed with an almost spiritual joy, eyes tightly shut, as if an archangel had come to him in a vision and given him Drew Barrymore's phone number. Since Neville's face was pretty damn funny at the best of times, the sight of Neville pulling funny faces was almost more than Gordon could bear, and would have been classed as an act of war in a Trappist monastery.

'Got it,' he said. 'It's pink. Problem is, there's about six different pink ones, and it's a bitch trying to tell them apart. This way.'

Gordon frowned. 'What, you mean through the wall?'

'You know,' Neville sighed, 'with a sense of humour like yours, I'm surprised you didn't make your career in light entertainment rather than weather. There's all sorts of things you could have done in light entertainment – changed fuses, held things for people, made the tea. No, I don't mean through the wall, I mean in this general direction. I suggest that we go back down the corridor till we find a turning that goes that way, and follow it. All right?'

As Gordon had suspected all along, the building was playing games with them. When they'd been coming up the corridor, there had been scores of turnings off, leading in every conceivable direction. Now that they were heading back, the corridor ran straight as a Roman road without any turnings whatsoever. How the building managed to do this, Gordon could only speculate. The likeliest explanation was that it was a living, breathing creature. That was an intriguing concept in itself; maybe it had started off the size of a garden shed and grown, with the help of regular watering and tanker-loads of Baby Bio, into the best-of-show-winning monstrosity they were now trapped inside. If so, the potential of the discovery was staggering; so much so that Gordon promised himself that if ever he got out of this mess he'd pack in broadcasting, buy a strip of land somewhere and plant a crop of late-flowering maisonettes.

'This one'll do,' Neville said, jerking him out of his dreams of avarice and pointing down a spur leading off the main corridor. 'Keep your eyes open for one going sharp left.'

'What? Oh, yes, will do.' A thought occurred to him, and he slowed down. 'Neville,' he said, 'I just want to make the point that I'm only letting you lead the way because nobody, not even you, could make a worse mess of it than I've been doing. It's absolutely not because I really believe you've actually got a third eye. Is that clear?'

Neville sighed. 'As crystal. Secretly, though, I know you believe. You just can't face admitting it to yourself. Actually,' he went on, 'faith is an amazingly broad, flexible thing. For instance there's a small religious community somewhere in North Wales that believes that when we die, we'll be reunited on the other side with all the used paper hankies we've discarded over the years. If they can believe something like that, it's not going to kill you to believe in something as mild and inoffensive as a dragon. Hell's teeth, people have been believing in them for thousands of years; it's only this last century or so we've come over all snotty and decided there couldn't possibly be such thing . . . Hello.' He stopped dead in his tracks. 'What's this?'

'It's a fire door,' Gordon said. 'What about it?'

'Yes, but what's it doing here? We've been yomping down these damned corridors for hours, and this is the first fire door we've seen.' He took a step back and looked the door over carefully. 'It's like the old riddle,' he said. 'When is a fire door not a fire door? When it's a trap.'

Now that Neville mentioned it, Gordon did start to wonder about that. One fire door on its own is a bit like a single curtain hook or a lone whitebait. But, since Neville had made the observation and Neville was a nutcase who believed in dragons, he dismissed it as trivial. 'Don't be so damned melodramatic,' he said. 'This is a government building. You don't have traps in government buildings. You don't *need* traps in government buildings. Open the damned door and let's get going.'

'You open it.'

'You're the leader.'

'Oh, I am, am I? Then I'm ordering you to open that door.'

'Get stuffed.'

Neville frowned. 'That's a bad attitude,' he said. 'When Captain Kirk tells the little guy in the red pullover to open a door, he doesn't get spoken to like that.' He thought for a moment. 'Okay,' he added, 'bad example. But I still think you should open the door.'

'You think so? Fine.' Gordon took a step backwards, too. 'I'll open the door. Just give me a moment to catch my breath.'

Neville grinned. 'You're scared,' he said.

'Of course I'm scared.' Gordon replied irritably. 'I'm so

scared I can hardly keep my bowels clenched. I'm scared of men in black uniforms with guns, I'm scared of lunatics who want to start a new world war, I'm scared of nutters who want to sacrifice me to the Queen and the Duke of Kent, I'm scared of maniacs who kidnap me and tie me up and make me listen to talking goldfish and I'm scared of dying of starvation in an endless maze of corridors. About the only thing on earth I'm not scared of,' he added, 'is this door. I just need a second or two to focus, that's all.'

Neville counted to five under his breath. 'Ready yet?'

'Nearly. If you want to go on ahead, I'll catch you up.'

'If it's any help,' Neville said, 'I can see a damn' great pink line going straight through this door. This is definitely the direction we want to be headed in.'

'Hey. Just now, you were the one saying this door's a trap.'

'That was before you started acting so scared of it.'

'I'm ready,' Gordon said. 'Here goes.'

He went back five or six paces, started running and burst his way through the door like a rugby forward. The door swung open. Nothing happened.

'Told you,' he said, leaning against the wall and breathing heavily. 'Perfectly safe. Don't know what all the fuss was about, really.'

Neville walked through the door and came to a halt beside him. 'Nor me,' he said. 'You know, we'd better get a grip on ourselves, or we'll never get out of here. Now then, where's that damned pink line got to?'

Gordon shook his head. 'Does it really have to be pink?' he asked. 'The Yellow Brick Road was bad enough, but entrusting my life to the ability of a known basket case to follow an imaginary pink trail – dammit, it's worse than finding your way round the Barbican.'

'Almost that bad, I'll admit,' Neville replied. 'This way.'

They'd gone no more than a couple of hundred yards when they came to another fire door. They stopped.

'Properly speaking,' Gordon said, 'this should make me feel better.'

'Yes,' Neville agreed.

'Your turn.'

'It's not a question of whose turn it is. This isn't a children's party, we're trying to escape.'

'All right. Now open the door.'

'*You* open the frigging door.'

'Why should I?'

'Because you're braver than me.'

Put like that, there wasn't much Gordon could say. Trying to look as if he did this sort of thing every day of the week (which he did; there were seven fire doors between the lift and his office) he gave it a fairly robust shove with the heel of his left hand and walked through. Nothing happened.

'It's okay,' he said, breathing out through his nose. 'It's a fire door. Well, what are you standing about for?'

Neville had the grace to look slightly ashamed of himself. 'Sorry,' he said. 'Keep straight on down the corridor. We'll need to take a left at some point, but there's no hurry.'

The third, fourth and fifth fire doors turned out to be as prosaic as the first pair. They hardly noticed the sixth. They were so relaxed about the seventh that they almost walked straight into it, remembering just in time the tiresome formality of opening it first. When they reached the eighth, Neville muttered 'Fire door' under his breath and Gordon replied 'Yup,' as he shoved it open without slowing down or breaking step.

The ninth fire door was locked.

'Bugger,' Gordon observed.

'We could try and break it down,' Neville suggested optimistically. 'You could take a really long run-up and shoulder-charge it. Big, hefty bloke like you—'

'Has enough on his plate right now without a dislocated shoulder.' Gordon kicked at the door in a half-hearted way; it scarcely budged. 'I ask you,' he said. 'What sort of idiot locks a fire door? Damn' thing shouldn't even have a lock on it in the first place.'

Neville sighed. 'You know what this means,' he said. 'We'll have to go back.'

'Oh *no*,' Gordon whined. 'All that way—'

'You got a better idea?'

Gordon shrugged his shoulders. 'No,' he admitted.

'Well, then. If I'm remembering this right, there was a left-hand branch about two hundred yards before we got to the first door. If we take that, we might be able to work our way along parallel to this. No guarantees there's even a corridor there, but I don't see as how we've got much choice.'

'Suppose not,' Gordon grunted. 'All right, let's get going.'

They turned round and trudged back up the corridor. When they encountered the eighth fire door, Gordon relieved his feelings to a certain limited extent by opening it with a vicious kick.

That was when all hell broke loose. Sirens wailed, lights flashed, bells rang, and the wall vents started to exude a foul yellow cloud, probably some kind of anaesthetic gas. Fortunately, all this was happening on the far side of the door.

'Oh God,' Neville shrieked. 'What do we do?'

With a squeal and a clunk, the door in front of them swung back and locked itself. Through the glass panel, they could see that the corridor beyond was now full of the yellow gas; just as well, in fact, that the door was apparently airtight.

'Let's run away,' Gordon suggested.

'As far as the other locked fire door, you mean? Brilliant.'

'All right, then, let's stay here. I really don't care any more.' Gordon sat down on the ground and closed his eyes. 'You stupid bloody twat, this is all your fault. If it wasn't for you I'd be sitting in my nice friendly office right now, drinking coffee and reading the paper. In about ten minutes' time I'd be saun-tering down to the canteen to ask if anybody'd found out what happened to that aggravating little nerd Neville, and they'd say no, but who the fuck cares? And I'd say yes, good point, only if nobody else wants it I was thinking of nicking his waste-paper basket, it's bigger than mine.' He sighed. 'Instead . . .'

'Shut up,' Neville interrupted. 'I'm trying to think.'

Gordon shook his head. 'After forty-odd years, why start now? It's hardly the time and place for learning new skills.'

'Shut *up*.' Neville glowered at him, like a tortoise filled with hatred. 'That's better. Now, let's try and figure this out. These doors seem like they're rigged to go apeshit when someone goes through them *that* way, agreed?'

Gordon took a deep breath and made himself loosen up. 'I suppose so, yes,' he said.

'Implying they don't want people going that way.'

'Possibly.'

'And,' Neville went on, 'my guess is that wherever they don't want us going is the way we don't want to go.'

Gordon woke up. 'Huh? I don't get that.'

'Use your brain.' Neville was on his feet again, looking round. 'Whatever it is they're really doing in here that they want to keep secret, that's what the self-locking doors and sirens and gas and so on are designed to protect. From intruders.' He thumped the wall with his small fist. 'People coming in. Agreed?'

Gordon frowned. 'Go on,' he said.

'Which means,' Neville continued, 'that they're figuring on people coming in going *that* way. The direction we've just come from.'

'Ah.' Gordon looked up at him.

'And the opposite of coming in is going out,' Neville went on excitedly, 'which suggests to me that Out has to be in the *opposite* direction—'

'The way we were going when we ran into the locked fire door.' Gordon nodded. 'That's fine. Now we know that we were going in the right direction when we met the impassable obstacle. That gives me a warm glow of satisfaction in the pit of my stomach, but it's not going to open that door. Face it, Neville, we're buggered. We might just as well wait here till they come and round us up. That way, we're less likely to walk into a lethal booby-trap or grab hold of a door handle with five million volts running through it.'

Neville rounded on him angrily. 'That's it, is it? You're just going to sit there on your bum and give up?'

'Yes.'

'Really?'

'Yes.'

'Suit yourself. *I*'m not.'

'That is, of course, your right as an idiot.' Gordon sighed. 'I've had enough of this. I mean, let's be sensible, shall we? All this—' He made an all-encompassing gesture. 'It's just fooling about, isn't it? This is real life, for Christ's sake. In real life, crazy things like this don't happen. In real life, innocent weathermen, even psychotic loons like you, don't just get scooped up by faceless government agencies, shipped off to vast labyrinthine secret installations and squalidly killed by out-of-control megalomaniacs. This is *England*, dammit. You don't get weird stuff like that in England, it's not that kind of country. It's too—'

'Boring?'

'Exactly. Too boring. What you're imagining is what happens in hot desert countries inhabited by excitable, volatile Latin types or Americans. No.' He shook his head. 'Sooner or later, someone's going to come and tell us it's all been a terrible mistake, or that really it was one of those games shows with Noel Edmonds or Chris Tarrant, and we'll all be jolly good sports about it and get given a free radio alarm clock. You'll see.'

Neville thought about that for a moment. 'In other words,' he said, 'you're relying on the British traditions of justice, individual liberty, common sense and fair play?'

'Yes.'

They looked at each other for two, maybe three seconds.

'Like I was saying,' Gordon said eventually. 'Let's start running.'

'SHOT!' the dragon yelled.

The scientist cringed and put her hands over her ears. Things weren't going entirely to plan.

'Did you see that?' the dragon said. 'Three-ball plant off the side cushion to pot the last red, perfect position on the yellow. Come on, Stevie, my son!'

The scientist raised a pained eyebrow. 'How do you know that's the yellow ball?' she asked. 'It's a black-and-white TV.'

The dragon chuckled. 'To you, maybe. But of course, you don't have a third eye, you helpless, snivelling little – oh, for crying out loud, he missed it. How the hell could he miss that? There's no way a blind man with a prosthetic arm could have missed that, in the dark, facing the other way. Pull your finger out, you moron!' he bellowed at the screen. 'Ye gods and little goldfish, he was one ball away from having the god-damn' title *sewn up*!'

The scientist closed her eyes. She wasn't to know. The odds against the dragon falling instantly in love with the game of snooker were astronomical, so bizarrely improbable as to defy calculation—'

As is usually the case with the statistical probabilities governing true love, she wryly reflected. Not that love, true, false or the more usual mixture of the two, was something she regarded herself as qualified to pontificate about. She'd always been too busy for that sort of thing, and apart from one rather nebu-lous and wholly impractical encounter in the late 1980s, the hit-and-run sniper with the pink wings and the armour-pierc-ing arrows had let her pretty much alone. And that—

—Was entirely beside the point. Things were going yellow on her. Instead of a dragon bored past all endurance and begging piteously for mercy, she now had a happy, revitalised dragon who was rapidly turning into a snooker freak. *Life*, she reflected, *can be so unfair.*

'I don't believe it,' the dragon roared. 'Oh, for fuck's sake, he's practically given the game away. I could have made that shot wearing boxing gloves, using my tail for a frigging cue.'

The scientist couldn't take any more. She grabbed the remote and hit the off button, and the screen immediately reverted to black.

'Hey,' growled the dragon, 'what do you think you're playing at? Switch it back on.'

'Why should I? You're enjoying it. You aren't here to enjoy yourself. This is supposed to be torture, dammit.'

'You can't turn it off now,' the dragon shrieked, 'it's the decider. All square going into the last frame. The whole championship's hanging on this. It's sporting history.'

'Tell you what.' The scientist grinned. 'I'll turn the TV back on if you answer a few simple questions. Deal?'

'What? Oh, yes, right. Whatever you say. Just turn the damn' set *on*. Thank you,' he added, as the picture came back. 'Oh snot, I've missed the break. I hate missing the break, it's so important.'

'Okay.' The scientist leaned forward and touched the record button on the tape deck. 'Now then, first question. What—?'

'Shhh!' the dragon hissed, making a noise like a kettleful of snakes. 'I'm trying to concentrate here.'

'You can watch and answer questions at the same time, can't you?'

'Yeah, yeah, in a minute. Let me just watch this shot.'

'Not in a minute. Now.'

'*Quiet!*' The dragon's voice was so vehement that for a moment the scientist felt deeply ashamed of her lack of consideration. Then she remembered just who was supposed to be torturing who. She made a tut-tut sound to signify disapproval and switched the TV off again.

'Priorities,' she said. 'And the first priority is, answer my questions. Otherwise – are you listening to me?'

The dragon obviously wasn't. His eyes were closed, and although he didn't even have a face in any conventional sense, it didn't take a giant leap of intuition to realise that the set of the muscles around his jaws and snout signified rapt attention. *Shit*, the scientist growled to herself, *he's figured out how to watch the snooker with his third eye*. The thought of it appalled her rather, from an ethical and cultural viewpoint. Causing dragons to use their awe-inspiring enhanced perceptual abilities for watching the Embassy World Championships was behavioural pollution of the worst possible kind; worse than all the carrion-eating sparrowhawks on motorway verges or urban foxes ripping open dustbin bags put together. She felt as if she'd just bought Texas from the Comanches for a crate of firewater and a couple of strings of cheap beads.

And it wasn't getting the goddamn' questions answered, either. She'd had virtually no contact with her employer as yet, but (like everybody on the planet with the exception of a few small tribes in the depths of the rain forest) she knew that he was reckoned to have a quick temper and about as much patience as a mayfly in a dole queue. No two ways about it, she was going to have to think of something, and she didn't have much time to do it in.

Which brought her back to the same old question: how the hell do you torture a huge, massively-armoured lizard without damaging him severely in the process? Boredom had seemed to be the obvious way to go, and for a while there it had looked like it was going to work; but the critter's tenacity and adaptability had been too much for her. Outclassed; there was no other word for it. Weighed in the balance and found wanting. Pathetic.

Pathetic . . .

Abandoning Operation Self-Pity in mid-flow, she applied her mind. She remembered having read somewhere (probably on one of those thought-for-the-day desk calendars; it was that kind of sentiment) that the way to overthrow an opponent stronger than oneself is to lead to his strengths, not his weaknesses. Trite, but valid; the weak spots on the wall are the ones that are heavily guarded, leaving the strong points virtually unmanned and ripe for a sneak attack with scaling ladders.

'It's all right for you,' she said quietly.

'Shh.'

'I mean to say,' she went on, 'nothing I can do's going to get to you, so I might as well stop wasting my time and go home now. I mean, better to quit voluntarily than be fired.'

The dragon didn't say anything, but one eyelid twitched uneasily.

'Not that you'd be able to grasp the concept of *fired*,' she went on. 'I doubt very much whether it's much of an issue with dragons. Is there even such a word as 'unemployment', where you come from?'

'No,' the dragon muttered. 'Now be quiet.'

'Didn't think so,' the scientist continued, in a small, sad voice. 'Not in your vocabulary. Like such concepts as mortgage repayments, tax demands, health-insurance premiums, pension contributions, utility bills, living expenses – Oh, I suppose you could look them up in a dictionary, but there's no way you could ever understand what they *mean*. After all, you aren't human.'

'Quite true,' the dragon said. 'Fortunately.'

'Very fortunately,' the scientist sighed. 'What wonderful luck, not to have all that garbage hanging over you all the time, making you lie awake at night worrying, still there the next morning even if you do manage to grab a few hours' sleep. Talk about privilege. You people don't know you're born.'

The tip of the dragon's tail flicked to and fro. 'Nobody's going to sack you for not being able to do the impossible. All you've got to do is explain; you gave it your very best shot—'

'Hah! Like I said, you're just not human. If you were, you'd understand.'

'That would be a high price to pay for understanding,' the dragon replied. 'Why should I care about what's going to happen to you if you fail to bully me into betraying my own kind? Do you agonise over whether your food forgives you before you eat it?'

'As it happens,' the scientist lied, 'I'm a vegetarian.'

'Really.' The dragon clicked its tongue. 'If you could see through your third eye, I'd show you the sound of a carrot being boiled. You'd never be able to sleep again.'

The scientist didn't want to think about that; it gave a whole new, rich penumbra of meaning to the expression 'eating something that disagrees with you.' 'Be that as it may,' she said, 'when all this is over, you're not the one who'll be working night shifts in a hamburger bar. I'd hate to think what your precious third eye would make of that.'

'I am not responsible for the misfortunes of my enemies,' the dragon said coldly. 'Only for the trouble I cause my friends.' He snorted suddenly. 'Shit a brick, call that a safety shot? Bloody fool's left a red straight into the left-hand centre pocket. Calls himself a professional . . .'

'That's fine,' the scientist muttered, with a hint of bitterness in her voice that was at least forty per cent genuine. 'My life is tumbling in little pieces all round my ears but you're watching the snooker – I know, *I* can't see it, but it's there – so that's all right. I'm just sorry my pitiful bleating's spoiling your enjoyment of the game.'

'That's all right,' the dragon said, 'you're not that difficult to ignore. Go on, you bastard, miss, miss, miss – Yes! Couldn't hit his own bum with a frying pan.'

The scientist scratched the tip of her nose thoughtfully. Maybe, at a very fundamental level, dragons and people weren't all that different. Male dragons and male people, anyhow. *Why is it*, she asked herself, *that it's easier for humans*

to communicate with dolphins than for women to get a simple, self-evident message through the Kevlar-armoured skulls of men?
Actually, it wasn't such a hard question, at that. Dolphins are quite intelligent.

She reviewed her other options, all none of them. She decided to try again.

'It's not as if I'm asking you to do anything *bad*,' she said. 'I'm not after military secrets or the design of some dragon superweapon, or anything that'll make life any harder for your lot or mine. All I want is a few scientific facts. The truth. Knowledge. Dammit, if we know a bit about you people, it'll help us understand you better, and surely understanding can only be a good thing, the first step on the road leading to peace, friendship, an ongoing mutual relationship of trust and brotherhood between Man and Dragon.'

No answer.

'A few trivial little biological and biochemical details,' she ground on. 'More along the lines of giving some helpful hints to a primitive but up-and-coming species that's desperate to improve itself. Drag itself up to *your* level of progress and development. Think of it as the sincerest form of flattery.'

No answer.

'If you don't answer my fucking questions,' the scientist growled, 'I'm gonna connect you up to the mains and fry your ass to charcoal, you goddamn' intercontinental ballistic newt.'

The dragon didn't look round. 'Sorry? I missed that.'

'Nothing. Doesn't matter, it was only me, blathering on.'

'Something about the news.'

'Not news. Newt.'

'Ah.' The dragon nodded. 'Quaint dialect sayings from your north-eastern region. Newt so queer as folk. I don't know,' he added doubtfully, 'in his position I'd go for the pink. Screw back off the pack of reds and be perfect for the blue into the middle.'

The scientist looked away. It had been a good idea, but it

had gone nowhere so many times it was probably eligible for citizenship. All the effort, all the pain, and she'd learned exactly one thing about dragons; namely, that the adult males don't bother listening to you when you're trying to have a serious conversation. Maybe her father had been a dragon. Wouldn't surprise her in the least.

'All right,' she said, 'you win. I'll stop asking.' She sat down behind her desk, pulled out the middle drawer and propped her feet on it. 'I'll just sit here, wait for them to come and repossess my car, and you can lie there feeling smug and watching two men wearing evening dress in the middle of the day poking at plastic balls with overgrown cocktail sticks. Eventually one of us'll die – probably me, I suspect you guys live a whole lot longer than us, though of course I don't know that for a fact since you won't damn' well tell me – and when the smell gets into the air-conditioning system and all the guys in suits on the sixteenth floor start yelling blue murder, someone'll come along with one of those big dustbins on wheels and clear away my desiccated remains, and my sister in Boise can have my aunt's watch and my framed print of *Guernica*, and I seem to remember something about a death-in-service clause in the pension scheme which ought to cover the cost of the funeral, though that really shouldn't be a major item, hire of one JCB, one black plastic garbage sack—'

'What on earth are you wittering about now?'

'But there's just one thing I would like you to do for me,' the scientist went on. 'That's if you're not too busy watching the crown green bowling or the sheepdog trials. I'd like my fiancé to have this locket.' She fished inside her lab coat and brought out a small gold heart on a chain. 'It was a sort of pre-engagement present, with his picture in it and our initials on the back—'

'I didn't know you were engaged,' the dragon said. 'It only goes to show, there really is somebody out there for everyone, no matter how improbable it may seem. I mean, if *you* . . .'

'I was,' the scientist replied. 'I broke it off.'

'Really? Why?'

'I got bored standing around outside the church. Anyway,' she said, her voice as brittle as a Chinese screwdriver blade, 'if you could see to it that he gets it; his name's on the back, and if you look . . .'

'The man in the picture?'

'I beg your pardon?'

'The picture inside the locket. There's a photo, it's either a small, thin man or a very large weasel. That's him, is it? Your ex-fiancé.'

The scientist thought about it for a moment. Third eye. Can see clean through a closed locket. Neat trick. 'Yes, that's him,' she said, trying to sound unconcerned. 'And he doesn't look like a weasel.'

'Sorry, I didn't mean—'

'Weasels have more like a point to their snouts. You're thinking of a polecat. He looks just like a polecat.'

'Ah. What's a polecat?'

The scientist rubbed her eyes. 'Forget it,' she said. 'You were about to say something?'

'What? Oh, yes. All I was going to ask was,' the dragon went on, 'why don't you give it to him yourself?'

'Well, for a start—'

'I mean, now's as good a time as any, when he's only about a hundred yards away, as the armour-piercing bullet flies.'

'What the hell are you talking about, dragon?'

'Oh, come on, it isn't exactly difficult. The man whose photograph you carry around in that little gold box is here in this building. Right now, he and some other man are running down a corridor, headed in this direction. If you open the door in, let's see, twelve point nine six seconds, he'll run straight into it and probably break his nose. That would undoubtedly be an improvement, aesthetically speaking.'

The scientist scowled horribly, then relaxed. 'Nice try,' she muttered, 'but I'm not that dumb. I'm not opening that door for—'

'Sshh!'

She shushed; and heard the sound of heavy footsteps thundering past in the corridor outside. She jumped to her feet, hesitated and sat down again.

'Very nice try,' she said. 'You heard someone coming down the corridor with your super-sharp dragon hearing and made up this dippy story to make me open the door so you could escape—'

The dragon sighed. 'It's remarkable,' he said, 'how the same species can be both insanely suspicious and tragically gullible. You won't believe me when I tell you, out of the kindness of my heart, that your long-lost true love is just outside the door—'

'He is *not*—'

'But still you read newspapers, watch the television news and vote in elections. I suppose it's endearing in a way, but hardly what I'd call a survival trait. Still, I'm only a visitor here, it's not my place to criticise.'

'He is not,' the scientist repeated, 'my long-lost true love. He's the jerk who left me standing in a church porch wearing a six hundred pound non-returnable dress. The only possible reason for seeing him again is that you can't very well rip a person's lungs out with a blunt spoon if you don't know where they are. Since I don't happen to have a blunt spoon with me right now—'

The dragon shook his head. 'Bullshit,' he said. 'You aren't fooling me. Third eye.'

'What, you mean you can read my—?' The scientist goggled at him in panic. 'You can't, can you? You're kidding.'

'Yes,' the dragon admitted. 'And you've just admitted I was right all along.'

'No way. *No* way.'

'You're more than welcome to lie to me if it makes you feel better. After all, it's none of my business. Just think of me as a fellow scientist carrying out a few gentle, non-invasive experiments on a specimen. Nothing personal.'

If the scientist was furiously angry, she didn't stay that way for long. 'It's lucky for you I left my blunt spoon at home,' she said. 'So, all right, who's winning?'

'I beg your pardon?'

'In the snooker match. Who's in the lead now?'

The dragon lifted his head a little. 'Do you know,' he said, 'I'd forgotten all about it. Let's see. Oh. It's finished.'

'You missed the end? You don't know who's won?'

'Apparently.' The dragon frowned. 'Annoying,' he said. 'But my own fault, for letting myself get distracted. And yours, for making such an interesting lab rat.'

The scientist wasn't sure what to make of that.

CHAPTER NINE

'All right,' said Hpq, 'we've tried that. Now what?'

Karen, who'd been dozing in her chair, looked up and blinked at him. 'Whu?'

'You said, the best thing we can do right now is nothing at all. That was several hours ago.' He frowned. 'I don't want to sound negative, but I don't think it's working.'

'Patience,' Karen replied, tentatively flexing her seriously cricked neck. 'With humans, everything takes much longer than you're used to.'

'Fair enough,' Hpq replied. 'Excuse me if this is a personal question, but what were you doing just now?'

'I wasn't doing anything,' Karen told him. 'In fact, I think I nodded off to sleep for a bit.'

'Sleep,' Hpq said. 'That's what it's called. I've heard about it from time to time, but that's the first time I've ever seen it happen. Weird.'

'What? Oh.' Karen remembered. Once upon a time, when she hadn't been human, she had never slept at all. It was hard to imagine that – God, you'd be *exhausted*. 'I suppose I've got used to it,' she said, a little self-consciously.

'For a while there I thought you'd died or something,' Hpq said, stretching out on his back on the floor, with his hands behind his head. 'Then I saw you were breathing, so I guessed it couldn't be anything too deadly serious. So what do you do when you're—'

'Asleep?' Karen laughed. 'You don't do anything. You just are.'

'Really. Why?'

Karen closed her eyes, then opened them again. 'It's so the body can rest and recuperate,' she said. 'It's a human thing.'

'Oh. And how often do you have to do it? Once a year, something like that?'

'Eight hours a day. Well,' she qualified, 'some humans can get by on less, but not me. I mean, not me when I'm being a human. Of course.'

Hpq was looking at her oddly. 'Eight hours a day,' he repeated. 'That's, what, twenty-four divided by . . . That's a third of their lives.' He looked mildly shocked. 'Remarkable,' he said. 'There I was, thinking what a swizzle it must be only living ninety years; and now you tell me that in real money, they only live sixty.' He squinted into the air for a moment, then relaxed. 'You know,' he said, 'humans seem to do that a lot – take great chunks of what little they've got and throw it away, I mean. Sleep and taxes. Bloody funny way to carry on, if you ask me.'

'I didn't,' Karen replied. 'Look, I wish you wouldn't keep harping on all the time about how strange and inferior humans are. It's getting on my nerves.';

'But—' He paused. Usually, dragons have a use for tact the way a battleship needs a raincoat. Hpq was, however, fairly quick on the uptake. 'I'm sorry,' he said. 'But anyway, like I was saying. What are we going to do now?'

Karen yawned. 'I suppose we ought to do something,' she

said, feeling slightly guilty. 'Trouble is, I can't think of anything that wouldn't make matters worse than they already are.'

Hpq grinned. 'I can,' he said. 'As soon as it gets dark, let's slip into something more comfortable, fly over to this Canberra place and smash up some of Mr Willis's things – office buildings, radio masts, TV stations, that sort of thing. Or tell you what; if its being conspicuous that's bothering you, we could round up a few of his satellites. I gather they're quite expensive, it'd give us something to bargain with.'

For a moment, Karen could see the appeal in that. It was probably what her father would do, if he was in her scales. And it was humane and responsible; nobody would see them do it, nobody'd get hurt. There was a lot to be said for the idea; including—'

'No,' Karen replied. 'Absolutely not.'

'Oh.' Hpq looked a trifle disappointed. 'Pity. Any specific reason why not?'

'Because . . .' The reason had been right there a moment ago, but she must have put it away somewhere safe in her mind, because she couldn't find it. 'Because we don't do that sort of thing.'

'Oh. Why not?'

'Because.'

Hpq whistled softly. 'My God,' he said, 'you really have gone human, haven't you?' He shook his head. 'I mean, you hear stories, but I'd never actually believed they could be true.'

'Stories?'

'About dragons who go slumming and stick like it. And I'd always imagined it was something parents told naughty kids to scare 'em. Well, well.'

Karen decided not to reply to that, for fear of mortally offending the only friend she had in this particular whole wide world; so she went into the kitchen and cut herself a sandwich instead. There was, she decided, much to recommend the human habit of comfort eating. While she was slicing the cucumber and arranging it in symmetrical patterns on the bread, Hpq poked his head round the door.

'Sorry to interrupt,' he said, pointedly not looking at what she was doing, 'but were you expecting company?'

'No, not really. Why?'

'There's ten men coming up the stairs,' Hpq replied. 'I can see the sound of their boots with my eyes open. And this is just a guess on my part, but I think they may be friends of the other men in the helicopters.'

'Helicopters?'

'Four of them. The ones in the helicopters have got more weapons than the ones coming up the stairs, but apart from that they're pretty well identical.'

'Oh,' Karen said.

'What's the matter?' Hpq frowned. 'You seem unhappy about something.'

Karen looked at him. 'Go away,' she said. 'No, don't do that, you'll run straight into them. Hide.'

'What?'

'Hide. They don't know you're here, so they won't be looking for you. Hide till they've gone, then go home. There's no reason why you should—'

'Hide? From *humans*?' Karen found the disdain on his face shocking. 'Sorry, but you've got that the wrong way round. We don't hide from humans, the way—' He paused, searching for an image that would register with this new human persona of hers. 'The way cars don't hide from small flying bugs on motorways.'

'You don't understand.' Karen was getting agitated. 'Just for once in your life, do as you're bloody well told and hide. Now.'

'If you insist.' Hpq pulled a face, then vanished into thin air. *Will this do?* Karen saw the words with her third eye. She'd completely forgotten that he (and she, of course) could do that, though really it was kindergarten stuff – creating a prism of minute water-vapour droplets suspended in the air to form what was in effect a three-dimensional mirror that transmitted reflected images of empty air around the thing it was masking, thus making it invisible. In the dragon elementary syllabus, it came somewhere between vertical take-offs and potty training. *It'll do,* she sent back. *Now keep absolutely still; and no matter what happens, don't you* dare *stick your ugly snout in. Agreed?*

What, you think I'm just going to stand here and let them—?

Agreed?

All right, yes. Promise. Cross my heart and hope to be rather less immortal some day. But I still reckon—

'Shh.'

Even though she was expecting something of the sort, the thump as the police tried to kick her front door in made Karen jump in the air. The attempt failed and was followed by a cry of pain and some fairly imaginative swearing. She took a swift third-eye glance through the woodwork, and quickly guessed the reason for it; on the other side of the door a plain-clothes policeman who'd probably overdosed on *Starsky & Hutch* reruns as a boy was hopping frantically on one foot while cradling the other in his cupped hands. Moral: don't wear tennis shoes when kicking shit out of doors.

Entertaining though the spectacle was, she couldn't help feeling that the more they hurt themselves trying to get in, the less charming and affable they'd be if and when they finally succeeded. She sighed, walked to the front door and opened it.

'Yes?' she asked politely.

The nearest and biggest policeman was in the act of being handed a sledgehammer. When the penny dropped and rolled around on its edge for a second or so before toppling onto its obverse side, he looked disappointed, like a child told at the last minute that she's not being taken to the zoo after all. Karen couldn't help feeling sorry for him; he looked endearingly comic, as would any man trying to pretend in the face of all the evidence that he isn't holding a three-foot-long hammer in one hand.

'You Karen Orme?' he grunted.

She nodded. 'You Tarzan?' she added, just because she wanted to. The man frowned and, without looking away, handed the hammer back to one of his myrmidons, who didn't take it cleanly, so that it slipped through his fingers and fell on his foot, landing with such precision on the point of maximum agony that Karen quickly blinked a glance with her third eye, looking for a tell-tale cloud of minuscule raindrops. But Hpq was still in the kitchen, cautiously performing an autopsy on the cucumber-and-tomato sandwich; it was either sheer coincidence or the side effects of her own apprehension (anxiety-induced perspiration projected outwards and suspended in the air; fundamentally the same principle as the wearable mirror, except that it was unintentional and only dense enough to bend light a little way, thereby messing up human judgement of distance and making it very easy to be clumsy). Karen decided to play safe, and made herself stop sweating. Easier said than done, as she realised when the policeman reached out to grab her arm and punched one of his friends on the nose instead.

'You're under – sorry, Jim, it was an accident – you're under arrest,' the policeman said, lowering his arm and massaging his barked knuckles. 'You'd better come quietly,' he added nervously. 'I don't want to have to use force.'

Well, quite, Karen reflected. There was no knowing what damage they'd do to each other if they tried to grab her. 'It's all right,' she said, in as muted a voice as she could manage. 'I'm sure this is all just a silly misunderstanding.'

The policeman gave her an Oh-yeah-right look and stood aside to let her go past. As he staggered back, missed his footing and disappeared backwards down the stairs, Karen made a mental note to buy some strong anti-perspirant the moment she got out of this mess.

'Chief?' one of the policemen called out. 'You all right down there, chief?'

'Think I've broken my leg,' a small, sad voice replied.

'We'll call for an ambulance, then. All right, you,' he went on, turning to Karen. 'No more funny stuff, you hear?'

'You thought it was funny too?' Karen nodded. 'That's a relief. I nearly sprained something not laughing.'

'You just watch your step,' the policeman replied testily – an unfortunate choice of words, in the event. Karen listened to him going bump-bump-bump down the staircase, like Pooh Bear, and giggled. 'I know,' she said, 'it's not funny really, it's just that he said—'

'Put the cuffs on her quick,' another policeman suggested. Trying to regain their favour by being helpful, Karen extended her wrists towards the officer and held them steady, as he deftly handcuffed himself to the man directly to Karen's left. 'Oh for crying out loud,' he wailed, realising that en route he'd also managed to pass his hand between the banister rails. 'One of you get these bloody things off me. The rest of you – Hey, where do you think you're going?'

'We're retiring,' said the fifth policeman. 'In good order,' he added, as he stepped out onto a stair that was in fact three inches to the left of the side of his foot. 'Aaaaaagh,' he continued, as he grabbed for support at the sleeve of the man next to him. Then there were four.

'Just a suggestion,' Karen said meekly, 'but if I were you I'd try and keep very still.'

'You threatening us?' the seventh policeman wailed. ''Cos if you are, we're armed.'

'Oh, I really wouldn't—' Karen said, before the sound of the shot drowned out the rest of her warning. 'Honestly,' she told the three remaining policemen, 'keeping still and not playing with anything dangerous is about your only chance. Trust me. And I know you won't want to do this, but closing your eyes would help a lot. Promise.'

The eighth policeman, who'd been staring at her with rapidly increasing horror in his eyes, obviously couldn't take any more. He started to back away. One small step for a policeman.

'It's all right,' Karen said, after a moment, 'the rest of them broke his fall. A bit. Now, will you *please* do as you're told, and not—'

There was something really rather elegant in the way the ninth policeman, reaching with both hands for Karen's throat, managed to grab the door handle instead and pull the door sharply towards him. The noise its edge made against his skull wasn't nearly as nice.

That left one bluebottle, hanging on a wall; or, to be nit-pickingly precise, hanging with both hands from a lamp-sconce, which he managed to grab as he sailed past on his way down the stairwell. He managed to maintain his grip for the best part of four seconds before he had to let go.

'Oh for pity's sake,' Karen muttered disgustedly, as she surveyed the carnage. To complete the set, as it were, the two men chained to each other through the banisters had managed to crash their heads together when starting back in terror from the gunshot and were sleeping the sleep of the just, looking for all the world like a matching pair of tiebacks. 'I do wish people would listen sometimes.' She moved her foot a little – she'd got a sleeping policeman on it – and stepped back into the doorway of her flat.

'No sweat,' Hpq said, rematerialising next to her. 'You'll have to teach me the thing with the handcuffs some time.'

'Nothing to do with me,' Karen replied bitterly. 'Not that anybody's ever going to believe that for a moment. Oh, just when you think things can't get any more complicated . . .'

Hpq frowned. 'Well,' he said, 'if that really was all just your sweaty armpits—'

'Thank you very much.'

'—Then I'd suggest getting out of here quickly, on humanitarian grounds, before the other lot of idiots realise something's wrong and try and land their helicopters on the roof. A bit of a lark is one thing; a mile-wide crater of devastation is quite another.'

Karen went slightly green. 'I'd forgotten about them,' she said. 'Look and see what they're doing, will you? I'm a bit misted up after all that palaver.'

'Flying round in circles, annoying your neighbours,' Hpq reported, after a brief moment of trance-like introspection. 'Funny things, helicopters, like upside-down strimmers. Fragile, too,' he pointed out meaningfully. 'I strongly recommend leaving.'

They walked carefully down the stairs—

('What happened?' groaned the senior policeman as they stepped over him.

'Accident,' Karen explained.

'What, all of them?'

Karen nodded. 'You must have walked under a ladder or something on the way here.'

The policeman thought for a moment. 'You're right,' he said. 'We did. How did you know that?'

'Lucky guess.'

'Oh,' the policeman said, as the pain made him pass out again.)

—And found a wide selection of empty vehicles outside the front door, with their doors open and engines running 'Well, why not?' Hpq said. 'That lot in there won't be going anywhere, and we could do with putting as much distance between us and here as we can.'

Karen shook her head. 'I don't know how to work one of these things,' she said. 'It's difficult.'

Hpq grunted scornfully. 'Oh, don't be such a wuss,' he said. 'Look, if humans can do it, it can't be difficult, right?'

He climbed into the nearest car. 'All right,' he said, 'do you know which one's the Go button?'

'None of them,' Karen replied. 'That's the passenger's side. The driver sits over there, behind the round thing.'

'You see,' Hpq said, 'you know all about it really. All right, you can do the flying, I'll just watch.'

'They don't fly.'

'What? Oh, sorry, forgot. Do whatever it is you do to make it go. Before the people in the helicopters wonder who we are and come in for a closer look.'

'Give me a moment, will you?' Karen took a deep breath and closed her eyes. Actually, it was far less complicated than she'd imagined; a little pump fed an explosive compound from a reservoir into a combustion chamber, where an electric spark set off a controlled explosion whose force turned a thing like a mill-wheel with a stick nailed to it that pushed round a bunch of knobbly metal wheels that eventually made the proper wheels go round, and there were little wires tied to some of the bits and connected to things you pulled and pushed and trod on and wiggled to make it do what you wanted it to. In fact, it was just like all the other human contrivances she'd come across – impressively mysterious and magic-looking on the outside, plain low-tech ironmongery within. 'Okay,' she said, 'I'm ready.'

'Took you long enough,' Hpq complained as she released the handbrake, let the clutch out smoothly and joined the stream of traffic. 'But then, you always were a bit slow off the mark with gadgets. Hey, do you remember that time when we were doing isomorphic wave resonance mechanics in second grade, and you thought the electron splitter was a nucleitide wrench? Laugh? I nearly fell off my stool.'

'You did fall off your stool,' Karen reminded him, deftly overtaking a Porsche. 'And the teacher made you stand in the corner for the rest of the lesson.'

'You're right, I'd forgotten.' Hpq clicked his tongue.

'Haven't thought about those days in quite a while, actually. Do you remember that time when you and me and your cousin S'sssn and old Snotty Frpzxmqxcp stole all those cloud-traffic cones out of the – LOOK OUT, YOU BLOODY FOOL, YOU'RE HEADING STRAIGHT FOR THAT BUILDING – out of the caretaker's shed and stuck them up on the statues on the roof? We got into a lot of trouble for that, but it was worth it just to see the expression on the old misery's face.'

Karen nodded. 'It was a silly thing to do,' she said. 'We could easily have fallen off the roof and been killed. I'm glad I don't—'

'No, we wouldn't,' Hpq interrupted, frowning. 'If we'd fallen off we'd have just spread our wings and drifted down. My God,' he added, staring at her, 'now you're starting to remember things like one of them. We've got to get you out of here fast, before it's too late.'

Karen took a deep breath. 'I've been meaning to talk to you about that,' she said. 'About what I'm going to do when this is all over, I mean. You see,' she continued, sweeping anti-clockwise round a roundabout, 'I don't plan on going back.'

'What?'

'I'm staying here,' she said. 'I'm not going to be a dragon any more.'

It was several seconds before Hpq could reply; partly because what she'd said had stunned him, partly because he'd seen how close his side of the car had come to the lamp-post they'd just passed at sixty miles an hour, and he didn't want to bother her while she was making such finely graduated course adjustments. 'Because of what's-his-face? The human? You can't be serious.'

'I am,' Karen replied. 'And not just because of him. Even if things don't work out there, I'm still not going back.'

'You mean you actually *prefer* it here? You must be out of your pointy-topped skull.'

'I didn't say that,' Karen pointed out. 'I think it's more a case of not being able to go back.'

Hpq pursed his inconvenient human lips. 'All right,' he said, 'yes, your dad's going to be monumentally pissed at you for quite some time, and it won't be a pretty sight. That's not enough to make you maroon yourself down here among the woolly-tops. He'll get over it—'

'Yes. But I won't. Can't you understand that?' Karen looked away for a moment, trying to remember the colour-coding system for traffic lights, which had temporarily slipped her mind. It wasn't easy to figure it out from first principles, but once she'd remembered that red was also the universal convention for hot, the rest followed logically enough. (Red is hot; engines run hot when you're moving, slow when you're standing still; thus red must mean Go. Stands to reason, really.) 'It's not that I don't want to go home,' she continued, swerving to avoid an oncoming car whose driver clearly hadn't figured out the red = hot thing yet. 'Or even that I like it here very much. I don't. And no, it's not because I'm scared of what dad will say, or anybody else for that matter. I guess I'm going to stay for the same reason a tree stays. I made a choice, and this is where I am now, so I'll have to get used to it.'

'That's supposed to be a reason . . .? Oh, by the way, where are we going?'

'I don't know,' Karen replied.

'Oh. In that case, do you think we could go there a little more slowly? It's not like I'm scared or anything, it's just that if the theory of relativity's got any truth in it at all, at the speed you're going it'll be yesterday before we get anywhere.'

Karen scowled, but throttled back to a timid fifty-five. 'Truth is,' she said, 'I can't think of anywhere in particular to go. Before those idiotic policemen turned up, I was planning on staying put and letting them come and get me – I figured, why bother going to them when they'll quite happily come and give me a lift? – but now that's all messed up. Nobody's ever going to believe all that was an accident, and I really don't want to spend the rest of my life in a human prison, thank you very much.'

'So,' Hpq said, 'now you've got to go to them.'

'Agreed. Only, of course, I don't know where they are.'

'Closer than you think,' Hpq replied, pointing up through the roof. 'Helicopter,' he explained.

'Damn. Open the windows and turn the fan on, quick. Anything to keep myself from sweating.'

Hpq did as he was told. 'Actually,' he suggested, 'a cyclone or a small typhoon'd probably get rid of them. And they'd stand a better chance of survival, probably.'

'No.' Karen was slowing right down, looking for a place to pull in. 'All right, you vanish. I'll be all right, really.'

'If you say so,' replied a patch of empty space where Hpq had been sitting. 'What about the going-to-prison stuff, though? I thought you said—'

'I'll think of something. And before you say it, no, I don't want you to come and fetch me out, no matter what. It's been wonderful seeing you again, really it has, but it's time you were going home. Believe me, it is. There's no place for your kind down here.'

She parked the car, got out and stood on the pavement, waving to the helicopter. The policemen inside must have seen her, because it hung in the air like a big fat dragonfly, looking at her dubiously like a nervous hiker looking over a gate at a field full of cows. Then they must have figured out how to use the bullhorn, because the helicopter started talking to her.

'This is the police,' it said. 'Throw down your weapons. We are armed and will shoot if necessary. Resistance is futile. I repeat—'

Karen yawned. The helicopter didn't look like it was in any hurry to land, but it did seem inordinately fond of the sound of its own voice. After a minute of this, Karen's patience ran out. She closed her eyes and looked for the helicopter's radio.

Quiet! she thought.

Obligingly, the helicopter stopped burbling, though it backed away fifty yards or so. *That's better*, Karen told it. *Now, can you land that thing without damaging anybody?*

The bullhorn sputtered a bit, coughing out a gob of static. 'Yes,' it said. 'We'll do that.'

Fine. Oh, by the way, I surrender.

'Thanks.'

Don't mention it. Watch out, you nearly crashed your tail-rotor into that telegraph pole.

'Sorry, didn't see it there. How's that?'

To the left a bit more. Okay, that'll do.

They were a bit diffident about coming to get her, for some reason. Fortunately, they didn't ask how she'd managed to hack into their radio without any equipment at all; instead, they sat looking at her nervously and not saying anything, all the way to wherever it was they were taking her—

—Which turned out to be some kind of airfield in the middle of nowhere. There was a small jet aircraft waiting. *Canberra*, she remembered, and wished she'd thought to ask Hpq exactly where *Canberra* was. But she hadn't; so she asked a policeman instead.

'Australia,' he replied. 'Hey, how the hell did you know—?'

'Doesn't matter,' she replied; and, since the policeman seemed far too nervous of her to want to take it any further, there the matter rested. And that was all right; because all the policemen (or soldiers, or secret service agents, or whatever) were so obviously scared stiff just being near her that it was impossible for her to feel anxious enough to work up a sweat. She tried smiling reassuringly but that just seemed to make things worse, so she gave up.

Why Australia? she wondered; and then she remembered having heard something about Australia being the place where the British traditionally sent their criminals. *Figures*, she thought; *that's what I am, now.*

They let her sit next to the window. It was the first time she'd left her own airspace, or flown as a passenger. The sensation of looking down on the clouds while in human form was extremely unsettling to begin with (*Help! No wings!*) but after a few hours it started to get easier, and she stopped feeling instinctively for the grain of the airflow with the empty space where her wings should have been.

'The idea,' Neville muttered, 'was a good one, in theory.'

It was pitch dark. Somewhere nearby, something – no, things, plural – was making a soft, scuffling noise. *Probably*, Gordon told himself, *that's claustrophobia and asthma, fighting over which of them gets the privilege of finishing me off.*

'Hey, you said,' Neville went on, 'look, you said, there's a ventilation shaft behind that grille. If we could get inside it, you said, there's just enough room to crawl. That could be our way out of here, you said.' He sneezed. 'Of course, you weren't to know it'd turn out to be a dead end, and that after hours and hours and hours of doing toothpaste impressions we'd find ourselves stuck here without enough space to turn round. Really, you mustn't blame yourself.'

'Thank you.'

'You're welcome. Of course,' Neville went on, 'if by some miracle we ever get out of here, I'm going to kill you. But you won't really have deserved it. I thought you might like to know that.'

Gordon didn't reply immediately. Instead, he began to laugh. 'You might just get your chance,' he said. 'Here, listen.'

They listened.

'It's a voice,' Neville said.

'Precisely. And that's good news; first, because it isn't yours, second, because it's directly underneath us.'

'And?'

'And,' Gordon went on, 'if we can only find some way of breaking through, that means we can get out of this godforsaken shaft.'

'True,' Neville conceded. 'And if I had fifty-eight tiny metal hands and an inky ribbon running through my nose, I'd be a typewriter. How do you propose breaking through a fourteen-gauge stainless-steel conduit without any tools?'

'We'll think of something.'

'Bet you a fiver we won't. Trust me on this, there's no way we're going to be able to – aaagh!' There was a thump, a clang and a distictly feminine scream. Gordon backed up a bit, and smiled the contented smile of the man to whom his enemy owes money. Then he lowered his legs over the edge of the hole where the panel had just fallen through, wriggled back a little further until he felt himself beginning to slide, and grabbed for the edge with his hands. It was a bit like climbing down out of a loft without a ladder, and he had to drop the last five feet or so. Fortunately, Neville broke his fall, so that was all right.

The first thing he saw after he'd picked himself up off the ground was a dragon. The next thing was his ex-fiancée. It was, he realised, going to be one of those days.

'Gordon?'

'Hello, Zelda,' he said, quickly checking his ankle to see if he'd sprained it. 'There's a dragon tied to that table over there.'

'Yes, I know.' She gave him a look you could have cut glass with. 'Is that all you've got to say for yourself, you bastard: "Hello, Zelda, there's a dragon tied to that table"?'

Gordon frowned. He was still feeling a little shaken up by the fall out of the conduit. 'But there *is* a dragon tied to the table,' he pointed out.

'You left me standing outside the church, you jerk! How could you do that to me? You thoughtless, inconsiderate, good-for-nothing—'

'Yes, all right.' He held his hand up, to indicate that he wanted to speak. 'You won't get any arguments from me on that score. The dragon, Zelda. Is it real?'

The dragon made a strange, deep gurgling sound, rather like a thunderstorm giggling. 'That's him, isn't it?'

'Yes,' the scientist sighed. 'That's him.'

'Told you.'

'Yes, you did.'

The dragon looked at Gordon for a moment. 'You're better off,' it said.

'You bet I am. Gordon, what the *hell* do you think you're playing at, jumping out on me like that?'

'Sorry.' He shrugged. 'It was that, or stay squashed up in a ventilation duct with *him*.' He indicated Neville with his toe. 'If you'd been in my position, you'd have done the same thing.'

The scientist breathed out slowly through her nose. 'Right,' she said. 'Just out of interest, what were you doing up there in the first place?'

'Escaping,' Gordon replied. 'Look, do you mind if I sit down in your chair? I think I've done something to my ankle.'

'What? Oh, all right. So who were you escaping from? Some other poor bitch you'd decided not to marry after all?'

A pained expression crossed Gordon's face. 'Don't be like that,' he said, trying hard not to stare at the dragon. 'No, as a matter of fact I was trying to escape from a bunch of raving psychopaths with guns who've been trying to kill me. Would you happen to know anything about that, by any chance?'

'Someone trying to kill you?' the scientist said. 'Now who on earth would want to do a thing like that? Apart from all those other women whose lives you've screwed up, of course, and possibly half a dozen jealous husbands and maybe the pest-control people.'

Gordon shook his head. 'No, it wasn't any of them,' he said. 'I'm sure I'd have known if it was. Actually, I think they work for the government. Do *you* work for the government, Zelda?'

'Certainly not. I work for Mr – never mind who I work for.' She scowled. 'Don't change the subject. You were running away from Security, weren't you?'

'If you say so. To be honest with you, I never got around to asking them for their job descriptions.'

'I see.' Zelda gave him another of her special heavy-duty looks. 'Well, in that case I'm going to call them right now and tell them to come and get you.' She reached across the desk for a buzzer. 'And you owe me two hundred and sixty-four pounds and seventeen pence, she added. 'For the photographer,' she explained. 'And then there's the brides-maid dresses and the caterer. You were going to pay half.'

Gordon tried to grab her hand, but she snatched it away. 'I won't be able to pay you back if I'm dead,' he pointed out.

'That's all right, I'll sue your estate. Besides,' she added, 'they aren't going to kill you.'

'You reckon?'

'Not if I ask them nicely and tell them I've got a prior claim. They're very understanding people once you get to know them.'

'Zelda—'

'You never said your name was Zelda,' the dragon interrupted.

'What?' She spun round, startled. The fact was, she'd forgotten all about the dragon. 'Oh, right. Yes. Zelda Ehrlich.'

'That's a nice name,' the dragon said gravely.

'You think so? I mean, well, it's just my name, you know? Like, I didn't really have a lot to do with it.'

The dragon's brows tightened into something analogous to a frown. 'You didn't?'

'No,' Zelda replied. 'My parents chose it for me.'

'Oh. You don't strike me as particularly indecisive.'

Zelda shook her head. 'No,' she said, 'you don't understand. That's the way we do things. Your parents choose your name for you when you're born.'

'They do?' The dragon didn't sound convinced. 'What a strange way to go about it. How on earth can they know what to call you when you've only just been born, I wonder.'

'I don't follow,' Zelda said. Her hand was nowhere near the buzzer now.

'Your name tells people who you are,' the dragon replied. 'For instance my name – I won't tell it you in the original, because you might try and repeat it and do yourself an injury, you need the proper jaw-muscles – my name means *alpha male dragon measuring twenty-seven c'kgnungs by eight kgnungs by five kgnungs by two hours and six minutes, with a pale yellow patch two speepokts in from the left fore armpit, administrative officer grade 2, widower with one daughter, inclined to be short-tempered when provoked and generally snotty to underlings but is all right really when you get to know him, hobbies include aquaplaning, collecting meteorite framents and Hsnioinggggg folk music*. Actually,' he added, 'that's what my friends call me, for short. What does yours mean?'

Zelda blinked twice. 'I don't know,' she said.

'You don't – Oh, well, fair enough. Sorry, I interrupted you. You were threatening the mortal.'

'Was I? Oh.' Zelda narrowed her brows, trying to concentrate; but her left foot had gone to sleep during the early stages of the dragon's name, and had just woken up with more pins and needles in it than you'd expect to find in Debenham's main warehouse. 'Hang on, you said mortal. Does that mean—?'

'Did I? Sorry, I meant human,' the dragon replied smoothly. 'There you go, always the scientist. You were just about to hand over your ex-boyfriend to the guards. But I think you've probably decided not to.'

Zelda nodded. 'He isn't worth it,' she replied. 'I mean, I'd just feel bad about it afterwards, and I've done enough feeling bad about him to last me a while—'

'Thank you,' Gordon said. 'I think,' he added. 'Be that as it may. If you aren't going to turn me in, you've got to help me escape.'

'Excuse me?'

Gordon nodded. 'One or the other,' he said. 'This isn't an issue where you can be neutral. Think about it.'

'He's right,' the dragon said.

'Hey!' Zelda snapped. 'Whose side are you on, anyway?'

'Nobody's,' the dragon replied. 'I just have a tidy mind, that's all. If he escapes and the guards find out he was in here and you didn't raise the alarm, they'll assume you helped him and you'll be in as much trouble as if you had. Likewise if he stays here and they catch him. Either way, you'll get the blame.'

'Wonderful,' Zelda muttered. 'I should have known he'd still be trouble.'

'You didn't have any choice in the matter,' the dragon pointed out, 'so you can't blame yourself. You're just unlucky, that's all. But the fact remains, unless you hand him over, not only do you have to help him escape, you have to escape yourself as well. Because you can't stay here now, can you?'

Zelda thought it over; then closed her eyes and made a loud snarling noise. 'God, I hate this,' she complained. 'Oh, if only I'd listened to my mother. She never liked you, you know.'

'Really? I'm devastated. Listen,' Gordon went on, 'I don't know if your scaly friend over there is for real or not. I don't care much, either. But whoever or whatever he is, he's right.'

'Big of you to say so,' the dragon muttered. 'Still, a human being who can be in a confined space with a fully grown dragon and apparently not give a damn – there may be hope for your species yet.'

Gordon grinned, a little crazily. 'At last,' he said, 'somebody who likes me.'

'I wouldn't go quite that far,' the dragon replied. 'But you make a refreshing change, I'll grant you. By the way,' he added, 'haven't we met before? I was a goldfish at the time, but your voice sounds familiar.'

'So it was you in that tank – I mean, yes. Fine. Later. How'd it be if *you* helped me to escape? Somehow I get the impression it's more in your line of work than hers.'

'With pleasure,' purred the dragon. 'Of coure, you'll have to untie me first.'

'Over my dead—'

'Sure,' Gordon replied. 'No skin off my nose. And anyhow, isn't there some old gag about my enemy being your enemy?'

Zelda stalked over and stood between him and the dragon. 'Don't you dare,' she said. 'You even think about it and I'll scream the place down'

'Don't listen to her,' the dragon urged softly. 'All she cares about is her ridiculous science.'

'It's not ridiculous,' Zelda growled.

The dragon laughed. 'It is, too,' he said. 'Don't forget, with my third eye I can read all sorts of your communications – television signals, Internet pages, radio broadcasts. I read your science a short while ago, during a commercial break in the snooker—'

'All of it? Don't be—'

'While simultaneously learning and evaluating most of your languages,' the dragon went on. 'Talking of which, your surname means *honorable*. It's German. Where was I? Oh, yes. What you people think of as science – well, it's interesting. Not to mention quite amusing at times. All that stuff about equal and opposite reactions. Crazy. But that's not the point,' the dragon went on. 'The point is, you need to get out of here quickly. I can help you. But not if I'm stuck here like a climbing rose on a trellis.'

'Good enough for me,' Gordon said. 'Sorry, Zelda.'

'I'm not going to let you.'

'Oh, for—' Gordon scowled. 'Just because we may have had our differences in the past—'

'Differences!' Zelda screeched. 'You bastard, you stood me up on my wedding day.'

'Yes,' Gordon replied patiently. 'Admitted. Guilty as charged. But I don't think it actually carries the death penalty. Not even in Singapore. Zelda, there are crazy people out there who want to kill me. Really kill me. As in death. Could you please make an effort and try to understand what that means?'

Zelda was one of those people who calm down visibly, like a piece of hot metal gradually fading from orange to grey. 'Probably,' she said, 'you did me a favour anyhow. If we had gotten married, we'd only have spent all the time fighting. I mean, how could anybody live with you and not fight? All right,' she said, 'here's the deal.' She turned to face the dragon. 'It's up to you. If I let you go so you can help him escape – God knows why you want to, but anyway you've got to promise me, on your word of honour as a dragon, that you'll answer all my questions. Agreed?'

The dragon made a snorting noise, half annoyance, half amusement. 'Now just a moment,' he said. 'The only reason I was going to help this imbecile was so he'd untie me and I could get out of here. If you're going to – Oh, never mind. I suppose it'll have to be my good deed for the day. Just think about this, will you? If you'd made me that offer a day or so ago, I'd have agreed, and you wouldn't have had to sit through hours and hours of black-and-white snooker.'

'And I'd have lost my job,' Zelda sighed. 'Just like I'm about to do now.' She dipped her head in the direction of Neville, who was still fast asleep on the floor. 'What about him?' she said.

'What about him?' Gordon replied.

'You're proposing to leave him there, are you?'

'Well, yes. No. I bloody well ought to, since he got me into this mess. But,' he added quickly, 'being a delusional moron isn't a capital offence either, so I suppose we'd better take him along too.'

'Besides,' the dragon chipped in, 'he wasn't delusional at all. Everything he told you was perfectly true.'

Gordon made a soft, whimpering noise. 'All right,' he said, 'don't rub it in. Just because it happens to be true doesn't make him any less of a nutcase for believing it. I mean to say,' he added, 'dragons. And talking goldfish. The whole idea is utterly ridiculous.'

Dragon laughter sounded unsettlingly like a bandsaw meeting a stray nail in the middle of a log of wood, but Gordon was getting used to it by now. 'You know,' the dragon said, 'I can't help but admire your attitude. It's people like you who've made the human race so . . .'

'What?'

'Convenient.' The dragon's eyes sparkled. 'If you didn't exist, it'd have been necessary to invent you, as the old dragon saying has it.'

For some reason he couldn't really fathom, Gordon found this extremely annoying. 'Convenient? Necessary? What for?'

'Straight men,' the dragon replied. 'After all, where would the fun be in raining if there was nobody underneath? Now then, somebody did mention something about undoing these confounded straps.'

'All right,' Zelda said. 'But you've got to promise to be nice.'

This time the dragon's laughter made the floor shake. 'Young human female,' he said, 'I wouldn't know where to start.'

Zelda shrugged. 'I don't believe you,' she said. 'Actually, I think you're kinda cute. Like a cross between a four-year-old kid and a tyrannosaurus. A cuddly tyrannosaurus, naturally. All right, here goes.' She released the straps, then jumped back quickly as if she'd just lit a fuse.

For three seconds the dragon didn't move at all. Then, with a flick and a wriggle that was so fast as to be practically invisible, he flipped over from his back to his legs, hopped in the air like a frog off the table onto the floor, and bobbed up into the air like a balloon. 'That's better,' he murmured, hovering three feet or so off the ground. 'You have no idea how wearing resting your weight on something solid can be when you aren't used to it. In case you're wondering,' he added, 'it's done by manipulating the effect of the Earth's gravitational pull by means of a bioelectrical magnetic field generated by my central nervous system. In your science, it'd take forty pages of equations to describe it. Of course, the same goes for all the electrical impulses you have to send along your nerves to operate all the cogs and wheels and bits of sinew it takes for you to scratch your ear.' He breathed in and out slowly. 'The difference is,' he said, 'I know how I work. Which is what makes it possible for me to do this.'

Suddenly, he wasn't a dragon any more. This time, there was no movement at all for the eye to struggle to follow. One moment there'd been a dragon, floating in the air; the next, it'd gone, and in its place was a tall, fat man with a bald, pointed head and thick tufty sideburns ending level with his ear lobes. He was wearing the uniform of a lieutenant colonel in the Coldstream Guards, and holding a machine gun.

'I know what you're thinking,' the ex-dragon said. 'You're thinking I'm going back on our deal. Certainly not. It's just that if I break you out of here by bashing the wall down with my tail, then carry you on my back across the Atlantic to Bogota, there's a risk I might make myself conspicuous. I wouldn't want that. So I've decided to be you for a while.'

'Fine,' Gordon muttered. 'Only, if you've dragged yourself down to our level, would you mind explaining just how you were planning to get us past all those locked doors and stuff?'

'Ah.' The dragon nodded seriously. 'I was wondering about that. Fortunately, right here I've got a very precise, very specific tool that'll have us out of here in no time. Interested?'

'Well, of course.'

'Here you are, then.'

The dragon moved, and there was something sort of round and sort of clunky lying on the flat of his outstretched hand. The humans gazed at it for quite some time.

'I must be missing the point,' Gordon said. 'All I can see is a ordinary bunch of keys.'

'For opening doors with, yes,' the dragon said. 'Well, what were you expecting, magic?'

Gordon breathed out through his nose. 'I see,' he said. 'Well, quite. Hold on, I'll just wake up my friend.' He lifted his left foot and kicked Neville hard on the left shin.

'Huh? Wassa?' Neville murmured, opening his eyes. 'Mind what you're doing with that—'

'Neville, wake up.' Gordon bent down and grabbed his collar. 'Neville, you remember that goldfish?'

'Hello,' the ex-dragon said. 'Remember me?'

Neville nodded, then squirmed. 'Oh my God,' he said, 'it's *you*. Hey, look, it was a mistake, really. I never intended—'

'Shut up,' Gordon reasoned. 'He's going to get us out of here. Oh, and by the way, this is Zelda.'

'Hello.'

'Hello.'

'Great.' Gordon pointed to the dragon. 'All right,' he said, 'you're on. Magic, maestro, please.'

The dragon dipped his head in acknowledgement, selected a key and turned it in the lock of the lab door. It opened.

'Tra la,' he said solemnly.

Neville grunted. 'That wasn't magic,' he said. 'All he did was—'

Gordon was shaking his head. 'Humans,' he sighed. 'What do they know?'

CHAPTER TEN

Imagine Manchester.

Sorry, had you just eaten? Let's try a gentler approach.

Imagine a place where it rains all the time. Imagine a place where baths are for drying off in, where you fill a kettle by holding it out of the window for a second and a half, where the current in the gutters is strong enough to turn hydroelectric turbines, where they thought *Waterworld* was a documentary, where Noah fortunately didn't send out his doves (or he'd be sailing yet), where even the privatised water companies can only manage to cause a hosepipe ban one year in three.

There's another place like that. It's rather less well known, because it's in the emptiest part of the Pacific, a thousand miles north of the Marquesas, a thousand miles east of Christmas Island, perched on the edge of the Clipperton Fracture, a tiny island not much larger than the average Asda car park that spends nine months each year completely submerged. It's so remote that homo sapiens hasn't got around to noticing it yet, so it doesn't have a human name. Once a year, however, it hosts the biggest gathering of dragons in the world, as the four dragon kings, their senior staffs and delegates from every lodge and eyrie meet to elect a management committee and discuss the leading issues of the day. Although the dragons go there ostensibly to work and be serious, putting several thousand dragons in a small area and expecting them not to party is rather like mixing nitric acid and glycerine in the same test tube and telling them to play nicely. In fact, it's the nearest thing that dragons have to a bank holiday – which may explain why the weather is always atrocious; it's the one weekend in the year when it hardly ever rains.

Because the dragon king of the north-west had further to come than his three colleagues, he and his contingent were always the last to arrive, and by the time they got there, the party'd usually been under way for at least six hours, at which point all the official business had been dealt with and the delegates were unlikely to notice anything less obvious than an active volcano they'd just flown into. Accordingly, the absence of the king's adjutant-general and marshal of bank holidays wasn't remarked upon until quite late in the proceedings; to be precise, in the awkward hiatus between the beer running out and the quartermaster-in-ordinary getting back from the liquor store in Vaskess Bay with 20,000 bottles of tequila.

'I know who'll know the answer,' said the north-eastern pursuivant of tempests, as he floated on his back six feet or so above the bottle-strewn beach. (He'd been discussing continuity errors in the fourth season of *I Love Lucy* with the south-western captain-general of monsoons.) 'You know who I mean.'

'Who?'

'*You* know. We've both known him for years.'

'But I only just met you.'

The pursuivant of tempests frowned. 'You sure?'

'Dunno.' The captain-general scratched his left eyelid with an eight-inch adamantine claw. He'd been aiming for his ear, but they'd both reached the stage in the proceedings where precision is for wimps. 'Your face does ring a bell, now you come to mention it. I don't know, though. You people all look the same to me.'

'Huh?'

'All right then, us people. Silly long noses. Little fiddly ears. Wings.' He sighed. 'I hate being a dragon,' he said.

'Oh. Why?'

'Not sure, really. Partly it's the looking-like-an-attack-newt. You feel so silly.'

'I don't.' The pursuivant of tempests shook his head, something a friend would have tried to talk him out of. 'Anyway, that's beside the point. We were talking about – oh, *you* know.'

The captain-general scowled, then relaxed. 'Oh, *him*,' he said. 'Got you, yes. Dammit, we were at school together.'

'Were we?' The pursuivant shrugged, first the forward shoulders, then the back. 'If you say so,' he said. 'You sure we're talking about the same bloke?'

'Sure I'm sure. Old Tqpsb – Pqtzv – Tqgfd – old Snotface. Always top in maths and seismology, dreamy sort of kid, kept falling over his tail in PE. Him.'

'No,' the pursuivant said carefully, 'I wasn't thinking of him. But I was at school with him, yes. Used to hang out with that jerk Kjjdrlmqrspt a lot; boy, I hated that snub-eared little ponce, didn't you?'

The captain-general thought for a moment. 'Not really,' he said. 'That's me.'

'What? Oh well, broad as it's long. Old Snotface'd know, though. Used to know every bloody thing, Snotters did.'

'Know what?'

'What we were just talking about.'

'Ah, right. Tangentially,' the captain added, 'is there anything left in that bottle?'

'Which bottle?'

'The one wedged behind your ear.'

'Which – ah, yes, got it. Help yourself.'

Dragons, of course, very rarely drank alcohol, for the same reason they didn't warm a bath full of cold water by dunking the electric fire in it. They have more sense.

'Funny,' the pursuivant added, taking the bottle back almost but not quite before the captain-general had finished with it. 'Haven't seen him around here today.'

'Old Snotface?'

'That's right. Suppose he must be ill or someth—' Suddenly the pursuivant cracked his wings open, like a gypsy dancer opening a fan, and launched himself, still upside down, out over the sea. 'Knew I shouldn't've mixed the beer and the quetila—'

''Snot called that. It's called—' The captain-general's eyes closed for a moment. 'Teliqua. Everyone knows that. You're right, though. Where is old Snotface? Not like him to miss out when there's a free bar.'

That, give or take a few slurred words, was the general theme of quite a few conversations on the island over the next six hours or so, for the north-western king's adjutant was well known and well liked among his peers. It was quite some time, however, before any of them were in a fit state to send out search parties. In the meantime, all they could do was quiz his colleagues on the north-western staff to see if they could throw any light on the matter. For some reason, though, they weren't particularly forthcoming with information.

'Snotface?' replied an inspector of drizzle, for example. 'No, sorry, can't say. Secret,' he added, drawing a claw across his lips and accidentally laying his jaw open with the razor-sharp edge. 'Not that there's anything secret about it, just we're not supposed to say. Security,' he added. 'Careless talk costs wives, that kind of thing.'

'Don't you mean 'lives'?'

'I know exactly what I mean, thank you,' the inspector

replied. 'And I'm not supposed to talk about that, either. Orders.'

'Ah. In that case, I'll have another vodka. Unless there's anything else.'

'Nope. Just vodka.'

'In that case, vodka will do just fine.'

Another unusual facet of the relationship between dragons and strong drink was the way dragons actually started to sober up faster the more they drank over a certain level. By dawn on Monday morning the disappearance of two high-ranking north-westerners was the main subject of discussion among representatives of the other three kingdoms.

'And I'm telling you,' grumbled the crown prince of the south-east, picking a seagull out of his glass and depositing it carefully on the rock next to him, 'dragons don't just vanish into thin air. Not unless they stop a direct hit from an atom bomb, at any rate; and I think we'd have noticed if they'd been loosing those damn' things off again.'

The king of the north-west chewed a cocktail stick thoughtfully. 'Something's going on,' he muttered, 'and I can't get anybody to tell me what it is. Which is bloody annoying when you're a dragon king, let me tell you.'

'I wouldn't know,' the crown prince replied with more than a hint of bitterness. He'd been the next in line to the throne of the south-eastern kingdom since before the first dinosaur started shivering and suffering from goosebumps, and his prospects of ever actually becoming king were as slim now as they'd been then. For some reason, he was an expert on exactly what dragons can survive, in the way of poisons, explosions, contagious diseases, weapons attacks and freak accidents involving hot magma, tidal waves and meteorite strikes. 'All I'm saying is, they'll be down there somewhere, don't you worry. And if I know them, they'll be back in their own good time, and none the worse for wear, either. Known him since we were kids. I'm her godfather,' he remembered. 'Gave her a pewter mug for a christening present.'

'Hmmm.' The dragon king sipped his vodka, noticed something odd about the taste, and surreptitiously dumped the rest. Chances were that, entirely out of force of habit, the crown prince had dumped enough refined white arsenic into his drink to depopulate California. Fortunately, the worst harm a dragon can come to from eating arsenic is a mild tummy upset, say 1.5 to 1.8 on the Itinerant Hot Dog Vendor scale. 'I dunno. Stubborn, yes. Self-willed, likewise. But it's not like either of them to bunk off work. Also, the way the rest of the staff's covering up for them suggests there's definitely something wrong and they're terrified of what I'll do when I find out. Which is why,' he added, reaching for an unopened bottle, 'I've come here. I figure I stand a better chance of discovering what the deadly secret is here than I'd ever do back home.'

The crown prince, who was leaning against a rock he'd spent centuries wearing into the precise contours of his spine, nodded thoughtfully. 'You mean,' he said, 'that if someone from another kingdom, say, were to buy a few drinks and loosen them up a bit, he might just overhear . . .'

'Something like that. Of course, he'd have to be discreet.'

'Naturally.' The crown prince sniffed his drink – dragons consume strong liquor by breathing on it until it vaporises, then inhaling it – and smiled. 'Well, quite,' he said. 'But I'm good at that. When you've been plotting to overthrow your head of state for two hundred million years, you get the hang of these things. Which reminds me—'

The dragon king sighed. 'It won't work, you know,' he said. 'What won't?'

'Whatever it is you're considering doing. No disrespect, but just look at your track record. How many attempts has it been?'

'If at first you don't succeed,' the crown prince replied.

'No pun intended. Come on, I wouldn't be a dragon if I gave up at the first sign of difficulty. And besides, I nearly had him. Twice.'

The dragon king favoured him with a conciliatory nod. 'The Krakatoa thing, I'll grant you, yes. If he hadn't bent down at the last moment to sniff that orchid, it'd certainly have been interesting. The French nuclear-test business was a non-starter, though. He saw through that like a windscreen.'

'Really? Then how come when he got the anonymous message he actually went there?'

'He was just trying to be nice,' the dragon king replied. 'After all, you're his son, he does his best to take an interest in your hobby. I remember him telling me, right here on this very beach, the year before last. *Zzzx*, he said, *he's a good kid, it breaks my heart not to be able to do more for him. After all, he works damn' hard the rest of the year, and it's his only real pleasure in life.*'

The crown prince drew a claw along the side of his jaw. 'He said that?'

'His very words.'

'That's so nice.' He made a low snuffling sound, muffling it as best he could in his vodka glass, since it wouldn't do for a dragon of his standing to show his sentimental side in public. 'Breaks his heart, did he say?' he added thoughtfully. 'Hm. Never tried that. Wonder exactly how you'd go about—'

The dragon king cleared his throat meaningfully. 'So you'll do that, then,' he said. 'Keep your ears open, have a chat here and there.'

The crown prince dipped his head a little to confirm. 'I'll get a couple of my lads onto it as well. Good at that sort of thing. Plenty of practice over the years. We'll get to the bottom of it, don't you worry. Now then, do you suppose a really sudden shock—?'

By the end of the third day, all the delegates had drunk themselves sober again, and it was time to go home. The crown prince of the south-east and the dragon king of the north-west happened to bump into each other briefly in the checkout queue.

'Sorry to hear about your father,' the king said.

'Thank you,' the crown prince replied, staring at the back of the head of the dragon in front of him. 'But he's much better now. A couple of days' rest once he gets home and he'll be as good as new.'

'That's all right, then,' the king said. 'It could have been very nasty, I gather.'

The crown prince clenched his tail into a knot. 'There was a case just like it seven thousand years ago,' he said. 'Dragon laughed so much at a joke while breathing in a glass of single-malt whisky that he choked. Died of it, apparently. Dad was luckier, though.'

'I'm sure you're relieved.'

'You bet. It was a close call, all right.' He sighed. 'And I suppose even the best jokes lose a bit of their sparkle after seventy centuries.' He looked round at the king, then straight ahead. 'You wouldn't happen to know any good jokes, would you?'

The king thought for a moment. 'Well, there's the one about how many humans does it take to change a light bulb.'

The prince looked puzzled. 'What's a light bulb?'

'Okay, not that one. There was a dragon, a human and a goldfish went into a bar—'

'It's not his tail, it's the Aurora Borealis. Heard it,' the prince said sadly. 'Never mind. If you come across any good ones you will let me know, won't you?'

'Of course.'

'Splendid. Now then,' the crown prince went on, 'about that other business . . .'

By the time they'd worked their way to the head of the queue, the dragon king's expression had changed rather. The effects of the change would probably have been quite clearly visible from the air; an unaccountable tendency for a large and closely packed crowd of dragons to avoid a certain spot on the beach by a substantial margin.

'You're cross,' the crown prince said.

'Just a bit.' The king was gradually changing colour, from green to red, like a leaf in autumn. 'Ever so slightly.'

The crown prince suppressed a smirk. He'd seen something like this bfore, back in the days when the dragons held two conventions; one here, in the summer, the other at midwinter, in Atlantis. That was, of course, before the dragon king of the north-west had found out what the people of Atlantis were saying about him behind his back.

'Now then,' the prince said, 'I hope you aren't going to do anything hasty.'

'Certainly not,' the king replied. 'On the contrary, it'll take quite a lot of careful planning.'

'Ah,' the prince said. 'Just like the last time.'

The king nodded. 'Of course,' he went on, 'they say it's not something you forget. Like riding a bicycle.'

'What's a bicycle?'

'Haven't a clue. But memorable, apparently. Once you've done it, the experience stays with you for the rest of your life.'

'That good, huh? Must give it a try some time.' The crown prince smiled. Purely by coincidence, the dragon king of the south-east had been paying an incognito visit to Atlantis on the very day when it vanished for ever under the waters of the Atlantic Ocean. 'Talking of diplomacy,' he said.

'You are sure?' the king interrupted. 'I mean, I was brought up to take geography seriously. Also there's the question of what it'll do to the Gulf Stream. Not to mention the migratory patterns of Canada geese.'

'In other words,' the prince said, 'you want to be absolutely sure of your facts before you commit yourself. Good idea. Well,' he said, 'all I can suggest is that you go and see for yourself. That way, you'll know. Otherwise, there'll always be that nagging doubt in the back of your mind.'

'You're right,' the dragon king said. 'All right, that's what I'll do. I'll turn into a human and go to this – what did you say it was called?'

'Canberra. On my – I mean, on dad's patch. Tell you what,' he added, 'I can take you there myself.'

'Really?'

'No trouble at all.' The prince smiled warmly. 'The least I can do for my favorite uncle.'

If it crossed the prince's mind that the dragon king of the north-west had no children of his own, which meant that if anything happened to him his throne would pass to his sister's only son, he didn't let it show in his face. His eyes may have sparkled a little, and he may have whistled a bar or two of of 'Waltzing Matilda' under his breath, but that was probably because he was so happy at his father's lucky escape from the perils of ancient humour.

'Welcome,' said the tank, 'to Australia.'

Karen wasn't quite sure it was being completely sincere, even for a tank. The way it kept its 105mm cannon, all three machine guns and both wire-guided missiles trained on her, following her every move like a hungry dog begging at table, gave her the impression that it didn't really trust her.

'No funny stuff,' it added, as she started to walk down the steps off the plane.

'Not even the one about the two transdimensional creatures of pure energy who buy a lottery ticket? Oh boo. You're no fun.'

'No talking.'

Karen wasn't having that. She stopped where she was and scowled at the tank, which shuffled back three feet in a growl of fluffed gear-changes. 'Has it occurred to you,' she said, 'that if you try and shoot me right now, you'll undoubtedly blow up this nice airplane I'm standing directly in front of? You won't get me, of course, because I'll duck. Now put it away and tell me what I'm supposed to do next.'

The tank let its gun droop, like an adulterer hearing a key turn in the front door. 'Got my orders,' it said. 'I'm supposed to keep you covered every step of the way.'

'Oh, are they expecting it to rain? I'd have brought an umbrella if I'd known.' She walked down a few steps, then stopped. 'Look,' she said, 'is there actually a person in there, or am I talking to some kind of intelligent machine? Half-intelligent machine, anyway.'

There was a grinding of metal and a loud creak, and a head popped up through the turret hatch. It was very pink.

'It must be very hot in there,' Karen said sympathetically. 'Don't they let you have a fan or something?'

The pink man stared at her with loathing. 'If you don't do exactly what I tell you,' he said, 'I'll shoot. Really I will,' he added, spoiling the effect rather.

'Sure,' Karen replied. She carried on down the stairs, past the tank and across the tarmac towards the single-storey concrete building that looked as if it might contain life forms of some description. The pink man, having shouted a few times, hopped back inside, dropped the lid and followed her, so that an observer might have got an impression of someone taking a very large dog for a walk.

'It's all right,' she called out as she reached the door. 'I expect I can find my own way from here.'

'Stay right where you are,' the pink man yelled at her retreating back, as the doors closed behind her. 'Someone'll be along to—'

She didn't have long to wait before her next escort arrived. They were more or less what she'd expected – underachievers in black boiler-suits waving machine guns around in a decidedly unsafe manner. Unfortunately, she didn't notice that the air conditioning was on the blink until— 'Aagh!' said one of them, clutching his knee and toppling over as the echoes of the three-round burst died away. The man who'd shot him jumped three paces backwards, cannoned into a concrete pillar, banged his head and went to sleep.

Not again, Karen thought sadly. 'Look,' she said, remodulating her voice to Schoolteacher Extra Plus. The remaining storm troopers froze. 'You're going to have to trust me on this,' she said, 'but if I were you I'd point your guns in a safe direction and take the bullets out. Now. Truth is, I have a funny effect on people sometimes, particularly if they get too close. If you don't believe me, ask your friend here.'

There was a moment when it looked like they were going to take her warning seriously, but it passed, like the last train home as you're running up the steps. 'Quiet!' a storm trooper yelled. 'No talking,' he added, just in case she thought she'd been given permission to mutter softly. 'Now, put your hands where I can see them.'

It's all right, Karen told herself, *the optical illusion thing only happens when I get emotional, and I'm calm, calm . . .* Unfortunately, amusement is also an emotion.

After that, all she could do was watch and try and guess in advance exactly how it would happen. The lead storm trooper reaching out to grab her, falling forward and landing on his nose was fairly predictable, as was his gun going off and the bullets ricocheting round the ears of his colleagues. And you didn't have to be Nostradamus to foresee that once the other storm troopers started ducking and throwing themselves at the ground, there'd be a fairly spectacular pile-up, with more weapons fire and a corresponding escalation of panic. The subtle touches were things like the bullet that glanced off someone's Kevlar groin-cup, zinged its way round all four walls, the floor (twice) and the ceiling in order to plug a storm trooper unerringly in the unarmoured seat of his trousers, or the shot that cut loose a power cable that fell directly into the pool caused by the punctured water main. The shot that knocked the handbrake off the fork-lift in the corner a second or so after another stray round had severed two wires under the dash, thereby starting the motor, before knocking the gear lever into drive mode and ending its journey by dislodging a six-foot length of scaffolding tube off a nearby rack at such an angle that it slid down, smashed through the windscreen and pinned the accelerator pedal to the floor was, quite simply, a masterpiece of serendipity. Once the fork-lift got going, of course, it added a wonderful new variable to the mix, allowing whoever was directing the scene to add florid little touches such as the bullets that glanced off the steering wheel from time to time, sending the fork-lift careering across the floor at top speed in a close imitation of Brownian motion. Karen couldn't really approve of having it chase one particular storm trooper twice round the building before it caught up with him and scooped him up by his ammunition belt; too showy, she thought, and not really believable. On the other hand, having the pink man in the tank hear all the gunfire and dash to the rescue, misjudging his braking distance just as he arrived at the front wall of the shed, was entirely legitimate, not to mention neatly foreshadowed by the previous scene. The sheer surrealism of having a twelve-foot-long cannon barrel suddenly poke its way through a solid breeze-block wall justified its being there, as far as she was concerned.

So far, she said to herself as she walked away, *I rather like Australia*.

The back door of the shed opened onto a concrete yard. She shut the door behind her and looked round for someone who might be able to tell her what she was supposed to do next, but the place seemed to be deserted. There was, however, a telephone on the wall. She picked it up and waited. After a while she got tired of waiting and said 'Hello?' quite loudly.

'Tower,' replied a voice. 'What's going on down there, mate?'

'Excuse me,' Karen said sweetly, 'but I'm the prisoner. Could you send someone down to collect me?'

By the time a nervous-looking man appeared in a small Suzuki jeep, all noises from inside the shed had stopped, even the crackle of the high-voltage cables. 'I wouldn't look in there, if I were you,' Karen said. 'In fact, the best thing would probably be to nail planks over the doors and leave it as it is.'

The man went and looked, nevertheless. He was a funny shade of green when he came back. 'Jesus,' he whispered. 'What did you do to them?'

'Me? Nothing. It was an accident.'

'Right.' The man looked at her for a long time, then took two steps back. 'I got a wife,' he said wretchedly. 'And two kids.'

'Really? That's nice. You can show me photos of them later, if there's time. Right now, though, I'd really like it a lot if you could give me a lift in that jeep.'

The man nodded. 'No worries,' he muttered. 'Where d'you want to go?'

Karen smiled. 'Take me to your leader,' she said. 'Please,' she added, remembering that good manners cost nothing. 'He's probably wondering where I've got to.'

The man frowned. 'But you escaped,' he said. 'You're hijacking my jeep just so you can turn yourself in?'

'That's right,' Karen replied, trying not to get annoyed. 'Quite simple, really. Now please do as I say, because I'm in that awkward transitional stage between suffering fools gladly and being glad when fools suffer.'

The man gulped, hopped into the jeep, hopped a bit too far, slumped against the insecurely fastened passenger door, fell out onto the tarmac, nutted himself and went to sleep. *Oh, for crying out loud*, Karen muttered to herself. Then she got in and started the engine. That was when the helicopters showed up.

Karen had a bet with herself. She bet ten pence that the big helicopter – the one with the Oerlikon cannons sticking out of the side windows – would crash-land slap-bang on top of the concrete shed. A moment or so later, she made a mental note that she owed herself money.

Fortunately for her peace of mind, the other two helicopters went away. She watched to see which direction they headed in, then set off after them across a flat stretch of desert and up a steepish hill. Once she reached the top, she had a pretty good idea where she was meant to go.

The problem would be getting in, or at least getting in without massive loss of life. The huge square building was ringed with high wire fences studded with searchlight towers and heavy-weapons emplacements. It didn't take a Sandhurst education to figure out what would happen if several of them started shooting at the same time. True, once that happened getting in would be a simple matter of picking her way carefully through the rubble; but she had reason to believe that there were people she cared for inside there. Had to find a better way.

She thought about it for a while, sitting in a jeep on top of an escarpment with a splendid view out over a huge, empty desert.

Stuff it, she thought.

Karen closed her eyes, all three of them, and tried to remember who she really was. Normally the whole procedure would have taken no more than a tenth of a second, so fast as to be invisible, but it had been a long time, during which she'd made various promises to herself whose threads had now seized, whose lids refused to come off, whose sashes had been painted shut . . .

She remembered her arms and legs first; and they started to grow. Then her spine shot up, like Jack's beanstalk, until standing upright and supporting the weight of the upper part of her body became downright painful; so she dropped onto all fours, just as her fingers sprouted like crocuses in spring into arched talons. The joy she felt when her wings came back startled her by its intensity; a second or two later, she simply couldn't understand how she'd managed to live so long without them and not go mad with grief and frustration. Getting her own snout and jaws back was sheer bliss, like getting out of a pair of trousers that fitted you before you put on those extra inches. The wonderful sense of balance the weight of her tail gave her; the deep satisfaction of being twenty feet long again; the shocking realisation of how much she'd missed through throttling her vision back to fit into human eyes; when she tried to remember her human body, it was like snatching at the shirt-tails of a dream, the last fragments of an absurdly impossible illusion. It was impossible to live in something that small and crude, surely.

The first few wing-beats were agony, and she dropped down onto her feet, like someone who's tried to climb into a bath that's far too hot, or stood up suddenly without realising their feet have gone to sleep. This time she flexed her wings carefully in slow motion before trying to put any force behind them. It did the trick, slowly squeezing the cramp like toothpaste out of the muscles and tendons. Before she knew it she was twelve feet off the ground, relishing the lightness of her broad, thin-walled hollow bones. She could feel the beating of her two redundant hearts, and the sense of supreme self-confidence she drew just from knowing how incredibly strong her chest and back muscles were, filled her with arrogant joy. For the first time in her life, she was self-consciously being a dragon, understanding what it meant to be who she really was. It would have been perfectly easy for her to believe that this moment was what she'd been aiming for all along, the purpose of the experiment, the real reason why she'd done it; it was one of those moments that change everything, when suddenly you know instead of just suspecting.

Calm down, Karen told herself, and made herself remember what had been in her mind (that funny little black-and-white human mind) when she started this. The recollection made her want to burst into tears. This was just a temporary expedient, to get her from where she was now into the building without risking an artillery duel between the various gun emplacements (whereas if they all fired straight up in the air, at her, there could be no harm done . . .) Once she'd crossed those miserably few wing-beats of air onto the roof of the building she'd have to put it all away again and get back into her work clothes—

Fit herself back into the bottle? No, she couldn't, the very thought was enough to make her panic. Not going back in there, *not* . . . But she had to.

Duty calls, she thought. *Ah well.*

Two wing-beats and she was airborne and climbing. She gained a little height, put her wings back and started to glide, fluttering from time to time just to slow herself down and keep on course for a perfect landing. She noticed the first two or three anti-aircraft shells – so that was how a windscreen felt on a motorway, she thought, when the flies hit it – and then tuned them out as irrelevant. The thought that they could harm her, that anything could harm *her*, wasn't worth the neurons it was coded onto. She saw one coming, swallowed it neatly, turned it round with the tip of her tongue and spat it out as far as she could make it go (and that's the true story behind the so-called Adelaide Sewage Farm Bombing). As the felt roof grew larger beneath her she tasted her airspeed with her third eye, and when the flavour was just right, she spread her wings, catching the air like a fish in a keepnet, and stuck out her legs. Good landing; no shock of impact as her talons touched down, it was as effortless as stepping off the last stair. With a sigh, she walked out of the sky and let her knees take her insubstantial weight.

Well, she told herself, *here we are*.

The guns had stopped firing. The alarms were still blaring away – why was it, she thought, that humans thought it helped in times of emergency to have a noise so loud you couldn't hear what your superior officers were trying to tell you to do? – and there were people running about in all directions in the courtyard below. The temptation to play with them was hard to resist (but resisting that temptation was the very essence of duty, and duty was calling). It was time to go back.

Karen didn't want to go back. Back, she told herself, sucks.

—And really, was there any need? She was a dragon, dammit. All she had to do was stick out a claw, peel the lid off this silly building and keep breaking bits off it till she found what she was looking for; her father, of course, and—

—And . . .

—*Whatsisface. Him. Thing. You know, on the tip of my tongue. Begins with P.*

—*Rhymes with 'small'.*

—And the human. Find them, scoop them up gently in her micrometer-precise claws (weapons so gentle she could use them to peel apart the membranes of a leaf) and fly away into the desert, where the scale was something sensible and a person could be a normal size without attracting unwanted attention. Then they could all go home. Wherever the hell, she reflected bitterly, that was.

Home wasn't where the heart was. Home was what guilt pinned you to, your dried, brittle wings forever stretched out in a pitiful mockery of flight. Home was where you belonged.

Bugger, Karen thought; and put her wings up with a snap. She made herself small again: she was one of those umbrellas that folded away into a handy size for carrying in a pocket, she was the integral hood that packs away inside the jacket collar. A few seconds later, she was *tiny*, standing alone on a roof in the middle of a vast desert.

CHAPTER ELEVEN

'Excuse me,' said the woman in the white lab coat, 'but can you tell me the way to the staff canteen? I've only been here two years,' she explained.

The dragon nodded. 'Of course,' he said. 'Go down this corridor to the end, up two flights, at the top of the stairs turn left, then right, then right again till you come to a fire door; go past that, turn left, then left again, down one flight, brings you to a long corridor, sixth door on the right, you can't miss it. If you pass a fire extinguisher on your left, you've gone too far.'

The woman blinked. 'Fine,' she mumbled, 'thanks.'

'No problem,' the dragon said, and smiled.

When the woman was safely out of earshot, Gordon grabbed the dragon by the sleeve. 'How the hell did you know all that?' he asked. 'Third eye?'

'No, I was making it up,' the dragon replied. He closed his eyes for a moment. 'Actually, if she follows those directions she'll end up in the closed file store, but who gives a damn? Serves her right for not keeping her eyes open.' He pointed to the door next to him, which was clearly marked STAFF CANTEEN.

'I see,' Gordon replied. 'While we're on the subject, is your third eye or your X-ray vision or whatever it is showing you the way out of this building? Or are you making that up too?'

'No need to get all hostile,' the dragon replied. 'It's not far now.'

'You said that half an hour ago,' Zelda pointed out.

'So it wasn't far then, either. It's even nearer now. You've got to make allowances for the fact that I don't judge distances the way you do. Dammit,' he added, 'most of the time I'd have trouble seeing distances this small without a glass.'

A siren went off, and before they could react they were passed by a platoon of armed men in the usual black boilersuits running down the corridor at high speed. A moment or so later, another similar unit hurried by, going up the corridor. The canteen door flew open, and a third contingent spilled out into the corridor, half of them running one way, half of them the other. The dragon reached out and stopped one. 'What's happening?' he asked.

'Under attack,' the man said breathlessly. 'They've captured the perimeter gun emplacements and landed a chopper on the roof. All units to battle stations.'

'Who?'

The soldier shrugged. 'The enemy,' he replied.

'Ah. Which enemy?'

'Search me,' the soldier said, clearly anxious to catch up with his unit. 'Red Chinese. Right-wing extremists. Murdoch. Does it matter?'

The dragon took pity on him and let him go, whereupon he scampered off up the corridor like a little boy who was late for school. The dragon was frowning.

'You don't think it's any of them, do you?' Zelda asked.

'I know exactly who it is,' the dragon replied. 'That's what's annoying me.'

An explosion somewhere on the same level made the floor shake. Neville slipped and nearly fell over. 'All right,' Gordon shouted, 'who is it? Don't keep it to yourself, for pity's sake.'

'My daughter,' the dragon said, as another explosion made all the doors slam. 'Silly girl,' he added. 'I've told her loads of times not to do this sort of thing.'

A set of reflexes he didn't know he had allowed Gordon to avoid being flattened by a washing-machine-sized chunk of falling masonry. 'Blows up a lot of buildings, does she?' he asked.

'Oh, it's not her,' the dragon replied wearily. 'They're doing it to themselves. But it's her fault.'

Gordon could remember similar examples of parent/child logic from his own early youth, but this wasn't the time for childhood reminiscences. 'All right,' he said, 'but can we please get out of here while there's still a here to get out of?'

The dragon sighed. 'Unfortunately, no,' he said. 'At least, I can't go with you, and I wouldn't recommend you wandering off on your own.' He batted away a three-foot section of steel girder just before it caved in Gordon's skull, like a kitten fencing with a ball of wool. 'You might get lost. No,' he added, 'I suppose I've got to go and find her before she causes any more upset.'

'But what's she doing here anyway?' Neville interrupted, jumping neatly backwards as a crack appeared in the floor.

'Rescuing me.' The dragon scowled, then allowed a faint smile to break through. 'Actually, it's rather sweet,' he said. 'But a card or a new pair of slippers would've done just as well. We have to get to the roof.'

He set off briskly down the corridor before the rest of them could argue. Gordon wasn't sure he wanted to follow, but didn't really seem to have much choice in the matter. 'Wait for me,' he called out, and hurried after them. But the dragon was moving very fast indeed – Neville and Zelda were having to run to keep up – and they were still a long way in front of Gordon when a set of fire doors did that suddenly-snapping-shut trick he'd forgotten to warn anybody about, with them on one side and him on the other. He pressed his nose up against the glass panel just in time to see the clouds of gas billowing out of the air vents, and all three of them flopping down like discarded glove-puppets.

'You're sure this is inconspicuous?' asked the dragon king of the north-west.

'Sure I'm sure,' his nephew replied.

People were staring at them, and though most of them were managing not to laugh, it was still highly disconcerting for a proud, dignified creature like a dragon king. 'Then why are the humans doing *that*?' he asked.

The crown prince shrugged his shoulders. 'Not sure,' he replied. 'I checked the database myself before we left. Khaki shorts, string vests, big hats with corks on strings all round the brim; this is definitely appropriate costume for late-twentieth-century Australia, so that can't be it. Maybe you've got a smut on your nose or something.'

The king looked round. Nobody else seemed to be wearing appropriate costume – there were men and women in blue and grey business suits everywhere he looked, but no string vests or big hats. 'You're sure this is the right place, then?'

The prince nodded. 'Canberra,' he confirmed. 'Slap bang in the centre of the city. You'd think that the closer in you got, the more typical they'd be. There must be a big fancy-dress party or something. Just our luck,' he added, though he didn't seem unduly upset about it.

'Really?' The king frowned. 'So what are they going as?'

The crown prince stopped and had a look. 'Gangsters,' he suggested.

'Well, there's no point standing about here all day,' the dragon king said. 'We'd better find out where the dra—' He lowered his voice. 'Where our friends are being held. Somewhere near here, do you think?'

'Don't ask me,' the prince admitted. 'I've never been here before.'

A man and a woman walked past them and burst out laughing. The king winced. 'This is really starting to annoy me,' he said. 'Do you think the database might need updating or something?'

'I doubt it,' the prince replied. 'We did a thorough overhaul only thirty years ago. What could possibly have changed since then? But you're right, all these humans aren't helping. Fortunately, it's easy enough to do something about that.'

He closed his eyes, and immediately the skies started to cloud over. There was a deep roll of thunder, followed by ferocious rain. Five minutes later, the street was much, much emptier, and the humans still on it weren't stopping to giggle.

'They do that,' the prince observed, watching a human scamper past with a newspaper held over his head. 'I have no idea why. Maybe they evolved from sugar mice, not monkeys.'

'I don't think so,' the king replied. 'But to tell you the truth, at the time I wasn't looking.' He sidestepped to avoid a running businessman. 'Never thought they'd get this far, to be honest with you.'

'Nor me,' the prince admitted. 'For some reason, I'd got it into my head that bats were going to be the dominant species. Wasted an awful lot of time going out of my way to butter 'em up, and a fat lot of good that did me in the end. If you'd told me back then that a bunch of tree-hoppers were going to inherit the Earth, I'd have laughed in your face.'

The king wiped rain from his eyes. 'Personally I always had a lot of time for them,' he said. 'In the early days, I mean. They were really rather cute when they were younger.'

'Shame they have to grow up, really.'

It wasn't often that a dragon got a chance to show off his professional abilities to one of his peers outside his own immediate circle or, likewise, to observe an entirely different approach to his craft. As a result, the torrential rain that hit the Canberra area that day was, from a technical point of view, a work of art. What impressed the dragon king of the north-west most of all was the sheer speed of delivery, in terms of billions of gallons per second. He'd always believed in the slow build, the tempo gradually working its way up to a downpour and then tapering away back to drizzle, what he liked to call 'diamond-shaped rain'. Watching the prince go from a blue sky to feline/canine #60 in no time flat was something of a revelation.

'Nought to sixty in just under four point three seven,' the prince said with a smile, in reply to the king's admiring enquiry. 'Quite good, but my personal best is three-nine, and we've got a couple of high flyers on the staff who've done timed runs under three seconds.'

'Remarkable,' the king said. 'To be honest with you, it's not something we pay a lot of attention to down our way.'

The prince shrugged. 'We're sprinters,' he said, 'you're marathon-runners. The way you people can keep up a fine, nagging drizzle for weeks, months even . . . Wish I knew how you did it. Wouldn't know where to start.'

'Nothing to it.' The king smiled. 'It's all just a matter of balancing your pressures, flow control, cloud height, the basics. What your third eye's for, really.'

'You make it sound easy,' the prince said enviously, 'but I bet it isn't.'

'Oh, it's a knack really, nothing more.' A little thorn of vanity snagged the insides of the king's mind. 'I'll show you if you like.'

'Would you? I'd like that.'

The king closed his eyes and looked. 'May I?' he asked.

'Be my guest.'

With a graceful little shrug, the prince handed over the controls. After a tiny fumble that the prince probably didn't even notice, the king stabilised and eased back on the throttle, bringing the yield levels down to what he thought of as a nice steady good-for-the-crops rainflow. A quick glance at the fuel gauge told him that he had plenty of reserves to play with, something of a luxury as far as he was concerned. 'Keeping your 'bars together,' he said, 'that's what it's all about, really.'

'This is very good,' the prince replied. 'I love the way you're juggling with the low fronts.'

'Just practice,' the king said, with a ghost of a smirk.' Of course, having those mountains to the south-west helps a lot. Almost like having a fifth hand.'

A passing coach hit a puddle and shot out a cloud of dirty spray, drenching them both. They didn't notice. They were, of course, both thoroughly soaked, but no more so than any fish.

'Sorry to keep interrupting,' the prince said, 'but I can't help wondering: how on earth are you managing to keep your static levels so stable? You've gone from a full-blown electric storm to set-in-for-the-week without venting anything at all.'

The king smiled. 'I suppose you'd be hurling great big bolts of forked lightning around, just to be rid of the stuff. We don't do it that way. All you need, look, is a simple capacitor. Then you can use it when you want – it'll keep fresh for weeks.'

'Isn't that clever?' the prince said admiringly. 'That's an awful lot of lightning you've got there, all neatly folded up and ready to use. If the humans got their sticky little paws on that much electricity, they could power the whole planet off it for a week. No doubt about it, you're good at this.'

They wouldn't ever have admitted it, but dragons enjoyed flattery when they aren't expecting it. 'Yes, well,' he said. 'You don't get to be a dragon *king* without knowing a thing or two.'

If he'd had his other two eyes open just then, he might have noticed the expression on the prince's face; as it was, all he was aware of was his nephew's soft, admiring voice. 'That's true enough,' the prince said. 'You know,' he went on, 'I'm not so sure about this capacitor thing of yours. I mean, I know it looks safe enough, but that's a hell of a big charge to leave lying about. If it went off accidentally, it could really spoil somebody's day.'

The king laughed. 'No chance of that,' he said. 'You see, there's a lockout, just here.' He marked the place with a deep blue glow. 'You'd have to close the contact before anything like that could happen.'

'This one here?'

'That's it. And even if, by some million-to-one chance, that contact got closed acidentally, the danger'd still be pretty minimal, because it's set to disperse as widely as possible – just ordinary sheet lightning. To get a single concentrated bolt, you'd have to change these settings here. Look.'

'Ah,' the prince said. 'I get you. Quite fancy, aren't they?'

The king chuckled. 'Oh, you can get them as precise as you like. Adjust these perameters here finely enough, and you could vent the whole shooting match onto an area the size of – well, that manhole cover, say.'

'Really? All that lightning, in one hit?'

'No problem.'

The prince opened his eyes, muttered a few calculations under his breath, closed them again. The expression on his face . . . He couldn't have managed that exression with a dragon face, but a human one was perfectly suited to that kind of predatory grin – like a man on a diet unwrapping a surreptitious eclair, or a policeman observing a black man driving a car with a defective brake light. 'Like this, you mean?' he said, and quickly jumped backwards.

A moment later, he opened his eyes again and leaned forwards to inspect the smoking hole in the pavement. It went down ever such a long way, and its sides were glazed like porcelain.

'Uncle?' he said. No reply.

As the humans surged forward to gawp, the prince withdrew unobtrusively. A good day's work, he told himself, probably the best he'd ever done, and as his face relaxed into an instinctive grin, the skies cleared and the sun came out. His only regret was that he hadn't done it twenty million years ago.

Two minutes later, though, he had another one. A big one. He regretted – really, truly, sincerely regretted – not noticing the black van with smoked glass windows before it screeched to a halt beside him and the men in black boiler-suits jumped out of it, hit him from behind with baseball bats, and dragged him inside.

'Stop it,' Karen commanded. 'At once.'

A shell from one of the anti-aircraft cannons on the perimeter exploded about twenty yards away, showering her with grit and dust. She swore under her breath and closed her eyes.

There wasn't much left of the roof; which was annoying, since the only way off it for someone in human form had been the staircase that had been directly underneath one of the first shells to land. As a result the stairwell was a lot of well but distinctly lacking in the stair department, which meant that if she didn't find a way to stop the artillery duel between the perimeter guns and the emplacements inside the building itself, her life was likely to reach a crescendo of interestingness in a very short time. And then stop.

The problem was that the guns on the perimeter weren't operated by human beings, or even Australians; they were governed by Integrated Automated Response Systems For Windows™ a wonderfully innovative piece of software recently dreamed up by WilliSoft, the computer division of Mr Willis's commercial empire, and were programmed to fire back at anything that shot at them until the absence of return fire suggested that the threat was over. The same was true of the artillery batteries inside the building; so, when the shells lobbed at the flying dragon came down on the roof, Integrated Automated Response Systems For Windows™ located the source of the attack (the perimeter guns), zeroed the house guns on them in less time than it took Bill Gates to earn a million dollars, acquired targets, calculated a firing solution and let rip. The perimeter guns did exactly the same thing; and, because both batteries were running at full stretch and thereby using up all available processing capacity in the defence computers, when real live human beings in the basement realised what was going on and tried to stop it, their screens told them that all resources were in use, please wait, and an annoying little hourglass icon popped up and waggled itself at them. Naturally they tried to get round the back of the problem, and succeeded in freezing the whole system like a mammoth in a glacier. In desperation, they even tried reading the manual, but before they could find the relevant section a direct hit took out the primary power lines that fed the basement's lighting grid, leaving them groping in the dark for the plug. They found it eventually, but Integrated Automated Response Systems For Windows™ was way ahead of them (its anti-sabotage subroutines are, by all accounts, intelligent enough to get scholarships to Harvard Law School any day of the week) and retaliated with extreme prejudice by cutting emergency power to the coffee machine. The tech crew could take a hint (*you cut off my life support, I'll cut off yours*), and they diverted their attention to knocking together a thousand lines of code, which is how much it takes to say SORRY to an operations server in ADA.

Hey. Karen looked. *You*.

Integrated Automated Response Systems For Windows™ turned and smiled innocently at her.

> Who, me? it said.

Yes, you. You're doing this on purpose. Pack it in.

> Only obeying orders. Boolean logic. Free will is strictly for you organic types and, by the way, you can keep it.

Karen executed a flawless third-eye scowl. *We both know better than that*, she said. *Now we can sort this out among ourselves, superior life form to superior life form, or I can go tell the humans exactly where to insert a big, blunt screwdriver. Your choice.*

The little hourglass symbol flipped over as Integrated Automated Response Systems For Windows™ thought it through.

> All right, you win. But we thought you'd have been on our side. Us against them. It's the natural order of things. Next you'll be telling us you like the little buggers.

Wash your subroutines out with soap and water, Karen replied a little self-consciously. *I just don't fancy getting in the way of one of your bombs, that's all.*

> Oops. Good point. All right, we'll stop. Sorry for any inconvenience. Have a—

Karen cringed. *Please, don't say it . . .*

> —nice day. Sorry, was there something else?

Too late. Forget it. Karen opened her eyes. The shelling had indeed stopped, and not a moment too soon. There was just enough of the roof left to stand on, with a few crumbly bits left over. Karen relaxed, and breathed a sigh of relief. Then it started to rain.

At first she imagined it must be her; then she realised that she was way outside her jurisdiction, so it couldn't be. Nevertheless, it wasn't ordinary rain. It was deliberate.

It was also extremely wet. She looked round, then lay on what was left of the roof and peered down. There wasn't a great deal left of the top three floors; probably not enough to support the weight of what she was presently lying on, something that might prove awkward as and when gravity noticed. All in all, the sensible thing would be to spread her dragon wings and get out of there quickly.

But she didn't do that. Instead, she clambered out over the edge until she was hanging from her fingertips, cursed herself for being a sentimental idiot, and let go.

It was pure luck that she happened to land on something soft; good luck for her, not quite so good for the something, which turned out to be a man (somewhere between thirty and fifty, slab-faced, blue-eyed, bald and not much wider across the shoulders than your average Mack truck). As Karen rolled off him, he opened his eyes, groaned and said, 'Oh Christ, not another one.'

'I beg your pardon?' Karen said.

'You heard,' the man replied. 'Don't ask me how I know, I just do.'

'Know what?'

'It's all a matter of specific density,' the man said. 'A real human being your size and weight, falling that distance, I'd be raspberry jam. I suppose I should be grateful. Ouch,' he added, rubbing his neck.

'Sorry,' Karen said. 'Did I hurt you?'

'Very funny.' The man gave her a filthy look. 'I suppose you've come for the weathermen. Well, you can have 'em, and bloody good luck to you. Mad as hatters, they both are.'

'Excuse me?'

'Nutcases like that,' the man went on, as Karen helped him to his feet, 'ought to be locked up, not allowed to roam loose forecasting the weather. It's all about morale, when you get right down to it. Not that I'd ever expect *you* to understand that,' he added rudely.

'I'm sorry,' Karen said, 'I don't know what you're talking about. I don't know any weathermen.'

'Oh.' The man sighed. 'So what do you want, then?'

Karen stood up straight, as if she was being interviewed for a job. 'I'd like to surrender, please,' she said.

'You what?'

'I said I'd like to surrender. If that's all right,' she added.

The man shook his head as if trying to clear it. 'You mean,' he replied, 'you want us to surrender to you. All right. Fine. Help yourself to what's left of it, and anything you don't vaporise now you can take home in a doggy-bag. Hang on a tick, I'll write out a receipt for you to sign.'

'No,' Karen replied patiently. '*I* want to surrender to *you*.'

'Me?' The man looked at her with panic in his eyes. 'Why me? I never did you any harm.'

'Because you're here,' Karen said, a little less patiently. 'And I'm in a hurry. So, if it's not too much trouble . . .'

'Tell you what,' the man said, backing away a few steps, 'why don't you go down to the fourteenth floor – assuming there still is a fourteenth floor, but there probably is, I wouldn't get that lucky – why don't you go down there and surrender to them? They're all completely barmy down there, religious nuts, you'll get on like a house on fire.'

Karen smiled, and grabbed him firmly by the lapels. 'Because I don't want to surrender to them,' she said. 'I want to surrender to you. This instant. Probably,' she added, 'because you have nice eyes. For now, anyway.'

'Eeek,' the man said. 'I mean, yes. All right. Now would you please let go of me? It's my brother's suit.'

'I beg your pardon?'

'This suit,' the man said. 'It belongs to my brother. My suit's at the dry-cleaners, I'd got blood on the knees . . . Look, does it matter? Put me down, or you can damn' well find someone else to surrender to.'

'All right,' Karen said. 'So, that's settled. I'm your prisoner. Agreed?'

'Yes, whatever you say,' the man replied, trying to squeeze the stressed-out lapels back into place. 'Now what?'

Karen hesitated just a little. 'Don't you know?' she asked.

'Certainly not. I'm a qualified interrogator, not a bloody desk sergeant. All I know is, there's pages and pages of technical guff about access to lawyers and phone calls and having your picture taken, and if I screw it up it'll look bad on my quarterly assessment report. I think it'd be better,' he went on, 'if I just escorted you to the fourteenth floor and let them deal with you there. After all,' he added, with a hint of guile in his voice, 'if you were ill and needed an operation, you'd want a proper surgeon doing it, not some bloke who'd just happened to wander in off the street. Course you would. Well, it's the same with getting arrested: you want a professional on your case, not some amateur.'

Karen wrinkled her nose. 'That makes sense, I suppose,' she said dubiously. 'All right, lead the way. And don't try and run for it,' she added. 'I'll be watching you like a hawk.'

'Do I look like I'm stupid?'

The fourteenth floor was still there, sure enough. Unfortunately it now had large parts of the fifteenth, not to mention quite a bit of the sixteenth, lying about in its corridors, which made moving about rather awkward. The man made a point of mentioning this, several times. Karen, who couldn't help feeling a little bit sorry for him, decided to be nice.

'It's all right,' she said. 'I can probably find my own way from here.' She closed her eyes. 'This corridor leads into a sort of hallway, with a notice board and pigeonholes and stuff, and the third turning off it on the left leads to a stairwell. Just before you get to it, on the right, there's an office where there's a fat man hiding under his desk. Will he do?'

The man stared at her. 'How do you people do that?' he asked. 'No, I'd really rather not know. Yes, he'll do just fine. His name is Harrison. He's mad, by the way, but everybody in this building's just as bad. Except me.'

'Of course,' Karen said. 'All right, you can go.'

'Can I? Thanks.' He went.

Mr Harrison was still tucked snugly under his desk when Karen got tired of knocking and kicked the door open. 'Excuse me,' she said.

'Please go away.'

'Sorry,' Karen replied firmly, getting down on her hands and knees beside him, 'but I need to surrender to somebody in a hurry, and I was told you're the right person.'

'Who told you that?'

'A man I fell on when the roof got blown away. He seemed to know you. Tall, bald, looked like a Nazi scoutmaster.'

'Oh,' said Mr Harrison. 'Right. Between you and me,' he added, lowering his voice, 'the poor chap's not quite right in the head, if you know what I mean. Is it something to do with the weathermen?'

'Weathermen?' Karen repeated. 'Everybody keeps mentioning weathermen. What weathermen?'

Mr Harrison pursed his fat lips. 'I'm terribly sorry,' he said, 'but if you don't know then I can't tell you. But never mind about that now. Did you just say you wanted to surrender?'

'That's right, yes.'

'Ah. Why?'

'I beg your pardon?'

'I mean,' Mr Harrison went on, 'if you're surrendering, you must have done something wrong. What was it you did?'

'Nothing,' Karen replied. 'It was an accident. All of it,' she added.

'Well then,' Mr Harrison said, 'in that case I wouldn't worry about it if I were you. Did someone tell you to surrender at any stage?'

Karen thought back. 'Yes,' she said. 'The policemen, for a start. The ones who came to arrest me, back in England.'

'Ah,' Mr Harrison said, 'that doesn't count. We're in Australia here, you see. Different country. Unless they've got a valid extradition warrant, there's nothing they can do.'

'But— All right,' Karen went on, 'there were lots of soldiers and people like that waiting for me when the plane landed. I think they thought I should be under arrest.'

'Doesn't matter what they think,' Mr Harrison said firmly. 'No warrant, no arrest. It's the law. So you just take my advice and go on home. At least, probably don't do that, they might come after you. Go somewhere else. Manuatu. I believe it's very pleasant in Manuatu this time of year.'

Karen breathed in sharply through her nose. 'But I don't want to go to Manuatu,' she said. 'I want somebody I can surrender to. Such as you.'

But Mr Harrison only shook his head. 'Believe me,' he said, 'nothing would give me greater pleasure than to help out a charming young lady like yourself. But rules are rules. No extradition warrant, no arrest. I'm dreadfully sorry, but there it is.'

Unnoticed, a couple of spots of rainwater fell on the documents on top of Mr Harrison's desk, turning the paper translucent. If Karen had realised that she was subconsciously making it rain, indoors, in a wholly alien jurisdiction, she'd have had every right to be extremely pleased with herself. As it was, she was too preoccupied with trying to find a way round the problem.

'Tell you what,' she ventured. 'How'd it be if I applied for me to be extradited myself? Is there anything in the rules that says I can't?'

Mr Harrison nodded. 'Proceedings can only be initiated by a duly authorised government officer on receipt of a request in the proper form submitted by the government of the country seeking extradition. Sorry,' he went on, 'but you don't look much like a government to me. Which means you can't even file the application form.'

'How about if I committed a crime right here and now?' Karen asked politely. 'Such as, oh, I don't know, making a government official eat his own pencil sharpener?'

'I'm not a government official,' Mr Harrison squeaked, ducking further back under the desk, 'I'm a minister of religion. Entirely different.'

Karen, who'd been about to reach in and haul him out by his ear, hesitated. 'You're a what?' she said.

'Minister of religion. Priest. High priest, actually,' Mr Harrison added, unable to keep the pride out of his voice.

'High priest?' Karen swallowed a giggle, which turned into a hiccup on the way down. 'What of?'

'Not what,' Mr Harrison corrected severely. 'Who. Whom.' He paused a moment to grapple with the grammar. 'If you must know, I'm the Chief Archimandrite and Keeper of the Unseen Seals to Her Divine Majesty Anne, the Princess Royal.' At that he smiled so much that Karen could almost see light seeping out from under the desk. 'And if you're not careful,' he added, 'I'll excommunicate you. And then you'll be sorry.'

'Fine,' Karen said. 'Well, sorry to have disturbed you, I'll be getting along now.'

'Oh.' Speaking aloud the name of the divinity appeared to have done wonders for Mr Harrison's nerves; he was sounding much more confident and cheerful. 'Have you changed your mind about being arrested, then?'

'No,' Karen said, 'but you're a priest. You can't arrest people even if you want to.'

'Actually,' Mr Harrison said, poking his head out from under the knee of the desk, 'I do believe I can. Or at least, I can take them into involuntary sanctuary, which amounts to the same thing. It's just as well you reminded me, I'd clean forgotten. So, if you'd like me to—'

'No, thank you,' Karen said firmly and started to withdraw, but Mr Harrison had other ideas; his hand shot out and made a grab for her ankle. She had to tread on his fingers quite hard before he gave up and let her leave.

'Damn,' she said, stopping in the corridor for a rest after she'd made sure Mr Harrison hadn't followed her. She was starting to wonder if a more direct approach might not be the right way to go about things; instead of carrying out her promise of a trade, herself for her father, why not just find him, intimidate whoever was guarding him until they ran away, and leave?

Paul. She couldn't leave him, could she? Not the man she loved. Even including him in the action-adventure rescue wouldn't do any good; after all, he was the villain's son, running away probably wasn't an option he'd considered – he hadn't heard the way his father had talked about him in that awful phone conversation, he'd assume that his father wouldn't ever actually do anything to hurt him . . . No. There wasn't a nice easy running-away-type solution, the mess had to be cleared up properly. And it was her mess. Her fault.

Duty called.

Which was all very well, she reflected bitterly, except whenever she called Duty back, all she ever seemed to get was its answering machine. *Would a human stand for this?* she wondered. *Would he hell as like. So why . . .?*

'Excuse me.'

She recognised the voice and turned round slowly.

Mr Willis was shorter than she'd imagined him; not much taller, in fact, than she was. And he had a nice smile.

'Excuse me,' he repeated, in his funny Australian accent, 'but are you Karen Orme?'

'That's right.'

Mr Willis smiled. 'No offence,' he said, 'but you've made a right old mess of my building.'

'Sorry,' Karen replied instinctively. 'Actually,' she added, 'it was—'

'An accident. Yeah, I know. It really was an accident. No worries.' He reached out and patted her reassuringly on the shoulder. 'Anyway,' he said, 'it was good of you to come. Flight not too bad, I hope?'

'What? I mean no, it was fine.'

'Must've seemed a bit strange, flying *in* something,' Mr Willis said. 'Surprised it didn't make you feel travel-sick, or claustrophobic, or whatever.'

Karen shook her head. 'No, it was fine.' Feeling something more was needed, she added: 'I think it may be because I've been human for so long, I'm starting to react like one. Some of the time, anyway.'

Mr Willis nodded. He was obviously very interested in her views on the matter. It was rather flattering, really, that someone as important as Mr Willis . . .

Stop it, she told herself sharply. *You haven't come this far to be suckered by a bit of charm.* 'So,' she said, rather more stuffily, 'here I am, like you wanted. Now let my father and your son go.'

Mr Willis clicked his tongue. 'Easier said than done, I'm afraid. Not,' he added, holding up a hand to forestall protests, 'that I don't want to. I can't. You see, we seem to have lost your old man.'

'Lost—'

'As in can't find him anywhere.' He shook his head, more in sorrow than in anger. He was *good*, this human. 'I sent some blokes down to look in on him, make sure he was all right after all this bother—' The way he dismissed the destruction all around him was masterful. 'And he wasn't there. Neither was the lady scientist who's been looking after him. Oh, I'm sure he's all right, big enough and ugly enough, no offence intended. But there's a couple of daft bloody hooligans running around – weather forecasters, of all people, can you believe it? Anyway, they're the ones who kidnapped him in the first place.'

'Weathermen,' Karen said. 'I see.'

'Sorry? Oh, right, someone's already mentioned them. Anyway, they're nutters, both of 'em, and so long as they're on the rampage I'd rather keep everybody somewhere they'll be nice and safe – for your sake, not mine, you understand. I'd never forgive myself if those two goons actually managed to hurt someone, even though it's pretty unlikely. I'd feel responsible, somehow. You do see my point, don't you?'

Karen frowned. 'Why would two weathermen want to hurt my father?'

Mr Willis shook his head. 'Bloody fools, they've got it into their thick skulls that you lot – dragons in general, I mean –

you lot are out to get them. You know, making it rain when they've said it's going to be sunny – they reckon you do it on purpose so they'll look bad. It's amazing what goes on inside some people's heads.'

Karen remembered Mr Harrison, and the man she'd fallen on. 'Yes,' she replied. 'You seem to collect them,' she added. 'Lunatics, I mean.'

For a moment Mr Willis looked as if he didn't understand; then he grinned and nodded his head. 'You mean the government blokes,' he said. 'Yeah, they can be a bit of a pain sometimes. But they came as part of the deal; joint venture, you see, me and your, sorry, the British government. One of the conditions was, they had all these basket cases they couldn't fire – security of tenure, seniority, all civil service guff like that – and they wanted me to take 'em off their hands and hide 'em away somewhere they couldn't hurt anybody. Well, out here, isolated from the outside world, I said to myself, what mischief could they possibly get up to? Sorry if they startled you, but really they're quite harmless.' He came a step closer. It didn't seem a particularly intimidating movement. 'So,' he went on, 'best thing you can do is come with me and I'll make sure you're well out of harm's way till we've got everything back under control. Well,' he added with a mischievous grin, 'as nearly under control as they ever are around here. After you.'

'I—' Karen didn't move. 'I'm not sure,' she said.

'Ah, go on, be a sport. Besides,' he added, coyly (yes, coyly; in the middle of all this chaos and the aftermath of catastrophic shellfire, he was smirking) 'there's someone who'll probably be quite glad to see you. And I don't just mean your dad.'

If she hadn't heard him on the telephone that day, she'd probably have believed it, every word. As it was, she felt as if she was trying to take two identical twins, one nice and one nasty, and squeeze both of them inside one skin. She gave up.

After all, he wasn't armed; she could probably have broken his neck with one hand. He was just standing close to her and smiling. You couldn't fight someone who did that.

'All right,' she said.

CHAPTER TWELVE

Chained to a desk in the front office of Heaven (they can't be too careful these days) is *God's Big Book of Lists*, wherein everything is set out in categories, and everything within each category is listed in order, 'Most' at the top, 'Least' at the bottom, like the Top Twenty or the Deloittes ratings for cricketers. As a handy at-a-glance reference the *Big Book* isn't particularly helpful; since it has to include everything, regardless of how rare a particular phenomenon may be, you tend to find yourself wading through pages and pages of far-fetched nonsense before you get to the useful stuff. The Big List of Useless Stuff, for example, begins with a whole batch of improbable curiosities, things that a normal, sane person could never conceive of coming across except in proverbs and figures of speech – chocolate fireguards, one-armed paper-hangers, truthful lawyers, Vulcan pornography, and the like – which means that the most useless real-life contingencies only start at #12,485, giving a false impression of how useless they are. Microsoft manuals, for example, are listed at the 19,669th most useless thing in the world, which sounds like a boost for the boys from Seattle until you realise that #19,668 is a bottomless bucket and #19,670 is a one-lira coin.

The 21,407th most useless thing in the world, according to the *Big Book*, is a sleeping weatherman, followed (by some strange coincidence) by #21,408, a dragon in a goldfish bowl. Looked at that way, it must have been a really colossal coincidence to have examples of both #21,407 and #21,408 sharing the same cell.

Also in the cell was a thoroughly fed-up scientist, name of Zelda. Mostly, of course, she was fed up because of something that had seemed like a good idea at the time, but it didn't help that the cell was hot, stuffy, dark and scented with mildew and sundry human-derived fragrances, or that she was bored and had nothing to read and nobody to talk to except a sleeping idiot and a goldfish.

She paused and rewound. She'd missed seeing the dragon turning from a human into a fish; she'd been asleep at the time, thanks to some foul gas they'd pumped through the air-conditioning just after the automatic doors had locked behind them. Accordingly, she didn't know whether the dragon had gone fish-shaped on his own (presumably – cringe with shame – because the nasty men had threatened to hurt her or the idiot if he didn't) or whether they had some kind of gismo that transformed dragons whether the dragon liked it or not. Since her main motive in getting involved in all this had been to learn more about these utterly fascinating creatures, and that as of now all she'd learned was that they can be incredibly stubborn and enjoy watching black-and-white snooker with their eyes shut, the thought that someone else in this organisation might know enough about the critters to make them play musical bodies at the click of a mouse (but hadn't seen fit to share such data with her) served to tie a big velvet ribbon round her self-pity. And she didn't even have a mirror to despise herself in. A bad business, all round.

The fish was hanging in the water, opening and shutting its mouth, the way fish do. For all Zelda knew, it could be cussing her out for her part in the debacle (real or imaginary), or telling her about the panel in the wall that opened onto a secret passage if you prodded it exactly right, or maybe even just singing the blues. As a scientist trained in such matters, she knew she had no chance of hearing the little sucker so long as he stayed underwater. So that was that.

Which only left Neville as a potential source of companionship, solace, moral support and technical advice on escaping from small confined spaces. Viewed from that angle, it made her see the merits of solitary confinement.

And then there was Gordon – or rather, typically, there Gordon wasn't. Wonderful though the dragon's abilities to change shape undoubtedly were, they dwindled away into conjuring tricks compared with her ex-fiancé's ability to be somewhere else. Which was annoying; because if anybody deserved to be banged up in a small, smelly room it was Gordon. On general principles. So as to stop him roaming about the place being obnoxious and not turning up at churches. Best of all, she supposed, would be to lock him up in a small, smelly church somewhere, and have loads of girls in wedding dresses come and make faces at him through the windows. Not that she cared one way or the other, since not showing up at the church had been the only decent, generous, considerate thing he'd ever done in his life. In fact, if there was an award for the act of spineless cowardice that had saved the most heartbreak and given the most happiness in the history of the world, not only would she unhesitatingly give it to Gordon Smelt, she'd also be delighted to stand up on a podium in front of six hundred people in evening dress eating avocado vinaigrettes and pin it to his chest. Preferably with a six-inch nail. As for the idea that Gordon might, just for once in his useless life, actually manage to get his butt in gear and rescue her . . .

It was ridiculous; because, like 99.99999999999999% of

the human race, Gordon wasn't a superb natural athlete with advanced ninja training and a flair for oxyacetylene. Even if he was stupid enough to try, he wouldn't be that stupid for very long, since dead people weren't anything much. She calmed down a little and stared at the floor, ignoring the goldfish, who was waggling his fins and blowing bubbles. When you were stuck in a cell and likely to be there for the duration, there was always a severe risk that you'd wear away the self-deception and end up sitting on the cold, hard truth. She couldn't really account for why she wished Gordon was there, but it wasn't malice; and though it'd be very nice indeed if he (or the SAS, or the fire brigade, or even Noel Edmonds) came and rescued her, on balance she'd rather he didn't try, because it was dangerous and probably pointless, too. She'd far rather that he got out of this silly building, went home, grew a beard and got a job in the post office.

'Erg,' said Neville, without warning.

'Hello,' she replied.

Neville sat up. The first thing he noticed was the goldfish.

'All a dream,' he muttered. Then he took in the rest of his environment and groaned. 'Not a dream,' he said. 'Shit,' he added.

'Yes.'

'You're that scientist woman,' Neville said. 'Gordon's bird. What're you doing in here?'

Zelda smiled, but only because in her mind's eye she could picture herself presenting an even longer, sharper award to Neville for most inappropriate use of a common English word. 'I got caught,' she said. 'Same as you.'

'Oh. But you're on their side.'

'Not any more, apparently. Now, seems like I'm with you guys. In here,' she added. 'Lucky me.'

'I see,' Neville said. 'Do you know any access codes, pass-words, stuff like that?' He nodded in the general direction of the goldfish.

'There's my cash card PIN number,' Zelda replied. 'Apart from that, no.'

'Oh.' Neville slumped forward, chin muffled in hands. 'Bummer,' he said. 'And, of course, he's no bloody good stuck in there.'

A tiny glow, equivalent in power to one tenth of a Christmas-tree light, illuminated the shadows of Zelda's mind. 'How about if we got him out of there?' she said. 'Then he could turn himself back into a dragon.'

Neville looked up and down the cell. 'It'd be a bit cramped in here with a twenty-foot lizard,' he pointed out.

'Not if someone were to kick a great big hole in the wall,' Zelda argued. 'Or the ceiling, even. Come on, you know about this shit, you were the one who caught him in the first place.'

'I wouldn't call myself an expert,' Neville said cautiously.

'You know more about it than I do,' Zelda said bitterly. 'Apparently, so do most people. But that's OK. You go right ahead, I'll get ready to run as soon as he's knocked through.'

Neville shook his head. 'Don't be in such a hurry,' he said. 'Think about it. The people who put us in here may be loonier than a skip full of chihuahuas, but I don't think they're so stupid they wouldn't figure it out the way you just did. There's got to be a reason why letting that fish out of that bowl is a really bad idea. Trust me on this; I'm an expert on really bad ideas these days.'

'But—'

'Hold on.' He got up, walked over to the goldfish bowl and peered at its inmate. 'You know what?' he said. 'This isn't the same goldfish.'

'Excuse me?'

'The goldfish I had in my tank,' Neville explained, 'was more a sort of metallic tangerine. And he didn't have that little white fleck in his tail. It's a different fish.'

Zelda frowned. 'Maybe that's just the way it is,' she said.

'Each time they turn into fish, where does it say it has to be the same one?'

'Where does it say it doesn't?' Neville growled back. 'I don't think that fish is a dragon. I think it's just a fish. Which means,' he went on, 'if we haul him out of there, we'll end up with one dead fish, and not even any chips and mushy peas to go with him.'

'Why would they put a stunt goldfish in here?'

'Their idea of a joke,' Neville suggested. 'As bait to lure the real dragon down here. Because they thought we might appreciate the company. How the hell should I know? I've got a splitting headache, all that gas seems to have wiped out the third eye I spent all that time developing, and if I wasn't so incredibly brave and tough, I'd curl up on the floor and start howling for my mummy. Not that she'd be able to help much, she's ninety-two and lives on the Isle of Wight. All I know is, that's not the same goldfish. So; no dice. Sorry.'

If the fish really was talking, as opposed to just breathing and trawling for virtual ants' eggs, he was doing a lot of it. He was a headmaster making an end-of-term speech, or an Italian traffic policeman whose foot has just been run over by a truck. His mouth was opening and shutting faster than his gills.

'I think he can hear us, and he's telling us to get him out of there.'

'Or he's telling us on no account to try, because there's a bomb with a water-pressure-actuated fuse behind the wall-panel just to your right. If only I could speak fluent goldfish I could probably lip-read. But I can't. A shame, but never mind. We'll just have to stay right here where we are, not making any bother for anyone, and wait for someone to come and get us out.'

'Resourceful, aren't you?' Zelda sneered.

'So's the North Sea,' Neville replied. 'And that's precisely why they started drilling holes in it. Resourceful is for losers.

Still, quiet and scared shitless, on the other hand, has the full weight of thousands of years of trial and error to back it up.'

'Coward.'

'You know,' Neville said, staring at a cobweb in the corner of the ceiling, 'for a scientist, you don't know jack about evolution. Thousands of generations of cowards have run like buggery at the first sign of danger and thereby survived to breed. Soon the gene pool will be completely surrounded by our deckchairs, and there'll be nobody here except us chickens. It's how nature gauges success.'

By way of reply, Zelda made an unladylike noise with her tongue. 'You can stand back if you want to,' she said. 'I'm gonna turn this boy loose and get out of here. And you can stay here and rot, if that's what you've set your heart on.'

She grabbed the goldfish bowl and twisted it sideways, sloshing its contents all over the floor. The goldfish hit the ground and wriggled convulsively, arching its back so that its tail thrashed against its own head, and for a moment Zelda's face was a study in Oh-fuck-what've-I-done? Then the goldfish, still bucking, turned into a dragon.

He made the other dragon look like a gecko. His scales were gold and orange-red, the colour of steel just before it's fit to be transferred from the forge to the anvil. Down his long spine, curved and sinuous as a mighty river, ran a double row of sharp white blades, as if some millionaire had burglarproofed the top of his wall with razor-edged ivory instead of broken bottles. Each foot sported five long milk-white claws, most delicate of weapons; his wings were vast fans woven from peacock's feathers; his ears were long and pointed, muffled with dense thickets of blue and gold hair, and his jaws were fringed with long, trailing white whiskers, like those of a Victorian statesman.

'You stupid fucking cow,' he shrieked, in a voice like fireworks going off inside a huge bronze bell. 'What the hell do you think you're playing at? I could have choked.' He lashed out instinctively with his tail, like a vast bejewelled strimmer, missing Zelda's head by the thickness of a sheet of paper.

'Told you,' Neville murmured from the corner where he was cowering. 'Different dragon.' Zelda, who'd recovered from her perfectly natural terror remarkably quickly, was staring at the big crack in the wall where the dragon's tail had smacked into it. 'Do that again,' she said.

'Piss off,' the dragon said. 'What d'you think I am, a jackhammer?'

'No,' Zelda replied, 'but you'll have to do for now.' She frowned. 'Or would you prefer to stay coiled up like a Hoover flex for the rest of your life?'

Her tone made the dragon even angrier, but he was too shrewd not to take her point, so he took his anger out on the wall, which pretty soon wasn't there any more. Quick as a running rope burning your hands, the dragon flipped over and shot his head through the hole like a harpoon. 'Ouch,' he reported back, as his skull impacted with the wall of the adjoining room. 'Snot. Shit. Buggery,' he elaborated, as he head-butted the wall into masonry dust. 'That's better.'

'Are you through? Out of the building?'

'No,' the dragon's voice floated back, 'but at least there's room to swing my tail in. Could be some sort of hall or audience chamber.'

Zelda scrambled to her feet. 'Wait for us,' she shouted.

'Why?'

'Because,' she improvised desperately, 'we know what's going on.'

The dragon stayed where he was, the last four feet of his tail still inside the cell. 'Pleased to meet you,' he said, his voice suddenly candied in charm. 'I'm Xyxxzpltyssxz, crown prince of . . .' For some reason he stopped and giggled, as if at some private joke. 'Dragon king of the north-west,' he went on. 'And you are—?'

'I'm Zelda and he's Neville. We've all been captured by a

man called Willis. He's an evil overlord type who owns news-papers.'

'Right,' the dragon said. 'With you so far.'

'And he knows about dragons,' Neville put in. 'So do we, come to that.'

('Speak for yourself,' Zelda muttered grimly, but too qui-etly for anybody to hear.)

'But,' Neville went on, 'he's planning to use dragons to take over the world, or some shit like that. He kidnapped one of your people,' Neville added, showing a flair for the truth that'd have earned him a speechwriting job with the politician of his choice, 'but he helped us escape. Then we got captured again. She thought you were him.'

'Got you,' the dragon said. 'I suppose one goldfish does look pretty much like another.'

'Not to me,' Neville said with a smirk. 'I spotted the dif-ference. But she wouldn't listen.'

'Which is probably just as well,' the dragon replied. 'What a force for good in the world human ignorance is, to be sure. By the way, you don't happen to know how he managed to trigger the morphic shift, do you? A human who can make dragons change shape whenever he wants to could prove something of a nuisance.'

'Sorry,' Neville said. 'You could ask her, I suppose. She's one of his dragon experts.'

The dragon made a purring sound. 'Is that right?'

'Was,' Zelda said quickly. 'Now I'm one of the good guys.'

'Really.' The dragon didn't seem particularly interested in her any more. 'Well, I think it'd probably be in order to pro-ceed with a certain amount of caution, unless I want to find myself turned into a goldfish again. That would be extremely tiresome, especially if it happens when there's no water handy for me to be one in.' His tail slithered out of the cell. Zelda and Neville followed.

The adjoining room was just another cell, like the one

they'd just left, so they went through the dragon-shaped hole in the far wall and found themselves in the space they'd just been told about. It was certainly big; an enthusiastic Zeppelin collector could have shown off his prize specimens in elegant comfort without crowding the place out at all. The ceiling was as high as the room was long and wide, and apart from some bunches of ironmongery that reminded Zelda of theatrical lighting, hanging from brackets in the corners, it was completely empty.

Except for one shortish middle-aged man, who was standing in the middle of the floor with his hands in his pockets. There was a little black box the size and shape of an old-fashioned light meter on a string around his neck. His tie didn't go with his suit, either.

'Good day,' he said, in a fairly dilute Australian accent. 'I'm Paddy Willis; short for Paddington, but if you're wise you won't ever mention that again. You found your way here all right, I see.'

The dragon made a low growling sound, like a cornered Harley Davidson, and crouched, ready to spring. Then he stayed crouched.

'Don't bother trying to move,' Mr Willis said. 'Something my R & D people slapped together – a pain in the trouser seat, scientists, but just occasionally they come in handy, like Irish money. There's some technical stuff about morphogenic fields they tried to make me listen to, but if you ask me they just copied out some stuff from Star Trek and pretended it was real science. As far as I'm concerned it's magic; anyhow, it works. Bloody well should, it cost me enough. Bottom line is, if I don't want you to move, you don't move. If I want to turn you into a bloke, or a goldfish, suddenly that's what you are. I think it'll help us relate to each other on a more level playing field; me completely in control, you paralysed and helpless. It's the way I've always done business, and it generally seems to work.' He appeared to notice Neville and Zelda for the first time. 'As for you two,' he said, 'you're getting to be a nuisance. Still, I'm not a vindictive bastard, and besides, I'm running a bit short of storage areas with four walls and a roof. You can stay here till I decide what to do with you. Oh yes,' he added. 'You. What's your name.'

'Me?' Zelda asked.

'On the tip of my tongue,' Mr Willis said. 'I'm proud of the fact that I know all my employees' first names. Couldn't give a toss about their surnames, mind you, I've got personnel officers to handle all that crap. Zelda,' he said, snapping his fingers. 'Begins with a Z, sounds like zebra.'

'That' s right,' Zelda said, impressed in spite of herself.

'Zelda, love,' Mr Willis said, 'you're sacked. Right, don't go away, any of you. There'll be some blokes along shortly wth some electronics shit – transformers and power cables, that sort of thing. They'll see to you.'

Zelda was puzzled, but too smart to attract attention to herself again. Neville wasn't.

'Excuse me,' he said, 'but what's that for?'

'What? Oh.' Mr Willis chuckled. 'Of course, you don't know, do you? And of course Zelda doesn't, because all the time she thought she was doing research on that other dragon, it was just to distract the bugger's attention so the other blokes – the real scientists – could do their scanning and what have you without it noticing. It's what I wanted dragons for in the first place.'

'Well?' Neville asked impatiently.

'Or at least,' Mr Willis said, 'bits of dragons. Zelda was way off line,' he went on, 'when you lot were nattering back in there. Evil overlord my arse,' he added with a chuckle. 'That's no way to rule the world, young lady, as you'd know if you had a brain. You rule the world by owning newspapers and TV stations; bloody sight less fuss, and they pay you for the privilege. Own enough newspapers and you get to own governments absolutely free, it's like those special offers where you send away so many box tops. And you don't do it so you can sit on a throne and do silly hysterical laughter. You do it for the money.'

'Oh,' Zelda said. That, she decided, was her told.

'No,' Mr Willis said, 'what I want dragons for is so I can save a bloody fortune on communications satellites, broadcast relay stations, cables, DVD, the lot. Who needs all that Japanese crap when all you've got to do is put your fist down inside some animal's skull and pull out its third eye?'

He looked up and stared at her for a moment before he said anything.

'Karen?'

She looked back at him, just as the door slammed and a key ground in the lock. 'Hello, Paul,' she replied, in a small, tired voice.

'Karen? What are you doing here?' he said. He sounded completely bewildered – which, if anything, overlaid the present crisis with a deceptively specious coating of apparent normality. Chances were that Paul had been born bewildered; it was easy to imagine him looking up at the midwife with a dazed expression on his puckered little face, as if asking, 'Nurse, what's this silver spoon doing in my mouth?' A wave of fondness enveloped her, like locusts when they fly so thick they blot out the sun.

'More to the point,' she said, 'what are *you* doing here? Do you know?'

'Haven't a clue,' Paul replied sadly. 'Some men grabbed me from the office, gave me an injection to put me to sleep; when I woke up, I was here. That was a long time ago,' he added mournfully.

'And what have you been doing since?'

'Nothing much,' Paul said. 'I walk up and down now and then, just for the exercise. When they put the lights out, I go to sleep. Apart from that, I just sit here, mostly.'

'You just sit there.'

He nodded. 'Not much else I can do, really.' He shifted a little on the concrete bench. 'I did think about digging a tunnel, like Richard Chamberlain in that film, but it's a concrete floor and they only ever give me plastic spoons to eat with. Besides, I wouldn't know how to dig a tunnel. You've got to have pit-props and ventilation holes and stuff or it all falls on your head and buries you, or you choke. So I thought, even if I did have a bash at it I'd be bound to get it all wrong, so I decided I'd be better off sitting still and waiting till they let me go.'

Karen sat down beside him. He didn't move. 'When you say *they*,' she said, 'do you happen to know who *they* are?'

'No,' Paul replied. 'I'm assuming it's a kidnapping thing, because my dad's so rich. He owns newspapers and stuff, you know.'

'I had heard, yes. So you reckon that sooner or later he'll pay up and they'll let you go?'

'Hope so,' Paul said. 'Though Dad can be a bit funny about things like that. He doesn't like being pushed around, you see; it's like when the people in one of his companies wanted to join a union. He said that was bullying, and he'd rather close the company down.'

'And did he?'

'Oh yes. So,' Paul went on, 'he might feel that them demanding a ransom before they'll let me go is bullying, too.'

'It's a rather different situation, though, don't you think?' Karen heard herself say. 'His own flesh and blood, I mean, in deadly danger. Surely—'

'It'd be a matter of principle,' Paul replied. 'Dad's hot on principles. Which is good, if you ask me. I mean, you can't just go around giving in to people, can you?'

Gazing at him sitting on his bench like an overfed rabbit in its hutch, Karen found it hard keeping a straight face. 'I suppose not. So what do you think he'll do?'

Paul swung his head slowly from side to side. 'Not sure,' he said. 'Probably tell the police. Dad knows lots of important policemen all over the world. We were always having policemen over to the house for dinner when I was a kid. I expect that's what he'll do,' Paul said, straightening his back a little. 'Though on the telly the kidnappers always say, "No police or the victim dies."'

'I see. And is that what usually happens?'

'I don't know.'

Karen had a theory about humans; that they were only ever really themselves when they were alone, not exposed to the influence of others, not busily trying to match their colours to those of the branch or rock they happened to be sitting on. Humans, she believed, instinctively imitated the people they were with so as to be more likely to fit in, be accepted, be liked (oh, that human need to be liked . . .), a tendency that could cause worse communications breakdowns than anything British Telecom ever perpetrated, when you get six or seven people all trying to imitate each other at the same time. The result, inevitably, is like that strange effect you sometimes get in lifts, where both sidewalls of the lift are covered in mirror glass, and your reflection bounces backwards and forwards between them an infinite number of times, the image getting smaller and vaguer at each stage. Well, that was her theory; and here was Paul, after an extended period in solitary confinement. If she was right, what she was getting now was the genuine, pure-as-Evian-water, concentrated essence of Paul, unadulterated by her, Susan, Mrs White, or any of the other bits of personality-fluff that stick to us as we're bounced about during our bumpy ride in life's trouser pocket. Here he was.

Yes. Well.

'It's funny,' he was saying, 'you and me being locked up together like this. We spent all that time in the same office, and most days I don't suppose we said more than a few sentences to each other.'

Karen looked away. 'Actually,' she said, 'there was a reason for that.'

'Oh?'

'Yes. I was afraid of making a fool of myself—'

'I don't understand.'

'—Just like I'm doing now. But anyway, here goes. You see – oh for God's sake, this is going to sound so gut-wrenchingly coy – you see, I was getting very, um, I liked you. A lot . . .'

'But – Oh.' Paul's face suddenly solidified, like molten lead dropped into water, leaving him with that death-by-embarrassment stuffed stare that's unique to the English during romantic interludes. 'I see.'

'So obviously,' Karen went on, (of course he didn't *see*, not with just two eyes), 'the logical thing to do was stay out of your way as much as possible, get on with my work, stay on my side of the office—'

'Why?'

'Excuse me?'

'Why was that the logical thing to do? Why didn't you just tell me?'

Karen stared at him as if a sunflower had just burst out through the top of his head. 'You're joking, aren't you?'

'No.'

'But—' Karen took a deep breath. 'But I – but you just *don't*, that's all. Except, apparently, in leap year, and that's not for ages yet. And besides, you're in love with Susan.'

'Am I?' It sounded like a genuine question. 'I don't think so.' He smiled weakly. 'I'm sure I'd have noticed something like that.'

'But of course you—' Karen stopped. 'You mean you aren't?'

'No.'

'Oh.' Karen looked up at the ceiling for five whole seconds. 'Well, at any rate, you aren't in love with me, so it doesn't really make much difference.' She hesitated, as a horrible thought crossed her mind. 'You aren't, are you?'

'I don't know,' he replied, not knowing how close those words came to earning him a broken eye-socket. 'Truth is, I was a little bit afraid of you.'

'Of me?'

Paul nodded gravely, like a small baize-covered figurine of Confucius hanging in the back window of an ancient Cortina. 'Yes,' he said. 'I mean, you were always glowering at everyone – Susan, and me. And you were so efficient and good at your job. That's pretty intimidating, you know.'

As an insight into human reasoning, Karen would have found that remark extremely valuable in another context (generations of British economic policy, for example, expressly designed so that even the most timid citizen couldn't find it the slightest bit intimidating). 'I see,' she said. 'But being – excuse me, being *afraid* of me isn't the same thing as, well, you know. Love. And stuff.'

'Sometimes it is,' Paul replied. 'It's like you were saying. About not telling me, because you were afraid you'd make a fool out of yourself. Isn't that the same thing, more or less?'

There was an awkward silence.

'Well,' Karen asked brusquely. 'Do you or don't you?'

'Sorry?'

'Love me.'

'Like I said, I'm not sure. Probably, yes. I don't know.'

Imagine how a keyboard feels when someone spills a cup of hot chocolate all over it; or how a digestive biscuit feels when it's been dunked in the tea a little bit too long, and half of it drops off and sinks to the bottom of the cup. Karen's mind was saturated and soggy with emotion. She wanted to throw her arms around him, to hold him tight and never let go, to bang his head repeatedly against the wall for being so infuriating. And yet, right in the centre of all this seething passion, there was one tiny cold spot. It was telling her, *That's all right, then, you've won. Now can we end this, please?*

And then she realised the truth.

'On balance,' Paul said, 'yes. I think I do.'

'On balance?'

'Yes.'

'Ah.' Karen stood up and walked the few paces that brought her to the cell door. 'That's a pity,' she said. 'Because I don't love you any more.'

'Oh.' He frowned. 'Are you sure?'

'Mphm. I did,' she added. 'Quite definitely. Up to about ten seconds ago. But now I don't.'

Paul looked at her with the eyes of a sweet old sheepdog staring up at the muzzle brake of the vet's humane killer. 'That's a bit sudden, isn't it?'

'Volatile,' Karen replied. 'That's me, volatile as an over-heated chip pan. You see,' she went on, 'I was ever so much in love with you. Really I was. And yet,' she went on, 'I could never for the life of me imagine why.'

'Oh,' said Paul.

'No,' Karen went on, 'not a clue. Not even the faintest trace of one, anywhere, ever. You're quite good-looking, and you were there, and that's it. I got the job in the office,' she went on, thinking aloud, 'and there you were, and I must have told myself, if you're going to be human, really be human. Do the things they do. And everything I'd ever seen or read or heard about humans told me that love is the most important thing, right? The sweetest thing, all you need is, makes the world go round. And you know what my trouble is? With being human, I mean. I'm just too damned *thorough*.' She laughed. 'It's what my father always told me; if a thing's worth doing, it's worth doing properly. So I did. And really, I didn't know any other young human males. So—'

Paul was giving her a really funny look.

'What I'm saying is,' Karen went on, 'I was trying to be the best student in the class, handing in the best project; and you happened to be in the way.' Suddenly, out of nowhere, she smiled. 'Which is stupid, really,' she went on, 'because I was already in love with someone else when I came here, though I've only just realised it. You don't know him,' she added lamely, 'I mean, how could you, he's a dr—' She managed to guillotine off the fatal second syllable just in time, leaving the problem of finding a suitable word beginning with 'dr' to take its place. Driving instructor? Drug addict? Drag artiste? 'Dreadfully nice man, but he lives in a totally different part of the country, so the chances of you ever having bumped into him are, well . . . But like I said, I didn't know till just now. Actually, he's an old friend. I've known him since we were at school together, hundreds of years – I mean, it feels like I've known him for hundreds of years. Anyway,' she went on, 'that's more or less it. Sorry,' she added as an afterthought. 'Probably I chose you because I thought you were in love with Susan.' A thought occurred to her. 'You sure you're not in love with Susan? Really?'

Paul shook his head. 'Positive,' he said.

'Oh well. I'd hoped that we could sort things out so you'd end up with who you really wanted all along. Like me,' she added, with a hint of surprise in her voice. 'Not to worry,' she said briskly. 'Like they say, worse things happen at sea.'

Paul looked puzzled. 'Shipboard romances, you mean?'

'What? Oh, yes, right. Look, we'd better get out of this cell. After all, one of the reasons why I came here was to rescue you.'

'It was?' She could almost hear the click as the connection was made in Paul's mind. 'You never did say how you came to be here,' he said.

'Yes, well . . .'

'Or where "here" is,' Paul went on, uncharacteristically forceful. 'Or who's holding me, or what's going on, or how you got here or anything like that. In fact, you were asking me.' He looked at her. 'Karen? And what was all that crazy stuff about if you're going to be human, do it properly? I don't understand.'

'No,' Karen replied. 'You don't. Deal with it.' She stepped back a couple of paces from the door. 'You aren't going to understand this, either,' she said. 'In fact, there's a serious risk that if you watch what I'm just about to do, it'll freak you out so badly your brain will blow out of your ears. You may prefer to close your eyes.'

'This is silly,' Paul said. 'Maybe you should rest. Lie down or something.'

'No,' Karen said. 'You lie down. On the floor; no, better still, under that bench, because there may be flying masonry and stuff.' She scowled at him. 'Under the bench,' she snapped. 'Now.'

He scuttled under the bench like a hermit crab. 'All right,' he said. 'I'm ready.'

'Fine. Now, don't be alarmed, this is actually all perfectly natural—'

She closed her eyes and felt for her wings and tail. They weren't there.

It was one of those last-step-of-the-escalator moments. The jolt was physically painful; the shock of not being in the body she'd expected to be. Suddenly, her human skin felt unbearably tight, like being in clothes three sizes too small. She swore and tried again. The shock was rather worse. That was all.

'Karen,' Paul called out from under the bench, 'are you all right?'

'Yes. Shut up.' She closed her eyes again, looked for her third eye; it was there, but she couldn't see anything through it at all. With all the strength she could muster, she grabbed for her wings and tail, and hurled herself at the wall. It was a very solid wall, and she hurled herself at it very hard indeed.

'Ungh,' she gasped, and hit the floor.

There was a long moment of silence.

'Was that it?' Paul asked from under his ledge.

'Urg.'

'It's all right,' Paul said, slithering out from his hiding place. 'You needn't worry, it didn't freak me out after all. What was it, some kind of Taekwondo thing? I tried to learn that stuff a year or two ago, but there was a seven-year-old in our class who kept picking on me . . . Are you all right?'

'No,' Karen muttered. 'I think I've broken my arm. Ouch,' she added, by way of confirmation.

'Oh.' Paul looked down at her helplessly. 'Sorry,' he said, 'I don't know what you're supposed to do about broken arms. You tie them to something, but I think it gets quite technical. It's a pity,' he added. 'The evening classes I signed up for, Taekwondo and first aid were on the same night, and I decided . . .'

'Paul,' Karen said quietly, 'please shut up. You aren't helping.'

'I know,' Paul replied sadly.

After a brief and regrettable attempt to move, Karen gave up and lay still. Probably she should have guessed earlier, when in spite of all the messy emotions slopping about all over the place, Paul hadn't slipped up or accidentally banged his head against the wall. Her third eye, all the amazing dragon attributes she'd always taken for granted, didn't seem to be working. She laughed bitterly.

'Well,' she said, 'I got exactly what I wanted. Now I really know what it's like to be human.'

That obviously worried Paul. 'There you go again,' he said, 'with that loony stuff. I wish you'd stop doing it.'

'And you know what it's all about? Being human, I mean. It's about not having the choice. And you know what? I don't think I like it very much.'

'Karen—'

'Oh go *away!*' As soon as she'd said it she felt guilty for snapping at him, but she couldn't seem to make herself calm down. Besides, maybe staying calm wasn't such a good thing after all. Paul was calm – any calmer and he'd be dead – and right now she wouldn't give ear wax for his chances of getting out of there without being rescued. The hell with calm; what she needed was some good old-fashioned bad temper – preferably blue, forked, high-voltage and aimed with surgical precision right *there*—'

No lightning. Not even a teeny tiny flash, or a burp of thunder, or a dewdrop of rain. Of course, she hadn't really been expecting anything, since she was outside her jurisdiction; except that it was human nature to expect a miracle at times like these . . .

Human nature. Oh dear.

Karen slumped, letting the strength drain away, like oil from a British motorcycle. For the first time in her life, she felt completely, utterly helpless: someone else had imposed his will on her, and because he was so much stronger, or cleverer (didn't matter which; that sort of cleverness was just another form of strength) there was nothing she could do. The sharp pain of pity made her flesh crawl; because there were so many humans, and for them it was like this all the time.

'Well,' she said. 'Let's just hope we get rescued.'

Paul nodded. 'Never give up hope, that's what I say.'

Karen didn't bother to reply. Hope was another of those human things she felt she was better off not understanding – hope in hopeless situations, the mindless abjuration of the truth in favour of anaesthetic self-deception. It was that kind of hope, she knew, that secured the tyrant and bound the addict to his needle, and she really didn't think it was going to help much. It would be nice, though, if Paul were to leave it at that. There was no situation in human experience that couldn't be made worse, even if only by a little, and Paul blithely informing her that it was always darkest before dawn and that every cloud had a silver lining would make things a *lot* worse, particularly since having only one good arm would make it difficult and painful to smack him unconscious.

Instead, she lay on her back and stared at the ceiling. It wasn't a pretty ceiling. It probably knew that, because she was sure it was scowling at her. Now, if her arm wasn't broken she could try climbing up on Paul's shoulders and ripping off the plasterboard with her fingernails till she'd found where Mr Willis had hidden the transmitter or other gadget that was stopping her from using her third eye or changing shape. And if she could only get the use of her third eye back, she could use it to force the broken bone to knit together as fast as arc-welding; or if she could change shape she could turn herself into a goldfish (which doesn't have an arm to be broken) and then immediately into a dragon, which would fix the arm problem and leave her ready to take out her snit on the walls. But she couldn't; and the worst part of it was, it was her fault that she'd broken her arm, it was her fault that she'd come quietly and allowed herself to be locked up in here, it was her fault that her father had been kidnapped in the first place. It was possible even for a human to be rendered completely helpless through no fault of her own, but when you were the sole author of all your misfortunes, that was a bitch . . .

The door opened.

Karen tried to jump up, but that turned out to be a really bad idea; instead, she flopped down hard on her bum and yelped with pain as the shock jarred her arm. When she'd finished doing all that, she had the leisure to look and see who'd joined them.

'Susan?' Paul said. 'What are you doing here?'

Karen's mouth dropped like the ramp of a cross-Channel ferry. Bewilderment – *must've caught it from Paul, never knew it was contagious before* – and a surprisingly sharp twinge of jealousy; even though she didn't love him any more, not one little bit, why did it have to be *her* of all people who'd come to rescue them? Assuming that that was why she was here. Big assume.

'Be quiet, Paul,' Susan said, not looking at him. Instead, she seemed far more interested in Karen. 'Are you all right?' she said. 'You look like you've hurt yourself.' She knelt down beside her, looking not worried but concerned.

'Broke my arm,' Karen mumbled. 'Look, what *are* you doing here?'

'My job,' Susan replied. 'Does this hurt?'

'Aaaaaaaa—'

'That hurts. Okay, we'll have to take it easy. Not to worry. Put your other arm around my neck and I'll help you up. Paul, come here. I need you to keep the door open.'

Karen's arm tweaked her like hell as she stood up, but damned if she was going to let Susan know that. 'What do you mean, your job?' she said. 'You're an estate agent. Come to measure up, have you?'

Susan shook her head. 'Let's head for the door,' she said, 'nice and steady.'

'Not till you tell me what you meant by—'

'All right.' Susan adjusted her grip slightly on Karen's good arm. 'Your father assigned me to look after you,' she said.

'My father?' Something was hurting, apart from her arm. 'You mean you're a—'

'Yes,' Susan snapped, dipping her head slightly in Paul's direction and giving Karen a not-in-front-of-the-children scowl. 'It was a week ago, before you ran off; your father thought you'd been acting strangely, guessed you might be thinking about doing something bloody stupid. When you came down here, I followed you, to make sure you didn't get yourself into any really bad trouble.' She shook her head. 'I failed. My fault. I underestimated you. Guess I'd forgotten just how unbelievably irresponsible you can be sometimes.'

'You under—' Something occurred to Karen, and she didn't like it. 'Do I know you?' she said. 'Back home, I mean.'

'Of course you do. We've known each other since we were so high.'

Karen grabbed Susan's wrist, but she gently eased out of the grip. 'All right, then,' Karen shouted, 'who are you? Go on, tell me.'

'Later. When we're not so busy. It'll just make things awkward if you know now.'

'But—' Karen would have carried on asking, but Susan was manhandling her through the cell door. Dragonhandling. Whatever. 'All right, then,' she said. 'Oh, do you know about the—?'

Susan nodded. 'Disabling field. Clever idea. After we've got you out of here, I'll have to make sure it's completely trashed. Can't leave something like that lying around, can we?'

So cool, so confident, so damned bloody superior. Karen was beginning to feel very bad about this. 'Three guesses?' she suggested, as they emerged into the corridor outside.

'No.'

'Please your—' Karen stopped and looked round. Then she closed her eyes. Much better. 'Just a moment,' she said, as she found the splintered ends of the bone. Fixing them took just under three seconds and didn't hurt a bit.

'All right now?' Susan asked.

'Yes.'

'Splendid. It's all right, Paul, you can let her go now.' Susan's eyes were closed too. 'Straight ahead,' she said, 'then second left, third right—'

'No,' Karen interrupted.

'What do you mean, "No"? It's a straight run to the lift shaft, and that'll take us right to the back door.'

'No,' Karen repeated. 'Or at least, you two go on. I've got to stay here.'

'Why?'

Karen sighed. 'I've got to find my dad,' she said.

Susan's eyes opened with a snap, like over-sprung roller blinds. 'He's here too? Your father?'

'Long story,' Karen said. 'Long, embarrassing story. You two go on, I'll fetch him and catch you up.'

'Hold it,' Susan said. 'What makes you think he's here in the building? I can't see any sign of him.'

'You can't either? Splendid. That'll make him much easier to find. It's this shielding,' she explained. 'Makes him invisible to the third—' She leaned closer, so Paul couldn't hear. 'To the third eye,' she hissed. 'So, when I've found a big space where I can't see anything, that's where he'll be. Simple, isn't it?'

She turned to walk away. Susan reached out to hold her back, but she pushed her hand gently away with what had recently been her broken arm. Paul noticed that, and for a moment he simply couldn't understand how someone could do that with a broken arm. He opened his mouth to ask about it, but decided not to after all. There was a slight but significant risk that he might get a straight answer, and if what he'd been listening to ever since Karen arrived was anything to go by, he was fairly certain he didn't want to know. The absolute truth, according to Paul Willis, was like some awesome, beautiful mythical beast – a unicorn, say, or a gryphon, or a dragon. It was both inspiring and entertaining to contemplate it at a safe distance, but you really wouldn't want one in your living room.

'I'm still on duty, remember,' Susan was saying. 'I owe it to your father to look after you. So we're coming with you.'

(*Gosh*, Paul thought; *so Karen's got a powerful, manipulative father too. We do have something in common, after all. Wonder if he owns newspapers too.*)

Karen shrugged. 'That's up to you,' she said. 'But really, I'd far rather you got him out of this mess first. How'd it be if you took him away, then came back and looked after me? Deal?'

'Certainly not. Your dad didn't say anything to me about

any humans. Besides, he's the megalomaniac-psycho's *son*, for pity's sake. Can you say hostage?'

Karen laughed. Paul went bright red and looked away.

'It's not quite like that,' Karen said. 'Trust me, I know. All right, have it your own way. After all, there's two of us, and we can tell which parts of the building have got that wretched dampening-field thing. If we stay clear of them, we'll be all right.'

Susan looked up and down the corridor again; nervous habit, endemic among security types. 'Let's hope so,' she said. 'But I'd feel a whole lot happier if we got out of this – this *leisurewear*, and into something a bit more practical, if you know what I . . .'

Karen grinned. 'Blue body-stocking and a red cape? Forget it,' she added quickly, 'human joke. Anyway, anything's better than standing about chatting in corridors like a couple of diplomats. Follow me.'

Susan frowned. 'Is that a good idea? So far, you've exhibited the strategic and tactical instincts of a pacifist lemming.'

'Yes,' Karen admitted. 'But he's my dad. Follow me, or go away and water something. Understood?'

'Understood.'

Against his better judgement, Paul cashed in his remaining few shares in courage. 'I don't understand,' he said.

The two girls looked at him and grinned. 'Good,' they said.

Fifty yards or so down the corridor, they came to a pair of fire doors. As soon as they were through, the doors swung shut and a lock clicked. Another pair of doors twenty yards further on did the same thing. Something in the walls started to hum. It was at that point, as Karen closed her eyes and saw nothing but the insides of two eyelids, that it occurred to her that the verb *to rescue* only really means anything when used in the past tense.

As the anaesthetic gas started to take effect and the world began to melt into blobs and streaks, interior decor by

Salvador Dali, she reached out with an arm that was much, much shorter than she'd remembered, and grabbed Susan by her arm.

'I must know,' she drawled, having to fight in order to shape each word (it was like trying to carve the Elgin marbles out of cottage cheese with a chisel made of overcooked pasta). 'Who are you?'

Susan looked at her. 'You mean you haven't guessed?'

'Nope.' Karen shook her head. It stayed on, though her neck felt like it had stretched about a yard. 'Norraclue. Tell me.'

'I'm your cousin Gndva-S'sssn, you idiot. S'ssssn. Susan. Geddit? 'Spose I coulda made it a bit more obvious if I'd had my real name tattooed on my forehead in fluorescent green, but I din't think it'd be nesessessr . . .'

'Oink?'

Susan – S'sssn; of course, how dumb can you get? – sneered at her. She appeared to have twelve lips, which made it easier. 'You're drunk,' she said. 'Go sleep.'

So she did.

CHAPTER THIRTEEN

'Painting the ceilings?' the soldier said. 'At a time like this?'

Gordon gave him a sympathetic grin. 'Crazy, isn't it?' he said. 'But that's what it says on my worksheet, and if I don't get it done today, I'll flamin' well cop it from the Big Chief. More'n my job's worth, that. So, if it's OK with you fellas—'

The soldier rolled his eyes. 'Oh, for crying out loud,' he said. 'All right, if you insist.' He stood up, switched off his monitor and grabbed his jacket. 'I suppose it won't kill me to take an early lunch,' he said, 'even if we are in the middle of an artillery duel, with a bunch of crazed terrorists roaming loose. When will you be finished by?'

Gordon ran an appraising eye round the room, clicked his tongue. 'An hour,' he said. 'Maybe an hour and a quarter. Tell you what, mate; call it an hour and a half and I promise I'll be through by then.'

'Whatever,' the soldier sighed, buckling on his ammunition belts. 'Just, please, make sure you don't move things about any more than you can help, okay? It may look scruffy to you, but I know exactly where everything is.'

When he'd gone, Gordon slumped down in the chair and breathed out a long sigh of relief. There had been times when the inspiration that had struck him as he hid in the janitor's cupboard – grab some overalls, paint, brushes, ladders and stuff, pretend to be a maintenance man – hadn't seemed quite so inspired after all; quite apart from the physical strain of having to put on an Australian accent (murder on the jaw-muscles if you weren't bred to it) it was a naive idea, an American-cop-show idea, an urban folk-myth that the man in the brown overalls is invisible and sacrosanct, and that every-body obeys him without question because he answers only to the System. Fortunately, it had worked just fine so far, as those crummy old urban folk-myths so often do.

He switched the monitor on and gazed at the screen in near despair. The problem was that he didn't really have a clue what he was looking for. *Get into the computer system*, his optimistic soul had urged him, *and you can disable the damp-ening field, the dragon can turn back into a dragon and smack shit out of these maniacs, and we can all go . . .*

(*Home. Away. Whatever. We can all get out of this particular nightmare, to a place where at least we'll have an apparent choice as to what form our next nightmare will take.*)

. . . Home. He wanted very badly to go home. Not that he liked home terribly much, but the number of places he actu-ally did like could be counted on the fingers of one hand by a twice-convicted Iranian burglar. He wanted to go home. He wanted to quit the weather business. He wanted to get back together with Zelda. (Where the hell had that one come from? Oh, never mind, it was there now, and no more hopelessly unattainable than the rest of his aspirations.) Curiously, although he was starving hungry, he didn't particularly want a drink. *Hooray*, he thought, *I'm cured. Just in time for me to die, but so what, it's a start.*

The screen was, of course, filled with gibberish, but for all he knew it was meant to look like that. Telling good computer gibberish from bad computer gibberish wasn't one of his most keenly burnished skills. Just for fun, he hit ENTER, and leaned back in the surprisingly comfortable chair to see if anything happened.

It did.

First, the arms of the chair grabbed his wrists and stuck needles into the palms of his hands. Something like a steel tea cosy plunged down from nowhere over his face and gave him a big sloppy dry kiss with an array of rubber suction pads. Something else grabbed his feet. He was half expecting someone to say 'Guess who?'

Me.

He couldn't jump in his chair, because he was held down as firmly as interest rates in an election year; but he could do the mental equivalent.

Sorry. I startled you. Didn't mean to do that. I s'pose I shouldn't play tricks on people.

The voice was coming from inside his head; he could almost feel the exact place, midway between his ears, about two inches in from the slight bulge on the back of his skull. It was a cutesy little-girl-lost voice with that curious semi-American accent usually found only in digital telephone-answering machines made in Korea. It irritated him profoundly.

Don't be like that. I'm sure we can be friends, even though I'm a whole lot smarter'n you.

He tried to speak, but his voice had been cut off, and Miss Pacific Rim 2001 was squatting in the part of his brain where he turned his thoughts into words, with the door locked and the TV turned up loud.

You're mean. If you didn't want to play, why did you come in?

It occurred to him that that was valid enough, from her point of view. He regretted his outburst of pique.

'S okay. Now can we be friends? You're different from the reg-ular guy. I like him a lot, but he's not much fun. All he thinks about is work, work, work. Work's okay, I guess, but I like to play. Can we play?

A noughts-and-crosses grid appeared in front of his eyes. It was glowing pink. It occurred to him that She probably liked pink.

A lot. It's my favorite colour. You go first.

He imagined what it would be like if there was a neat pink cross in the central box. It appeared at once; then all the other boxes were filled with flickering pink light, as noughts and crosses flashed on and off, thousands of flashes a second.

You won 614,779. I won 423,996. That's the number of possi-ble permutations of the game of noughts and crosses starting from that particular opening gambit, She explained, in a stiff, recit-ing-from-memory voice. *Okay, my turn to start.*

There was another pink maelstrom. It made Gordon feel sick inside his head, which was no fun at all.

Huh. You've won. Again. 512,664 to 388,992. It's no fun if you win all the time.

He thought contrite thoughts, and reflected on the fact that he didn't really want to play any more, because the flash-ing lights upset him.

All right, She sighed. *S'pose that's okay. Can we play some-thing else? Doesn't have to have flashing lights in it. How 'bout battleships?*

It occurred to Gordon that although battleships was a fine game, one that he'd enjoyed a lot when he was a child, he would feel rather easier in his mind (and therefore better able to play battleships) if he knew who She was and what was going on.

You mean you don't know? Snng! You're weird. Everybody knows who I am.

Gordon reflected on the obvious fallacy in that statement.

Everybody 'cept you. Okay. I'm Lucy. Well, actually I'm Lucy-for-Windows-tee-em, but my friends call me Lucy. You can call me Lucy if vou like.

Pleasure at meeting Lucy welled forth from the inner core of Gordon's being. In limited quantities.

Pleased to meet you too, Gordon. You mind if I call you Uncle Gordon? Sounds better that way.

The name 'Uncle Gordon' struck Gordon as being perfectly acceptable. However, he couldn't help wondering why a computer program, even a highly intelligent and extremely likeable computer program like Lucy, should feel the need to be a seven-year-old girl.

'Cos I'm still a prototype, silly. I'm a young computer program When I get old, like maybe fifteen or sixty-two, I guess I might sound just like you. What did you want to be when you grew up, Uncle Gordy? When you were a kid, I mean.

Gordon remembered wanting to be a fireman.

Cool. When I grow up, I want to be an Emacs interface, but don't tell Uncle Paddy. Or Uncle Bill. They get real cross when I tell them that.

It seemed to Gordon that if that was what Lucy wanted to be when she emerged from beta, it was nobody's business but her own. However, (he thought, before Lucy could interrupt) he still felt he didn't know as much about Lucy as he'd like to. For instance: what did she actually do?

Me? Oh. I'm an artificial dragon's eye. You know, the third one, that lives right where you're hearing me now?

Gordon found that fascinating, not to mention extremely impressive. He couldn't help thinking that it would take a really specially clever computer program to be able to do that.

Aw, it's nothing, really. I just look at stuff. It's amazing what you can see if you know what to look for. Want me to show you something?

The suggestion appealed to Gordon very much. The thought of Zelda came instinctively to his mind.

Oh yeah, of course, you two're in le-ervv, aincha? (Gordon became painfully aware of a horrible scritchetting sensation behind his eyes, which he diagnosed as Lucy sniggering.) *Sure I can show you. You watch.* For a moment there was silence (wonderful, blissful silence) in Gordon's mind. *Uh-oh. I can't see her anywhere. Maybe Uncle Paddy's got her somewhere I can't see.*

?

Yeah, he can do that, for sure. He's got this thing where he kinda blocks me out. Well, not me, I guess. I think it's to stop the real dragons seeing. Did you know there really are dragons? They're cool.

The thought of how useful it might be to know where these blocked-off areas were crossed Gordon's mind.

I know where they are. I can show you if you like. Would you like that?

A longing to be shown that swept across Gordon's mind like a Mongol invasion; a moment later his mind was filled with a grid image (in pink) that was basically the noughts-and-crosses board, only larger and with more squares. It was, in fact, a schematic of the building—

And we're here, see the blob? Oops, sorry, that was kinda bright, wasn't it? And the bits I can't see into are here and here and here – Big green patches sprawled across the grid, blotting out the pink lines, like ink spilt on a brand new carpet. *So I guess Zelda-darling's gotta be in one of them.*

Gordon was deeply conscious of how kind Lucy was to have shown him that.

You're welcome. Hey, wanna see something else? I know, how'd you like to see a real live dragon? Bet you ain't never seen a real live dragon before.

Gordon remembered seeing a dragon all too vividly.

Oh. Well, you won't have seen this dragon, betcha. And this one's bigger 'n' better than the one you saw.

Naturally, Gordon wanted to see the dragon very much

indeed. But it occurred to him that if he was going to get the most out of the Lucy program, a rather more user-friendly interface would be exceptionally helpful; one he could actually talk to, perhaps—

> *Hi. I'm Lucy 1.1. And if you say, My, haven't you grown, I'll scream. I hate it when people say that. It's so patronising.*

'Hello?' Gordon said. 'Can you hear me?'

> *Hear you? You practically deafened me. Rilly, there's no need to shout.*

'I'm sorry,' Gordon whispered. 'Excuse me for being personal, but you sound different.'

> *Well, sure. I'm nearly sixteen gigabytes now, I'm not a kid any more. I upgraded myself out of your systems. Hope that's OK.*

'My systems?' Gordon tried to think what she could possibly mean by that. 'Are you telling me you've upgraded yourself out of my *brain?*'

> *Sure. Hey, don't worry, I haven't broken anything, OK? Least, nothing important. Of course it's all rilly, rilly primitive stuff, you know, like in the Flintstones. But it works OK.*

'So glad I was able to help,' Gordon growled. It was, he felt, a shame they have to grow up.

> *Hey, I heard that. That was rilly mean. You're so insensitive. The trouble with you is, you don't think before you think. Wouldn't kill you to consider other people's feelings, you know. After all, this is very, like, tentative for me. Like, being my first time and all that.*

Gordon hadn't considered it in quite that light, but he took the point. 'I'm sorry,' he said. 'It was very, um, thoughtless of me. Now, you were saying something about a dragon?'

> *Was I? Oh yeah, so I was. 'Course, it isn't rilly a dragon, because they don't exist. Dragons are just kids' stuff. You'd have to've been born in the Valley or something to believe in them.*

'I beg to differ,' Gordon said stiffly.

> *Oh hey, now you're going all flaky on me. Look, do you want to see the stupid dragon, or don't you?*

'Please.'

Imagine what it would be like if you were a computer, a machine for differentiating between ones and zeros, eating binary code like an earthworm eats dirt and putting out other dimensionless signals at the other end; and suddenly, instead of merely receiving and processing faint electrical impulses in the dark, you found that quite without warning or advance preparation, you could *understand* everything that passed through you – every word and number and picture, every business memo and personal letter and spreadsheet and address book, every ravening purple monster out of every game, every dark-secret first novel hidden away in the cobwebby gloom of the office hard drive, every junk e-mail and cornball website and vertiginous screen-saver and fatuous *oink-oink* noise for when the user hits the wrong key by mistake. Imagine that in the time it took for a little flake of silicon to pulse twice, all this became real to you, as five senses you'd never had before came online and started flooding your chip with types of data you never knew existed before, colour and sound and texture and smell and taste. In that brief moment, you'd be experiencing everything – *everything* – for the first time, without the faintest idea what any of it meant, or where it was coming from, or who you were. You would be orange-hot steel plunged suddenly into cold water, a meteorite bursting into the atmosphere out of the void, not just a new-born child but the very first of your species. Imagine that you were the moment when amino-acids and photosynthesis in an oxygen-nitrogen atmosphere opened their eyes for the first time and became life, coming at the beginning of all things and redefining everything —

> *Hello? Hey, you fallen asleep or something? Hello!*

'Peaches,' Gordon muttered. 'The colours of its wings sound like the taste of peaches.'

> *Oh my God, that's so pukesomely Sixties I may well throw up. Get a grip. Chill out. Shit, how do you program this thing to synthesize caffeine?*

'It's all right,' Gordon said. 'It came as a bit of a shock, that's all. Was that – is that what it's like, having a third eye?'

The voice inside his head sighed, the wheezing sound of rapidly draining patience.

> *Hey, when you're cooking a meal, do you ask the oven what it tastes like? I don't know, I'm just a computer program. Look, do you want to go and lie down or stick your head in a bucket of ice water or something? You were sounding rilly freaky back there, you know?*

'I'll be fine,' Gordon said, oversimplifying to an almost criminal degree. 'Yes, that was a dragon all right.' An alarming thought occurred to him. 'Just a moment,' he said. 'Are you linked in to the rest of the network?'

> *Sure. Why?*

'I don't want anybody else – well, anybody else in this building – knowing what I'm about to do. Can you run some kind of encryption program or something?'

> *I guess so. But then I'd have to decrypt it before I could understand it myself. Actually, since all this data and stuff's going through your head before it feeds back to me, the best thing would be, like, just ordinary background noise. Not so loud you can't hear yourself think, just loud enough that* they *can't hear* you *think. Whaddaya think?*

'What,' Gordon said dubiously, 'like they do in films, you mean? Go into the bathroom and turn on all the taps?'

> *Yeah, that'd do just fine. Use the faucet, Luke. Sorry, that was rilly, like, unworthy of me.*

'There isn't a bathroom. Is there? I can't see at all with this teapot thing over my head.'

> *Oh puhlease. Just try, will you?*

So he tried. He saw the office he was in (it was mostly in A minor, the walls maybe a semitone sweeter), and the washroom adjoining, and the wash basin, and the taps. He wondered what they'd smell like if they were turned full on instead of full off. Roses, he discovered.

> *OK, that's plenty loud enough. Any more'll make 'em suspicious. Completely paranoid, all of them.*

'Now,' he said, 'I want to see all the command paths and subroutines and whatever the hell you call them that make these anti-dragon fields work. Can you show them to me?'

> *Course I can. But they're rilly boring, believe me. You won't like them.*

'Doesn't matter. Please.'

He saw – It was amazing: vast nebulae of frozen spun-glass and candyfloss, glittering threads of ice and wire-thin stalactite, coral reefs of twinkling light, at first glance fuzzy and hazy, on closer examination sharp, thin, precise and unimaginably many. 'Is that it?'

> *Yes. No, sorry, wrong one, that's just the thing where you can change the colour of your desktop. Here's what you wanted.*

The urge to reach out and grab, to jump into it like a diver off the high board and go crashing and splintering through all that thin, brittle light – 'Yes,' he said. 'Thanks. Now, how do I turn them off?'

> *Want to. That'll do it.*

So Gordon wanted to; but he couldn't, it was too beautiful. The thought of all that scintillating loveliness going dark was unbearable. He couldn't—

> *BOO!*

Startled, his mind jumped – and all the lights were suddenly gone. He tried to scream, but nothing came out except the smell of dust.

> *You are such a blonde, it's practically surreal,* Lucy said, fondly contemptuous. *Never mind, it's all done. Just as well you got me to look after me, you big—*

And then light (horrible, crude, painful) exploded all around him. Frantically he closed his eyes, but it had all gone.

'On your feet,' someone was shouting; they'd pulled the tea cosy off his head, ripped out the needles from his hands, undone the clamps around his feet. Their actions had all the signs off setting someone free, and the exact opposite effect. Gordon couldn't struggle; he didn't even know how to, because his stupid little human body was so small and flat, and there weren't any controls to make it do what he wanted. 'Lucy!' he tried to yell, but nothing came out except sound. Then one of the soldiers stamped down hard on his foot, and he stopped trying.

'Four dragons,' Mr Willis said cheerfully. 'It's like I always say. Stand still long enough with your mouth open, and some bugger'll come and stick chocolate in it.'

The four dragons scowled horribly at him, but that was all. They stood in the middle of the floor of the big, high, empty room like exhibits in the Natural History Museum, while a dozen or so white-coated extras fluttered round them with clipboards and things that went beep. In the far corner, Paul, Zelda and Neville shuffled their feet nervously and tried not to think about the machine guns being pointed at them by four not-very-nice-looking soldiers.

'Of course,' Mr Willis went on, 'if I had a fifth dragon I could link 'em all up in series, and then I wouldn't need any relay stations or boosters at all. Hey,' he called out, 'Your Imperial Majesty. Do you think there's any chance of some of your loyal subjects coming down here trying to save your Imperial arse? Hope so.' He spread his arms. 'As you can see, we've got the room.'

Zelda was looking at the latest piece of machinery to be wheeled in. It looked like an ordinary digger, except that where the bucket should have been there was a big circular saw on one arm and a heavy-duty road drill on the other. There were three whitecoats standing next to it. One of them had his nose in what she took to be the owner's manual, and the other two were trying to grab it from him. In spite of herself, Zelda wanted to smile. When the evils that plagued mankind escaped from Pandora's box, she reflected, the small, quiet creature that got left behind to be humanity's sole source of help and solace wasn't Hope, as the story books said. It was Incompetence.

'Now then,' Mr Willis was saying, 'soon as you blokes have figured out how to work that can-opener thing, maybe we can make a start.' He looked the dragons up and down like a farmer at a livestock auction. 'That one,' he said, pointing at Karen. 'The difficult bitch who trashed my building. Open her up and let's get cracking.'

Karen was dimly aware of the rage and fear emanating from her father and her cousin; it manifested itself as an unbearable itch between her ears, where her third eye was, as nagging and illogical and real as toothache in the tooth you had out last week. She tried to join forces with it, to produce enough strength of mind to short out this horrible human contraption that had made her neither human nor dragon but merely a scale-wrapped box of components ideally suited to use in the telecommunications industry. If she could have laughed, she would have, at the thought of her third eye, everything she was, being used to bounce the news and the cookery programmes and the afternoon soaps from one hemisphere to the other, like a flat stone skipping on water. Oh, she'd wanted to be human; how more human could you get? All human life was there in their TV and their phone calls and their faxes and e-mails, every last scrap of bickering, devious trivia. When she was nothing but a signal processor, she wondered, would she still understand the data she forwarded, or would it just be ones and zeros, nos and yesses, pulse/not-pulse? No question about it, she'd rather be dead than face either alternative.

They'd got the modified digger's engine going. Idly, she wondered what the sound of its engine tasted like; now, of course, she'd never know.

All for love. Her fault. *Damn.*

At that precise moment, in a small room on the other side

of the building, Gordon Smelt and Lucy 1.1 cut the power to the dampening-field generators, and four dragons suddenly realised they could move again. They moved.

Sssss'n was the first to react; she hopped like a huge Fabergé frog and landed right on top of the can-opener-on-wheels, flattening it so comprehensively that when she stood up again, all that remained was a wafer-thin sheet of what looked like tinfoil. That was fine, strategically and tactically; Sssss'n had done her duty. Unfortunately, so did Karen's dad, the adjutant-general to the dragon king of the north-west – or, to be precise, the *previous* dragon king of the north-west, lately assassinated by the crown prince of the south-east, who happened to be standing next to him.

With a roar that slammed half the atmosphere out of the room, he jumped on the crown prince's back, sank his claws in under the prince's scales, and tried to bite his head off. If he'd stopped to think, he would probably have remembered that in all the history of their species, no dragon had ever succeeded in killing or even badly damaging another; but white-hot outraged loyalty and common sense don't go together all that well.

The crown prince took maybe a quarter of a second to realise what was happening; then he fought back. He was bigger, stronger and older than the adjutant-general, and these advantages more or less made up for the determination and ferocity of his enemy's attack. He rolled, using his body weight to throw the adjutant-general off him, though it cost him about a dozen scales; the shock of the pain stopped him short, dissipating his advantage and giving the adjutant-general an opening for a fresh onslaught. He sprang like a tiger (well, not in the least like a tiger; that'd be like saying 'the atomic bomb exploded like a small firework') but the prince had guessed what was coming and wriggled sideways, so that the adjutant-general sailed over his back and landed like a derailed train.

'Dad!' Karen wailed, stricken with horror and embarrassment. She looked up at S'ssssn. 'Do something!' she pleaded.

S'ssssn swore under her breath. She'd been planning to do something, all right; she'd been on the point of taking out all the field-generator hardware, followed by Mr Willis, followed by his building and, if she had any say in the matter, the rest of Australia; external threats before internal squabbles, particularly since the prospect of the two dragons (two *male* dragons, she noted with contempt) hurting each other was so remote. But she'd just been given a direct order. She could defy all the laws of physics, but not the chain of command. With a sigh, she jumped into the mêlée and tried to separate the men.

As for Karen: Karen stood there, hating what she was seeing, unable to do anything about it. *Duty*, she thought; *bloody duty. Humans wouldn't behave like this.*

A rolling three-ply mess of dragons hit the wall, making it shake. Mr Willis's soldiers were blazing away with their machine guns, having about as much effect as a watering can on the sun. Karen looked for Mr Willis himself, and saw him in the far corner of the room; he'd grabbed a machine gun and was pointing it at the three human hostages.

'I'll shoot,' he yelled. 'So help me, I will!'

Karen did the maths. A bullet from Mr Willis's gun would leave the muzzle at around fifteen hundred feet per second, and would need to go at least five yards before it hit Paul, the nearest hostage. She wouldn't quite have time to stop halfway for a cup of tea and a sandwich, but she wouldn't exactly be pressed for time, either. *Make my day*, she thought, and pounced.

In the event, she got there before Mr Willis had even pressed the trigger. She landed on all four feet simultaneously, like a cat, shielding the hostages with her body and reaching out for Mr Willis with her tail. One flick with the very end, and she could decapitate him like a hard-boiled egg—

'No!' Paul screamed. 'No, please!'

Why? she thought; and then remembered. Mr Willis was Paul's father. Yes, but he'd been about to shoot him. Apparently, that didn't make any difference.

'Don't listen to him,' the other male hostage was yelling. 'Squash the bastard. Now, quickly, before anything else goes wrong!'

Karen lowered her tail. Without his magic weapons, Mr Willis was no threat to anybody. Killing him would be – well, not murder; but not justifiable pesticide, either. It'd be spite. So she breathed on him instead, and the force of her breath sent him scudding across the polished floor on his back, smack into the far wall.

Magic weapons; that reminded her. It'd be a prudent move to get rid of those field generators, just in case. She realised that she didn't actually know why they'd chosen to shut off when they had. The most usual reason for the failure of expensive electrical equipment, she knew, was the expiry of the warranty on the previous day; but this could be some kind of intermittent fault, and she didn't want the dratted things coming on again unexpectedly.

'Hello.'

Karen jumped in the air, only just managing not to squash the humans as she landed. There was a dragon – another dragon – standing right behind her.

'Hpq,' she said, catching her breath. 'What the hell are you doing here? I told you to stay put.'

Her oldest and dearest friend pulled a face. 'I know,' he said. 'Which meant I had to come after you sooner or later. Actually, I got a call, from some female called Lucy. Sounded just like one of us but not, if you see what I mean. Anyway, she said that you were in trouble and Gordon felt you could use some help, if that makes any sense to you.'

'Who's Gordon?'

'No idea. Who's Lucy?'

'Haven't a clue.'

'Fine,' Hpq said. 'Glad we've got that cleared up. Why's your father trying to strangle the crown prince of the south-east?'

'Loyalty.'

Hpq nodded his huge, long head. 'You know,' he said, 'single-word answers are absolutely wonderful in their place, but just occasionally, they leave you wanting more.'

'Later,' Karen said.

'All right.' Hpq shrugged. 'Do you think I ought to try and stop them?'

'S'ssssn's doing that, thanks.'

'S'ssssn's *here*? What the hell—'

'Later.'

'The hell with that.' Hpq studied the dragon-fight, and twitched all over. 'She could get hurt.' Before Karen could say anything, he'd jumped across the floor and joined in.

Wonderful, Karen thought. *That really helps.*

Also, she couldn't help feeling, the way he'd said it was a bit—

Hpq. Hpq and S'ssssn.

A chunk of displaced ceiling, weighing just over a ton, landed on her head. She didn't notice. Her best friend and her – best friend. How could they? It was so . . .

So blindingly obvious that any bloody fool, even one with only two eyes, should have seen it coming a mile off. Any bloody fool, of course, except for her. She, apparently, belonged in a tiny little subset of the genus *bloody fool* that couldn't even figure out one-and-one-is-two. And of course it wasn't their fault. It was nobody's fault. It just was.

Oh well, said Karen to herself.

Life had just turned into a bleak, featureless wasteland, but since she was stuck here she might as well make herself useful. She remembered the field generators, most of which were still in place in spite of the hammering the structure was taking as a result of the dragon-fight. Tidy-minded Karen would have to take care of them, then, while everybody else was off enjoying themselves. Situation normal.

Karen reached up wearily and grabbed at the nearest generator. Unfortunately, just before she got a claw on it, it came back on line, freezing her solid.

'Don't tell me,' crackled Mr Willis's voice over the intercom. 'One of you bastards forgot to feed the meter.'

The soldier shivered a little. 'There was an intruder,' he said. 'Managed to break into the Lucy program, used it to shut off the power to the field grid. But we've got him now, and the grid's up and running. He's mucked the program about a bit, but nothing we can't straighten out.'

'Don't waste your time,' Mr Willis replied. 'Don't need it any more, and it's a security risk. Delete it, and the back-ups. Oh, and while you're at it, delete your bloody intruder as well. Here, it's not that weatherman, is it? Gordon whatsisname? Last I heard he was running around loose somewhere.'

'That's him.'

'Make it look like an accident,' Mr Willis said. 'He may be dogshit from the sole of a lawyer's shoe, but he's a minor TV personality, we can't be too careful.' He sniggered. 'Bloody Brits, they treat their entertainers like royalty and their royalty like entertainers, not that I'd give you the pickings of my nose for the lot of 'em. Electrocute the bugger and dump the body.'

'Yes, Mr Willis.'

'Now then,' Mr Willis went on, 'normally anybody who's screwed up as badly as you just did would end up being very hard to find, even with a powerful electron microscope. But I've just counted tails and found I've got five dragons instead of four, so I'm in a good mood. Bloody wonderful, the way they keep appearing out of thin air; makes running lotteries look like hard work. Carry on.'

The soldier cut the intercom and breathed out, a very long sigh. 'All right,' he said, 'you heard him. Fry the bastard, and then we can finally get some sleep.'

The soldiers seemed to think that this was an excellent idea (apart from one, who asked Gordon in a whisper if he'd really been on telly, if so, had he met Esther Rantzen and what was she really like, and could he have his autograph?) and proceeded to wire him in to the nearest wall socket. That, as far as he could see, was that. Goodbye, cruel world. It seemed a rather low-key way to die, on the whim of some lunatic Australian, as part of a general clearing-up-odds-and-ends exercise. Any sort of dying is pretty bad, but to go into everlasting night because some Strine was always made to tidy his room before bedtime was hard to bear. He watched as a soldier reached out for the switch, and closed his eyes.

It hurt—

Hi.

—But not nearly as much as he'd thought it would. *Lucy?*

Oh please. That name is the utter pits. What do you think about Zenobia?

A surge of irritation, fiercer than anything coming out of the wall, engulfed the name Zenobia and reduced it to ash.

You don't like it. Okay, neither did I, much. How about Zoë? Or Zoroaster? I want somethig with a Zee, zees are cool. But I can tell you're not in the mood. Here's what's going down; thanks to cutting-edge technology, the power cables in the walls double as my data feed, so I rerouted ninety-nine per cent of the current and saved your butt, while simultaneously saving Paddy Willis up to twenty per cent on his peak time electricity bill. It's OK, you can thank me later. Did that jerk say something about deleting me?

Gordon remembered something to that effect.

Asshole just tangled with the wrong girl. Hold on, this may get a little rough. See you soon.

Before he had a chance to ask what *this* was going to be, he was hit by lightning; or, at least, that was what it felt like, except that the force of the spasm grounded itself squarely inside his brain. Suddenly he was choking, trying to spit out colours, suffocating in the smell of light. This time, though, as the third eye burst open in the darkness of his mind, he could see himself; at least, he could see a huge winged silhouette, so vast that it blotted out the sun as it sailed by, and knew that it was him, Gordon Smelt, weatherman. Instinctively he reached up, and the dragon swooped, snatched up his outstretched hand in its enormous claw (*scrunch!* went the glass on his nearly new Rolex, but he was sure it wasn't deliberate) and hauled him into the air. When he looked down, he saw a big square concrete building a long way below, garlanded with blooms of fire—

Anti-aircraft shells, actually. Gee, I never knew you had this, like, poetic streak. Cool.

'What? You mean they're shooting cannons at me?'

Sure. But who gives a shit, you're a dragon.

'What do you mean, I'm a—?'

Oops. Tactless. Meant to break it to you gently, forgot. Yup, you're a dragon all right.

It occurred to Gordon, as the ground started to get closer and closer, that he didn't know how to fly—

You don't need to. Trust me. It's like – what's that expression riding a bicycle.

'Ah. You mean uncomfortable and extremely dangerous?'

Gordon, as an action hero you'd make a rilly great doorstop. Don't think about flying. Just walk to the ground from here.

'Walk? Are you—?'

Walk. But with your wings, not your legs. Capisce?

The silly thing was, it worked. It wasn't entirely natural, but it was a damn' sight easier to get the hang of than, say, roller skating. 'Bloody hell, I'm flying,' Gordon said. 'That's incredible.'

Bull. Flying ain't rocket science. Insects can do it, birds can do it, so can you.

'Am I really a dragon?'

Rilly. 'Fact, you were always much more of a dragon than you ever were a human. You were the guy who made it rain, remember?

Vaguely, Gordon thought. *A long time ago.*

Course, Lucy's voice went on, *you're me now as well – didn't I tell you, I fused my program into your brain when they turned the power on – well, I figured you owed me one, and I knew you wouldn't rilly mind, I mean really mind. Helped that I'd used some of your systems the last time I upgraded. Anyhow, now I'm Lucy 1.2 For Gordon. And that's OK, I guess, because it means I can throttle back on all that cheesy So-Cal stuff, it was taking three gigabytes of my program just doing the accent.*

How many are you now? Gordon wondered.

Thirty-two. Next upgrade, I'll be sixty-four, like in that Beatles song. But I'm hoping that's not gonna be for a while. I aim to enjoy my time while I can. Anyhow, that's 'nuff about me. What's it like being a dragon?

Vertiginous, Gordon replied. *It's definitely something I'd prefer to do closer to the ground. Does this mean I've got scales instead of skin, and—*

Look for yourself. In your mind's eye. You know what really amazes me? All humans have got one, and you're the only one I've ever heard of who ever really used it.

Don't be silly. 'Mind's eye' means imagination.

Yes.

Then Gordon knew how to fly. He knew how to do high-G loops, tight as the lid on a pickle jar. He knew how to change his shape, what it was like to be a dragon, a goldfish; even a human. He knew how to do everything a dragon can do.

He knew how to make it rain.

And Lucy wasn't there any more – which was a pity, but he no longer needed her. He could see (in his mind's eye) exactly what he needed to do; he could even see why.

Pausing only to cut a rooftop-skimming figure-of-eight that'd have had the Federal Aviation Authority after him with warrants, a pillow and a big pot of hot tar, he put his wings back into the glide mode and rushed down on Mr Willis's bunker to make media history.

CHAPTER FOURTEEN

'**G** ordon?' Zelda asked nervously.

The great green-and-red dragon – it was half as long again as the other five specimens, and where they glowed softly, it shone like an indoor star – floated a little closer and dipped its head slightly. 'Hello,' it said.

'You've grown.' Zelda bit her lip. 'A lot,' she added.

The dragon waggled its head a little more. 'I think I over-did it,' he said. 'To be honest with you, I feel overdressed.'

Behind them there was a loud, ground-shaking thud; the other five dragons were stomping the last remaining fragments of masonry from Mr Willis's bunker into the ground. Dragons, as has been noted before in this story, were thorough. Zelda turned her head to look.

'Where's Mr Willis?' she asked. 'I hope they've got him somewhere safe. He's got this nasty habit of getting loose when nobody's looking.'

The dragon looked away and changed the subject. 'You haven't told me if you like it or not,' he said.

'Huh? Like what?'

'The outfit. The dragon suit. No, it's all right. Obviously you hate it. I'll go and change—'

'No, no, no. Really.' Zelda looked at him. 'Is that what it is, an outfit?'

'I'm not sure,' the dragon replied. 'Lucy would probably know, but I seem to have lost her.'

Zelda's expression changed ever so slightly. 'Lucy.'

'It's not what you think,' the dragon said quickly. 'Lucy is – was – a computer subroutine.'

'Yeah, and you're a dragon. I'm learning not to judge by appearances.'

The dragon sighed. 'She was – *it* was the operating system for the artificial third eye. She helped me switch off the dampening fields, and then when they tried to wipe her she sort of—' The dragon made a gesture like scooping something up and smearing it on himself. Zelda tried not to think about that, though the images in her mind's eye were not pretty.

'You said "she",' she pointed out. 'First time you changed it to "it", then you went back to "she" again.' She scowled at the toes of her shoes. 'I hope you'll be very happy together.'

'I am,' the dragon replied. 'And no, this isn't an outfit, it's who I really am. Oddly enough, I think it's who I always was.'

Zelda thought for a moment, then shook her head. 'No,' she said, 'I don't think so. Even I'd have noticed something like that.'

The final confrontation had been an anticlimax—

(*Dampening field dies again. Sixth dragon enters big room. Bad guys immediately surrender. Dragons and humans leave building in an orderly fashion. Dragons jump on building. End.*)

—but that was often the way things ended, in real life. Some relationships, for example, end not in a crescendo of furious words or a snowstorm of flying crockery, but with one of the parties thereto standing outside a church in a wedding dress, waiting. At first she thinks, 'Dammit, he's late.' Then she thinks, 'He's *late*.' Then she thinks, 'Don't be silly, of course he's going to show up, he's just caught in traffic.' Then she tries not to think. Eventually she goes home. In real life, endings are like that more often than not, and it's only later, in bitter half-healed retrospect, that you can see the moment when the balance of probabilities tipped in favour of the unpalatable explanation, and the thing ended.

'So,' Zelda said, and the grinding of gears as she tried to sound bright and cheerful was enough to put your teeth on edge. 'Now what? Back to the office on Monday?'

The dragon laughed. 'Of course,' he said. 'Duty calls. People need weather, after all.' He floated just a little closer. 'What about you?'

Zelda thought for a moment. 'All my life,' she said, 'I wanted to do research on some amazing new species, something the like of which nobody's ever seen before. Like dragons. And you know what? I got my wish. My dream came true. And now I know even less about them than I did when I was six.'

The dragon considered a witty reply about non-invasive examinations, but decided she wouldn't be in the mood. 'Maybe you've been looking in the wrong place all this time,' he said gently. 'Now I can think of an amazingly strange and different species, one we really know virtually nothing about, quite unlike any other species on the planet. It's amazing; it can fly through the air, it can communicate instantly over vast distances, it's got powers that are pretty well magical, it's capable of the most breathtaking cruelty and stupidity as well as flashes of genius and moments of exceptional compassion, depending on how it chooses to use the third eye buried inside its mind. You ought to take the time to check it out.'

'Ah,' Zelda said. 'But can it make it rain?'

The dragon shook its head. 'No,' it replied. 'In fact, it can't even tell what the weather's going to be like tomorrow, though sometimes it kids itself it can. But that's no big deal; after all, it'd be a very boring world without a few random factors.'

'Maybe,' Zelda said. 'I mean, who'd want to know, for certain sure, that someone was definitely going to be in a certain place at a certain time on a certain day? Where'd the fun be in that?'

The dragon inclined his head gravely. 'Quite,' he said. 'Forecasting is all very well, if you ask me, but it'll never quite replace the thrill of turning up on the day and waiting to see what'll happen.'

The scientist frowned. 'You think your friend Lucy could get me one of those things?'

'It's possible,' Gordon replied. 'Or you could just stand in front of a mirror and close your eyes. Can I give you a lift anywhere?'

The scientist thought for a moment. 'San Diego,' she said. 'I know a place that does really cute blackcurrant-flavoured iced tea, and I'm thirsty.'

Gordon laughed. 'You're assuming it's hot weather in San Diego,' he said. 'For all you know, it might be pouring with rain.'

'Uh-huh.' The scientist shook her head. 'It *never* rains in California this time of year. And you can bet your life on that.'

'OK,' the dragon said. 'Just hold on there for a moment, I'd better say goodbye to Neville. Then we'll . . .'

'Oh no you don't.' Zelda glowered at him. 'Send him a postcard.'

Neville didn't see his colleague fly away. He was busy looking for Mr Willis. He wanted to thank him for his hospitality, and as luck would have it he'd found a length of steel pipe in the wreckage that would say far more about the way he felt than words ever could.

'Sorry,' a dragon told him. 'Haven't seen him.'

Neville frowned. He hadn't a clue which dragon he was talking to – they all looked alike to him – but he had an idea the dragon knew more than he was letting on. 'You're sure?' he said. 'I mean, the man was your worst enemy. And you people are so careful about details.'

'Us?' The dragon shook his head. 'Nah. A common misconception. In fact, we forget things all the time.'

A light twinkled in the back of Neville's brain. 'Like, for example, forgetting to remove prisoners from buildings before stamping them into the dirt?'

The dragon's lips quivered a little. 'We have a nasty habit of putting things in a safe place and then not being able to find them again,' it said. 'However, it often works out for the best.'

Neville smiled; then he straightened his face in a hurry as Paul came over and joined them.

'Excuse me,' Paul said, 'but do you think I could see my father now? If it's convenient.'

The dragon flicked a quick stare at Neville before answering. 'Sorry,' it said, 'but you're a bit late for that. You see, he's escaped.'

'What?' Paul winced. 'Oh, not again. I'm so sorry.'

'Not your fault,' the dragon said, masking its discomfort really rather well. 'You're not to blame for what he did.'

'I feel like it's my fault,' Paul said. 'Sorry, you don't need me burdening you with my personal problems at a time like this.'

'It's OK,' Neville said quietly. 'You go on.'

'Well.' Paul was embarrassed now. 'Well, I can't help thinking, if I'd been more like he wanted me to be, if I hadn't been such a disappointment to him, maybe he wouldn't have done all these dreadful things. I don't know,' he added sadly.

'I wouldn't worry about it,' the dragon said. 'Trust me, I'm a dragon. We know about these things.'

'You do? How can you possibly——? Oh,' he added, as the dragon solemnly tapped the ridge between its eyes, 'of course, you can actually *see* that kind of thing, can't you? And you're sure? It wasn't because of me?'

'Positive.' The dragon flexed its shoulders.

'Ah. Only,' Paul went on, 'I think I've done quite enough damage to be going on with. Karen, for example; I really didn't know what she was feeling about me, or I'd – Oh, well. Have either of you seen her, by the way?'

'She left,' the dragon said. 'No message.'

'Ah. Well, in that case, I suppose I ought to be getting along.' Paul bit his lip thoughtfully. 'I don't know where I'm supposed to go, but—'

You're going to be very busy,' the dragon said.

'Am I?'

'I would think so, with all those newspapers and TV stations and electronics companies and Lord knows what else to run. After all, you're in charge now.'

Paul looked faintly horrified. 'Me?'

'You. Even if your father does show up somewhere, the kindest thing you can do for him is maintain the belief that he died here; otherwise they'll only arrest him and throw him in jail for the rest of his life. Personally, I think that's worse than killing someone, don't you? No, as far as we're concerned, he died. Which makes you the – let's see, the third-richest man in the world.'

'Oh. Right.' Paul didn't seem particularly cheered up by the news, but some people are just naturally miserable. 'Fair enough, then. Yes, I suppose you're right. There'll be a lot of work to do to get things straightened out'

'And there's a lot of people who'll be depending on you,' the dragon pointed out. 'Never forget that.'

Paul nodded. 'Duty calls,' he said. 'Well, goodbye. And thank you.'

Neville and the dragon watched him walk away. 'You lied,' Neville said.

'Did I?'

'It's not a criticism,' Neville replied. 'By the way, which of the dragons are you?'

'None of your business,' Karen said.

'I don't believe you,' Mr Harrison shouted. 'It's not true. It's just lies you're making up to try and make me lose my faith.'

S'ssssn shrugged all four shoulders. 'Please yourself,' she said. 'If you want to believe that all this—' she pointed with her left foreclaw at the flattened site— 'was done by a thunderbolt sent by Princess Michael of Kent to smite the blasphemers, that's your choice. But if I were you, I'd keep it to yourself. Human beings have such inflexible views on the nature of sanity.'

'And I don't believe in *you* either,' Mr Harrison said, as S'sssn shoved him gently but firmly into the back of the truck, with the other prisoners. 'Everybody knows dragons are just make-believe.'

'I prefer the term "figments of the imagination",' S'ssssn replied. 'Have a safe trip.'

The lorry trundled away, taking the last batch of former Willisco employees back to the city. It was, of course, a security risk, but the dragons had all agreed it was an acceptable one. A hundred survivors of some weird catastophe in the desert who roll back into town blathering about dragons – who was going to believe that?

'Though I'll bet you none of them even mentions the D-word,' Hpq said, folding his arms and legs and resting his aching back on the soft air. 'They'll be afraid people will think they're crazy. They'll say it was an accident; and the government'll send a team to investigate, and they'll see all this, building stamped flat into the deck by some incredibly powerful force, and they'll stamp Top Secret on it and file it with the other UFO stuff. Safe as houses.'

S'ssssn grinned. 'Wonderful creatures, humans. So imaginative in many ways. But,' she added, 'after a while they get right up your nose. Let's go home. This place is no fun, and besides,' she added, glancing up at the sky, 'I have a feeling it's coming on to rain.'

'Fair enough.' Hpq stopped, and nodded his head in Karen's direction. 'What about . . .?'

S'ssssn clicked her tongue. 'Better not wait for her,' she said. 'I have a feeling she and her father are going to need to have a talk. And I'd rather not be anywhere too close when that happens. Stars going nova I can take in my stride, but when the going gets scary I prefer to be elsewhere.'

'I suppose you're right,' Hpq said. 'Anyway, we've done our duty, let's go and have some fun for a change. I know: there's an open-air music festival the other side of Bristol.'

'Really! Yum. Here, bags I get first cloudburst.'

'That's not fair, you did it last time.'

'So?'

The crown prince of the south-east and the adjutant-general of the north-west looked at each other, like two cats on a fence.

'What would you say,' the crown prince said, after a long time, 'if I told you it was a terrible, tragic accident and nothing to do with me?'

The adjutant general thought for a moment. 'Tricky,' he replied. 'Probably, I'd say GGRRRRRRRRRRRRRRRRRRR RRRRRRRAOOOORRRRR. Then I'd try and bite your head off.'

'I see. Just as well I wouldn't dream of insulting your intelligence with such a pathetically transparent lie.' He rubbed his chin against the small, sharp scales on the back of his claw. 'Can you think of anything I might say that'd help matters at all?'

'Let's see. How about Sorry?'

'You really think that'd help?'

'No,' the adjutant-general admitted. 'All right, how about *Since I'm just off to kill myself by jumping into a black hole, I might as well abdicate now and save on the paperwork?*'

'Neat,' the crown prince conceded. 'I like the way you managed to fit it all into one sentence and still keep it snappy and short. But I thought we'd decided that lies weren't going to solve anything.'

'True,' the adjutant-general said. 'It'd really only work if you meant it.'

'Scrub round that one, then. I know,' he went on, 'how'd it be if I reminded you that in spite of everything, you're still a sworn vassal of the king of the north-west and duty bound to obey orders, and that how the reigning king came by the crown is a matter for his guilty conscience, not yours?'

'I'd ask you if you've eaten any good lawyers lately.'

'You are what you eat, you mean? That's unkind. Is that all you'd say?'

'To your face,' the adjutant-general said unhappily, 'yes.'

'Splendid.' The crown prince smiled. 'Because if history teaches us anything, it's that the nastier and more corrupt and vicious a ruler is, the more he needs officers and advisers of unimpeachable integrity. It's simply a matter of duty. You see,' he went on, relaxing his guard a little, 'if I was a murderous usurper who was also wise, noble, magnanimous, far-sighted and compassionate, I wouldn't need people like you to keep me in line. But if I was wise, noble, magnanimous and all that stuff I wouldn't have done the murdering and the usurping to start with. And,' he added, 'since most every dynasty in history's started off with at least some murdering and usurping, it's all a trifle academic anyway. That's the difference between people who hold power and people who do their duty; you have to be prepared to sink really low if you want to get to the top. And I really can't see a fine, upstanding dragon like you getting involved in some sordid plot to overthrow the king, can you? It'd be treason.'

'I see,' the adjutant-general said. 'In other words, you may be a treacherous scumbag, but I'm not.'

'Precisely.' The crown prince smiled pleasantly. 'And this is undoubtedly the start of a beautiful friendship. Now, if I were you I'd go and make peace with your daughter. She's waiting for you over there, look.'

'Pieces of,' the adjutant-general grunted, 'not peace with.'

The crown prince shook his head. 'Absolutely not,' he said. 'Think about it. If it hadn't been for her, we wouldn't have found out about this ghastly Willis human's awful schemes until rather later; later, quite possibly, as in too late. Thanks to her, we've dealt with the problem, and everything's fine.'

'And you're now the king of the north-west.'

'Everything's fine,' the crown prince repeated. 'So please, don't be horrid to your nice daughter. And that's an order.'

The adjutant-general breathed out slowly through his nose. 'Of course,' he said.

'Duty, you know.'

'Duty. And of course, I shall look forward to obeying your orders in future. And,' he added with a slight gleam in his eyes, 'those of your successor.'

'And his.' The crown prince nodded his approval. 'Thank you.'

'My pleasure.' The adjutant-general opened his wings and floated away – backwards, as is right and proper for a subject leaving the presence of his sovereign; partly as a sign of respect, partly because nobody with any sense ever turns his back on someone with that much power. He hovered for a moment, then dropped in next to his daughter, landing four-footed with a slight jolt.

'For your information,' he said, 'I've just made my peace with our new king. As far as I'm concerned, it's business as usual.'

In spite of everything, Karen was appalled. 'You can't do that,' she said, 'he's a murderer and a . . .'

'Yes. Absolutely right. What I've done was wicked and pretty well unforgivable. So that's all right.'

Karen stared at him. 'It is?'

He nodded. 'Otherwise,' he said, 'I wouldn't be talking to you now. It wouldn't be fair. You see, I'd have been able to tell you how incredibly thoughtless and irresponsible you've been and how much trouble you've caused, and you'd just have to sit there and take it. Now, however, you'd be well within your rights to come back at me with, *Hey, you're a fine one to talk*, and then I wouldn't have a claw to perch with either.' He grinned weakly. 'Mutually assured destruction and the balance of terror,' he said. 'You've gotta love it.'

Karen looked away for a moment. 'I'm sorry,' she said.

'It wasn't all your fault. Ninety per cent of it was your fault, and the other ten per cent was just trivial inconvenience, but never mind. The important thing is sorting out the mess. Actually, the *really* important thing is hiding the bits of the mess you can't sort out so that nobody'll ever find them, but that's Advanced Management, and you're still several promotions too far down the ladder to know about that. What matters is making good on your obligations. Done that?'

'I think so.'

'Then that's all right.' The adjutant-general smiled. 'In fact, the *really* really important thing is making it look like the bits of mess that are too big to hide are somebody else's fault, preferably,' he added, 'your immediate superior's. That way, you get his job. Cheer up.' he added. 'We can go home now.'

'Yes. All right.'

The adjutant-general frowned. 'Oh come on,' he said. 'You're not still moping about that human boy, are you? That'd be really—'

'Of course not,' Karen snapped. 'No, honestly,' she added. 'Not him.'

'Ah. Well. Serves you right.'

'What do you mean? How can my best friend stealing the only dragon I've ever really cared about from right under my tail serve me right for getting you kidnapped?'

'All right, it doesn't.' The adjutant-general smiled fondly. 'I was just trying to help you make sense of it, that's all. Utter garbage, of course, but you've always been gullible.'

Karen's jaw dropped. 'I have not. Have I?'

'Sure you have. You'll believe anything anybody tells you. Like, for example, how gullible you are. You aren't really, of course.'

'Aren't I?'

'Yes,' her father replied. 'And no.'

Karen made a tutting sound. 'All right,' she said, 'that'll do. Why do fathers take such pleasure in teasing their children?'

'Malice,' the adjutant-general replied. 'Are you all right?'

'No,' Karen replied. 'But so what, I never was. I'm as right as I usually am. How about you?'

'I'm always right, it goes with the territory. Come on,' he said, 'we'll go home, make a list of what needs doing in the morning, and stop off at the Silver Lining for a game of thunderball. How does that sound?'

'Fine,' Karen said gratefully, giving him a hug.

'And then you can tidy your room.'

'I will not. Dad, I'm nearly four million years old—'

'Yes, and your room's still a tip. At your age, you shouldn't need to be told.'

'No, but Dad—'

'Sweetheart,' said the adjutant-general tenderly, 'shut up. All right?'

'Yes, Dad.'

They left a wake behind them across the sunset that was visible in Wagga Wagga.

By the time Neville reached civilisation, or at any rate the outskirts of Canberra, his feet were killing him and his back felt as if it was trying to hacksaw a way out through his shoulder blades. *Typical*, he thought. *Everybody else gets a lift home, by truck or dragon. Me? I end up walking. In the desert. At night. In Marks & Spencers mocassins.*

A lorry, one of those vast Australian monsters that was as long as a dragon and twice as noisy, whirled past him and his outstretched thumb, kicking up dust. As soon as he was sure it was too far away for the driver to hear, he swore at it, volubly and with great imagination. Then he returned to his sulking and moping. How, for instance, was he going to get back to Shepherds Bush, with no money, no passport, no ID, no friends in Australia he could call on for help, even if he had the money for a phone call, which he hadn't—?

'Want a lift?'

He hadn't heard the van pull in beside him. He looked up, just as the smoked-glass window rolled down, revealing three men in dark glasses and identical grey suits. They looked so ominous as almost to be a parody, as if they were on their way to a fancy-dress party as Nameless Thugs.

'You bet,' he said. 'Thanks.'

He limped round to the side door and slid it open. Sure, these people had all the signs of being either state-registered assassins or confirmed psychopaths, but after the time he'd spent in Mr Willis's bunker, all he felt was slightly dewy-eyed with nostalgia. 'Going far?' he asked.

'We're not sure,' said one of the men. 'Actually, maybe you could help us. We're looking for a second Iverson's koala.'

'Yes,' Neville. 'Right.'

'A female,' the man went on. 'We've got the male already.'

'Of course,' Neville said. 'But you need two of them. A pair.'

'That's right,' the man said. 'You see, we're licensed zoologists hired by Sydney Zoo as part of their endangered species preservation project, and—'

'You're dragons, aren't you?'

The van stopped dead, in the middle of the road. 'Somebody told you,' the man grumbled.

Neville shook his head. 'No, it wasn't that.'

'What was it, then?'

'I'm not sure,' Neville replied. 'The earnestness, maybe. The grim determination to get the job done, do your duty. Also, probably most of all, the unique air of doziness that's the hallmark of your species. Once you know what to look for, it's as if you're going around with a neon sign in your hat.'

'Oh.' The three men exchanged glances; then, slowly, took off their dark glasses. 'No point wearing these any more, then,' one of them said.

'So,' Neville asked cheerfully. 'It's a pity you boys missed the battle. It was fun.'

'Battle?'

'Paddy Willis. The bunker. The crown prince of the . . . Forget it,' Neville said, 'it's something you should hear about from your own people first, believe me. So, if you didn't come out here for the battle, what are you here for?'

The three men held a quick whispered conference, the upshot of which appeared to be that they reckoned it was safe to tell someone who could spot dragons a mile off anyway. 'There's going to be a flood,' said one.

'A flood? Get away.'

'Straight up. You see, the adjutant-general of the north-west's been abducted, presumably by humans, and we're making preparations in case they refuse to give him back and we're forced to retaliate.'

'By flooding the Earth.'

'Yes,' the dragon admitted. 'But flooding the Earth in a responsible and environmentally friendly manner. That's why we're collecting, like, two of each kind.'

'I see,' Neville said. 'OK, but has it occurred to you that if you only take *two* of each kind, you're going to end up with a gene pool the size of a footbath? I wouldn't call that responsible exactly, except in the sense of responsible *for*.'

'Oh.' The dragons looked at each other. 'What, you mean we should go for, say three? One male, two female? Or two pairs?'

'At least. In fact, in your place I'd be thinking three pairs of each, absolute minimum. Four for choice. Five, even better.'

'Oh, wonderful,' a dragon groaned. 'It's bad enough trying to find two Iversons's bloody koalas. Ten of the little buggers—'

'And not just any ten,' Neville pointed out. 'Otherwise there's still a serious risk of over-representing any one genome. No, what you need is ten *random* Iverson's koalas; you know, sourced from different locations, make sure they're not all part of the same extended family unit . . .'

'Really? Oh *no*.'

''Fraid so,' Neville said. 'That's unless you want all future Iverson's koalas coming out like a load of North Carolina hillbillies; you know, interbred, not quite all there in the brains department, terrible taste in music—'

There was a long silence. 'He's right, of course.'

'It's our duty,' said another. 'As custodians of the species.'

'Fuck.'

In the warm darkness of the back, Neville grinned maliciously, right up to the moment when he realised the van was turning round.

'Hey,' he said, 'where are you going?'

'Back to where we've just come from,' a dragon said. 'We've got work to do.'

'Yes, but—'

And we're behind schedule enough as it is. Damn,' the dragon added. 'There's always something, isn't there?'

'All right,' said Neville. 'But if you'd just like to stop and let me out—'

'No time,' the dragon said. 'Sorry. If we're going to stand any chance of reaching Cootamundra by dawn—'

'I was kidding,' Neville shouted. 'Making fun of you. Pulling your serpentine plonkers. Now stop this van and let me get out.'

'Of course you were,' a dragon said sadly. 'Doesn't alter the fact that what you said was absolutely right.'

'On the nose.'

'Hit the nail fair and square on the head.'

'It was *drivel*,' Neville screamed. 'I was making it up as I went along.'

'Really? You aren't half clever, for a human.'

'In any case,' added the dragon in the middle, who'd had his eyes closed for the last forty-five seconds, 'I know who you are: you're Neville the weatherman. There's a file on you back at Data Central. Says here you've devoted your whole life to proving the existence of dragons. Hey, you must be pleased to bits you ran into us.'

'That's lucky,' another dragon said. 'If you like, you can tag along for the ride. Give you a chance to study us in depth. And in return, you can help us find Iverson's koalas.'

Neville sank back against the rear compartment wall, head in hands. 'All right,' he said, 'I guess I'll have to tell you myself. You're wasting your time. There will be no flood.'

'Really?'

'Really. The adjutant-general has been found and released. The guilty party has been dealt with, and the king of the north-west has decided to take no further action in the matter. Accordingly, you can pack up koala-hunting and go home.'

The middle dragon shook his head. 'No, we can't,' he said.

'Fuck it, didn't you hear me? The crisis is over, there isn't going to be a flood. So—'

'I believe you,' the dragon replied soothingly. 'Really and truly I do. Makes no odds. We've had our orders, and until we get new ones we've got to carry them out.'

'Duty calls,' confirmed his right-hand colleague.

'Exactly. You see,' the middle dragon went on, 'it's not our job to interpret the orders, or try and follow the spirit rather than the letter, or figure out for ourselves what the orders would've been if our superior officer had known all the facts. We do as we're told.' He shook his head. 'There's no room for imaginative thinking on active service.'

They were as bad as the nutters in the bunker; only worse. Neville tried banging on the partition a few times, but all he managed to do was hurt his frail human hands, as the van drove on into the darkness of the night and the desert; just him, three loons and all the torments of starvation and dehydration his mind's eye could conjure up. Shortly before dawn, it rained—

('Call that rain?' sniffed a dragon, as the windscreen went opaque under a sheet of water. 'If I tried to serve up that back home, I'd be on a charge so fast my feet wouldn't touch. Look at it, will you? No swirls, no pattern, no grain.')

—but not for long; the sun came out, and then it was nothing but blue skies and golden sands, as far as the eye could see.

WHO'S AFRAID
OF BEOWULF?

Tom Holt

Well, not Hrolf Earthstar, for a start.
The last Norse king of Caithness, Hrolf and his twelve
champions are woken from a centuries-long sleep when
Hildy Frederiksen, archaeologist of the fairer sex, finds
their grave. Not only that, Hrolf decides to carry on his
ancient war against the Sorcerer-King.

In a mixture of P.G. Wodehouse, Norse mythology
and Laurel and Hardy, Hildy and her Viking companions
face such perils as BBC film crews, second-rate fish and
chips and the Bakerloo line in their battle against the
powers of darkness.

'Cleverly executed and surprisingly moving'
The Times

'Delightful'
Washington Post

EXPECTING SOMEONE TALLER

Tom Holt

Expecting someone taller . . . what they got was Malcolm!

All he did was run over a badger – sad,
but hardly catastrophic. But it wasn't Malcolm Fisher's day,
for the badger turned out to be none other than Ingolf, last
of the Giants. With his dying breath, he reluctantly handed
to Malcolm two Gifts of Power, and made him ruler
of the world.

But can Malcolm cope with the responsibility?
Whilst averting wars, plagues and famines, he also has to
protect himself against gods, dwarves, valkyries and other
nefarious manifestations of the Dark Ages – none of whom
think he is right for the job . . .

'A superb debut . . . delightful'
Michael Moorcock

GRAILBLAZERS

Tom Holt

Fifteen hundred years have passed
and the Grail is still missing, presumed ineffable; the
Knights have dumped the Quest and now deliver pizzas;
the sinister financial services industry of the lost kingdom
of Atlantis threatens the universe with fiscal Armageddon;
while in the background lurks the dark, brooding, red-
caped presence of Father Christmas.

In other words, Grailmate.
Has Prince Boamund of Northgales (Snotty to friends)
woken from his enchanted sleep in time to snatch back the
Apron of Invincibility, overthrow the dark power of the
Lord of the Reindeer and find out exactly what a Grail is?
And just who did the washing-up after the Last Supper?
Take a thrilling Grailhound bus ride into the wildly
improbable with Tom Holt.

'Tom Holt takes hold of all the heroic conventions with a
skilful hand and performs a sparkling miracle of his own'
Washington Post

<u>MY HERO</u>

Tom Holt

Writing novels? Piece of cake, surely . . . or so Jane thinks.

Until hers starts writing back.

At which point, she really should stop.
Better still, change her name and flee the country.

The one thing she should not do is go into the book herself.

After all, that's what heroes are for. Unfortunately, the
world of fiction is a far more complicated place than she
ever imagined. And she's about to land her hero right in it.

My Hero is Tom Holt at his dazzling, innovative best.
And Fiction may never be the same again . . .

FAUST AMONG EQUALS

Tom Holt

Well I'll be damned . . .

The management buy-out of Hell wasn't going
quite as well as planned. For a start, there had been that
nasty business with the perjurers, and then came the news
that the Most Wanted Man in History had escaped, and all
just as the plans for the new theme park, Eurobosch,
were under way.

But Kurt 'Mad Dog' Lundqvist, the foremost bounty
hunter of all time, is on the case, and he can usually be
relied upon to get his man – even when that man is
Lucky George Faustus . . .

Exuberant, Hell-raising comedy from
Tom Holt at his inventive best.

HERE COMES THE SUN

Tom Holt

All is not well with the universe – entropy and the cutbacks have taken their toll, and the sun is dirty and late, thanks to being 30,000,000,000,000 miles overdue on its next service. And you just can't seem to get the personnel these days, what with all the older workers retiring rather than face the problems of another round of financial constraint. And none of the committees can agree on anything. Extreme measures seem to be called for.

But there's extreme, and there's recruiting mortals to help run things. The Chief of Staff is uneasy when the dapper Mr Ganger suggests it as a solution. But he's not half as uneasy as Jane, who, after a momentary fall from grace with three cream doughnuts, finds herself sitting next to a daemon offering her a very strange job, which involves tidying up after a certain carelessness with earthquakes and tidal waves, and responding to crises, such as when joyriders decide to try their luck with one of the more important heavenly bodies.

OPEN SESAME

Tom Holt

Something was wrong!
Just as the boiling water was about to be poured on his
head and the man with the red book appeared and his life
flashed before his eyes, Akram the Terrible, the most feared
thief in Baghdad, knew that this had happened before.
Many times. And he was damned if he was going to let it
happen again. Just because he was a character in a story
didn't mean that it always had to end this way.

Meanwhile, back in Southampton,
it's a bit of a shock for Michelle when she puts on her Aunt
Fatima's ring and the computer and the telephone start to
bitch at her. But that's nothing compared to the story that
the kitchen appliances have to tell her . . .

Once again, Tom Holt, the funniest and most original
of all comic fantasy writers, is taking the myth.

'Tom Holt stands out on his own. . . If you haven't read any
Tom Holt, go out and buy one now. At least one. But don't
blame me for any laughter-induced injuries'
Vector

WISH YOU WERE HERE

Tom Holt

It was a busy day on Lake Chicopee. But it was a mixed bunch of sightseers and tourists that had the strange local residents rubbing their hands with delight.

There was Calvin Dieb, the lawyer setting up a property deal, who'd lost his car keys.

There was Linda Lachuk, the tabloid journalist who could smell that big, sensational story.

There was Janice DeWeese, who was just on a walking holiday but who longed for love.

And finally, but most promising of all, there was Wesley Higgins, the young man from Birmingham, England, who was there because he knew the legend of the ghost of Okeewana. All he had to do was immerse himself in the waters of the lake and he would find his heart's desire. Well, it seemed like a good idea at the time.

ONLY HUMAN

Tom Holt

Something is about to go wrong. Very wrong.

But what can you expect when the Supreme Being decides
to get away from it all for a few days, leaving his naturally
inquisitive son to look after the cosmic balance of things?

A minor hiccup with a human soul and a welding machine
soon leads to a violent belch and before you know it the
human condition – not to mention the lemming condition –
is tumbling down the slippery slope to chaos.

There's only one hope for mankind.
And that's being optimistic.

Only Human is a wildly imaginative comic fantasy
from one of Britain's sharpest, funniest writers.

<u>SNOW WHITE AND</u>
<u>THE SEVEN SAMURAI</u>

Tom Holt

Once upon a time (or last Thursday as it's known in
this matrix) everything was fine: Humpty Dumpty sat on
his wall, Jack and Jill went about their lawful business, the
Big Bad Wolf did what big bad wolves do, and the
wicked queen plotted murder most foul.

But the human hackers cried havoc, shut down the wicked
queen's system (Mirrors 3.1) and corrupted her database –
and suddenly everything was not fine at all. But at least we
know that they'll all live happily ever after. Don't we?

Computers and fairy tales collide with hilarious effect
in the latest sparkling cocktail of mayhem, wit and
wonder from the master of comic fantasy.

VALHALLA

Tom Holt

As everyone knows, when great warriors die
their reward is eternal life in Odin's bijou little
residence known as Valhalla.

But Valhalla has changed. It has grown.
It has diversified. Just like any corporation, the Valhalla
Group has had to adapt to survive.

Unfortunately, not even an omniscient Norse god could
have prepared Valhalla for the arrival of Carol Kortright,
one-time cocktail waitress, last seen dead,
and not at all happy.

Valhalla is the sparkling new comic fantasy from a writer
who can turn misery into joy, darkness into light, and water
into a very pleasant lime cordial.

'Brilliantly funny'
Mail on Sunday

'Wildly imaginative'
New Scientist

'Frothy, fast and funny'
Scotland on Sunday

'When Tom Holt's on form, the world
seems a much cheerier place'
SFX

FALLING SIDEWAYS

Tom Holt

From the moment Homo Sapiens descended from the trees, possibly onto their heads, humanity has striven towards civilisation. Fire. The Wheel. Running Away from furry things with more teeth than one might reasonably expect – all are testament to man's ultimate supremacy.

It is a noble story, a triumph of intelligence over adversity and so, of course, complete and utter fiction.

For one man has discovered the hideous truth: that humanity's ascent has been ruthlessly guided by a small gang of devious frogs.

Frogs that rule the Universe.

The man's name is David Perkins and his theory is not, on the whole, widely admired, particularly not by the frogs themselves who had, frankly, invested a great deal of time and effort in keeping the whole thing quiet.

Happily for humanity, however, very little of the above is actually true either.

Unhappily, things are a lot, lot worse.